WESTERN

Rugged men looking for love...

Fortune's Faux Engagement
Carrie Nichols

The Rodeo Cowboy's Return
Kathy McDavid

MILLS & BOON

Carrie Nichols is acknowledged as the author of this work
FORTUNE'S FAUX ENGAGEMENT
© 2024 by Harlequin Enterprises ULC   First Published 2024
Philippine Copyright 2024   First Australian Paperback Edition 2024
Australian Copyright 2024   ISBN 978 1 038 92177 2
New Zealand Copyright 2024

THE RODEO COWBOY'S RETURN
© 2024 by Cathy McDavid Books, LLC   First Published 2024
Philippine Copyright 2024   First Australian Paperback Edition 2024
Australian Copyright 2024   ISBN 978 1 038 92177 2
New Zealand Copyright 2024

® and ™ (apart from those relating to FSC®) are trademarks of Harlequin Enterprises
(Australia) Pty Limited or its corporate affiliates. Trademarks indicated with ® are
registered in Australia, New Zealand and in other countries.
Contact admin_legal@Harlequin.ca for details.

MIX
Paper | Supporting
responsible forestry
FSC® C001695

Published by
Harlequin Mills & Boon
An imprint of Harlequin Enterprises (Australia) Pty Limited
(ABN 47 001 180 918), a subsidiary of HarperCollins
Publishers Australia Pty Limited
(ABN 36 009 913 517)
Level 19, 201 Elizabeth Street
SYDNEY NSW 2000 AUSTRALIA

Cover art used by arrangement with Harlequin Books S.A.. All rights reserved.

Printed and bound in Australia by McPherson's Printing Group

Fortune's Faux Engagement
Carrie Nichols

MILLS & BOON

Carrie Nichols grew up in New England but moved south and traded snow for central AC. She loves to travel, is addicted to British crime dramas and knows a *Seinfeld* quote appropriate for every occasion.

A 2016 RWA Golden Heart® Award winner and two-time Maggie Award for Excellence winner, she has one tolerant husband, two grown sons and two critical cats. To her dismay, Carrie's characters—like her family—often ignore the wisdom and guidance she offers.

Visit the Author Profile page
at millsandboon.com.au for more titles.

Dear Reader,

This was my first time writing in the world of the Fortune family. I enjoyed Heath and Jade going from a fake engagement to having genuine feelings for one another. I especially loved writing about Jade's basset hound, Charlie. If you're familiar with my other stories, you know how much I love my canine characters, and Charlie was no exception. Dressing him up in a Halloween costume was such fun. Too bad he didn't agree! I hope you enjoy reading about Charlie and his humans, Jade and Heath.

Let me know what you think. You can reach me at authorcarrienichols@gmail.com. I always love connecting with readers. And check out my website, carrienichols.com, for updates on new releases.

Thanks, and happy reading!

Carrie

DEDICATION

With gratitude to Dan Carney for his help with the agricultural technology ideas, and to Pippa Roscoe for the memory box idea, and to Jill Ralph for the traveling carnival idea.

CHAPTER ONE

JADE FORTUNE'S FEET skidded to a stop the moment she spotted the shiny black Mercedes G Wagon. She wouldn't have been surprised if her favorite red Chuck Taylors had left skid marks on the pavement.

Heath Blackwood must be in town. Her heart began pumping faster.

It had to be him. Heath was the only one she knew in Chatelaine, Texas, who drove that particular color and model of SUV. Not only did he drive a G Wagon, but it had been showroom clean every time she'd seen it. Just like the one parked in front of the Daily Grind.

"I can barely manage dust-free for a day. And I'm not just talking about my truck," Jade muttered, glancing down at her companion, who'd been forced to stop when she did. "How do you suppose he does it?"

The answer was a short, baying bark.

She nodded. "You're right. It is a mystery."

Charlie looked up at her with his soulful basset hound eyes as if wondering why she was carrying on this particular conversation with him. Considering it didn't involve any of his favorite words—treat, walk, ride or nap—he wasn't interested.

"Sorry, but this is what happens when you're thirty-three, single and haven't had a date in ages. You end up carrying on most conversations with your dog," she told him.

He shook his head, his long ears flapping noisily. He'd also succeeded in scattering doggie drool everywhere.

"Ewww." Jade pulled a paper napkin from the front pocket of her jeans. When you owned a basset, you learned to be prepared. She swiped at her pant leg. "Drool or no, we've been together longer than any of the guys I've dated, and you've been the most loyal, so you're forgiven."

Charlie wagged his tail and gave her a cheerful bark.

"You're right, I have no business complaining. I'm in a good place in my life. I don't need a man to prove that."

After a dozen years of drifting through life and a series of dead-end jobs, she was settled. And content. Living on the Fortune family ranch and updating and expanding the petting zoo kept her busy. She also set up workshops and day camps to teach school children about animals and agriculture. Both were more rewarding and fulfilling than anything she'd ever done.

Sure, she had experts guiding her with the zoo part, but she was as hands-on as possible, even picking up a rake or shovel and cleaning up after the animals when necessary. She spent a lot of time studying so she could teach many of the offered workshops herself, depending on subject matter and the age of the students. Jade also tracked down and invited experts to come to lecture whenever possible. That approach worked best for older kids who might require more in-depth knowledge than she could provide.

Her work life might be stable, but she doubted her single status was about to change anytime soon. With Dahlia and Sabrina happily ensconced in loving relationships, her mother and, to a certain extent, her sisters were now trying their best to matchmake her. She'd gone on a couple of casual dates but wasn't likely to become serious about anyone else while she had this pesky crush on the utterly gorgeous, utterly unobtainable Heath Blackwood.

Yes, she was happy and in a good place but…

Sometimes, late at night when she couldn't sleep, the thought of Heath Blackwood's broad shoulders and deep blue eyes gave her tingles and—

"Nope. I've got to cut that out. I'm sure he doesn't even know I exist." She tossed the napkin in the trash can in front of her original destination, Longhorn's Farm & Feed.

Jingling the leash, she said, "C'mon, Charlie, let's get this poster inside the store before you slobber all over it too."

Standing in the entrance to the feed store, she allowed herself another glance across the street to the Mercedes parked in a prime spot at the coffee shop. Well, the Daily Grind was Chatelaine's version of a coffee shop. Granted, it had a barista and sold a variety of coffee concoctions along with yummy pastries just like the iconic shops in Dallas or Houston, but that's where the resemblance ended.

The shop was located in a modest bungalow that had been converted into an eatery in the 1930s and hadn't changed much since except for the wide porch that ran the length of the front of the building, which now acted as take out for coffee and pastries A few tables were scattered there for customers who preferred to sit outside to enjoy their coffee.

That parked Mercedes meant Heath Blackwood was probably in the shop. So close. She made an impatient sound with her tongue and turned away to continue into the feed store but paused in the doorway to adjust to the dimmer interior after being in the bright October sunshine.

Inside the store, Jade unrolled the poster and brought it to Phyllis Castleberry, who was manning the cash register today. Phyllis was reputed to be in her seventies, but her age was not a subject you discussed with her or with anyone else if you knew what was good for you. Same with her teased and sprayed bottle-blond helmet of hair.

"Hey, Phyllis, can I leave this with you? It's all about Halloween Happenings at the petting zoo. Starting in the middle of the month, we'll be offering hayrides, pumpkin decorating fun and a costume parade for kids and their pets."

Phyllis raised one of her pencil-enhanced eyebrows. "Pets in costumes? I gotta see that. Are you dressing Charlie up?"

"Of course. It's part of his duty as grand marshal of the parade," Jade told her and glanced at her beloved pooch, who plopped his butt onto the floor with a long-suffering sigh. Jade would swear that Charlie's canine brain understood a lot more of what was said than most people gave him credit for.

Phyllis put her arms on the counter and leaned over so she could get a look at Charlie. With her short stature, she needed the boost and to brace herself to see him on the floor. "Such a sweet thing. If a trifle slow."

Yup, that's what Jade was talking about. She glanced down at Charlie, who looked up at her with what Jade considered a dog version of an eye roll. She nodded in commiseration. If she thought it would do any good, she'd correct Phyllis, but in the short time she'd known the woman, Jade had learned nothing short of an act of God could get the older woman to change her opinion. On anything.

Best to change the subject. "So, about the poster. Can I leave one here?"

"Of course, dear." Phyllis glanced at the poster, her lips moving as she read. "Ooh, that sounds like fun. I'll be sure to bring my granddaughters on my day off. I hope you realize how much we appreciate all you're doing for the young people in town."

"Thanks," Jade said, and she did mean it. She liked Phyllis, the other woman's opinion of Charlie's intelligence notwithstanding. "We really believe in giving back to the community and—"

"It's such a shame," Phyllis interjected with a sigh.

"What is?" Jade braced her hand on the counter and stood. Had something happened that she didn't know about? News traveled at the speed of sound in Chatelaine, but Jade wasn't always paying attention.

"You." Phyllis hitched her chin toward Jade. "You're obviously so good with kids, it's too bad you don't have a few of your own. You really ought to get married and start a family."

The older woman reached under the counter and pulled out a roll of clear tape. She lined up the edges of the poster along the top of the counter and taped the poster to the glass countertop. "You should think seriously about starting a family. You're not getting any younger, ya know. After all, the Good Lord gave us a finite number of child-bearing years."

"Thanks. I'll be sure to give it some thought," Jade said, working hard to keep her voice level. Thirty-three wasn't *ancient*, she wanted to shout but didn't. And she had to admit that every so often, she swore she heard a faint ticking and feared it might be her biological clock. Too bad she—

No. She wasn't going to fall into that trap. There was nothing wrong with her or her life. She was content and fulfilled, and that was a lot more than some married people could say.

Phyllis made marriage and kids sound easy, but first Jade would have to find a guy who was interested in doing that with her. And they weren't exactly coming out of the woodwork.

"There." The other woman smoothed the tape over the poster. "I know Chatelaine isn't like the big city, but we have our share of single men. Take Heath Blackwood, for instance…"

An image of broad shoulders and smoldering sex appeal sprang forth in Jade's mind. Looks, money and success all in one package. Yeah, and for those reasons, he was on the radar for every single female within a 150-mile radius. Probably some married ones too. What sort of chance did she stand?

You can't expect to attract a man if you don't put forth some effort in your appearance.

Jade shoved her father's caustic comments back into the box she kept them in and slammed the lid shut. She had never been able to compete in the looks or elegance department with her beauty queen mother or her two younger sisters. So she'd stopped trying ages ago.

Her mother, Wendy, maintained that Casper, her father, had loved his children and only ever wanted the best for them and that's why he could be harsh. Whether that was true or not, Jade would never know now that he was gone. She tried not to dwell on the past and the regrets she had when it came to her relationship with her dad.

"Or there's always Carl Evens, the greens keeper at the country club. No, wait. Shari at GreatStore says he started dating someone. Ooh, speaking of which, I think there's a new assistant manager working there. Maybe—"

Charlie chose that moment to bark. Standing, he tugged on the leash, his nails clicking on the cement as he headed toward the exit.

Thank you, Charlie. Who says you're not the smartest dog ever? "Well, I guess we'd better get going. Thanks for your help with the poster."

"Of course, dear, anytime."

Once outside, Jade blinked against the bright sunshine and glanced across the street before she could think better of it.

The luxury SUV was still parked in front of the Daily Grind.

"That must be some sort of sign. Right?" Jade mumbled. "Quick change of plans, Charlie."

The dog woofed as if he didn't like the sound of that.

"I think I could go for a latte," she told him. He whined but fell into step beside her as they crossed the street. Latte. Yup, that's the only reason she was heading to the coffee shop. And maybe a pastry. Nothing at all to do with the man who was inside.

The walk-up window on the porch was Chatelaine's version of a drive-through.

"You wait right here." She tied Charlie to the post in the small area out front that the owner of the shop had made for dogs. There were several filled water bowls. Charlie began to snuffle as she turned away, but Jade was ready for him and handed him an emergency dog bone she kept in her purse before he could let out an embarrassing full-blown basset howl at the indignity of being left behind.

She had just reached the top step when she spotted Heath sitting at one of the tables on the porch. She quickly and, she hoped, *smoothly* did a course correction toward the walk-up window at the far end of the porch, getting in line behind several people. No sense going inside if Heath was out here, right? And besides, if she stayed outside, she could keep an eye on Charlie.

Her gaze went back to Heath. He wore a pair of black-framed glasses as he sat hunched over his open laptop. She'd never considered glasses sexy…until now.

He seemed to be absorbed in whatever was on his laptop, a coffee cup and an untouched Boston crème donut

perched beside him. Maybe after getting her latte, she'd
say hello and tell him about her workshops. She'd been
at the table when he'd been introduced to his triplet sisters, but they hadn't spoken. She liked to think he'd been
so caught up in meeting the Perry triplets that he hadn't
acknowledged her. For sure she'd taken notice of him. To
think he had noticed and immediately dismissed her was
too depressing.

Either way, she could ask him if he'd be interested
in giving a lecture to her kids at one of the ranch's day
camps. She knew his tech company worked with farmers and ranchers. Yeah, that sounded like a good reason
to approach him.

"Are you sure this is the right place?" a woman who'd
gotten in line behind Jade asked.

"The sign said the Daily Grind," answered another
woman. "That's what they told us back at the spa."

"It doesn't look like any coffee shop I've ever seen,"
the first one scoffed.

Jade couldn't help grinning at their conversation. She
had to agree that the Daily Grind was unique, but so was
Chatelaine. And that was fine with her.

"Remember, we're not in Dallas anymore," the other
woman pointed out.

The line advanced, and Jade shuffled forward as the
two women's conversation flowed behind her. Something
about them reminded her of the snobbish girls from her
high school days. Her family's money had not spared her
from the castigating tongues of those girls. So, she had
spent her high school years trying to blend into the background, to avoid detection. Getting noticed for any reason
meant becoming a target.

But, considering she'd reached her full adult height of
five foot nine by the time she'd even started high school,

it hadn't been easy. Making it worse was the fact most of the boys had not yet grown to their full height, so she towered over many of them, including her twin, Nash. He eventually flew past her and now loved patting her on the head and calling her a good *little* sister to make up for those early days.

"How do people stand it? How do you live in a place with no Nordstrom? It's practically barbaric," said one of the women with a condescending snort.

Chatelaine might not be as large or upscale as Dallas or Houston, but it was now Jade's hometown, and she was proud of it. The people here had welcomed her and her family. She'd never seen her mother so excited or happy as she had been since moving here. In fact, the last time Jade had been with her mother, the woman had been positively glowing. Jade never remembered her being like that in the past. Of course, times had not always been easy during Wendy's marriage to Casper Windham, but she'd made the best of it. Yet this…this was *different*. Wendy's happiness wasn't just her putting on a good face. You couldn't fake radiant.

"Well, I'm going to blame you if this coffee is crap," one of the women griped to her companion. "Why couldn't you have waited until we got somewhere decent to feed your caffeine habit?"

That's I*t!* She'd heard enough out of these women. Chatelaine may not have a Nordstrom, but they had damn fine coffee.

Plastering on a smile, Jade turned around. "You don't have to worry about the coffee here, ladies. I've had coffee in Dallas and Houston, and I'd put the Daily Grind's coffee up against those bougie shops any day."

Now, standing face-to-face with the women, Jade regretted her outburst. Heat rose to her cheeks from the uncharacteristic tirade as she tried to figure out why they looked familiar. One was a blonde with hair cascading down around her shoulders, the other a brunette, her shiny hair cut in a symmetrical bob.

The blonde, dressed in a couture designer outfit, looked trim and elegant despite the warm sun and her advanced state of pregnancy. The diamonds in the rings on her left hand sparkled in the sunlight, and Jade was tempted to caution her not to blind anyone. Also dressed in a chic outfit, the brunette carried a large, brightly patterned Dolce & Gabbana tote bag.

Jade did a double take when the head of a tiny dog popped over the top of the designer bag. The red toy poodle blinked at Jade. She'd bet that dog didn't drool all over everything and silently apologized to Charlie for even thinking it. She vowed to give him an extra dog treat when they got home. "Cute dog."

The brunette patted the poodle's head but pulled her hand away when the dog began kissing her fingers. "This is Zaza."

Jade nodded, but before she could say anything more the blonde was saying, "Jade? *Jade Windham*, is that you?"

Pocket-size dog forgotten, the hair on the back of Jade's neck stood up. How did…? Oh God, it was Alexis Baker and Nina Carpenter. No wonder they looked familiar. They were her high school nemeses, but she hadn't seen them since graduation. And she could have gone happily for the rest of her life without crossing paths with them ever again. They'd been just as snobbish back then. Not to mention, they'd made Jade's life miserable with their cutting comments disguised as helpful advice if others were present and just plain mean digs if they managed to get her alone.

"I'm not surprised you ended up in the back of beyond," Nina, the brunette, said with a brittle smile.

Jade's cheeks flushed. What was wrong with her? She was a grown woman. High school was fifteen years ago, middle school over twenty. So why did she feel like she'd been thrown back into second period biology with the school's ultimate mean girls?

"Actually, it's Jade Fortune now." *Oh no.* Why did she have to say that? She didn't want to get into that and not with Alexis and Nina of all people.

Jade had, along with her brothers and sisters, changed her last name to Fortune when their mother learned she was related to the well-known Texas family. They'd done it mostly to please Wendy. And it wasn't as if Jade had been close to Casper Windham and would miss using his name.

"Oh, that's right. I heard something about all that. Y'all found out you were Fortunes. May as well take advantage of the situation, right?" Alexis tossed her long blond hair over her shoulder, ignoring the woman behind her, who sputtered when that hair slapped her in the face.

Yeah, not much had changed.

"We decided to embrace our family connection," Jade answered, keeping her voice as even as possible. Why hadn't she minded her own business? They might not have noticed her. But, no, she had to stick up for her new home. Now she'd called attention to herself and had to suffer the consequences. Felt like high school all over again.

Remembering their snide comments about the town, she asked, "What are you both doing in Chatelaine?"

"We were invited to enjoy the spa at Fortune's Castle," Nina told her.

Jade did her best to hide her surprise. Her mother was redoing Fortune's Castle, turning her inheritance into an exclusive resort and spa. Last time she'd spoken with her, Wendy had mentioned that she'd invited Heath to stay at the hotel in one of the finished penthouse suites. She'd also invited some women to come for a day to sample the services of the spa. Too bad her mother included these two in her invitation.

"You were invited?" Jade asked and winced. Did that make her sound pathetic?

"Of course, we were on the list." Alexis said with a sniff. "Nina is a major social media influencer, so she was invited. And she asked me to come along as her guest."

"I wouldn't have wanted to come way out here by myself," Nina said with a shudder.

Jade ground her back teeth but ignored the biting comment.

"A last girls' trip before Junior is born," Alexis said and patted her stomach.

It wasn't easy, but Jade smiled and found her manners. "Looks like it won't be too long. Congratulations. A boy, you say?"

"Thanks." Alexis waved her hand, holding it so the diamond-studded engagement and wedding bands were on display. "Yes, Conrad and the whole family are thrilled to death. I'm carrying the first grandson."

"How wonderful." Jade nodded. Why had she given in to temptation and come over here? Oh yeah, in hopes of running into Heath Blackwood. And here he was, sitting right over there and could probably hear everything these catty women were saying to her. Would he agree with them? Was it her imagination, or had the place descended into silence?

"Is it true what we heard today? You're running some sort of animal thing?" Nina asked.

"A petting zoo," Jade clarified.

"Who would have thought you'd end up running a zoo of all things? But I'm sure there's a lot more to it than cleaning up animal dung all day." Nina giggled. "At least you're wearing the right footwear for the job—"

"Jade?" Candace, the barista manning the window, leaned out. "You're next. What can I get you?"

The ability to click my *heels and be home at the ranch would be nice.*

Jade managed to smile. "A Royal English Breakfast latte, please. Oh, and I'd love a Boston crème."

"Sorry. Out of those donuts. How about a double chocolate chip muffin instead."

"No, that's okay. But thanks, Candace."

Maybe if she didn't turn back around, Nina and Alexis would leave her be and go about their own business. *And maybe pigs would fly.*

Nina snapped her fingers. "That reminds me, I assume we'll be seeing you again next weekend."

"Next weekend?" Jade racked her brain trying to figure out what they could be talking about. Her mother hadn't mentioned anything else going on at Fortune's Castle.

Alexis nodded. "Our fifteenth high school class reunion. You are planning to attend, aren't you? You can tell everyone the exciting ins and outs of running a petting zoo. I'm sure everyone will be fascinated to learn what it's like to scoop poop all day."

The two women giggled, and Jade clenched her hands. She loved her job, and they were making fun of it. "My boyfriend wasn't sure if he could get away to come with me, so I hadn't made plans yet."

Oh no. Where had that *come from?*

"You have a boyfriend?" Nina gave her a critical once over.

Jade wiped at the damp spot on her jeans from Charlie's drool. "My fiancé actually."

*Oh, Jade, where is your head at? When you're in a hole
you are supposed to stop digging, not get a bulldozer.*

"Fiancé? Really?" Alexis giggled.

"That's him right over there," Jade said and made a
vague motion with her head in the general direction of
Heath's table. What were the odds that they'd know him?

"Say what? You can't mean *him*. That's Heath Blackwood," Nina squeaked.

So much for not knowing him.

Alexis *tsked* her tongue. "You couldn't possibly be engaged to someone like Heath Blackwood."

"Oh, it's not official yet or anything, but he asked me,
and I said yes. So…" Had she taken leave of her senses?

Nina gave someone a saccharine sweet smile. Jade
turned her head to see who she was looking at.

Heath, no longer hunched over his laptop and intent on
his screen, was watching them. His forehead wrinkled in
a frown. Had he overheard the conversation?

Shoot me now.

Or worse. Maybe he knew Nina and Alexis. Perhaps
he was business associates or golfing partners with their
husbands, and he was coming over to say hi to them. And
they would rat her out.

She groaned inwardly. Why oh why had she opened
her big mouth and let all those stupid lies spew forth?
Maybe her dad was right. There was something seriously
wrong with her.

Where were the Four Horsemen of the Apocalypse her-
alding the end of the world? She'd just claimed to be Heath
Blackwood's fiancée. That surely was the end of *her* world.
Because if anyone had overheard her, her life in Chatelaine was over. She'd be laughed out of town if anyone
got wind of this.

And it would be her own damn fault.

JADE FORTUNE.

Heath had spotted her as soon as she came out of the feed store and crossed the street. Dressed in worn jeans, a T-shirt and red sneakers, Jade was long and lithe but round in all the right places. Seeing her made him catch his breath.

He'd been mentally kicking himself for not introducing himself since seeing her that day in the coffee shop. But he'd been caught up with meeting his sisters. Digging into his mother's past and meeting his sisters had been the reason he'd come to Chatelaine.

But not speaking to Jade that day didn't mean he hadn't noticed her so now he felt like doing a fist bump when she got in line for the takeout window. At first it appeared she'd been planning to go inside but changed her mind at the last minute to stay outside. Had she noticed him? Is that why she'd decided to line up at the window?

Ego much, Blackwood?

Maybe he should go up and actually introduce himself this time. Then they could talk. He huffed out a short laugh. This wasn't one of those Jane Austen type movies his mom had watched all the time. No need these days for a formal introduction in order to speak to her. Except the thought of talking to her made his mouth go dry. Made him feel like he was in his youth. When the girls hadn't paid any attention to the gangly, fatherless boy from the wrong side of the tracks.

But, man, they'd sure noticed once he'd achieved success with his start-up tech company and he'd shot up into the tax bracket he now occupied. Except all the females who threw themselves at him now left him cold. Probably had something to do with the fact that his success is what drew them.

He came to the decision to suck it up—hey, he was a

grown man, not a tongue-tied teen—and go over there. Damn. Now she was talking with those two women, so he stayed seated. He didn't want an audience in case he stumbled over his words. Why did Jade make him feel so awkward?

Truth was, she was the only one he was interested in talking to, so he may as well wait. From the first moment he'd laid eyes on her in town, he'd been fascinated. She could only be described as authentic. Each time he'd seen her, she'd been wearing jeans and a T-shirt or flannel, depending on the weather. Her long shiny hair had been tied back in a no-nonsense style instead of puffed out and sprayed, like so many of the socialites at the country club. Jade didn't seem interested in putting up a front, not like the two women behind her. He'd swear those two were all show and no substance.

He admired what Jade was doing for the children of the community. As a boy, he'd attended the sort of workshops she provided. They were free or very little cost, so his mom could afford it, and they satisfied his thirst for knowledge. Those workshops had also fueled his imagination, and he credited them with helping him, a fatherless boy, reach his potential, fulfill his dreams and beyond. He'd created his own innovative company to help farmers and ranchers. His first idea had made him millions. It had been a special weather forecast application useful for both farmers and ranchers.

Moving on from weather apps, he'd been researching drones and lasers, wanting to take his company in a new direction. He liked the idea of using drones, along with artificial intelligence, to target and kill invasive weeds with lasers. This was an up-and-coming technology for farmers, and he wanted in on the ground floor, dumping his profits back into research for this technology—

Hang on. Did someone just mention *his* name? Glancing around, he brought his thoughts back to the present and the coffee shop.

The blonde who was carrying a purse that looked large enough to stock a small country was staring intently at him. A tiny red curly-haired creature popped its head out of the large tote. Was that a *dog*?

The two uppity women glanced his way, and Jade was looking increasingly uncomfortable. Was something wrong? It might not be any of his business, but he decided to pay closer attention to the conversation because it was affecting Jade.

From what he could gather, the ladies were acquainted with Jade, but he'd never seen them around town until today.

He caught enough of the conversation to be angry on Jade's behalf. Running the petting zoo was not something to be denigrated. It wasn't just the kids who benefited but the entire town. In the short time he'd been part of it, he'd come to like the people who lived here.

What the...?

Intent on preventing those women from humiliating Jade, he pushed his chair back so quickly it fell over with a clatter. All three women turned at the sound.

He tossed his glasses onto the table and stalked across the porch, coming to Jade's rescue his only goal.

"Sweetheart, I've been waiting for you," he declared as he approached.

Jade's eyes widened. "Well, I—"

He threw his arms around her, cutting off what she'd been about to say and pulling her close.

Leaning down, he whispered in her ear. "Play along."

She parted her lips as if to speak but his mouth claimed hers before any words came out.

CHAPTER TWO

IT WAS SUPPOSED to be a quick peck on the mouth, but once his lips met hers, he couldn't move away as quickly as he planned. He savored the feel of those soft lips against his. At the beginning of the kiss, she'd held herself stiff against him, but she began to relax, her softness molding to his hardness. As if she belonged there. For a moment, he wished she did. The kiss was invigorating, like the hint of autumn that was in the air today.

"You can't be serious," one of the women sputtered and broke the spell Jade had cast over him.

He pulled his mouth away from Jade's but kept a proprietary arm around her waist. "Why not?"

"Because you're so important and...and I don't see a ring," the blonde one said with a smug expression, as if she'd caught them in a lie. She flipped her hair over her shoulder.

Well, she had caught them, but he wasn't going to turn on Jade now.

"We're getting it sized," he lied smoothly. He turned to Jade. "Sweetheart, aren't you going to introduce me to your...friends? I don't know them, although they seem to know all about me. Or think they do."

"Of course they know you. You being so important and all," Jade said with an amused grin.

Ah, she had a sense of humor. He liked that and silently saluted her. Tapping a finger to the end of her nose, he retorted, "And you didn't believe me when I tried to tell you that."

Jade laughed, and his gut tightened again, but for a very different reason this time. She had a clear, robust laugh and he loved it, wanted to hear it again. Wanted to be the one making her laugh.

Still smiling, she held her hand out toward the other two. "Heath, this is Nina Carpenter and Alexis Baker."

"Actually, it's Alexis Heede now," the blonde said with a disdainful sniff.

So not *a gracious loser*, he thought dryly. He could be all wrong, but he imagined Jade being well mannered, even in defeat.

Evidently, Alexis figured she was important enough for that information to be common knowledge. Yeah, he had made the right choice to back up Jade's lie even though he didn't condone lying.

"And I'm still Carpenter, but that's all about to change next year. That's part of why we were checking out the spa at Fortune's Castle. I'm deciding on venues for a bachelorette party. It's going to be a fabulous blowout. My fiancé said to spare no expense. He is such a dear. But I'm sure you know him, Heath. He's Trevor Trudeau of Trudeau, Fitch and Wilson."

Heath made an exaggerated grimace. "If I admit I don't know him, will that change my status as someone important?"

Jade gave him a playful slap on the arm. "You are such a tease. I'm sure he knows all about your husband, because Heath isn't just important, he knows everyone who *is* important."

Touché. Heath met Jade's gaze and silently indicated that he knew what she'd done there, because he hadn't known her two former classmates.

The barista stuck her head out the window. "I hate to break up this reunion, but your latte is ready, Jade."

Heath stepped forward and pulled out his wallet. "I've got this. You can sit at the table I saved for us, sweetheart."

"Speaking of reunion, can we expect to see *both* of you next weekend at the class reunion in Cactus Grove?" Nina asked, her smug gaze bouncing between them.

Jade shifted her feet. "Well, I...that is, we—"

"We wouldn't miss it. I'm looking forward to meeting the rest of Jade's friends," Heath said. After that kiss, he wasn't about to let Jade Fortune slip away before he had a chance to get to know her better. He'd been attracted to her since first laying eyes on her shortly after he'd arrived in town, but that intoxicating lip-lock had been a game changer. Talk about chemistry.

Jade looked up at him, her expression surprised. "You are?"

"Now who's teasing?" He gave her a quick kiss. He did it because he'd been dying for a repeat performance and wanted to see if he could recreate the zing he felt when his lips had first touched hers.

Yep, still there. Not a fluke. And it felt...*right*. More right than anything else he'd experienced with a woman.

The barista stuck her head out the window. "Are you ladies ready to order? You're holding up the line."

"Well, we'll let you place your order. Hope to see you both next weekend," Heath said and led Jade to his table. He carried her drink in one hand and placed the other on the middle of her back in a proprietary gesture. Those two women weren't the only ones whose gaze was glued to them, but he didn't care.

There was only a scattering of customers on the porch, but that's all it would take for word to get around town about him and Jade. The gossips would be linking their names together. He thought about that for a moment and realized he didn't mind being linked with Jade, a woman he admired and who inexplicitly made his pulse race.

"I can't tell you how sorry I am about all this," she was saying as she slipped into a seat at his table.

He set her drink in front of her. "Don't worry about it."

"How can I *not* worry about it? You realize these people—" she paused and glanced around "—overheard most of that. I've probably ruined your life."

He barked out a laugh, which he regretted when he saw her misery was genuine. He covered her hand with his. "You have done no such thing. If anything, you've raised my status."

"How do you figure that?"

"Being engaged to a Fortune can only help me in Chatelaine."

She quirked a brow. "Is that why you didn't tell them I made it all up?"

He had a much more specific reason for not contradicting her, but he wasn't ready to share that. Not yet anyway. So, he shrugged.

"Oh, geez." She clapped a hand over her mouth.

"What? What's the matter?"

She took her hand away from her mouth and waved it around. "I just realized. What if you are involved with someone, and they hear about this? I've probably messed—"

He grabbed her flailing hand. "There's no other woman. At least those two got something right."

"You're sure?"

"I'm positive." He squeezed her hand before releasing it.

"Thank goodness," she muttered and peeled the cover off the drink, pulled out a tea bag and squeezed it. She wore no rings, and her nails were trimmed and unadorned, but he found her hands appealing. What would they feel like on him? Would her touch be bold or tentative?

He shook his head, hoping to scatter those thoughts. She stirred the drink, mixing the foam that floated on top.

"What is that?" he asked.

"A Royal English Breakfast tea latte."

"That's a thing?"

"Like I told Alexis and Nina, the Daily Grind can hold its own with any bougie shop out there."

He grinned. "You did, didn't you?"

She heaved a sigh. "I should have kept my mouth shut. Maybe they wouldn't have even noticed me."

"I find that hard to believe." He'd noticed her from across the street.

She brought the tea to her mouth and blew on it before taking a sip. "Why would you say that?"

"You're very noticeable, Jade Fortune." His focus the last time they'd been together at the coffee shop had been on meeting his sisters for the first time but that didn't mean he hadn't noticed her even if he hadn't said anything.

She laughed and shook her head. "You say that like it's a good thing."

"Believe me, it is."

"I'll bet you're sorry I noticed you and dragged you into my mess like something straight out of a high school drama club production."

"Like I said, I was happy to come to your rescue." And he meant it. When he'd gotten up and walked over, he'd intended to just divert the women's attention, but once he opened his mouth, he'd found himself backing up her claim.

"How can you be so cavalier about this?"

He shrugged because he wasn't sure he knew the answer to that himself. He didn't want to admit he was drawn to her. Not yet anyway. "If I hadn't come to your rescue, I might never have found out how important I am. So there's that."

She laughed. Oh man, he liked that laugh.

"I would have said they were hitting on you by appealing to your ego, but they're both attached so…"

Now he laughed. "Even if they were trying to flirt with me, do you think I'd fall for it?"

"I don't know. I wouldn't have expected you to back up my outrageous claim, but you did."

He frowned. "Why is it so outrageous that we could be involved?"

"Well, because…because…" She shook her head. "We don't even know one another."

"We can change that. We have week before the reunion."

Her eyes widened. "You mean you really intend to go?"

"I told those snobs I was, so I will." And he could use that occasion as an excuse to get to know Jade Fortune. Not that he needed an excuse, but he liked to cover his bases.

Jade seemed to give it some consideration and finally nodded. He let go of the breath he'd been holding and smiled. "Good."

"So, you're the one who grabbed the last Boston crème," she said, pointing her chin at the uneaten donut on the table and sighed. "Lucky you."

She wanted the pastry, that much was clear. Did he want to just be a gentleman and give it to her or… "I'm willing to share."

"No. Honestly." She blushed. "I shouldn't have said anything."

He rose and took several steps back to the counter that held napkins and creamers and scooped up a cellophane-wrapped napkin and plastic cutlery packet. Sitting back down across from Jade at the small square table, he ripped open the packet. "There. I even have a knife to divide it."

"You're my hero," she said then blushed as if realizing what she'd said.

"That's good to know." The blush highlighted a smattering of freckles across the bridge of her nose. He hadn't noticed those before, and he shifted in his seat as he took note of them now. He'd love to take his time counting them, punctuating his exploration with kisses and the tip of his tongue.

Damn. If he didn't knock this off, he'd be blushing too. To concentrate on something other than those alluring spots, he cut the pastry in half. Some of the pastry cream filling squirted onto the plate from the donut.

"Sorry. I seem to have made a mess of this," he muttered. He should have known better than to try and divide it with such a heavy-handed movement. He should have just given the donut to her, but for some silly reason, sharing the pastry seemed more intimate than just giving her the entire thing.

"That's okay," she said and stuck a finger in the cream and brought it to her lips.

He cleared his throat and shifted in his seat, unable to take his eyes away from her mouth.

"You've got some…" he said, and before his good sense could take over, he reached out and touched a fingertip to the corner of her mouth and wiped off the spot of filling.

Her eyes widened at his touch, and he quickly drew away, bringing the finger to his own lips. Damn, what was he doing?

What was it about this woman that not only piqued his curiosity but had his imagination in overdrive?

OH NO! WHAT in the world was she doing scraping the filling up with her fingers? Jade had no choice now but to taste the pastry cream. Talk about being obvious. She ate it then wiped her hand on the napkin.

She swallowed hard. Twice. It was either that or drool. And it certainly wasn't the pastry causing it. The donut was delicious but couldn't compete with the delectable man seated across from her. And he was watching her every move.

Maybe he was afraid of what she might say or do next. Not that she could blame him. She certainly wasn't acting like the Jade Fortune who was awkward around men.

"I'm so sorry. I don't know what made me say that we were engaged," Jade said, trying not to let her misery show on her face. She thought about that kiss. Had he done it to be kind? Pity was the absolute last thing she wanted from Heath Blackwood.

"It's okay," he replied with a negligent lift of one shoulder.

Why was he being so nice about this whole debacle? It just made her feel worse. If he'd been angry or gave her a hard time, she'd feel a whole lot better about the situation. "No, it's *not* okay. I never should have made that claim. What was I thinking? Oh, wait. I wasn't."

"Yeah, I got the feeling maybe you were just reacting to the vitriol those two were throwing at you."

"They used to bully me in school," she admitted. Oh, why had she said that? Talk about looking pathetic in front of the hottest guy in Chatelaine. Maybe she should have checked her horoscope before leaving home today. It might have warned her not to open her mouth.

"I hate dealing with bullies."

"I can't imagine you have to deal with them."

"Believe it or not, I wasn't always this important," he said with a lopsided grin.

She pressed her palm against her chest. "No! Say it isn't so."

He laughed and she joined him. It felt good to be sharing not only a pastry but a joke with a handsome man.

See, Dad, maybe I'm not such a failure after all.

"But it is true that I didn't grow into my greatness until much later. I was referred to as a shrimp well into high school," he confided.

"I had the opposite problem. I reached my full height in eighth grade."

He winced. "Ouch, you must have towered over the boys."

"That's for sure."

"I'm not sure I would have let that stop me if I'd known you in high school," Heath murmured.

"Oh, you would have. I wasn't exactly Miss Popularity."

"Don't be too sure. You have a lot of appeal."

"Those two didn't seem to think so." She hitched her chin toward Alexis and Nina, who were walking back to a white Range Rover. Unlike Heath's SUV, theirs was dusty, and Jade got some perverse pleasure out of that. That was pretty juvenile, but she couldn't help it.

"Forget about them. Tell me more about yourself."

"Not much to tell. You may find this hard to believe, but I don't always go around claiming to be engaged to strange men."

"Wait." He drew back. "How did I go from important to *strange*?"

Her cheeks heated. "Let me rephrase that. I don't claim to be engaged to strangers."

"Then I'm honored you chose me."

"Again, I apologize. I still don't understand why you didn't tell them the truth."

"And humiliate you? No way." He looked over her shoulder for a moment as if deciding on something. "When I was in elementary school, I won a statewide science award. Some of the other boys, I'd say they were male versions of Alexis and…"

"Nina."

"Right." He paused for a moment as if deciding something. "As I was saying, they used to make fun of me because I never had a dad come to anything. I told everyone they'd get to see my father at the ceremony for that science award."

She put her hand on his arm and squeezed in sympathy. She'd had a dad, but he didn't always come to things like that. Not that she'd done anything outstanding like win a science award. "What happened?"

"Well, since I didn't have one, he obviously couldn't come. Luckily, my mother, bless her soul, saved the day and told the others that he'd been called out of town on important business. She spared me from public humiliation because those kids couldn't imagine my mother backing me up." He huffed out a breath. "But that's because they didn't know my mom."

"I'm glad it worked out."

He shrugged. "It did and it didn't."

"How so?"

"She saved me but, in the process, I hurt her. Even though we didn't talk about it much, I knew she felt guilty because I didn't have a father. And I'm sure she knew I always longed for one, especially when I saw the other boys with their dads. Playing ball, going fishing, stuff like that. So, with my lies I piled on more guilt. That was my bad." He looked straight ahead, but his gaze was unfocused, as if he were lost in the past.

"You were a kid. I'm sure she took that into consideration. On the other hand, I don't have that as an excuse.

I'm an adult and should have handled that whole situation better. Again, I'm truly sorry I dragged you into it."

"Those girls were giving you grief you don't deserve. I think what you're doing for the kids and this town is terrific."

She swallowed. "You do?"

A tingle ran down her spine. Heath Blackwood knew about her camps and classes. Talk about catching her off guard!

"Why are you so surprised?"

"It's just that I drifted for a long time, but this feels right. Yet at the same time, I sometimes wonder if my family felt sorry and just gave me something to do. Patted me on the head and said, 'Sure, make a zoo.'"

"It's not just the zoo but those workshops you're doing. They meant so much to me as a kid."

"Really?" Maybe she wasn't just wasting her family's time, space and money with her zoo and activities on the ranch after all.

"Yes, really." He grinned. "I went to a lot of them as a kid. Where do you think I got the idea for my start-up company? I used to daydream about the stuff I learned and about making it better."

"Well, you've been very successful. Would you be willing to come and talk to the kids sometime? Let them know a little bit about what you're doing." *Please say you'll come.*

His smile lit up his blue eyes, and they resembled the sky on a sunny day. "I thought you'd never ask."

"I… I would have asked earlier, but I wasn't sure if you'd be interested. I know how busy you are."

"Not too busy to help the next generation of innovators."

"I can't thank you enough. First for pulling my butt out of the fire and now this. How will I ever repay you?"

"Have dinner with me?"

Her heart skipped a beat. "You want to have dinner with me?" She'd imagined this scenario ever since she'd realized she had a crush on him, but those had been pipe dreams. This was *real*.

"Yes, that's why I'm asking."

"But…but…"

"Why wouldn't I want to have dinner with you?"

Yeah, why? She might not be able to compete with her mother and sisters in the glamour department, but she was honest enough to know she was attractive. And fishing for compliments was beneath her. But this whole situation had her flummoxed. "Well, because—"

He tsked. "Jade, don't tell me you let those women get inside your head."

"I wasn't going to let them, but then it was like I was back in high school and feeling all awkward. How could I have let them do that to me? And to involve you was unforgivable."

"It's easy to get sucked back into situations from the past. And I involved myself. I could have denied even knowing you, but as I mentioned before, I know what it's like to be bullied." He winked at her. "And what matters now is that you're giving back and helping kids. What are those women doing to help shape the future?"

"Nina is an important social media influencer."

"I rest my case." He laughed.

Glancing at his watch, he scowled. "Unfortunately, I have to get back. I have a video meeting with my research and development team this afternoon."

"Okay."

"About tonight…"

Jade kept her smile in place. He was probably coming to his senses and going to cancel. "It's—"

He pulled out his phone. "Give me your number and

I'll program it in and text you so we'll have each other's numbers. But if you don't hear from me, I'll pick you up at seven."

"Uh, do you know where I live?" she asked.

A spot of color appeared high on his cheeks. "Yeah, I guess that would help."

She gave him her address and he typed it into his phone.

After doing that, Heath leaned down and gave her a peck on the cheek. "Until tonight."

Jade sighed, admiring Heath's confident, loose-limbed stride as rushed down the steps of the coffee shop. Did all of that just happen?

She brought her fingers to her cheek, touching where his lips had been.

On his way out, Heath passed a couple with a baby coming up the steps as he was going down, but she only had eyes for him. She stood up to clear off the table before she left.

"Jade?"

She glanced at the couple on the porch and quickly revised her original assessment. The man was her brother Ridge. He and the woman with him, Hope, weren't a real couple.

As far as Jade knew, Ridge had found Hope passed out in his barn back in July. No one knew if Hope was even her real name because she claimed to have amnesia.

No, wait. Using the word *claimed* wasn't fair. Jade truly believed Hope was telling the truth about her lack of memory. Jade had come to know the mysterious woman in the past three months and didn't believe her capable of deception. She was definitely a good mother and took excellent care of baby Evie.

But that didn't prevent Jade from worrying about her brother. She could see how much he was starting to care of

Hope and the baby. Given their matching tiny birthmarks and how much the baby resembled her, it seemed obvious that Hope was the infant's mother.

What if Hope recovered her memory and discovered she was a married woman? A husband and family could be searching for her at this very moment. Jade hated to think of Ridge falling for Hope and the baby only to be heartbroken when the truth was discovered. And the truth *would* eventually come out. She couldn't imagine a woman and child going missing forever and no one noticing.

"I thought that was Charlie tied up out there." Ridge came over and gave Jade a brotherly one-armed hug. "Evie recognized him too. She started cooing and kicking her feet."

Jade hugged Hope and kissed the top of baby Evie's head. She couldn't help but fall in love with the sunny, smiling baby. Maybe someday she'd—

"Was that Heath Blackwood with you? What were you two doing together?" Ridge gave her an assessing look.

"We…uh, we were just chatting. He's interested in giving a workshop for my kids sometime." And that was the truth. Or *part* of it.

"Well, rumor has it he was kissing you."

"Oh…um, that." Heat rose in her face. She should have known that little incident wouldn't go unnoticed.

"Maybe your sister would like her privacy," Hope suggested gently.

Ridge huffed out a short laugh. "Then they shouldn't have been kissing in public. Jade?"

Great. She was going to have to confess. The whole of Chatelaine would probably know about all this by tonight anyway, so what did it matter? How the heck could she have gotten herself into such hot water? She'd love to place the blame on Alexis and Nina, but she was the one who'd opened her mouth.

"Would you mind going ahead and ordering for us?" Hope asked him. "I would love a Boston crème."

Ridge glanced between the two women. "Fine, but I expect a full explanation when I get back."

It was a reprieve at least. Time to get her thoughts together. Maybe find a way to tell them what had happened without making herself look foolish. Yeah, right. "A word of warning. Those donuts are all gone. Heath and I shared the last one."

Ridge raised his eyebrows at her. "You two split a pastry?"

Why, oh, why, hadn't she kept her mouth shut?

Hope touched Ridge's shoulder. "I'll have an eclair with my latte. Can you hurry before they're all gone too?"

Ridge grumbled but went to the walk-up window.

"Thank you," Jade told Hope as her brother strode away.

Hope laughed and sat down, settling Evie on her lap. The baby was drooling and gumming a teething ring. "Don't thank me yet, I'm just as curious as he is. After all, this is Heath Blackwood we're talking about."

"You'll get the whole sordid tale. I promise." Jade sat down in the chair she'd recently vacated.

"Ooh, this is sounding better and better," Hope said, rubbing Evie's back in soothing circles.

"While we wait, why don't you tell me how you've been? I've been thinking about you. Are you still having those dreams?" Jade asked, although they sounded more like nightmares.

Hope had told her about her dreams of a middle-aged couple holding their arms out to her and the baby, but when Hope doesn't turn over the baby, their faces become mean.

A woman came out of the coffee shop with a giggling

child darting ahead carrying a pastry box. "Give me that," the woman called in an exasperated tone.

Hope's face drained of all color. Jade reached over and placed her hand over her friend's. "Hope, what is it? What's wrong?"

"I don't know." She began to shiver and wrapped her arms around Evie and clung to her. "I want to go home. Now."

Evie started to fuss and squirm, and Hope kissed the top of the baby's head, rubbing her cheek against the baby's fine hair. "Shh, sweetie, it's okay. I won't let anything happen to you."

Now it was Jade's turn to shiver. She couldn't imagine what horrific event put that much fear into Hope. Whatever happened was bad enough that she'd blocked it out, and it was giving her nightmares and panic attacks.

"Nothing is going to happen to either of you," Jade promised, trying to comfort her friend. "What do you want me to do?"

Hope gnawed on her lower lip. "Tell Ridge that Evie and I need to go home. Right now."

Jade nodded, wondering where Hope meant when she said "home." Had the other woman regained her memory? Did she want Ridge to take her home, as in where she came from? Or did Hope consider the Fortune family ranch to be home?

The baby continued to fuss. Probably picking up on her mother's stress. And Hope was certainly stressed. Her face had drained of color, and her gaze darted about as if she expected something to happen.

Jade was torn between soothing mother and baby and getting her brother's attention as quickly as possible. She could have stayed with Hope and yelled across the porch to him, but she figured that hot kiss had caused enough of a spectacle in the Daily Grind to keep the gossip flying around Chatelaine for the foreseeable future.

CHAPTER THREE

RISING FROM HER CHAIR, Jade touched Hope's shoulder in a reassuring gesture that mirrored the loving pats Hope was giving the baby. As worried as Jade was about Ridge getting hurt because of his deepening tenderness toward Hope and baby Evie, she herself was developing feelings for them too.

As much as Jade wanted to, up to now, she'd refrained from giving Ridge any unsolicited advice. She knew how it felt to have her family all up in her business, and she was sure they would be all over this whole fake engagement thing.

"Ridge, Hope wants to go home." Jade told him.

Jade patted Evie. "I have to get home, too. Got lots to do."

"Got a big date planned, Sis?" Ridge joked.

For once she could answer in the affirmative. At least she guessed it was a date. Heath was taking her to dinner, so of course it was a date. Wasn't it? Or were they as fake as the engagement?

"Sis?"

"Well, I…"

"You do." Ridge peered at her, then glanced over to where Heath's Mercedes had been parked. "With Heath Blackwood?"

The questions and speculation had already started, and Ridge didn't even know about the fake engagement, just tonight's date. "Look, you better get Hope home. We'll talk later."

"We definitely will," Ridge promised.

Yeah, she had a lot of explaining to do. Maybe her family hadn't heard about what happened in the coffee shop today.

Nope, that's not a likely scenario. The whole town probably knew about it by now. At least Heath had backed her up, saving her from public humiliation.

Grinning, she went to fetch Charlie and go home to get ready.

She'd barely gotten the basset settled into his special car seat in the dusty pickup she used for ranch business when her phone started buzzing with calls and incoming texts. She checked Charlie's harness and pulled out the phone from the pocket of her jeans. Most of the messages were from her family, asking about a rumor going around town about her and Heath Blackwood.

Despite the barrage of messages, she grinned all the way home. She had a date! An honest-to-goodness date. When was the last time that had happened? And that date was with the gorgeous Heath Blackwood. Simply saying his name under her breath sent a tingle down her spine. As if that wasn't good enough, it was October but still warm enough to wear the dress her mother had insisted Jade buy for the annual Ranchers' Reception at the LC Club this summer. She could bring a shawl or shrug with her in case the evening turned cool. If she couldn't find something in her closet, she could ask one of her sisters. One of them would certainly have something appropriate…

Yeah, she had a bit of explaining to do. Why, oh why, had she opened her big mouth and spouted off all that nonsense about being engaged to the gorgeous newcomer? If she was going to be thrown back into adolescent behavior, why couldn't she have invented a boyfriend who conveniently lived in Canada?

That was something a kid in middle school would do, but she'd acted like one, so why not?

JADE PRESSED THE remote for the gate to the driveway of her home. Each one of the six log homes she and her siblings occupied had its own entry gate. She wasn't sure what the purpose was for the gates, but they were there when they moved in.

She groaned. The gates certainly didn't serve to keep people out because she spotted three golf carts lined up in front of her home. She hadn't expected the in-person third degree from her family to start quite so soon.

"They didn't even give us a chance to get home," she said to Charlie as she passed the carts so she could pull her truck closer to the house.

One of the carts was decorated with large dahlia flower decals, so she assumed her sister Dahlia was among the visitors. She'd bet the other two were her mother and sister Sabrina.

"I should have known this whole fiasco wouldn't stay a secret for long," she moaned as she pulled into the driveway.

As she always did when arriving home, Jade took a moment to thank her mother for buying the 3,500-acre ranch that she and her siblings now lived on. In addition to the ranch home and offices, the place had six magnificent log homes surrounding the shore of one side of Lake Chatelaine.

When Wendy had first discussed purchasing the ranch and invited all her children to move to what she was calling the Fortune Family Ranch, she'd said there were log cabins available for each of her children. Jade soon discovered that "log cabin" was a bit of a misnomer. Yes, they'd been constructed using logs, but they were large and luxurious, well beyond the realm of cabins. More like the ones she'd seen featured in slick magazines about those exclusive ski resort communities in Colorado.

Jade had felt guilty at first, as if her family was handing her charity by giving her the home, but when all her siblings moved into their respective log homes, she decided her guilt was misguided.

Charlie perked up and wagged his tail and began barking. The one Jade called his happy bark. She followed to where the dog was looking. Sure enough, her mother and two sisters were seated on her porch.

"Nothing like being obvious about butting into my business," she muttered to Charlie, who barked a response. When the siblings moved onto the ranch, it was understood that everyone would be afforded their privacy. The log homes had been built far enough apart to give the illusion of being alone in the Texas countryside.

Jade parked her battered ranch pickup at the end of the driveway and got out. She went to the passenger side and opened the door, unhooked the dog's harness and hefted all sixty-five pounds of him out of the seat.

"You need to grow longer legs or lose a few pounds," she told him with a grunt as she set him on the ground.

He went running over to the porch to greet his visitors as fast as those short legs would carry him. Jade's mom and sisters greeted him, showering him with affection and, Jade suspected, dog treats. Dahlia was the only one who owned a dog, an Australian cattle dog named Tripp, but they all carried dog biscuits, and Charlie knew it.

"Hey, to what do I owe the honor?" Jade asked as she approached the porch that wrapped along the length of the house. As if she didn't already know the reason for the welcoming committee.

"We just wanted to chat," Wendy said with a cheerful smile.

Her mother was doing her best to look and sound like this was some innocent visit. And failing *miserably*, because they all knew this was a mission. A mission to find out the truth about what they'd heard. And, considering how rampant gossip in Chatelaine was, there was no telling what they'd been told. The truth, fantasy or something in between. Jade voted for in between. She may not have been in Chatelaine for very long, but she had lived here long enough to know the gossip was like that old game of telephone. As the story got passed along, each person added their own spin on it so that it grew with each retelling.

"You know you could have gone inside," Jade told them and hopped up the two steps to the porch.

"We may all live on the same ranch, but we didn't want to barge in and invade your home." Wendy rose and gave her daughter a quick hug. "We respect your right to privacy, dear."

Jade returned the embrace and laughed. "And yet I suspect you're all here to do exactly that. Invade my privacy."

"Oh, no, don't say that." Wendy frowned. "We just—"

"Jade's right," Dahlia interjected and stood. "Come clean, Mom. We're all here to find out the truth about Jade's supposed engagement with Heath Blackwood."

"'Supposed'? You make it sound as if that's impossible," Jade said, feeling defensive. The fact that she would have thought so too before the incident at the coffee shop didn't stop her from being annoyed. They were right, but it still sounded a bit insulting.

Of course, that meant she and Heath needed to play this out. If they didn't attend the reunion, everyone would assume the engagement was fake. Alexis and Nina would be sure to spread the word to her former classmates. So backing out of this whole thing wasn't feasible.

"Not impossible at all, dear, except you never once mentioned him, and I don't believe you two are acquainted enough to get engaged. If it's true, you've done an excellent job of keeping your relationship a secret."

"How did you even hear about any of this?"

"The barista is one of Miriam Stemple's granddaughters, and she told her mother, who told Miriam."

"And Miriam is...?" Yep, the game of telephone.

"We go to the same beauty salon and—"

"Never mind, I get it." Jade heaved a sigh and opened her front door. "Might as well come in so I can explain what's going on."

Her mother and sisters trooped into the house, along with Charlie, who went from one guest to the other, greeting them and checking to see if anyone had any handouts.

"Hey, I saw that," Jade said and pointed at Dahlia. Her sister had taken a dog biscuit out of her pocket for Charlie. "I was just telling him he needed to cut back."

"But who can resist that face?"

"Evidently nobody which would explain why he gets excited anytime y'all come to visit."

"Oh, here. I almost forgot." Wendy paused to pick up the insulated soft-sided cooler she'd left on the floor next to her chair on the porch.

Jade took the package. "What is it?"

"Lasagna. I was in a mood today and made way too much."

"In a mood? Before or after you found out about my fake engagement?"

Wendy gave her a smile and a pat on the arm. "Does it matter?"

"I suppose not." But Jade knew the answer. "Feels like there's a lot here. I live alone, Mom."

"I know you do, dear, but you can divide it into smaller portions if you want and freeze it. Or—" Wendy paused as if for effect "—you could invite someone to share it with you."

"And would that someone go by the name of Heath Blackwood, hmm?"

All three women grinned at Jade. Now that her two younger sisters were happily attached, Jade knew her mother would be wanting that for her. Heck, she wanted that too. But claiming a fake engagement probably wasn't the best way to go about that.

They followed Jade into the spacious open kitchen of the log home and gathered on stools along one side of the long granite-topped island. She put the lasagna in the refrigerator and removed the gallon jug of apple cider. She set the cider and cups on the island along with a box of cinnamon sugar donut holes she'd splurged on. At least she wouldn't be tempted to eat the entire box.

After Jade got through telling them what had happened at the coffee shop, Wendy shook her head slowly and said, "I never liked those two girls."

"Yeah," Dahlia agreed, wiping her hands on a napkin. "I remember them from school. They wouldn't have anything to do with underclass students."

"That was so nice of Heath to come to your rescue and back you up," Wendy said.

"Well, I…" Jade started but Sabrina jumped in.

"Why should Jade feel grateful? Maybe Heath Blackwood is the one who should be thanking his lucky stars that the beautiful and talented Jade Fortune picked *him* to be her fake fiancé. I'm sure there were plenty of other guys in the coffee shop," Sabrina said.

"I doubt if there were plenty, but Sabrina's right, Mom," Dahlia put in.

Sabrina glanced over at her sister. "Of course I am."

Wendy looked startled for a moment, then smiled. "Yes. You're absolutely right."

Jade glanced at the women in her family and was appreciative of the support. She blinked back tears. As annoying as they could sometimes be, Jade was grateful for her family. Apart from her father, they'd always had her back, even when she was stumbling along trying to find her place in the world.

"Thanks. But Mom is sort of right. I really put my foot in my mouth with that claim," Jade said. "I was lucky Heath didn't leave me stranded and humiliated in front of those two."

Sabrina shook her head. "But he didn't. He stood up for you, and he's even agreed to go to the reunion, hasn't he?"

"How did you know that he agreed to attend my reunion?" Jade asked, narrowing her eyes.

Her sisters laughed. "Have you forgotten this is Chatelaine? The customers of the Daily Grind were given a play-by-play, and every last one of them couldn't wait to spread every juicy tidbit."

"So, my original point still stands. He wouldn't have done any of that if he didn't like you," Wendy said with a smile at her oldest daughter. "Sounds like he may like you a lot."

"And why shouldn't he? What's *not* to like?" Sabrina and Dahlia asked at the same time.

She quickly steered the conversation onto other topics, but after her mother and sisters left, Jade contemplated what they'd said. Was it possible Heath liked her as much as they seemed to think?

HEATH PARKED HIS SUV in the lot of Fortune's Castle, the rambling mansion Wendy Fortune had inherited from her grandfather Wendell when he died. He gazed up at the structure as he exited his SUV. Fortune's Castle was aptly named because it was a replica of a medieval castle complete with ornate pointed arches, flying buttresses, gargoyles, and stained-glass windows. The result was odd while at the same time strangely impressive. It was something you'd expect to find in France or Germany, not Texas.

He certainly hadn't expected anything like it when he'd come to this dusty little town to make contact with his sisters. His mother's death had prompted him to begin his search in earnest for his biological father. Although he was still trying to fit the pieces of the puzzle that were his background. Why had he been separated from his sisters? Why had his mother chosen to leave Chatelaine?

His cell phone buzzed as he made his way across the parking lot to the cobblestone pathway that lead to the entrance. The phone screen identified the caller as his sister Lily, who, with her marriage to Asa Fortune, was also a member of that elite family. Chatelaine might be small, but it felt as though it were crawling with Fortunes.

"What's this I hear about you and Jade Fortune being engaged?" Lily asked before he could even say hello.

"Good afternoon to you too." He should have known word of what happened at the Daily Grind would spread through Chatelaine at the speed of sound.

"Sorry." She sighed into the phone. "It's just that we've been going crazy wondering what this sudden engagement was all about."

Now that he had found his half sisters and made contact with them, he would have to get used to having others taking an interest in his personal life. "'We'? You mean as in you and Asa?"

His sister was gloriously happy with her marriage to Asa after a bit of a rough start. He didn't know the whole story, but he did know her marriage had started as a marriage of convenience, like something from one of those romance novels his mother loved. But according to both his sister and Asa, it was now a real marriage and both couldn't be happier about it. And Heath was thrilled for them both.

"I mean 'we' as in me, Tabitha and Haley," she clarified. "I have a feeling Asa will tell me to mind my own business."

Heath grinned even though he knew his sister couldn't see him. "Smart man."

"Hey, I resent that," Lily shot back.

Heath winced. Damn, he was still navigating this whole brother and sister thing. He was grateful he'd found his half sisters and even more so that they were able to start forming a bond despite having three decades lapse before they met. "Look, I'm sorry. I didn't mean to—"

"Hey! I was just teasing. I'm told it's something siblings do a lot of. I'm just as new at this as you. We may not know exactly what happened thirty years ago, but now that we've all found one another, I thought we were going to be real siblings."

"And by 'real siblings,' I take it you mean teasing and getting into one another's business?"

"Well, yeah. I think it's a requirement or something." She paused and sighed again. "And to be honest, Heath, it's because we care about you. You're our big brother."

According to his research, he was two months older than his triplet sisters. *Half sisters*, he amended, then regretted the amendment. They might not have shared the same mother or even grew up together, but the bond they were now forming was as strong as if they had.

"Thanks for the concern, and I apologize for the remark about getting in my business."

"Apology accepted, but that doesn't let you off the hook. I was appointed spokesperson," Lily informed him. "I'm supposed to find out what the heck is going on and report back."

"In other words, you drew the short straw."

She laughed but didn't give him an answer, and he wasn't going to press.

Heath sighed. He should have known this was coming. But frankly, he was still getting used to having sisters, to having any extended family. With his mom gone, there wasn't anyone to take an interest in his personal life. So he decided to go with the truth. "It's just a cover story."

"Cover story? Cover for *what*?"

He tried to think of a way to explain the situation so that no one thought poorly of Jade. Because he hated to think his sisters might blame her for taking advantage of a situation. "Jade got a bit carried away when confronted with some nasty women she'd gone to school with and claimed we were engaged."

"And you simply went along with it?" Lily asked, sounding skeptical.

He leaned against the G Wagon and crossed his feet at the ankles. "It was entirely my choice to back her up."

"Oh?"

It was just as he'd feared. He tried again to explain without having to get into the whole background of what prompted him to go along with Jade's assertion. "Would you rather I denied it and humiliated her in the Daily Grind?"

"Well, no. I can't claim to be close friends with her or anything, but I do like Jade."

"So do I," Heath admitted gruffly.

"Oh?" This time, Lily made that one-word sound totally different. Gone was the skepticism to be replaced with curiosity.

"Yeah," he said with a hint of a challenge in his voice. "I like Jade."

"And there's absolutely nothing wrong with that unless…"

"Unless what?"

"You don't have a wife stashed away somewhere, do you?" Lily asked.

"Nope. Not even a girlfriend or sometime girlfriend." The last woman he'd dated had dumped him when a better prospect had come along. She'd hinted around about marriage, but he hadn't taken her up on it. Yet he hadn't even dated Jade Fortune, and he'd jumped in to lay claim as her fiancé. What did that say about his feelings toward a woman he barely knew?

"But why did she claim you two were engaged?"

Heath explained the confrontation with those two snotty women at the coffee shop.

"Well, I'm proud to call you brother, Brother," Lily said after he'd finished his explanation.

Warmth filled his chest. He quite liked being a big brother. If only he could figure out why his mother had never told him about his biological father or that he even had half sisters. What was so wrong that she'd left town and never told James Perry he had a son?

LATER THAT EVENING, Jade did a pirouette in front of the full-length mirror in the dressing area of the master bedroom, letting the fabric swirl around her thighs. The black dress, which ended at her knees, had bright gold and orange flowers tossed across the full skirt and a round neck with extended shoulders and front princess seams.

She didn't wear dresses very often, but she had to admit this one was flattering, even with her less than generous curves. And her mother and two older sisters wouldn't be there to outshine her, so it was all good.

Jade frowned at her reflection. "That was uncalled for," she told herself firmly.

It wasn't as if her closest female relatives went out of their way to make her look like the frumpy wallflower that she was. Her mother had been a beauty pageant winner in her younger days and was still a gloriously attractive woman. And the fact was that both of her sisters took after their mother in the glamorous looks department.

She shook her head. No time for a pity party, because she had a date with Heath Blackwood. The thought made her giddy and she laughed at her reflection. If this was a dream, she never wanted to wake up.

A knocking sound sent her rushing into the hallway and toward the front door. Several feet before she reached it, she slowed down. *Eager much, Jade?*

She inhaled deeply, trying to center herself. She could see the silhouette of Heath's broad shoulders through the inset frosted and beveled glass of the red painted door. Smoothing her dress, she smiled and threw open the door. "Welcome."

"Hi," Heath said and handed her a bouquet of sunflowers.

The paper wrapped around the flowers crinkled as she accepted the gift. She couldn't resist sticking her nose in the circle of blossoms. The subtle fragrance was natural and irresistible, whisking her back to her childhood. "Oh, thank you. I love these."

"I wasn't sure what to get, and those looked…uh…as good as any," he said, a faint blush high on his cheeks.

"I think sunflowers look happy. How can you not smile when you see them?" And how could she resist smiling at him. Tonight, he wore a light blue Oxford style shirt, black dress slacks, and shiny black Cole Haan pinch tassel loafers.

He slipped his index finger under his shirt collar. "Yeah, I guess I was thinking that too."

"Is that what you were going to say? It's okay to admit that they made you smile," she teased.

He chuckled. "Are you sure someone won't come and demand my man card?"

The delicious sound of his deep chuckle sent tingles down her spine. "We just won't answer the door if they do. Problem solved. Let me put these in some water before they wilt. C'mon in."

"Nice place you have here." He stepped inside and glanced around at the expansive living room with its soaring ceiling.

"It sorta comes with the job or the family, depending how you look at it. Another reason this ranch is perfect for us. It's not a bad perk, and each one of us has a mini mansion cabin like this."

"It is impressive. I love your fireplace."

She turned toward the two-story fieldstone wood-burning fireplace set between two soaring windows that went from floor to ceiling. "I love it too. I just wish I had more opportunities to use it. If the cabin was in someplace like Montana or Wyoming, it would come in handy a lot more."

"That's true, but then you wouldn't be here in Texas, and we wouldn't have met."

She didn't have a regular flower vase—when was the last time she'd gotten flowers?—so she filled a decorative antique pitcher with water. "And you wouldn't be forced to explain a fake engagement to your family."

Heath grinned. "A small price to pay, and my sisters seem to think it's all very romantic."

"Sounds like my sisters." She set the pitcher with the flowers on the mantel.

He walked over to her floor-to-ceiling windows. "This home is perfectly situated to capture the views of the lake."

"Yes, I know I can't complain. I'm really lucky. When my mother first bought this ranch, I was skeptical, but now I think it's the best thing she did."

"Do you like living so close to family?"

"Yes, and we're not so close that we trip over one another. If Mom had her way, we'd get together as a family to share a meal once a week," she said and tried to interpret the look that came over his face at her comment. But the expression disappeared almost as soon as it had appeared. If she hadn't been looking closely, she would have missed it. Did it have to do with Heath not growing up with his sisters? But, from what she understood, the Perry triplets didn't grow up together either.

"Yeah, thirty-five hundred acres gives humans and animals plenty of space to spread out," he said and smiled when she gave him a quizzical look. "I've spoken with your brother about using some of my company's technology for the ranch."

"That's right. I forget your technological advances have real-world applications." And that he was just as rich or more so than the Fortunes. And Casper Windham. Was Heath like her father? More interested in business and money than family or the people around him? She didn't think so, but then, she had to believe Casper had courted Wendy at some point. Why else would she have married him?

Heath glanced at his watch and she got the hint. "I need to let Charlie in before we leave. He has a secure and fenced area, but I don't like to leave him outside while I'm gone," she said, moving to open the side door.

Charlie came bounding inside. Probably knew they had a visitor and was hoping to get some more treats.

Her smile turned into a frown as he rushed past her, because the parts of him that were supposed to be white weren't. He was covered in some sort of brown grime.

"Charlie! What in the world did you get into?"

"Is there a problem?" Heath asked from somewhere behind her.

Charlie perked up at the sound of a new voice. Her pet loved meeting new people. Well, more like he loved meeting potential victims for his mooching. Each new person he met might fall for his "she's starving me" act.

Afraid of what was coming next, Jade made a grab for him, but Charlie slipped through her arms like a greased pig. But not before he'd transferred whatever muck he'd rolled in onto her dress.

The dog made a beeline for Heath, who was standing only a few feet away.

"Watch out," Jade yelled but it was too late.

Before Heath could move out of the way, Charlie had his muddy front paws on Heath's formerly cleaned and pressed slim fit chinos.

Jade closed her eyes as if that could block out the disaster. So much for her fairy-tale night. Her dress was a mess and she was sure once she dared open her eyes, Heath's pants would be in a similar state as well.

"Well, hello, there. You must be Charlie," Heath was saying.

Even though he was being a good sport, Jade's heart sank just the same. First, she ambushed him in the coffee shop by announcing their nonexistent engagement, and now her dog was getting mud all over him. She wouldn't blame him at all if he left and wanted nothing more to do with her.

"Heath, I'm so sorry."

"Don't worry about it." He continued to rub Charlie's head and around his ears, sending her dog into a state of ecstasy. While the fastest way to her dog's heart was food, lavish praise and attention ran a close second. "It'll all come out in the wash. Fortune's Castle has a good laundry service."

Jade was confused at first but remembered that's where Heath had been staying. The luxury hotel wasn't officially open yet, but the rooms on the top floor—the luxury penthouse suites—were completed. Wendy had told Jade that Heath had approached her and asked if he could stay in one of those suites during his time in Chatelaine. He'd said he didn't mind the ongoing construction on the lower floors, and her mom had agreed, letting him stay at a reduced rate. She informed Jade that it gave her staff someone to "practice" on.

"I'll be sure my mother sends me the bill," Jade told him.

He dismissed it with a wave of the hand. "Not necessary."

"I don't know how you can act so casual. He's ruined our evening."

"I highly doubt that was his intention, and the evening's outcome has yet to be determined."

Either Heath Blackwood was the mellowest guy she'd ever met, or maybe the evening didn't mean as much to him as it meant to her. Had she been reading more than warranted into tonight? She blinked rapidly, hoping to prevent the tears that threatened to break free.

CHAPTER FOUR

HEATH PANICKED WHEN he saw how distressed Jade was. He was not good with emotional females. And the thought of having to witness Jade so upset was more than he could take.

"Hey, hey," Heath said and patted her back awkwardly. Despite the polished exterior he'd worked hard to pull around him like a cloak, deep down he still felt like that nerd he was in high school. Maybe that was another reason he'd jumped to Jade's rescue and why he was attracted to her. She wasn't artificial and slick like those two women today, like many of the women who vied for his attention. Even before his success with Blackwood AgriTech, women had shown interest. He wasn't vain, but he knew the face he saw in the mirror every day was attractive to women. But they were drawn to him until they realized he was just a computer gadget geek in a nice package. Many then lost interest.

Sure, when he'd made his first million, he'd dated women like Alexis and Nina like it was a rite of passage or something. But the truth was, they'd left him cold. He'd take Jade's down-to-earth personality any day. Still…

What had he gotten himself into? Maybe he should have denied her claim about the engagement back there at the Daily Grind. He'd let his crush on Jade overcome his common sense. He hadn't simply backed Jade up on her claim of an engagement with him, but he'd taken it one step further and agreed to attend the reunion. When those catty women had asked if they were attending, he could have ended it then and there by saying no. But he hadn't. Why? Because after that kiss, his thinking was muddled, and he'd agreed to attend.

Jade sucked in a quavering breath. "How can you be so calm?"

The dog plopped down in front of him and looked up, his soulful canine eyes seeming to beg for forgiveness.

Heath reached down and patted the dog on the head again. "It's okay. You didn't mean to ruin anything, did you boy?"

"How can you say that? Look at us." She pointed first at her muddy dress and then his dirt covered pants. She sighed. "I'll bet Zaza doesn't roll around in the mud."

"Zaza? Who—"

"Nina's dog."

"Ah, the red one in the tote bag." He had nothing against small dogs in general or that dog in particular, but like Jade, he preferred Charlie.

"That's the one." She nodded and frowned. "I'll bet he doesn't get covered in mud or drool all over everything."

"I'd take Charlie over him any day," Heath said because he didn't want Jade to cry or to call a halt to the evening. Both would be disastrous. "Charlie seems like a robust dog."

Robust? Now you're just babbling, Blackwood.

"That he is." She winced. "But he can also be stubborn and disobedient as you can see."

Heath laughed despite the turn the evening had taken. They wouldn't be making their dinner reservations at the LC Club, but maybe that was a good thing. Playing out this fake engagement in public might not be the smartest move. He genuinely liked Jade and didn't want her to have to face too much public scrutiny when the fake engagement ended.

He had to remember that the number one priority in his personal life right now was solving the mystery surrounding his birth and his biological father. That had to come first.

Jade was watching him, and he realized he'd lost the thread of the conversation. What had they been talking about? Yeah, the dog and the insipid comment he'd made about Charlie being robust. "I meant he's not afraid to roll in the mud, get dirty."

"If those are the guidelines, then, yeah, I suppose Charlie is the most robust dog in Chatelaine. He's not afraid to get dirty, and he's not afraid to spread the love. As evidenced by tonight's episode."

At least this silly conversation had gotten her mind off what had happened. Her melancholy seemed to have lifted. "See, now you can't say that about that other dog. Don't get me wrong, he looked nice enough, but I'll bet Charlie is more authentic. Like you."

She narrowed her eyes. "Are you comparing me to my *dog*?"

That's exactly what he'd done, but he didn't think she'd appreciate it if he said so. Damn. He needed to salvage this. He wasn't the smoothest operator when it came to women, but most females overlooked that because of his bank balance. Except Jade didn't think like that, and that's the biggest reason he liked her.

So what he liked best about her might be his undoing. And he did like her. He might not be in a place in his life for a permanent relationship, but that didn't stop him from admiring her.

"You're taking this all wrong." No, you're *saying* it all wrong, a voice in his head chided. "I meant that when I look at you, I see a real person, not just an image you're trying to project."

She looked down at her muddy dress. "Yeah, definitely not the image I was going for tonight."

"I happen to like real people." He stalked over to her and lifted her chin with his thumb. "I happen to like you, Jade Fortune. Mud and all."

She swallowed. "Y-you do?"

"I do." His gaze landed on her parted lips. He needed another taste of that desirable, kissable mouth. The one sip of those exquisite lips at the coffee shop wasn't enough to satisfy his hunger. Would he ever get enough of this woman? "May I?"

She nodded and he leaned down and hovered with his mouth just above hers. He could feel her breath mingling with his. Heath eased forward until his lips touched hers, then cupped his palms around her face, angling her head so he could deepen the kiss. He drew the tip of his tongue along the seam of her lips and—

A howl pierced the air.

Jade pulled away and Heath let her go. The dog had ruined the moment, and he couldn't decide if Charlie's ill-timed interruption had spoiled his evening or had acted as a good reminder that this whole thing was fake. The engagement wasn't real, and he needed to remember that.

Charlie howled again and Heath knew why basset hounds had a reputation for being noisy. He'd researched the breed when he realized how important Charlie was to Jade.

He looked down at the dog. "Some wingman you turned out to be."

"Charlie, that was rude," Jade admonished.

"Maybe he doesn't like the idea of you kissing someone. Or is it *me*?" Talk about sounding needy. He hadn't anticipated wanting the approval of a dog. A woman's family maybe, but certainly not a floppy eared canine.

"He's never seen me kissing anyone," she admitted, then turned red as if realizing what her comment was revealing.

He couldn't prevent the grin spreading across his face. "That's good to know."

"Is it?" She suddenly smiled too.

"Yes, for sure." That bit of information, whether she'd wanted him to know it or not, made him happy. It probably shouldn't, because this wasn't real, but in this moment he didn't care.

"What about you?"

"I doubt Charlie has ever seen me kissing someone," he said, hoping to lighten the mood.

"Very funny. That's not what I meant."

"At my age, I've been in some relationships, but nothing terribly serious." Nothing that felt like this, and this—whatever this was growing between him and Jade—wasn't even a real relationship. Yet she was like a ray of sunshine cutting through the gray fog that had enveloped him since he'd started the quest to find out the truth about the circumstances of his birth. When he was with Jade, he wanted to know the truth of those circumstances for his own peace of mind. Jade might not care but he did.

Heath leaned toward her again, but Charlie shook himself, sending particles of dirt and mud flying.

"Yikes. I need to get him into a bath before he starts ruining everything. Ha! What am I saying? He's already ruined the evening."

As disappointed as he was, Heath wasn't going to let a dog chase him off. Even if that dog belonged to Jade. He was made of sterner stuff than that. "Nothing is ruined. Just modified."

"Modified?"

"Much of my best work was accomplished by running into a roadblock and having to alter my original plans." And that was the truth. One setback didn't mean the end.

"So you're not angry with the way this evening is going?"

"I got to kiss you…again. How could I be angry? And to set the record straight, I apologize for not asking before I kissed you the first time in the coffee shop. But the situation called for action. I hope you didn't mind."

"I had no objection." She shook her head slowly. "To be honest, I quite liked it."

He gave her a lopsided grin. "So did I."

Charlie chose that moment to lift his head and let out another long, loud howl. Maybe the basset hound was the smart one here, reminding them that this wasn't real.

"Charlie, no. Be quiet." Jade told him in a stern voice, but he continued to make noise. "He's doing this because he heard me say the word B-A-T-H."

"Charlie, quiet," he ordered.

The dog stopped and went over to Heath and sat.

"Good dog. Now, shake on it." Heath put out his hand and Charlie gave him his paw, but he'd forgotten the dog's paws were muddied. If he didn't know better, he'd swear that look Charlie gave him resembled a smirk. He'd bet the dog knew exactly what he was doing.

Heath stood and wiped his hand on his pants. They were already covered in dirt, so a little more wasn't going to matter.

"There," he said trying not to sound smug. "He's ready to get cleaned up."

"I don't believe it! What have you done with my dog?" Jade looked from Charlie to Heath and back. "If not for all that dirt, I'd think he was an impostor."

"You have to say it and mean it," Heath said, but he

was as surprised as she that Charlie had obeyed him. And eternally grateful.

"Uh-huh, I'll try to remember that. Impostor or not, he needs to get clean." She turned her attention from the pooch to Heath. "Again, I'm sorry about the ruined evening."

"It's not ruined," he said and meant it. He was spending an evening with Jade; the rest was just window dressing. "We'll have something delivered and eat it here, if that's okay with you. You can give Charlie a bath while we wait."

True to form, Charlie howled at the word *bath*.

"Quiet," he said and held his breath.

The dog obeyed, but Heath decided he'd quit while he was ahead. He didn't want to push his luck. "I guess I proved my point. Now, about that delivery—"

"Delivery? Have you forgotten that this is Chatelaine?" Jade shook her head. "And if that isn't bad enough, the Fortune ranch is way off the beaten path. It'll be impossible to get someone out here."

"It's been my experience that nothing is impossible. I'll start calling around and see what I can come up with."

"You could, but why don't I save you the trouble? My mother sent over some homemade lasagna earlier today. I could heat that up, and I have the ingredients for a salad. If that is okay with you? The lasagna is big enough for two."

"More than okay. I can't remember the last time I had a home-cooked meal." But as far as he was concerned, any meal was a bonus to getting to spend an evening with Jade.

"Let me just get a towel so you can at least wipe off your pants. Sorry I don't have any spares to lend you."

"I've had worse on me. I test my gadgets in the real world of farms and ranches. A little mud from a dog is not that big a deal." And wasn't that the truth? Working ranches could be filthy, smelly places. But he liked to be hands-on with his projects. Hiring someone to do the dirty work for him didn't sit well with him. "Just point me in the direction of the bathroom, and I'll get washed up."

"Okay and I'll pop the lasagna in the oven, clean up Charlie and get changed. The lasagna should be heated through by then."

"Do you need any help?"

"No, thanks. It's bad enough Charlie got you dirty, you don't need him getting you wet too. Which is what would happen, believe me."

"Good point. I hope your dress isn't ruined." He'd only seen her wearing jeans, and he'd enjoyed that, but he had to admit it was also nice seeing her legs. She had sexy legs.

"Well, the dress says it's washable, so fingers crossed it all comes out."

"How about before I get cleaned up, I check out the yard and see what he got into. Not sure what I can do about a mud puddle, but I can make sure you don't have a leak of some sort. Or a break in your fence."

"Good idea. I hadn't thought of a break in the fencing. I'd hate for him to get out again if the backyard area isn't secure."

Heath nodded and let himself out the door she had used to let the dog in. He knew how fond she was of Charlie, and if he could prevent any harm coming to the dog, he'd do it. This so-called relationship might be fake, but he had to admit not all of his feelings for Jade were.

JADE LEANED OVER and lathered up the dog, who complained with more than a few disgruntled snuffles and snorts. At least he didn't try to escape. Probably knew it was futile.

After her mother and sisters had left, she'd done the one thing she'd managed to resist despite her crush on Heath—she googled him. Besides lots of business articles about his successes with his company, she'd picked up a few more personal tidbits. Only one of them had her fretting.

Heath was thirty years old. That meant he was three years younger than her. It didn't matter. At least that's what she was telling herself. And it didn't. Not to her anyway. But what about Heath? He had to know. After all, he'd agreed to accompany her to her fifteenth-class reunion, so the math was simple. Could it be that he didn't mind?

After bathing the dog, she went into her bedroom and changed into dry clothes. Not exactly what she'd planned for the evening, but she found a white button-down blouse to pair with dry jeans. Maybe in some weird way, it was for the best, because she needed to remember the handsome entrepreneur was doing all this as a favor to her so she could save face with Nina and Alexis.

She found Heath in the kitchen, washing his hands at the sink. He turned and smiled at her as she walked in. At least he was still here. He hadn't stomped off when Charlie had gotten mud all over his pants.

"You had a bird bath that had gotten knocked over. That's what caused the puddle. I righted the bath and refilled it. You might want to supervise him until the puddle dries up."

"Thanks. I'll be sure to do that," she said as the timer went off on the stove. "The lasagna is almost done. It needs to sit on the counter for a few minutes so it will stay together when cut."

He helped her set the table and sliced cucumbers and tomatoes to add to the bagged salad she had on hand. She had to admit working alongside him in her kitchen was just as much fun as going to the country club. Maybe more so because she had Heath to herself for the evening.

Before they sat down to supper, she got a new chew bone out of one of the cabinets and handed it to Heath.

He accepted it with a raised eyebrow. "Thanks?"

"Maybe if you give it to him and tell him to go lay down with it, he'll obey."

Heath chuckled. "You're really putting me on the spot."

"You're the one with the special powers."

He showed Charlie the bone and brought it over to the dog bed in front of the fireplace. "This is for you to enjoy while we eat. Got that, buddy?"

Charlie took the bone and laid down to enjoy it. Heath glanced across to where she stood watching them.

"Impressive," she said. "It probably won't completely prevent him from begging for handouts at some point, but it might help some."

"You could have stopped at 'impressive,'" he said and made a noise with his tongue.

"Sorry," she said and set the casserole dish on the table.

"My reputation is in your paws, buddy," he told the dog and went to join Jade at the table.

The conversation came easily during supper. They decided to tell anyone who asked at the reunion that they'd seen one another when Heath came to Chatelaine on business. At least that was partly true. They'd been introduced last month when he first came to Chatelaine, but there was no need for them to go into an explanation about Heath looking for his half sisters and information about his biological father. That wasn't anyone else's business even if most people in Chatelaine knew he and the Perry triplets were half siblings.

"So, your sisters know the truth about this engagement?"

"Yeah, it would have been difficult to convince them I was truly engaged."

"Oh?"

"They know how important it is for me to find out the

circumstances surrounding my birth before I could make that sort of commitment to anyone."

And especially to someone like her, Jade finished for him, channeling her father's voice. She needed to remember Heath was doing this as a favor for her. So she could save face after making that outrageous claim at the Daily Grind. If only she had kept her mouth shut, she wouldn't be in this mess now.

But was it really a mess? Or the most exciting thing to ever happen to her? The whole engagement might be a farce, but getting to spend time with Heath wasn't. She needed to learn to live in the moment, savor the present and let the future take care of itself.

The conversation had died down a bit after Heath made his pronouncement about needing to learn the truth about his birth before he could contemplate being in a serious relationship.

Not wanting the evening to end on a sour note, Jade decided to change the subject. "Tell me how you got Charlie to obey you so easily."

He exhaled as if he too was glad to change the subject. "It wasn't hard. I gave him a clear instruction and he obeyed."

"I know that but—"

"Haven't you done obedience training with him?" he interrupted with a frown.

"I have. Several times. He washed out each time." *A lot like me.* Thinking about her college days was too depressing, so she concentrated instead on the man she was spending the evening with. After all, growing up with Casper Windham and his brand of parenting, she'd had lots of practice pushing aside unpleasant thoughts.

"Maybe he obeyed because he knows I'm only temporary," he remarked.

She couldn't lie, his words hurt even if they were the truth. But she did her best to keep her emotions off her face and to keep her tone even. "Why would that matter?"

"I won't be around long enough to make him obey long term."

"I guess that makes sense." She needed to change the subject because the thought of not seeing Heath after the reunion was too depressing. "So, exactly what is it that you do for a living? I heard something about agricultural tech, but I'm not sure what that is."

"It means my company works with farmers and some ranchers to develop applications and tools."

"Doing what? Or is it a secret?" she asked.

He shook his head. "Not a secret in the broad sense. Some of our methods and equipment are proprietary, but not necessarily what the tools and apps do."

"Someone said something about using AI."

"Yeah, that's what we're working on now. I originally improved the weather apps used in farming equipment."

"Is that how you made all your money?" Jade slapped a hand over her mouth, but it was too late. The words were already out. "Oh, God, I'm so sorry. I didn't mean that. How gauche. Please ignore that. You don't have to answer."

Instead of being offended, he laughed. "It's okay. I already know I'm rich."

"That may be, but normally I have better manners."

Still smiling, he shook his head. "If it will make you feel any better, I can ask how it feels to find out you're a Fortune."

How was she supposed to answer that? She had all sorts of feelings, many of which were conflicting. "To be honest, I'm still getting used to it."

"But you changed your last name. It's my understanding that all of you changed from Windham to Fortune."

"Yes, we all did, but we did it more for our mother than any other reason. At least I did. Mom said it was entirely up to each of us, but I knew she really wanted it. I confess I didn't need a lot of convincing."

"Daddy issues?" he asked and flinched. "Now it's my turn to be gauche. I apologize. It's really none of my business."

Just goes to show that this isn't a real relationship, Jade thought. If they really were engaged, he wouldn't be saying that. They'd feel free to share things like that with one another.

She sighed. It was true that she still had a lot of unresolved issues involving Casper Windham. At first, she'd balked at the idea of changing her last name but came to the consensus her siblings did that her mother was here, and their dad wasn't. She didn't want to damage her relationship with her only living parent. Not that her mother would have pushed. "It's complicated, but you're not far off."

"Would it help to talk about it?"

"I don't know. It's probably pretty boring, and I don't like to play the poor little rich girl card." Even during those years after high school when she'd been drifting, she knew she was lucky. She had family and resources to fall back on. That's why now, when she'd finally landed on her feet, she did all she could to help the kids who attended her day camps.

"That's right. You were rich even before you became a Fortune," Heath was saying. "Your dad was Windham Plastics."

She couldn't have put it better herself. Her dad lived and breathed his company, even to the point of ignoring his family. But the business was why she had the resources to do what she, her mother and her siblings were now doing, so she had no right to complain. But that didn't prevent some feelings of resentment when she thought about her father and his attitude toward her. "It meant everything to him."

"Ah, I'm getting a vibe here. Does some of that have to do with the tension I sense when Casper is mentioned?"

"You could say that," she acknowledged.

His lips twisted into a grimace. "Not that I'm defending him, but businesses take a lot of time and care…successful ones even more. And from what I understand, Windham Plastics was extremely successful."

"It was, and I know I shouldn't complain since it gave my brothers and sisters and me a comfortable upbringing. We were able to move to Chatelaine and make the Fortune family ranch into something we can all be proud of."

"From what I hear, you have every right to be proud of the petting zoo."

She laughed, unsure if he was serious. "Right."

"I'm serious. Between that and the camps and workshops you're doing, you have a chance to change the lives of a lot of children in Chatelaine."

"Thank you, but I hardly think I'm changing lives." She shook her head. Sure, she enjoyed what she was doing, and she was doing her best to adhere to ethical guidelines when it came to the animals in her care, but she doubted she was transforming anyone's life but her own. She wasn't struggling to find her place anymore and that felt good. Which was why she felt baffled by her behavior in front of Alexis and Nina. Seeing them and listening to them had thrown her back into the dark days of high school. And she'd managed to drag Heath into her drama.

"Don't be too sure. Programs like yours changed my life, and look where I am today."

She pulled back in surprise. "You can't be serious."

"But I am. As the child of a single mother, there wasn't

a lot of extra money, but I was able to enjoy attending free lectures similar to the ones you sponsor. That sparked my interest in technology being used for farming and ranching."

"So, maybe I'm creating your competition with my little camps?" she teased.

He laughed, sending tingles down her spine. She couldn't remember any man causing her spine to tingle. She liked it. A lot. Maybe that explained her behavior at the Daily Grind.

"I'll forgive you. There's room for everyone," Heath told her.

"That's pretty magnanimous of you."

Grinning, he shrugged. "It'll be a few years yet before I'll be looking over my shoulder. The ones you teach are pretty young still."

"Yes, but you're pretty young to be such a success as well." *And to be so rich*, she thought and frowned. That truly didn't matter to her.

"Are there any kids that stand out that I should be worried about?"

"Well—" she dragged out the word "—there is one that's quite smart. His name is Billy Connor. He lost his dad about a year ago, and his mom has been bringing him around a lot."

"I'd be happy to meet with him, if you want."

"I'll bet he'll be thrilled," she said without thinking. She'd been concerned about Billy. She knew him as a quiet and respectful boy, but lately he'd been disruptive during her presentations.

He frowned. "Forgive me. Did I sound pompous?"

"What? No. Sorry. My mind was elsewhere for a minute. Billy hasn't been himself lately, and I'm not sure why.

I didn't mean to come across as sarcastic." The last thing she wanted to do was take out her frustrations on Heath.

He touched her arm. "I have a feeling we're both a little on edge."

"It's all my fault for opening my big mouth and claiming we're engaged," she said thickly.

He lightly squeezed her arm. "Considering I went along with you, I'd say we're in this together."

"I'm not such a martyr as to accept the full blame if you're willing to accept half." She laughed, feeling much lighter. "So, yes, I suppose we are in this together."

"Maybe we need to establish some ground rules," he said abruptly, dropping his hand.

She missed the warmth of his touch. "Ground rules?"

Of course he wanted ground rules. Her head may have been in the clouds regarding this fake engagement, but his certainly wasn't. And why should it be? *He* wasn't spinning dreams around her rash statement. *She* was the one doing that.

Jade pushed those unproductive thoughts aside and inhaled, waiting for what Heath was going to say.

Don't buy trouble, she told herself.

He drew his hands through his hair and, after a long palpable moment, finally spoke. "I like you and want to be honest with you, Jade."

"I like you too, and I'm all for honesty." She might want the truth, but that didn't prevent his words from causing her to feel a bit anxious about what he might say next. Sounded like trouble was coming of its own accord.

"I want to explain what I meant when I said I didn't want to get involved."

"If you don't want to get involved, that's your right. You don't have to explain—"

"But I want to because you're special, Jade."

Oh my. His words did funny things to her insides. She didn't think anyone had ever called her special before.

Before she could respond, he continued. "You know that the Perry triplets are my sisters—well, half sisters."

She managed a shaky smile. Just because he'd called her special didn't negate the fact that he was explaining why he didn't want to get too deeply involved with her. At least he offered an explanation. A lot more than most guys would. Maybe this wouldn't be so bad after all. It wasn't like he was telling her anything she didn't already know. "I think the entire town knows."

"Yes, well, like I said, I'm trying to find out the true reason I never knew about them, nor they about me. I realize their circumstances probably made it impossible since they were so young when their parents died. But my mother also never told me the truth."

"How did you find out that you even had sisters?" Having grown up with her five siblings, she could not imagine what it would be like to only discover them now as an adult. Her heart went out to him and his sisters.

"After my mother passed, I realized I would never get any answers from her, so I took a DNA test. I was matched with one of my sisters. Fortunately, I was able to contact her and found out I had not just one but three sisters." He shook his head, his expression conveying he was focused on something only he could see.

This time it was she who reached out to touch him. "I can't imagine how that must feel, but I'm glad you've finally found one another."

He seemed to come back to himself and turned his attention back to her. "Yeah, it answers some questions but raises a bunch more."

Those questions probably had to do with his biological father. Did he hope to find answers here? "So, finding your sisters is how you ended up in Chatelaine?"

He sighed. "Yeah. We've been trying to find out what happened, but it hasn't been easy."

"Have you been able to learn anything about the circumstances surrounding your birth?" For all the problems she'd experienced in the fraught relationship with her father, at least she'd had one. She and he hadn't had time to settle any differences between them before he died, but that didn't weigh as heavily on her now as it once had. She still minded, but not nearly as much.

"We've managed to learn very little. Doris Edwards— I'm not sure if you know her—knew my mother before I was born. She's a greeter a couple days a week at Great-Store. Except the woman is now suffering from bouts of dementia and isn't always lucid. For example, she told my sisters that we were quadruplets, but that's impossible because I was born two months before them and in a different town. Those are undisputed facts. My sister Haley confronted her, and she claimed that my parents were taking me to the hospital the night they were killed in that accident. But that's impossible unless my mother lied to me. As an infant, I would not have been in Chatelaine. I would have been with her in Cactus Grove. It makes no sense."

"I'm sure the DNA would show you're not full brother and sister." She could tell that he was bothered by all this conflicting information, and she couldn't blame him.

"Yes, so I knew going in that they were going to be half siblings, but I still want to know what happened. This Doris woman seemed to be the only one who knew there were four of us babies fathered by the same man."

"But she hasn't been able to explain how?" Jade wished she could help him. He had stood up for her when she made her engagement claim, and she wanted to return the favor. But how?

"Not yet. But I'm not giving up. She has her lucid moments, and she's indicated that knows something even if she can't remember exactly what she knows."

"Quite a conundrum."

He laughed. "Yeah, that's one way of putting it."

"So, exactly how does this affect our situation?" She called it a "situation" because she wasn't sure how else to refer to it.

"I'm good with keeping up the pretense of us being engaged until after your reunion."

But don't make the mistake of thinking it's real, she finished for him.

She needed to repeat that as a mantra because her simple crush on Heath Blackwood was starting to feel like something more. Something real. Something dangerous to her heart.

CHAPTER FIVE

HEATH WINCED. WHAT was he doing pouring his heart out to Jade? Like she'd be interested in all his birth mystery drama. He was pretty sure Jade's two classmates would have fled the scene by now, bored to tears. Or they would have offered empty platitudes before steering the conversation to something else.

But not Jade. She expressed genuine interest and sympathy, he argued with himself.

While he was engaged in his internal debate, she got up and started to pick up their dirty dishes.

Remembering his manners, he stood and picked up his plate. "Here, let me help."

"That's not necessary."

"I insist. You fed me. I'll help clean up." He wasn't so far removed from his humble beginnings that kitchen work was beneath him. His merit scholarships didn't always cover his living expenses or books, and he'd bussed tables to earn money during college.

"But it was my dog that ruined the date."

"Will you stop saying he ruined it. Poor guy's going to get a complex. He didn't ruin our evening. Unless…" Had she wanted to go to the LC Club? Maybe he was wrong about Jade not caring about appearances. He hoped he was wrong.

She frowned. "Unless what?"

"Maybe you would have preferred going to the country club? Would you have preferred being seen tonight?"

"Being *seen*? I don't understand what you mean by that." Her tone held a note of suspicion.

"Some women prefer getting dressed up and going out so they can be seen by others." He might be insulting her with his assumptions, but he needed to know before he got too involved.

Wait. What was he thinking? He had no plans to get involved beyond a few dates and the reunion. He was going to say something to that effect, but she was already answering him.

"Believe me, that's not me. I got dressed up because I didn't want to embarrass you, but the part about being seen doesn't interest me in the least."

"Let's get one thing straight. Jade Fortune, you would never embarrass me. I'm proud to be seen with you, whether you're wearing jeans or a dress." And that was the truth. He found her refreshing and he was relieved by her attitude.

She gave him a look he wasn't sure how to interpret and nodded once. "Thanks. How about I make some coffee, and we can take it to the back patio? The moon is pretty full tonight, so we might even see it reflected off the lake."

"Sounds great. Your place really is well situated here," he said as he stacked the last plate into the dishwasher and closed it. "Do you want to run the dishwasher?"

"Yeah." She rummaged in the cabinet under the sink and pulled out a detergent packet, put it into the holder in the door and started it. Going to the faucet, she ran water into an electric teakettle.

He grimaced at the thought of instant coffee, but to his relief, she pulled a French press off the shelf under the kitchen island. While the water heated, she measured ground coffee into the pot.

Heath watched her quick, economical movements. Once again, he found himself contemplating her hands. They were unadorned but they fascinated him. He frowned when he recalled that one woman's comment about Jade not having a ring despite the engagement. Well, he'd have to do something about that before the high school reunion. He took a closer look at her fingers. That's when he noticed a nasty cut on her index finger. "How did you do that?"

"Do what?" Jade asked as she measured ground coffee into the French press.

He took her hand in both of his. "That looks like a serious cut."

"Not bad enough for stitches, but I did some serious bleeding."

"I hope you're up to date on your tetanus shot."

She rolled her eyes. "Of course. I live on a ranch and work at a petting zoo."

Yeah, he got it. He was making a fool of himself, but he couldn't help worrying about her. Instead of responding, he brought her hand to his lips and kissed it before letting go.

They stood facing one another, neither one speaking. Finally, Heath cleared his throat and stepped back. He needed to stop this. Getting involved too deeply with anyone at this time wasn't a good idea. Once again, he reminded himself that finding out the truth about his father and the mystery surrounding his birth was his first priority.

But what if he didn't like what he found? He pushed the disturbing thought aside. First things first.

"Let me finish getting the coffee ready," she said and turned away, busying herself with pouring the hot water over coffee grounds and stirred. She replaced the plunger into the pot and set it aside to steep.

"I see you have some torches around the patio. Would you like me to light them?"

"That would be great. Most have citronella to help ward off bugs." She opened a drawer and pulled out a barbecue stick lighter.

They sat in comfortable wooden rockers facing the lake with a small table between their chairs. The flickering torches gave the setting a warm ambience. Even better than an evening dining and dancing at the country club. The one downside was that without dancing, he didn't have an excuse to hold her in his arms. There were always other times, he consoled himself.

"Is there something I should know about you before the reunion?" Jade asked. "I know about your job and family, but I'm talking about something that might not be common knowledge. Like Twizzlers or Red Vines?"

"Neither. What about you?"

She shot him a look. "What? How is something like that even possible?"

"Because I'm more of a Jelly Belly guy," he said and waited for her reaction.

"Ooh, I like those too. All those flavors. I guess I'll have to give you a pass on the licorice."

"Damn right, you will." The conversation might be silly, but he was enjoying sitting with Jade and wanted to know more about her. "Aside from this thing about red licorice, is there anything else I should know about you?"

She sighed. "If you must know, my phone is full of pictures of Charlie."

"So?" He stifled the laugh that bubbled up. The only light on the patio came from the torches, but from what he could see, she was blushing. He couldn't remember the last time he'd been with a woman who blushed. He quite liked it.

Her eyes widened. "You don't think that's strange?"

"Should I?"

"I'm sure Nina and Alexis would think so."

"Why should you care what they think?"

YEAH, WHY SHOULD SHE, Jade wondered. Heath had a point. She shrugged. "I guess that day in the coffee shop, I was thrown back into high school."

He shook his head. "Those of us who weren't popular in high school have moved on. Some people reached their peak back then. That's the real shame. Their glory days are behind them. On the other hand, ours are ahead of us."

"I'm not sure I have glory days ahead of me, but thanks for thinking so."

He made a sound with his tongue. "Don't discount what you're doing, Jade. How do you think I got my start?"

"At a petting zoo?"

He chuckled, sending her pulse racing.

He turned toward her. "All those workshops you do. Like I said before, I attended some like that when I was young, and it encouraged me to pursue my dreams of using technology to help farmers and ranchers."

Her eyes widened. "You seriously did attend ones like I give?"

"I haven't been to any of yours, so I don't know if they're exactly the same, but I'm sure you could be inspiring the next generation of innovative farmers and ranchers."

"The next Heath Blackwoods, you mean?"

He laughed and touched the end of her nose.

"Are you still interested in speaking at one of my workshops?"

"Of course. I'd love to," he replied. "Just let me know when and I'll be there."

"Thank you so much. This will mean a lot to the kids."

He flashed her a grin. "I'm not sure they'll even know who I am, but I'm happy to help."

That grin made her heart do some sort of stumble thing but she managed one of her own. Albeit a shaky one.

"Right," he said with a glance at her mouth before continuing, "I'd better get going."

With that he gave her a distracted nod, turned, and left, leaving her wondering if that last part was meant for her or himself.

After Heath left for the evening, Jade knew she was going to have to remember that this was a fake engagement. She needed to keep that in mind at all times or risk getting her heart broken. Heath was doing her a favor by going along with the fake engagement. She might be falling for him, but he was definitely not falling for her, and she'd do well to remember that.

Charlie came over, stood next to her and whined, deep in his throat.

"Don't you start falling for him too," she cautioned him.

THE NEXT MORNING, while Jade went about her chores at the Fortune Family Petting Zoo, the previous night's date kept crowding out her other thoughts. She had to acknowledge that her little crush on Heath Blackwood was no longer little. And that could create a problem. A *big* one.

It wasn't easy, but she pushed thoughts of Heath out of her head so she could concentrate on her project. She had turned an old, disused aluminum rowboat into a small pond with a fountain.

Jade turned on the water pump to be sure it worked. Thankfully it did, and the water in the aluminum rowboat and water sprayed up through the small fountain she'd placed in the middle. The boat was battered, but she'd repaired the rust spot enough for the craft to hold water.

While the rowboat might not be lake worthy, it made a wonderful swimming pool for the ducks.

"What a clever idea."

Jade turned to see Hope standing there watching the proceedings with avid interest.

"Thanks," she said and wiped her hands on her jeans. "I saw an example of this online and thought I'd try it for the baby ducks."

"I love it. Can't wait for Evie to see it with ducks in it."

Jade glanced around but Hope seemed to be alone. "Speaking of Evie, where is she?"

"Ridge has her. She's fascinated by the baby chicks in the incubator." She smiled. "Your brother is very good with her."

"I know," Jade said.

It never ceased to amaze her how comfortable Ridge was with the baby. He'd taken to fatherhood like…well, like a duck to water. Except he wasn't that baby's father. And that was what bothered her, because he could be heading for a world of hurt if he didn't put the brakes on.

Pot? Kettle?

Yeah, she didn't have room to criticize. Look at the dangerous game she was playing with Heath. He wasn't really her fiancé, and no amount of wishing was going to make that true. He'd rescued her from humiliation in front of those snotty girls and was doing her a favor by taking her to the reunion. But she needed to remember that when the clock struck midnight, her carriage would turn back into a pumpkin.

"So, I thought I'd take a moment to explain…"

Hope's words brought Jade back to the here and now. "Explain what?"

"What happened at the coffee shop?"

Jade shook her head. "That's not necessary."

"No. I don't want you to think I'm some sort of flake. Freaking out the way I did." Hope heaved a sigh.

"I would never think that."

"All I remember is that when that woman started chasing after her child, I panicked. I had a memory flash of a middle-aged couple smiling at Evie but suddenly turning mean and saying I had to hand my baby over." Hope shuddered.

Jade put her arm around the other woman, hoping to comfort her. She didn't know what else to do. Saying everything was going to be okay sounded disingenuous because Jade had no idea what had happened in Hope's past. Without knowing the woman's situation, how could she be sure things would work out? Jade was convinced that Hope was Evie's mother, but that fact alone didn't mean she had rightful custody of the baby. Any number of things could have happened.

"I know it was just a memory surfacing, but it scared me," Hope was saying and pulled Jade back to the conversation.

"I can understand how that could happen. Please, don't think anything of it." Especially after what she herself had done in that coffee shop. People could react in extreme ways in certain situations.

"There you are," Ridge strolled over and stood beside Hope. He had Evie securely on his hip, his arm around her. "See? Mommy is right here. I told you she couldn't have gotten far," he crooned to the baby.

Evie reached out her chubby arms to Hope, who took her from Ridge and hugged her close.

Ridge gave Jade a playful swat on the shoulder. "Hey, Sis."

"How's it going?" Jade asked, hoping she'd managed

to keep the doom and gloom she felt over his situation from her voice.

"Great. Did you put this together?" he asked, pointing to the makeshift duck pond.

Jade puffed out her chest. "I did."

"So that's why you wanted that old boat." He squatted on his heels to examine her creation.

"I told you I had a use for it," she said, waiting to see if he found anything wrong.

"You did, and I confess I lacked the imagination to picture this."

"I guess I was a bit vague in my explanation. I wanted to be sure I could pull it off." She was so used to being a failure in front of her family that it was old habit to keep things from them.

Ridge stood. "Well, you certainly pulled it off. Great job."

Jade smiled. She really had found her calling with this petting zoo.

Ridge chucked her on the shoulder. "But was there ever any doubt?"

"I imagine there was a lot. I haven't exactly been the most successful member of this family."

Ridge gave his sister a quick one-armed hug. "*Pfft*. So what if you took a little longer to find your way? You're doing a bang-up job with the zoo and the day camps for kids."

"Thanks." It felt good having her family see her as successful.

"Uh-oh, I think this little girl needs a diaper change," Hope said and wrinkled her nose. "How such a sweet thing can make such a big stink is beyond me."

"You can take her over to the family area. We have facilities there." Jade pointed to a small outbuilding painted barn red.

Ridge watched Hope walk off, then turned to Jade. "Did she say anything more to you about what happened at the Daily Grind? I know she felt bad leaving like that. She insisted on coming to explain."

"She apologized again, but I assured her it was okay. I guess something someone said sparked a partial memory. Has she regained any more substantial recollections?"

He nodded. "After we got home and we were unpacking the diaper bag, she had another flash."

Jade noticed how he'd casually used the word *home*. She knew they weren't living together, because Hope and the baby were in a small cabin close to Ridge's. But the way he'd said it indicated to Jade that he was getting deeper and deeper with Hope. "Can you tell me about it?" she asked.

"It wasn't very detailed, but she said she recalled throwing things in Evie's baby bag and rushing to a car. She remembers constantly checking the rearview mirror as she drove away."

Jade put her hand on her brother's arm. His muscles were bunched stiff. "Oh no, Ridge. This sounds pretty serious."

He shook his head and looked at Jade, a bleak expression in his eyes. "Sounds like she was running from someone. But who? An abusive husband?"

"Give her time and space. I'm sure her memories will come back." Jade wished she could believe her own words. But what else could she do? Ridge was an adult. All she could do was pray things would work out for him. If not, she and the rest of the family would be there for him.

"Thanks. I'm sure they will too."

They were silent for a moment.

"I'm just afraid what those memories will reveal," he whispered, "but I'm all in no matter what happens."

Jade squeezed her brother's hand. Even when she was drifting along trying to find her place in the world, her siblings had been there for her. No matter what Casper said or did, Jade knew she could count on her brothers and sisters. "You know we'll be here for you and Hope and baby Evie. No matter what."

"It looks like this might work out," Jade said as she watched Dahlia's lamb exploring the new enclosure Jade had built when her sister had approached her about the lamb.

"It's not a permanent solution, but I'm glad to have someplace safe for it," Dahlia said.

Her younger sister had been taking care of a lamb that had been rejected by its mother. Jade had two other lambs, and Dahlia thought being with others might help the baby. They stood by the fence and watched the lambs getting to know one another.

"Has Ridge said anything more about what's been going on with Hope?" Dahlia asked curiously.

"He and Hope were here this morning with the baby." Jade debated how much to say but, in the end, opted for the truth. Ridge was Dahlia's baby brother too.

"I just pray he knows what he's getting into with all this," Dahlia muttered after Jade had told her what she knew.

"Me too."

"Speaking of relationships, I saw Heath driving through town this morning," Dahlia said.

"Huh." Jade's stomach tightened. Had Heath said something to her sister? "Did you talk to him?"

"No. I didn't get a chance to do more than wave. I was coming out of the feed store when he went by."

Jade nodded, secretly relieved that they didn't have a chance to chat.

"But Phyllis did. Talk, that is."

Jade groaned.

"Yeah, she asked all about you. Kept asking me about the engagement and how sudden it was. Seems you were in the feed store gabbing with her and didn't mention anything about an engagement even when she mentioned Heath's name to you."

"What did you say?" Jade hated putting her family on the spot, but there wasn't much she could do about her impulsive lie at the moment.

"I reminded her what a private person you were," Dahlia said and grinned.

"And did she believe you?"

Her sister noisily blew air between her lips. "Hardly. So I started talking about Rawlston, and she took the bait, asking all sorts of intrusive questions. You owe me, big-time."

Jade winced. It wasn't that long ago when Dahlia and Rawlston were the hot topic when they came back from Vegas married, of all things. Everything worked out in the end, and they were deliriously happy now. But some people still liked to speculate on what actually happened in Vegas.

"Doesn't Phyllis know that what happens in Vegas stays in Vegas?"

"Evidently not."

Jade heaved a sigh. "Sorry about that. Like you said, I owe you."

Dahlia leaned against the fence and turned her head to look at Jade. "Then tell me what's bothering you?"

"What makes you think something is bothering me?"

"Because you had a weird look on your face when I mentioned Heath. Are you two still planning to go through with the trip to the reunion?"

"Yes. Mom has agreed to watch Charlie while I'm gone. It's only for the day, but you know I don't like leaving him on his own without some backup plan." And considering what had happened when she'd let him into the yard unsupervised the other night, she had all the more reason to be concerned.

Dahlia grinned. "Yes, we all know he's your baby. At least for the time being."

"What's that supposed to mean?"

"Nothing, except I'm sure some day you'll get married and have human babies too."

Jade wished she could be as confident about her future as Dahlia seemed to be. She was happy with her life as it was, but that didn't mean she didn't want a family of her own someday.

"C'mon, Sis, spill it. I can tell something's on your mind."

At the risk of having her sister laugh, Jade told the truth. "I realized I'm three years older than Heath."

Dahlia gasped. "Oh my God! How did I not know about this shocking bit of information?"

Jade opened her mouth to speak, but Dahlia beat her to it. "I don't understand why you felt you weren't able to confide in us. I mean, this is just shocking. My sister, a cradle robber."

"Very funny. Are you done?" Okay, maybe she was making more of this than was necessary. Three years wasn't much at all. And she probably wouldn't even have thought much of it if she hadn't also wondered why Heath was interested in her. But she wasn't gorgeous like her sisters or sophisticated like Alexis and Nina. No matter what she did, she couldn't rid herself of the awkward girl she used to be. That girl was buried deep inside Jade.

"Am I done? Hmm, let me think." Dahlia tilted her head to the side and tapped a finger on her cheek.

"Dahlia," Jade said, a note of warning in her voice.

"Okay, I guess that's all I've got. If I come up with something else, you'll be the first to know."

"I can hardly wait." She snorted. "Maybe you should take that show on the road."

"C'mon, Jade. Lighten up." Dahlia playfully bumped shoulders with her. "And seriously, three years is not a big deal."

"What if he thinks it is?" That's what had been bothering her. What did *Heath* think about it? Why hadn't he mentioned it?

"He must know it if he's agreed to take you to your fifteenth high school reunion. I'm sure he's done the math. Have you asked him?"

"No."

"Why? Afraid of the answer?" Dahlia asked.

Jade rolled her eyes but didn't respond, because her sister had gotten it right.

"He must've known when he told those brats that he was going to the reunion with you. Face it, Jade, the man is a genius. I'm sure he can do math in his head. Has he said anything about it?"

"No." But then neither had she.

Dahlia shook her head at Jade. "Then why are you turning it into an issue? If it's because someone else said something, then stop this nonsense right now."

"Nonsense?"

"Yeah. Until or unless you hear directly from Heath that the age gap matters to him, it's a nonissue."

Dahlia made sense and Jade wanted to believe her. And she did…mostly. Still, there was that small part of her, the part where Casper's caustic remarks took up residence, that found it hard to believe Heath didn't care.

CHAPTER SIX

HEATH LOOKED UP from the laptop on his table on the porch at the Daily Grind. He was beginning to think of this table as his spot since he'd taken to spending time drinking coffee and doing research here. Plus, it reminded him of his first official meeting with Jade. Both a blessing and a curse. He loved spending time with her, but it was getting harder and harder to keep in mind that theirs was a fake relationship.

Today, like the other day, he'd taken advantage of the spot to conduct some research and some business, such as answering business emails. He couldn't let his personal searches regarding his past overshadow his business concerns. After all, he'd worked too hard to get where he was to let this issue cause him to lose his edge over the competition.

He glanced across the porch to see his sister Lily. She was climbing the steps to the porch. Spotting him, she waved.

"I thought I might catch you here," she said as she approached the table.

"I didn't realize you were looking for me." He stood and gave her a quick hug.

"I was at the feed store and spotted your SUV, so I decided to take a detour and come here before heading back home."

"Well, I'm glad you did."

"Have you made any progress?" she asked, hitching her chin toward his laptop.

He knew she meant in his research regarding their biological father. "No. I think I've just about exhausted anything I can find online. I'm thinking about taking another shot at Doris Edwards. Maybe I can catch her in a lucid moment."

"We could try that, or maybe we should talk to her daughter," Lily said. "Phyllis at the feed store said her daughter has been caring for her mother for the past year. Veronica takes her mother to and from work."

"I still find it surprising that the woman still holds down a job." He knew Doris was still employed by the Great-Store.

"She likes it and I imagine greeting people as they come in to shop is good for her. Besides, it's only a few hours a day and a couple days a week. I'm glad the management of the store allows it."

Heath nodded. "Chatelaine seems like the kind of place that takes care of its own."

As little as six months ago, he would not have seen himself living in such a small town without the conveniences he was accustomed to, like twenty-four-hour food delivery. Although the evening with Jade had been enjoyable, thanks to her. He even smiled a little as he remembered one of those women who'd been snotty to Jade had likened the place to a vast wasteland because it lacked a Nordstrom. But since getting involved with Jade, he had grown to like the place, and settling here permanently no longer seemed like such an outlandish idea. These days, with the internet and various technologies to connect people, working from a remote location, even one as remote and small as Chatelaine, was very doable.

"I can contact Veronica, if you'd like. I was on a parade committee with her last year and have her number."

"Do you think she can give answers that Doris won't or can't?" Was finding out about his past going to be that simple? He cautioned himself not to get his hopes up. They'd been dashed enough times already.

His sister shrugged. "I don't know, but it's worth a shot."

Lily pulled out her phone and thumbed through her contacts. "I'll arrange a meeting for you with her."

She smiled at him while she waited for her call to go through. He thought about how lucky he'd been with his sisters. They'd readily accepted him and had set about forging bonds despite only learning about a brother after they'd found one another. Lily, Tabitha and Haley had been separated as babies after the tragic death of their parents and had also come together as adults. But as full-blooded sisters and triplets to boot, their bond was much stronger. His link to them was more tenuous, especially since they didn't know why he'd never been told about them or his father. Perhaps if the cancer hadn't taken his mother so quickly after being diagnosed, Anne might have given him an explanation. But that didn't happen, and he had to accept it.

Lily ended her call and looked at him. "Veronica says she can meet with you this afternoon at the real estate office where she works."

"Will you—" He stopped and cleared his throat. "Would you like to come with me? This involves all of us."

There. Phrasing it that way didn't sound quite so needy. Not that he wouldn't go alone. He'd been doing things by himself most of his life. His mother had worked two jobs to put a roof over their heads and food on the table. He'd helped out as soon as he was able, and of course once his start-up company was making a profit, he'd done his best to make his mom's life comfortable, but the cancer had taken her so quickly. He hadn't had a chance to do all the things for her that he'd wanted.

"Sure." Lily dropped her phone back into her purse. "I'd love to come. I know Haley and Tabitha are both busy today, but I'll let them know if we find out anything worthwhile."

"We have some time to kill, so why don't you sit and have something while I finish my coffee."

"Sounds good. Let me go to the window and order something."

Heath jumped up, "Let me get it. A thank-you for coming with me today."

"No thanks necessary. We're family."

Warmth bloomed in his chest at her simple statement. Lily told him what she wanted, and he went to place her order. As he waited next to the walk-up window, his gaze went to his sister sitting at the table. He'd told Jade that he wasn't ready for a committed relationship while the story of his birth was still a mystery, but he wondered now if that was completely true. He treasured his burgeoning relationship with the triplets. So what made his feelings regarding Jade so complicated?

Maybe they'd learn something important today from Doris's daughter, and he could figure out his feelings for his fake fiancée.

He picked up Lily's mocha latte and brought it to their table. As they sipped their drinks, they talked about ranching and some ideas Heath had for devices to make life easier for ranchers. Heath had worked closely with Lily's husband, Asa Fortune. Asa's ranch was a dude ranch, but he and Heath had thrown some serious ideas around. Today's meeting loomed, but neither wanted to dwell on what-ifs.

The real estate office where Veronica worked was located along the main street in Chatelaine. Veronica was alone in the office when they arrived. After greeting and seating them around a small table in what looked like a conference area, she offered them coffee.

Lily chuckled. "We just came from the Daily Grind, but thanks anyway."

"I can't compete with the fancy stuff they sell anyway. We only recently upgraded to one of those coffee makers that uses those coffee pods," Veronica said with a smile.

"Yeah, we're lucky to have such a great coffee shop in Chatelaine," Lily murmured.

Lily's comment threw Heath back to the day Jade claimed they were engaged. She had defended the town's somewhat unusual coffee shop.

Yes, he was on this journey of discovery for himself and his siblings, but Jade and a possible future with her was always there in the back of his mind.

"I'm not sure why my mother has told you the things she has, but I need to clear up some of what she's been saying," Veronica said, not wasting time on small talk.

"You mean the things she's been saying about me as a baby being with my father? That bit of information had shaken me the most," he said. If it were true, why hadn't his mother ever mentioned it?

Veronica nodded; her features masked in sadness. "About you and that night. The night your father was killed, one of my mother's neighbors came to ask if I could come over and babysit her daughter. Megan Shaw lived next door and I occasionally babysat her six-year-old daughter Tiffany. Megan's husband had been hurt at work, and she needed to go to him at the hospital. The woman was pretty upset and worried. So was Mom. Anyway, as it turns out, that was the night James Perry and his wife were also killed. I didn't know it at the time, but Mom knew about him because of her friend Anne. Your mother. I think she's confused the two things in her mind."

"Well, that makes sense," Lily said and glanced at Heath as if for confirmation.

He nodded, trying to digest this information. At least he now knew his mother hadn't kept this tidbit of information a secret from him. It seemed more logical that if she left Chatelaine, she hadn't had any more contact with James Perry. Of course that didn't mean she never told him that he had a son. That was still a possibility, depending on the nature of their relationship. Or their *lack* of one. Perhaps the simplest explanation was a one-night stand, but that didn't explain how close in age he was to his half sisters.

"I'm sorry if she's upset you or made things more difficult," Veronica said.

Heath shook his head. "It's not her fault. I'm just sorry she's so confused. I know how hard it is when it's your mom that's being ravaged by a cruel disease."

Veronica's expression told him how much she appreciated his words. "If I could help you, I would, but I didn't pay a lot of attention to that sort of gossip at that age. I was more into boys and clothes. I babysat to earn money to buy clothes. But what am I doing telling you all this stuff? Not like you're interested. I just wanted you to know I'd help if I could."

"You've already helped by debunking the story about me being with my father that night."

Veronica nodded. "I can talk to my mom about Anne and let you know if she tells me anything new. She has good days and bad. If I can catch her on a good day, I might be able to find out something. She has talked a few times about a memory box, but I have no idea what she means. I'm sorry."

"Thanks, we really appreciate your time," Heath murmured.

A telephone rang in the outer office.

"Sorry, but I need to get that," Veronica said and rose from her seat.

"We won't keep you any longer." Heath and Lily both stood, and he reached out his hand toward Veronica. "Thanks again. We know this isn't easy on anyone and we appreciate your willingness to help."

After they got back into his SUV, Heath sat for a moment and looked at the modest brick ranch home typical of the sixties and seventies that had been turned into a real estate office. But he wasn't really seeing the house. This had been another dead end. Did Doris even know his mother? It's not as if Anne ever talked about her or even her time in Chatelaine. It wasn't until his DNA was matched with the triplets that he was aware of the dusty little town.

Would he ever find out the truth so he could put it behind him? He groaned.

A hand touched his arm. He was startled. He'd almost forgotten that Lily was with him. Poor girl. He always seemed to be dragging her into his drama.

"It's a setback but not a dead end," she told him.

He ground his back teeth. He didn't want sympathy, but instead of reacting, he inhaled deeply. Lily was his sister, one of the only relatives he had, and he didn't want to do anything to alienate her. And if he succeeded in damaging his relationship with her, his relationship with his other sisters would suffer too. That was the last thing he wanted. He found he quite liked being a big brother. Not something he ever thought he'd be.

"Thanks for coming with me today," he mumbled and gave her a quick hug.

She patted his chest. "No thanks necessary. We're family now."

He turned his head and met her gaze. His chest tightened with emotions he couldn't name. Maybe they didn't grow up together and were bound together by a man neither of them had known, but none of that mattered now that they'd found one another. Their bond was unbreakable. "We are, aren't we?"

"Growing up, I always dreamed of having a family." She laughed. "And now I seem to have them coming out of my ears."

"I'm going to assume that's a good thing."

"Very. I'm definitely not complaining." She nodded with a smile. "What about you? Are you happy to have extended family?"

"I am." He might still be getting used to having sisters in his life, but he was grateful for them.

After dropping Lily off, Heath ran an errand, then headed for the Fortune Family Ranch. He didn't think he'd gotten his hopes up, but the disappointment he was feeling belied his thoughts. Maybe seeing Jade and talking with her would help him put things in perspective. Knowing he'd be in her presence soon lifted his spirits. He patted the box in his pocket and glanced at the back seat to what he'd put there a few moments ago.

A faint voice in his head issued a warning that all he and Jade had was a fake relationship. Something based on a lie. So why did it feel so real when he kissed her?

He chose to ignore the voice and the warning. For now.

"CHARLIE, WILL YOU please let me put this on you," Jade pleaded, but the dog once again managed to wriggle out of the Sherlock Hound costume before she could get it fastened.

She'd purchased the getup off a website and now wondered what drugs they'd given the dog who'd modeled the costume. Or how many people it had taken to wrangle the dog into submission. She'd been trying for over half an hour to get the costume on the dog. He wasn't cooperating. Normally a very laid-back type of pooch, it appeared Charlie drew the line at dressing up for Halloween.

It had been two days since her date with Heath. She hadn't seen him since, but he'd texted and called, apologizing for not being able to see her in person and explaining that he'd had leave town to meet with new investors.

But he'd called a short while ago, said he was back and asked if he could stop by because he'd missed her. Jade held his words to her like a precious gift. He'd *missed* her. She'd confessed to missing him too.

After speaking with Heath, her package with Charlie's costume had been delivered, and Jade had thought she'd let him model the outfit for Heath. If she couldn't get the dog to wear the costume, never mind showing it off to Heath, what was she going to tell the kids? She'd promised them a fun Halloween parade at the zoo with Charlie as the parade marshal. The children all loved Charlie and were excited to see him in his special outfit.

"C'mon, Charlie, you don't want to disappoint all those kids, do you?"

The basset shook himself and backed away from her and the dreaded costume.

"I'll bet the kids will have so much fun they'll want to shower you with love and—" she looked him in the eye "—extra treats."

He perked up a bit at the word "treats," but then his gaze landed on the costume, and he backed up another step. Evidently the lure of dog biscuits wasn't enough to convince him to wear the outfit. Why hadn't she thought of Charlie refusing to cooperate when she promised the kids a dog costume parade?

Maybe her dad had been right. She didn't have whatever it took to be a success. At anything. She'd attended college but hadn't kept at it long enough to earn a degree. She'd tried her hand at several jobs, but most hadn't worked out either.

Maybe she—*No!* She was doing a good job with the petting zoo and running the day camps for the kids in town. And Heath had praised what she was doing, had said a similar program helped him. She may not ever be as rich or successful in business as her dad or Heath, but if she could help some other child reach his or her potential because of what she was doing, she'd call that a win. And she could live with that. She didn't think money was the only way to measure success.

She looked at Charlie and gave it one more try. "You get to be the grand marshal. That means you get to lead the parade. Wouldn't you like being the leader?"

"Not everyone is cut out to be a leader."

Jade twisted around at the sound of the familiar voice. Her heart skipped a beat when she saw Heath standing in the doorway of the barn belonging to the petting zoo. Seeing him made her realize how much she had missed him. And it had only been two days. Oh man, she was in trouble. She stood and smiled. "And you think Charlie is a born follower?"

Charlie ran over to Heath as if he were expecting salvation. Heath bent down and greeted the dog by rubbing his ears and running a hand over his long, squat body. The basset snuffled and squirmed in delight.

Dressed casually in worn jeans and a faded dark blue

Henley with the sleeves pushed up to his elbows, Heath looked like every woman's dream. As if that wasn't enough, he also had on a pair of worn Ropers. The state of his boots told Jade that he was the real deal, not just some wannabe wearing the clothes. Something about that went straight to her heart.

And he was here to see her and had agreed to accompany her to the high school reunion. How lucky could she get? Even Nina and Alexis were envious. It didn't matter that she'd made up the whole engagement, Heath had backed her up, and they were forced to believe it.

He drew her attention away from her thoughts when he rose and hooked his thumbs into the front pockets of his jeans. "What is it you're trying to get him to do?"

Her cheeks grew warm. What if he laughed at her? "I need him to wear a costume in the Halloween parade I'm planning for the zoo. The parade and the party that follows it is the grand finale of all the Halloween Happenings I've got planned for the kids."

He raised his eyebrows. Although he didn't say anything, his expression was saying, *Are you freaking kidding me?*

"It's a cute dog costume." She looked at it. "And it cost me a pretty penny too." Jade held up the double-brimmed deerstalker cap and the brown houndstooth plaid trench coat trimmed with satin. The outfit was actually quite clever and well made. But along with Charlie not wanting to cooperate, she wondered if the kids had even heard of Sherlock Holmes.

Heath shook his head and looked at Charlie. "I gotta say, bud, I wouldn't be feeling it either. Costumes haven't been my thing in a long time."

"Oh great, encourage him, why don't you." She twisted

her lips. If she was looking for an ally in this whole thing, it obviously wasn't Heath.

He rubbed a hand over his mouth and cleared his throat.

She knew he was hiding a smile, and she couldn't blame him. The whole thing *was* silly, but she still had an ace up her sleeve. "It's all for the kids. They'll be so disappointed. I know how much they've been looking forward to this."

He looked down at the dog and spread his hands and palms out in supplication. "What can I say, bud? It's for the kids."

Charlie whined and hung his head as if he understood but still didn't want to cooperate. The look he gave Heath said he felt like he'd been double-crossed.

"I feel you, Charlie, but sometimes we have to do things we don't want to please the people in our lives."

Jade's insides tightened. Was he talking about taking her to the reunion? Was he doing it simply to please her? Of course he was. It wasn't like he wanted to attend a function with a bunch of strangers.

You didn't think he really wanted to go with you? said a voice in her head that sounded suspiciously like Casper Windham.

She had to clear her throat before she could speak. "You don't have to go. It's okay. Really. I understand."

Heath's head snapped up; his eyes tight in the corners. "Are you talking to me or Charlie?"

"You." Now she felt miserable. She'd managed to convince herself he wanted to go with her. Not just to help her out but because maybe, just maybe, he enjoyed being in her company.

"Why do I get the feeling that I'm talking about dog parades and you're not?"

She swallowed. Hard. Was it possible that he really *was* referring to Charlie's refusal to put on the costume? She didn't want to create a whole misunderstanding by not getting clarity. "It's just that—"

He cut her off by covering her mouth with his.

His actions caught Jade off guard, but she soon melted against him. How could she not? The way his lips explored hers had her eyes threatening to roll back in her head. His actions may have been swift when he began the kiss, but now he was taking his time. *Savoring* was the only way to describe what his mouth was doing to hers.

The kiss was not some fantasy kiss; it was so much more. There was nothing sweet or gently seductive about it. The lip-lock was all about primal masculine desire and fiercely controlled passion. The kind of kiss a man gave a woman when he set out to make it clear he wanted her.

She knew there were only two possible responses to a kiss like that: she could return it with equal ardor or she could break free and step back. She doubted there was any middle ground. And in that moment, she knew she was *all in*. Wrapping her arms around his neck and kissing him back with a sensual hunger she'd never experienced, excitement sent adrenaline coursing through her.

By the time he freed her lips, she was hot and cold, breathless and a little shaky. She clutched him, savoring his scent and the hard feel of his unyielding body. When she kissed the warm skin of his throat, he exhaled deeply. Was it a sigh of pleasure, surrender or exaltation?

He used one finger to raise her chin, His mouth came back down on hers in another intense kiss. She could feel the heat of the fire that smoldered just beneath the surface.

She wanted the moment to go on indefinitely, but that wasn't realistic. And she had to keep reminding herself that this was a fake relationship even if the embrace was real. She knew guys didn't always have to have deep feelings for a woman in order to engage in a sexual relationship.

A loud braying bark spoiled the mood and Heath lifted

his head. They stared at one another, each breathing heavily, for several moments before he stepped back.

Charlie lifted his head and howled.

"I think we're embarrassing Charlie," Heath said and contemplated the dog.

"Sorry about that. He's a very opinionated dog." Jade tried to keep the disappointment over the abrupt ending to that mind-blowing kiss out of her voice.

"It appears Charlie doesn't have one romantic bone in that low-slung body of his."

The dog hung his head as Heath squatted down and picked up the costume. "How about we do a little negotiating? I'll bet you enjoy going for rides. Most dogs do."

"Next to treats and naps, it's his favorite thing," Jade chimed in.

"I have a proposition for you, Charlie, my man. Put the costume on, and I'll take you for a ride in my G Wagon. How does that sound?"

Jade took a step toward them. "Oh, I don't think that—"

Heath stopped her with a finger pressed to his lips and a shake of his head.

"Deal?" he asked the dog.

Charlie seemed to consider the idea, then sat down with a sigh. Heath took that as a yes and put the costume on him, including the deerstalker cap.

"Wait. Let me get some pictures." Jade pulled her cell phone out of her pocket and began snapping away. If Charlie refused to put the costume on again, at least she'd have something to show the kids. She made sure to get some with Heath in the photo too. Sort of a memento of that unforgettable kiss.

"What is he's supposed to be?" he asked.

She heaved a sigh reminiscent of Charlie's of a moment ago. "He supposed to be Sherlock Hound."

Heath studied the dog. "Okay. I see it. Clever."

"No, it's not. If you didn't recognize the costume, there's no chance the kids will either. What was I *thinking*?"

"Hey, don't give up. We can explain it to them."

Jade picked up on his use of the word "we" and felt better, but that didn't solve the problem of a cute but unrecognizable costume. "Wanna bet most of the kids have never heard of Sherlock Holmes?"

Heath gently rubbed his knuckles across her back. "Consider it a teachable moment."

"They're a little young for Sherlock."

He snapped his fingers. "But not too young for Encyclopedia Brown."

"Encyclopedia Brown? I remember loving those books. I enjoyed helping solve the mysteries and fancied myself being a girl detective."

Pulling out his phone, Heath said, "I saw you were giving out prizes to the kids. How many kids are you expecting?"

"I'm not totally sure yet." She hadn't gotten back all the signup sheets yet.

He waved his hand in a dismissive gesture as he studied his phone. "No matter. I'll order seventy-five copies. That should cover it. Any extras we can donate to the school."

"Any extras of what?"

"I just ordered sets of the Encyclopedia Brown series. I think the kids will enjoy them, and we can explain that Sherlock Holmes is also a detective, albeit an adult."

Leave it up to Heath to come up with a solution. "You're a real problem solver, Heath Blackwood. No wonder your company is so successful. How can I ever thank you?"

"No thanks needed, but I think we need to give Charlie his reward."

His tail wagging, the basset watched Heath.

"We can take my ranch truck. Not much can harm that old thing," Jade said.

Heath shook his head. "That wasn't the deal. Was it, buddy?"

The dog woofed in agreement.

"But…you may not realize this, but Charlie is a drool monster."

Heath brushed his mouth lightly against hers. "I've been around him enough to know he drools and sheds."

"And loves to roll around in the mud," she added.

He laughed. "Can't forget that."

Squatting down, he started to remove the costume and looked up at Jade. "Unless you'd rather I keep this on him?"

"No. Take it off. No telling what could happen to it if we leave it on." She gave him a wary look. "Are you *sure* you want to take your Mercedes for this ride?"

He chuckled and rubbed the dog's ears. "Positive. I have an important bit of business to conduct." After finishing his task, he stood and handed the folded costume to Jade, who put it on the workbench in the barn. She picked up the leash from the bench and clipped it to Charlie's collar. The dog barked and danced around, his tail wagging. "What sort of business? Where are we going?" she asked.

"We're going to the lake, by the dock. And it's important business," he said.

She gave him a narrow-eyed stare but decided to be patient. He seemed to be in a good mood, so she tried not to worry. She doubted he'd take her for a ride to the dock at the lake if he had some bad news, like he wouldn't be continuing their fake engagement.

"Important business?" she repeated.

"Very," he responded with an eyebrow wiggle and a wink. That wink made her heart do all kinds of foolish things.

CHAPTER SEVEN

"Now, TRY TO behave yourself in Heath's car," Jade told Charlie as they followed Heath to his Mercedes.

"I'm sure he'll be fine," Heath said over his shoulder, and opened the door to the back seat.

"What's that?" She pointed to the back seat.

"Oh. That?" he said with a wide grin.

"Yeah, that. It looks like an animal car seat, but you don't have a pet." Maybe he was thinking of getting one or had recently had one. She'd felt close to him since their date, but the fact was she didn't know as much about him as she thought. She actually knew very little of his life outside of Chatelaine.

"Not me personally, but I know someone who has a dog that means a great deal to her." His eyes held a certain gleam. "I did it for her."

Warmth flooded Jade's chest. Had she heard that right? "Don't tell me you got that for Charlie?"

"I did." He nodded and widened his grin. "I saw that you had one, so I decided to get one too."

"But...but you don't want Charlie riding in your car on a regular basis."

He gave her a puzzled frown. "Says who?"

"Me. His owner. You experienced firsthand what mayhem and destruction he can cause."

"If you're talking about our first date, I beg to differ. I think the evening turned out quite well."

"He ruined all your plans," she reminded him, but her protestations were getting old even to her.

Heath narrowed his eyes. "How do you figure that?"

"You had the evening arranged at a nice restaurant. I can't imagine that staying home and eating lasagna and sitting on the porch listening to the cicadas and watching for fireflies could compare to what you had in mind when you asked me out."

"The only plan that mattered was spending time with you. Considering that, I got exactly what I wanted from the evening, with the bonus of home-cooked meal."

"You did?" His words were making her insides go all gooey.

He captured her chin between his thumb and index finger. "I got to spend it with you, Jade, which was the only thing that mattered. And your mom makes great lasagna."

"It was a great evening for me too, and my mom does make great lasagna."

"Then Charlie didn't ruin anything at all. I think everything turned out the way it was supposed to. Maybe he's a lot smarter than you're giving him credit for."

"Perhaps you're right." Jade smiled at Heath. "Do we have any plans for this ride?"

"I haven't driven around the lake yet and I'd like to. I believe there's an open field near the boat dock. Charlie might like to explore. What do you say, bud, ready to go for that ride?"

Charlie barked and did a little dance, letting Heath know he was all in for this adventure.

A moment later, Heath picked up Charlie and put him in the special car seat, making sure he was secure.

"Did I do it right?" he asked, and moved aside so Jade could double-check it.

"It looks fine," she said and took a step back and bumped into Heath. "Sorry."

"I'm not." He steadied her and turned her in the circle of his arms.

Being in Heath's arms felt so natural, and when he leaned down and kissed her, she fell even more under his spell. The kiss was short, but to Jade, it felt like a promise. A promise of more to come.

He rested his forehead against hers and sighed. "Please tell me I'm not in this alone."

"You're not in this alone," she said in a breathless tone.

He gazed into her eyes. "That's good to know."

Charlie barked and they both laughed.

"I guess we'd better get going," Heath said and opened the passenger door to assist Jade into the seat.

He went around the hood of the vehicle and slipped into the driver's seat.

"You said you had some business," Jade reminded him as he started the finely tuned engine.

"I'll explain when we get to our destination."

They drove the short distance to the dock area of the lake, and he parked in the gravel lot. He lifted Charlie down from the SUV. The dog shook himself and tugged on the leash wanting to explore.

Meandering around the area, they followed the basset hound as he went from place to place and sniffed. They reached a small barbecue area, and Heath suggested they sit on one of the picnic benches.

Once seated, Heath reached into his pocket and pulled out a small box. A *jeweler's box*. The kind that held a ring.

Jade's breath caught in her throat. Why would he be giving her a ring? Despite the fevered kiss of a few moments ago, this was still a fake relationship. Attempting to remain calm and rational over this, she went over everything he'd said since he arrived.

He had told the dog he had business to take care of. Is this how he saw giving her the ring? As a piece of business? Because the engagement wasn't real.

Don't start fantasizing just because his kiss knocked you for a loop. He was a good kisser, and they might even have chemistry, but that didn't mean he saw this engagement as anything other than a face-saving favor.

He opened the box and showed her the ring nestled inside. The white gold ring had a sapphire in a prong setting. The round cut enhanced the gemstone's natural sparkle and color. She gasped at the beauty of it. "I couldn't possibly accept something like this."

"Why not? Don't you like sapphires?" He sounded surprised by her refusal.

"Of course I like it. What's not to like? It's a gorgeous ring." Its magnificence had everything to do with her decision. How could she in good conscience accept jewelry knowing their relationship wasn't real? Why was he even offering it to her?

"Then what is the problem?" he asked, his jaw tightening.

Her heart sank. Insulting him was the last thing she wanted to do. "It must have cost a fortune. I can't accept such an extravagant gift under false pretenses."

He frowned. "False pretenses?"

"You said yourself you can't be in a serious relationship with anyone until the mystery of your birth is solved." She needed to get ahead of this and explain her side.

"And your point is?"

"To be perfectly honest, this looks like a serious ring."

"It might look like it, but believe me, it's not." He shook

his head. "I think it would be a good idea to wear it for the reunion. Help sell our story to your classmates."

His explanation sounded logical, but did they really need help selling their story? "I'm no expert in jewelry, but I know sapphires can be pricey."

"Not all of them."

She'd take his word for it. What else could she do? "Was there a reason you picked a sapphire?"

"It's supposed to be a perfect gemstone for hazel eyes."

Her heart thudded. He'd picked out a ring because of her eye color? She'd bet some of the guys she'd known would have been hard-pressed to even remember her eye color.

"I promise to take good care of it. I'm sure you'll want it back after...after..." The thought of their fake engagement coming to an end made her queasy.

Get used to it, she cautioned herself. This isn't real. None of this is real.

"Let's not worry about that."

"Okay," she agreed. She was most certainly setting herself up for heartache in the future. But the keyword here was *future*, and she decided today wasn't a good day to worry about it. She'd enjoy being with Heath, and if today was all she was getting, then so be it.

HEATH WANTED TO give himself a good kick. That didn't go *at all* like he'd planned. He'd assumed Jade would have jumped at the chance for a ring like that. He'd probably have to explain it as part of their engagement story, but then he'd offer it and she'd accept. End of story. But Jade was different, and that's why he was having trouble remembering that this whole thing was temporary. He'd take her to her reunion and then what?

Maybe he'd solve the mystery surrounding his birth father before the reunion, and he could get on with his life, depending on what answers he'd receive.

"So, you'll wear the ring...for now at least?" The truth was, he wanted her to have it. As for why, he hadn't a clue. He didn't understand his own reasoning, so how was he expected to explain it to her?

"If you want me to, I will." Her tone was solemn, as if she were making a vow.

Was she making a vow? He pushed that thought aside, just as he had the crazy notion of going down on one knee before giving Jade the sapphire ring.

Instead of kneeling, he gently took her left hand in his and slowly slipped the ring onto her finger. He squeezed her fingers as he seated the ring in place. It looked right, as if it truly belonged on her finger. As if she truly belonged to him. The thought made his heart stutter.

He led her over to a picnic table so they could sit and watch the dog.

"Charlie looks like he's running out of steam," he said.

The dog had been running around the grassy area but had taken to lying under a tree.

"Yeah, he's not known for his endurance. He likes to run around for short bursts, but then he's ready for a nap," Jade said with a chuckle.

"That's a good philosophy to embrace," Heath said and got the reaction he'd been going for. Jade laughed. God, how he loved that laugh.

They bundled Charlie back into the car. Securing the dog into the special animal car seat made him think about what it would be like to have a family of his own. A family with Jade. Did she even want kids? Did he? How could he bring a child into the world until he knew the secret behind his birth story?

They got into the SUV, and he pulled out onto the road leading back to the Fortune ranch.

"What made you pick this model of car?" she asked curiously.

He glanced at her for a second before turning his attention back on the road. "Pardon? What do you mean?"

"I just wondered what drew you to it."

He shrugged. "I liked it."

"Fair enough."

Was she simply making conversation? "Why? What's your dream car?"

"Promise not to laugh?" she asked.

He felt her gaze on him. "Promise."

"It *was* a Maserati Quattroporte."

"Was?"

She had made him promise not to laugh, but then she did so herself. "It sounded so exotic to me, then I found out Quattroporte just means four—"

"Doors," he finished for her. He managed not to laugh but couldn't prevent the smile that curled his lips.

"See. You're making fun of me. It lost some of its luster when I learned the mundane English translation."

"I most certainly am not making fun. As a matter of fact, you have great taste in luxury cars." He knew Casper Windham had been worth a lot of money, so Jade and her family had never been poor. Not like he and his mom. But despite the privileged upbringing, Jade was very down to earth. Which is what had drawn him to her in the first place.

"Yeah, well, I couldn't have one with Charlie." She heaved a sigh.

"Why? Does he object to Italian luxury cars?"

She laughed. "No, but he'd want to go every time I drove anywhere, and you've seen how much he drools."

He waved a hand. "You worry too much about that."

"But you keep your car so clean."

"I like to take care of the things I have. I didn't have a lot growing up and take care of the things I have now in my life."

"You appreciate them," she said softly.

"I guess you could say that. I don't like to take anything for granted."

"You started the Anne Blackwood Foundation to help disadvantaged kids stay in school and get a higher education."

"How did you find out about that? I don't publicize it." Heath didn't do it for the kudos. He'd simply seen a need and decided to fulfill it. The project helped him honor the legacy his mother had given him. He wasn't able to help her now that he was rich, but he could help others in her name.

"You've been googling me?"

She shrugged but didn't deny it. "Why don't you like to take credit for it?"

"I don't deny its existence, but I don't need accolades to accomplish what I want."

"I admire you for that. You're nothing like my father was."

"And that's a good thing?" he asked but was pretty sure he knew the answer. He noticed Jade was not comfortable talking about her father.

"A very good thing," she said, but didn't elaborate.

Her words gave him conflicting feelings. He was glad she admired the things he'd accomplished, but it also made him wonder how she'd feel if he discovered negative reasons why James Perry had never acknowledged him.

JADE HELD OUT her left hand and admired the sapphire ring. She'd been doing that ever since Heath had given it to her.

After he'd left yesterday, she'd told herself she would wear it to the reunion and only then. Her family knew the truth, so there was no need to pretend in front of them.

At least that had been the plan, but she'd been unable to bring herself to take the beautiful ring off. Every time she started to remove it, she heard Heath saying he'd picked a sapphire to complement her hazel eyes.

"Jade? I saw your message and thought I'd come and check on the lamb."

Jade turned at the sound of her sister's voice. Dahlia was walking across the grass toward the barn.

Glancing at her left hand and the ring, she grimaced. Too late to remove the ring without calling attention to it.

"How is he doing?"

"Yesterday he was disappointed after speaking with—" Jade broke off abruptly. She had to assume her face was probably a nice candy apple red by now. Of course Dahlia had meant the lamb, but Jade's mind was so full of Heath that she'd answered automatically.

"Oh, wow! He speaks? That'll be a big draw for the petting zoo." Dahlia was obviously working hard to keep a straight face.

"Ha ha. I was talking about—"

"Heath Blackwood," her sister said without trying to hide her grin. "I was going to inquire about him next, but we can start with him first if you'd like."

"We'll talk about the lamb and only the lamb, if you don't mind."

Dahlia raised an eyebrow. "And if I *do* mind?"

Jade rolled her eyes at her younger sister's antics and briefly wondered if Heath teased or got teased by his sisters. Had their relationship evolved to that point? Did meeting your sibling as an adult change that dynamic? They might—

"So, about the lamb?"

Dahlia's question chased away Jade's musings over Heath. *Get out of your head, Jade.*

"The lamb is doing much better since I removed him from the petting area."

"What was the problem? Did one of the kids do something?"

Jade shook her head. "No. I think he found all the attention from humans stressful, so I moved him to the barn."

Dahlia made a face. "The poor thing. First his mama rejects him and now this."

Jade patted her sister's shoulder. "Don't fret. He's been befriended by one of the baby goats, and I'm keeping them together. They're both doing much better, but I may not be able to keep them as part of the actual petting zoo. But don't worry, I will look after them regardless of that."

"You're such a soft touch with the animals. I think you've found your true calling, Sis."

"I'm grateful to the family for this opportunity."

Dahlia smiled over at her sister. "We're grateful to you for taking it over and making a success of both the zoo and the children's workshops in such a short time and—"

Jade glanced at Dahlia, wondering what made her stop.

"Oh my God, Jade, where'd you get that sapphire? That's some *serious bling.*" Dahlia grabbed Jade's left hand to get a closer look at the ring. "It looks like an engagement ring. Jade? Are you holding out on us?"

Jade pulled her hand out of Dahlia's grasp. "What do you mean? It's just part of the fake engagement story, not a real engagement ring."

"It might not be a real engagement, but that ring is the real deal."

"Well, of course it's real. I'm wearing it, aren't I?" Jade told her sister, but she started to get an uncomfortable feeling in the pit of her stomach. Those weren't butterflies swarming in there but bats. Enough bats to make the citizens of Austin envious.

"I'm not a jeweler, but that ring didn't come from a cereal box."

Was it possible that Heath bought a real ring for her to wear? Real, as in expensive? Of course he was wealthy, but he didn't seem like the type to throw his money around. The only thing flashy about him was his car, and even that wasn't all that flashy. She'd seen plenty of soccer moms driving G Wagons at the country club.

"I think this guy is serious," her sister said.

"Really?" Damn, she wanted to kick herself for sounding so needy.

"And why not?"

"I'm not exactly the type of woman a billionaire picks."

Her sister narrowed her eyes. "What's that supposed to mean?"

"Rich, successful men want beauty queens on their arms," Jade said, repeating something Casper had said to her on more than one occasion. In the past, Jade hadn't cared because she didn't want a rich, successful man. And now?

"That's bull crap."

"No, that's Casper Windham."

Her sister put her arm around her. "I know Daddy did a number on you, but he was wrong. Dead wrong. About a lot of things but especially about you, Jade. Look what you've done with this place."

"The zoo didn't have any animals left, but the buildings and such were already here."

"Don't undercut all you've accomplished," Dahlia admonished her. "You've done a wonderful job."

"I renovated the place and brought it up to date with a

lot of help from others," Jade said, but her sister's praise gave her a warmth that spread across her chest.

"You've given it *heart*. But enough about the zoo. Let's talk about that ring."

Jade looked down at the dazzling sapphire. "You're sure it's real?"

"Positive, and I'm positive about what I see when Heath looks at you."

Even after Dahlia had left, Jade couldn't stop thinking about what her sister said about Heath. Was it possible that he was falling for her as hard as she was falling for him?

CHAPTER EIGHT

HEATH STEPPED INSIDE Fortune's Castle after returning from a meeting with investors in Houston. He loosened his tie as he strolled inside and crossed the grand entryway with its black-and-white checkerboard floor tiles. As always, he glanced up at the elaborate wrought-iron candelabra hung from the ceiling painted with a Byzantine-style mosaic of peacocks and birds.

Would he ever not be taken aback by the opulence of the place, he wondered, shaking his head at the black torch-shaped sconces interspersed with paintings of medieval lords and ladies in outdoor landscapes lined one wall.

It felt good to be home. His last thought caused him to stumble, but he caught himself before falling and embarrassing himself.

When had he started thinking of Chatelaine as home? When he'd first arrived, he planned on staying only long enough to meet with his newly discovered sisters and to find answers to the questions surrounding James Perry. But those plans had started to morph once he met Jade Fortune and agreed to be her fake fiancé for her reunion. He had a feeling that Jade had a lot to do with his thinking of Chatelaine as home.

The hotel might not be fully operational yet, but staff had been hired and were obviously being trained. He halted as a group of trainees followed a member of management through the lobby. He glanced over at the reception counter and the desk clerk waved at him.

The woman, who appeared to be in her mid to late twenties, also called out. "Mr. Blackwood, sir?"

He changed direction and went to the counter instead of the bank of elevators. "Something wrong?"

The woman gave him an engaging smile. "No, sir. I found this on the counter when I came back from getting some copy paper from the back room."

She held up a plain white envelope with his name printed in shaky block letters.

"Do you know who left it for me?" he asked. This was all very odd, but he did have to admit that the entire population of Chatelaine probably knew he was staying at the Castle even if it wasn't formally open.

"Not a clue. I'm sorry, but our security cameras aren't hooked up yet. But it must be someone who knows you're staying here."

He took the envelope and grunted. "I'm sure that's the entire town."

She laughed. "Pretty much. Not many secrets in Chatelaine. That's for sure."

Except for the mystery surrounding the circumstances of his birth. Why he never knew his father, and his mother felt the need to keep it a secret. He should have pursued it more forcefully with Anne. He would have if he'd had any inkling that she would have been gone so soon and so quickly. The cancer that took her had worked fast. He'd tried to press her a few times, but when he saw how agitated the subject made her, he backed off. So that was on him. But truly, how could he hound a dying woman? And he didn't want her to think she hadn't been enough. She'd asked him that once when he'd prodded her for details on his father. After that, he'd let it go. And the information she'd had was buried with her.

He appreciated that she hadn't had an easy time of raising him as a single mother but he had never lacked for love. They may not have had a lot of luxuries but she saw that he always had the basics. He missed her and wished he could've had more time to spoil her once he started making large sums of money.

"Is there a problem, sir? As I said, the envelope was here when I got back from my errand."

The desk clerk's question pulled him out of his morose thoughts, and he gave her a vague smile. "No problem at all." After a quick glance at her name tag, he added, "Thanks again, Sara."

He glanced at the envelope as he walked toward the elevator. Strange. Despite his curiosity, he decided to wait until he reached his room to open it. No telling what it contained.

Once inside his suite, he dropped his briefcase on the desk and tore open the envelope. There was a single sheet of paper inside. It was plain white copy paper. On it was a handwritten note in the same shaky block letters.

Your mother was deeply in love with James Perry, but he did her dirty.

Heath turned the note over, but it was blank. The note was also unsigned. Had it come from Doris Edwards? She had said something similar when Heath had gone to see her for the first time with his sisters.

He debated with himself for a minute but decided not to tell the triplets about the note. He didn't want to taint whatever they thought of their father. They might have been too young for any personal memories of him, but people had shared their memories with the girls, and he wasn't going to mess with that. Besides, he didn't know the whole story.

Would going to see Doris again help? He remembered how she'd ended up rambling the last time. He wasn't sure he was interested in engaging in that frustrating exercise again. Maybe at some point he would, but not at the moment.

According to the note, his mother had been in love with his father. Was that a good thing or not? Heath wasn't sure. Had James Perry truly taken advantage of his mother? Or had she just fallen for the wrong man? Considering how close in age he was to his half sisters, a mere two months, had he led two women on? Obviously James had married his sisters' mother. What about Anne? Had he simply dropped her despite her being pregnant? Or maybe his time with his mother had been an extramarital affair. Was James the kind of man who found it impossible to be faithful? Heath knew the type but, despite having James Perry's blood and DNA, didn't think he could be that cruel as to cheat on a spouse.

And if James *had* cheated with Heath's mother, how would his sisters feel about that? Would they somehow feel Heath's mother was responsible for the way their father treated their mother?

Now that he'd found his siblings, Heath did not want to sever the bond that was being forged between them. Maybe he shouldn't even be *on* this quest. He would have to share his results at some point, but the last thing he wanted to do was hurt Haley, Lily or Tabitha.

He decided to change out of his business clothes and go to see the one person who might help him make sense of this. She made everything in his life feel different.

"What is it you're doing?"

Jade's stomach somersaulted at the sound of his voice.

She'd set up a table in the doorway of the largest barn at the petting zoo so she could work on her craft project for Halloween Happenings. She set down the pair of pliers in her hand and drank in the sight of Heath. Today he was wearing faded jeans, a denim work shirt and a pair of scuffed black Ropers. A tingle ran along her spine. This feeling was becoming a habit whenever she was with him. Would it always be like this? Or would she get used to being with him?

Get used to being with him?

Where did that thought even come from? Theirs wasn't a real relationship. Heath was doing her a favor by not telling everyone how she'd lied about their engagement.

Heath stood next to a sawhorse, and an image of him astride a horse came unbidden into her mind, threatening to leave her breathless.

"Do you ride?" she blurted out before she could stop herself. He was going to be convinced she didn't know how to carry on an intelligent conversation if she kept asking him outlandish questions.

"Depends on what you're talking about riding."

Warmth bloomed in her cheeks, and she could only pray that she didn't resemble a ripe tomato. "Horses."

"Yes," he said, drawing the word out so it had three syllables.

"Why am I sensing a 'but' in there?"

"Maybe because that's what gets sore when I ride," he said, his lips twitching.

"I meant the *but* with only one *t*, but I guess you answered my question." She laughed. At least he wasn't calling her names for inciting inane conversations, like the one about the English translation of Quattroporte. "So am I to understand you don't like horseback riding?"

"Depends on who I'm riding with. If you're asking, then I'm willing."

"Sore butt and all?" She'd have to check with Nash or Ridge and perhaps they could arrange a riding date.

"I figure it would be worth it. When did you have in mind?"

She wasn't about to tell him that the whole thing stemmed from a vision she'd had of him as a cowboy astride a horse. "I didn't have any specific time in mind. I was just curious. After all, this is a ranch, so I'm sure we can scare up some horses."

"Let me know when and where, and I'll be there." He squatted on his haunches next to her Halloween project. "Now, what is this going to be?"

"It's something I saw online and thought it would be great for the costume party and parade I have planned for the kids." She pulled out her phone and searched for what had given her the inspiration.

She found it and handed him the phone. He took it from her, and when he did, his fingers brushed against hers. Again with the tingles from the skin-to-skin contact.

"Very clever."

"I thought so."

Then Jade showed him what she was doing with the tomato cages. She'd turned them upside down and twisted the bottom spikes together and tied them. Using a Styrofoam ball, she stuck it onto the gather spikes. Then she wound a string of clear lights around the cage. She covered the entire thing with a precut square of white cloth.

"Whadaya think?" She sat back and checked out her creation.

"I think it needs some eyes."

"That's right! I almost forgot." She checked the bag of

supplies she'd brought with her and pulled out two circles cut from black felt. "I'll need to glue them on."

"Can I do it?"

"Sure." She handed him the felt circles and the fabric glue she'd picked up at GreatStore, along with the other supplies to make the ghosts.

"We'll need to plug them in," he said as he put the cap back on the glue.

"I brought some power strips and extension cords." She pointed to the plastic bags stacked against the side of the barn.

"How many did you plan on making?"

"I'm not sure yet. I decided to try this one first and see how it came out before I committed myself to half a dozen."

He nodded. "Let me get this one hooked up so you can see how it looks."

She watched him walk into the barn and couldn't help but admire him. Tall, loose-limbed and totally delicious. And he was all hers.

What? No, no, no.

Get that thought out of your head right now, Jade Fortune. This is all make believe. Your feelings might be real, but the situation isn't.

"So, how does it look?" Heath asked as he came back out of the barn.

"What?"

"Your ghost. How does it look?" He gave her a scrutinizing look.

How could she have forgotten the ghost? She studied her creation with a critical eye but had to admit it looked pretty good.

This is what you need to concentrate on, she told herself. Forget building make-believe castles and fairy tales.

HEATH WATCHED JADE CLOSELY. Before he entered the barn to plug in the extension cord, she'd been excited about her project. He saw it in the gleam in her eyes, the glow on her cheeks. He could have planned his future on that smile and the soft expression in those hazel eyes. But when he emerged from the barn, she had changed. As if a switch had been flipped. She was still smiling, but he detected something different. It didn't light up her eyes as it had before. He sighed, thinking how in tune he was to her various moods. Not a good sign if he expected to walk away from this phony relationship with his heart intact.

"The kids are going to get a kick out of them." She came to stand beside him. "What do you think?"

Jade's scent filled his senses with a combination of soap, shampoo and what he suspected was laundry detergent or fabric softener. She didn't need cloying perfume to smell good or to catch his eye. Everything about her grabbed his attention from the moment he'd spotted her leaving the Daily Grind as he drove through Chatelaine for the first time. Maybe that's why the coffee shop had become a favorite—

"Heath?"

"What?" He pushed his thoughts aside. "Sorry. What did you say?"

She gave him a speculative glance. "I asked what you thought of my ghost."

"I love it, and I'm sure the kids will too."

She nodded. "Thanks. I agree. I'll use up the rest of the supplies and make some more."

"Would you like some help?" He had assembled the prototypes for his drone and laser weed zappers and was pretty sure he could handle some tomato cage ghosts.

"I'd love it. Thanks." She glanced at him with an unreadable expression. "You're sure you don't mind? I know how busy you are."

"Not too busy to help you," he told her, then added, "Like we told Charlie, it's for the kids."

"Right. For the kids," she said in a monotone.

Great. Why did he have to tack on that last bit? Yes, part of him was doing it for the children, but a very small part. Mostly he was doing it because of Jade.

She'd begun assembling another ghost, so he chose supplies to make his own.

"How was your trip to Houston? Did you accomplish what you set out to do?" she asked as she wound lights around the tomato cage.

"I think so. The investors are definitely interested," he said, but his thoughts while there had been on what waited for him upon his return.

"But?"

He looked up from his partially finished ghost. "There was a strange letter waiting for me at the hotel."

"A notice from the management?"

"No. It was an anonymous note. It said, and I quote, 'Your mother was deeply in love with James Perry, but he did her dirty.'"

Heath stuck the Styrofoam ball onto the spike ends of the tomato cage. Stepping back, he checked to be sure he hadn't damaged the Styrofoam. He'd used a bit more force than had been necessary. Thank goodness his rough treatment hadn't harmed anything.

"Oh, wow. That is disturbing. Any clue who sent it. Was there a postmark?"

He began stringing the tiny lights around the structure. "It wasn't sent through the mail. The desk clerk at the hotel said she found it on the counter addressed to me.

She didn't see who dropped it off, and their security cameras aren't hooked up yet."

"Do you think Doris Edwards wrote it?"

"That was my first thought, but I don't know how she would have delivered it to Fortune's Castle."

Jade shrugged. "She could have had someone give her a ride or got someone else to bring it. My mother has begun employing a lot of locals so someone could have dropped off the note for her."

"I guess it doesn't matter how it got to me. The fact is it did." He finished wrapping the lights and made sure they were secure.

"And its contents are bothering you?"

"Yeah." He exhaled loudly. "Plus, I hate having to keep something from my sisters."

"Why would you feel the need to hide it from them?"

"It doesn't exactly paint James in a very good light. I hate to be the one giving them sketchy information about their biological father. Who says the note is even right?" He'd always been afraid his mother was the villain in the story, but the note made it sound like *she* was the victim.

"But the truth is exactly that…the truth. That note may be nothing but a lie, but whatever you find out, you can't protect them from the truth."

He nodded mutely, letting her words sink in.

"I'm sure they understand that whatever you find out about James Perry and his relationship with your mother doesn't affect your relationship with them," she added.

"Are you sure about that?"

"Not one hundred percent, but I didn't have a great relationship with my father while some of my siblings had a much better one with him. I don't hold that against them." Jade shrugged. "How could I? It wasn't their fault the way Casper treated me. And it's not your fault, or theirs, the way James treated your mother. Your sisters are smart, they'll understand that too."

As usual Jade knew how to make him feel better, and he trusted her judgment.

Ignoring his common sense and following his instincts, he moved toward her. Putting his hands on her slender shoulders, he pulled her to him and brought his mouth down on hers. Although his actions had been abrupt, he soon gentled his kiss, exploring her mouth with his. He drew the tip of his tongue across the seam of her lips, and she opened for him. His tongue slipped past her teeth to slide against hers.

An alarm sounded in his brain, and he took a step back. Not because he wanted to put distance between them. He did it because he *had* to. The situation was starting to get out of hand.

He should probably explain why he pulled away but wasn't sure he could. Instead, he waited a moment for his insides to settle back into place and for some oxygen to return to his brain.

"I, uh…" He blew out his breath.

She was breathing heavily. "Yeah. Me too."

"So I'm not in this alone?"

She shook her head.

"That's…reassuring."

She blew out a breath and laughed. "Yeah. It is."

"Maybe we should work on finishing these ghosts." He hitched his chin toward the table scattered with supplies.

"Good idea." She got back to work on the half-finished ghost. Clearing her throat, she asked, "Does the fact that I'm older than you bother you?"

"You're older than me?" He placed a hand across his chest in a theatrical gesture. Her age didn't bother him, but he wasn't entirely sure how she felt.

"Yes. You must have realized it when—you're teasing me."

"Now, Jade, this is hardly a matter for levity. I'm involved with an older woman. That's rather shocking, don't you think?" he asked, trying his best to keep a straight face.

"You ought to get together with my sister Dahlia," she muttered.

"Well, she is younger than you, but I have a feeling that her husband Rawlston might not take too kindly to that." He'd heard that Dahlia and Rawlston's marriage had had a rocky start, but everyone in Chatelaine agrees the couple is deeply in love. Nothing and no one were coming between those two.

"Very funny." Jade narrowed her eyes at him, but her lips twitched as if fighting a grin.

"I'm not so sure this is a laughing matter. I'm assuming Dahlia agrees with me about this troubling turn of events." He couldn't remember the last time, if ever, he'd teased a woman. He liked it. His whole relationship with Jade was different than any other.

Maybe because it's not real, a voice in his head taunted, but he pushed it aside. The engagement might be fake but this moment with Jade was real—*she* was real—and he was going to enjoy it.

"Are you sure it doesn't bother you?"

"Cross my heart," he said.

"I—"

He cut her off by placing two fingers across her lips. "Not another word. Ever since I had a crush on my second grade teacher, I have had this thing for older women."

"You had a crush on your second grade teacher?" she asked.

"I don't remember much except she had long blond hair and wore red high heels."

"Wow. That's specific."

He laughed, shaking his head at the memory. "About the only thing I remember about second grade."

She laughed too. Boy did he love that sound. It was getting harder and harder to remember that this relationship was temporary.

But it had to be until he was able to solve the mystery surrounding James and Anne's history.

AFTER HEATH LEFT, Jade called the school to let them know that Heath would be teaching the next workshop, which happened to be the following day. The school staff was excited and asked if they could send more than one grade to the ranch.

Heath, true to his word, arrived at about the same time as the school kids and their teachers. Also arriving were what appeared to be an abundance of parent chaperones, mostly mothers. Looked like the kids weren't the only ones excited by Heath's appearance. Not that Jade could blame them. The day was sunny and crisp, a perfect autumn morning. It was as if even the weather wanted to cooperate for Heath's demonstration.

Jade watched the children file obediently into the bleachers that had been set up several months ago for the workshops.

The only one not cooperating was Billy Connor. The boy and his mother had visited the petting zoo many times before. Jade knew how much he loved the zoo and the day camps he'd come to. The boy's teacher, Mrs. Miller, had taken him aside, so Jade sauntered over.

"I'm not sure what's wrong," Mrs. Miller confided to Jade, "but he's lost his chance to see the animals today," she said in a voice loud enough for Billy to hear.

Jade tried to get him to talk to her, but he shrugged his

shoulders and hung his head. She did notice he was paying close attention to everything Heath said.

After the workshop and the drone demonstration, the kids, all except for Billy, raced off to see the animals at the petting zoo. The chaperones followed closely behind, but a few of the women glanced back at Heath. Jade couldn't blame them. Not one bit.

Heath nodded to Jade and headed over to where she stood with Billy and his teacher.

"Do you know Mr. Blackwood?" Billy tilted his head to look at Jade.

"As a matter of fact, I do," Jade told him and grinned when Billy said, "Cool."

Heath approached, glancing at Billy, who was busy trying not to look awestruck, and raised his eyebrows in inquiry.

Mrs. Miller reached out her hand to the boy. "Billy, thank Mr. Blackwood for today's lesson, and then you come with me and give him and Miss Jade some privacy."

Warmth crept into Jade's cheeks. Evidently Billy's teacher had heard the gossip that was racing around town.

Billy thanked Heath and rippled with excitement when Heath reached out and shook his hand.

"You can go hang out with Charlie if that's okay with your teacher," Jade suggested and motioned with her head when the teacher nodded. "He's in the barn. He's in timeout today too."

"Dogs get time-out too?" Billy asked, his eyes wide.

"When they misbehave, they do," Jade told him.

Mrs. Miller took Billy by the hand and led him into the large red barn.

Heath glanced around, and with no one in sight, he leaned down and gave her a quick kiss. It was over almost before it began, but Jade still felt a tingle race down her spine at the contact.

"So, what's the deal with Billy?" Heath asked.

"He misbehaved on the bus over here and lost his petting zoo privileges. He was always such a good kid, but lately not so much. His mom and his teacher have both spoken with me about his behavior." Jade sighed. "I know how much he loves coming here. He's interested in the animals at the petting zoo. He even mentioned one time that he might want to be a veterinarian. I don't understand the change in him."

Heath's brows dipped toward the bridge of his nose. "I hate to hear that."

"I don't know what's wrong, but I could see he was paying attention to everything you said and did," Jade said and paused. Was she really going to do this? "He looks up to you. Maybe you can find out what's bothering him, and we can take it from there."

He seemed to consider it.

Jade shook her head and touched his arm. "I'm sorry. I shouldn't have put this on you. Forget that I even asked. This is above and beyond anything I should expect from you."

Heath put a hand on her shoulder and gently squeezed. "No. I want to help. He was curious about the drone. I'll offer to give him a closer look and maybe he'll open up."

"Thank you. And please, if he's not forthcoming, don't worry about it."

"I'll see what I can do."

Jade's heart skipped a beat as Heath sauntered over to where Billy was squatting down, talking to Charlie. Even if he couldn't find out what was bothering Billy, at least he was trying. More proof that Heath might be rich, successful and driven like Casper Windham had been, but that's where the similarities ended. He had proved time and time again that he cared about more than his business or making more money. Of course, that knowledge made her admire him even more. If she wasn't careful, she could end up falling in love with him. She shook her head, determined not to let that happen if she could help it. But the question was, could she help it?

Maybe you're more than a little in love already, a voice whispered in her head.

HEATH HAD OFFERED to help Jade put out juice boxes and cookies for the kids, but she'd shooed him away, saying she could handle it. He assumed she'd done that so he could use the opportunity to approach Billy. Normally, he wouldn't get involved, but he couldn't say no to Jade. And if she thought he could help, he'd at least give it a shot, although he didn't expect the kid to actually talk to him about anything personal.

Now, he stood next Billy, who was petting Charlie. The dog wagged his tail and greeted Heath like a long-lost friend.

"Hey, Mr. Blackwood, Charlie knows you," Billy said.

"He seems to know you too."

"Yeah, me and my mom love to come to Miss Jade's zoo," the boy told him.

The teacher smiled at Heath. He nodded at her unspoken question, and she said, "I'll go over and help Jade while you talk to Mr. Blackwood, but you have to promise to behave, Billy."

"I will. I promise." Billy said and stuck his chest out. "I really like your drone. Maybe someday I can do stuff like you and get to use one."

"Would you like me to show you up close how I use it?" Heath saw how fascinated Billy.

Billy's eyes were the size of saucers. "You mean it, Mr. Heath? You're gonna show me how to work the controls of the drone?"

"Yes, but you have to be very careful. It's not a toy."

"Oh, I'll be real careful. I promise."

Heath demonstrated how the controls worked and let Billy try it. "Miss Jade tells me you haven't been behaving yourself during her workshops lately."

"I'm sorry. My mom made me apologize to her already. Do I need to do it again?" The boy's lower lip trembled a bit, but he squared his shoulders.

"No, I don't think that's necessary, but I hope you will listen to her in the future. You know I got my start at workshops like the ones Miss Jade gives."

"Huh? What did you start?" Billy scrunched up his face.

Heath chuckled. "I started my company. I got lots of good ideas at those workshops, but that's because I paid attention."

"I promise to pay attention from now on."

"That's good. I think you disappoint others when you don't behave."

"I know but…" The boy hung his head.

"But what?" Heath asked gently but continued to show him how to work the controls rather than confront him directly. He wasn't sure if that method would work, but it was worth a shot.

"I dunno," Billy said and shrugged. "Do you have a dad?"

"Not really. My father died when I was a baby." If James Perry had truly been his father and must have been because DNA didn't lie. Not like people.

Heath's answer seemed to have caught Billy's attention. "So, like, you didn't know him at all?"

"No. I never met him." Heath didn't realize how much it would hurt to admit that.

"My dad died a couple years ago when I was little." Billy kicked his foot in the dirt. "But I can't remember what he sounds like anymore. Does that mean I'm gonna forget all the other stuff about him too?"

"Even if you forget some things about him, he'll always be here." Heath tapped Billy's chest. "He'll be in your heart."

"I guess. Is your dad in your heart even if you didn't meet him?"

Heath thought about it for a moment. "Yeah, I guess maybe he is."

Once the boy rejoined the group, Heath was able to let Jade know what had been bothering Billy. She said she'd be sure to speak with Mrs. Miller, who in turn could discuss it with the boy's mother.

Long after the kids had left, Heath thought about his talk with Billy and his answer to the kid's question. He carried James Perry's DNA, but what else did he carry? Had James really done Heath's mother dirty, or was there another explanation for what happened?

He really needed to find out the truth before he could form a meaningful relationship with Jade. It was only fair.

CHAPTER NINE

JADE HAD PUT this meeting off for as long as she could. She would have loved to delay it indefinitely, but she knew that wasn't going to happen, so she may as well get it over with. Her mother, as well as her sisters, wanted to take her shopping before the reunion. They would be taking the opportunity to give Jade a makeover.

Didn't they understand that she'd never be glamorous like the three of them?

She walked into the Cowgirl Café and immediately spotted her mother and two sisters in a booth. Wendy had extended the invitation, but Jade was pretty sure her mom had recruited Dahlia and Sabrina as reinforcements. Jade huffed out a breath. The way her mother and sisters were acting, you'd think she'd been invited to attend Cinderella's ball. If not for the debacle with Alexis and Nina, she wouldn't even be going.

Yes, the reunion was being held at a swanky country club and, considering most of the students came from well-to-do families, it would be a classy affair. But it hardly merited the battle plan that Wendy Fortune was sure to propose.

Jade had the urge to leave, but they had already spotted her, and her mom was waving her over.

"You made it." Wendy looked relieved to see Jade.

"I told you I was coming," she said as she slipped into the booth next to Sabrina.

"She was afraid you'd come up with an excuse to cancel at the last minute," Dahlia told her, picking up her coffee and blowing on the steaming brew. She cautiously took a sip.

"Dahlia, please," Wendy frowned at her daughter.

"What? It's the truth." Dahlia set her coffee mug down. "We know Jade doesn't like all the fuss."

Hannah, the waitress, appeared next to the booth. "Hey, Jade. Can I get you some coffee while you decide?"

"Yes, please, and I don't even have to check the menu. I'll have French toast and bacon."

Hannah stuck her order pad into the pocket of her white apron. "Extra crispy on the bacon?"

"You got it." One of the benefits of living in a small town. The waitresses knew what you liked to eat.

"Heard you and Heath Blackwood are gonna tie the knot." Hannah paused before walking away to place Jade's order. "That true?"

And that was the *downside* of living in a small town. Everyone not only knew your business, or thought they did, and weren't shy to ask all about it.

Jade unfolded her napkin and set the silverware next to it. "We haven't made any official announcements yet."

The waitress nodded. "Well, let me add my congratulations. You two make a cute couple. Be right back with the coffee."

Jade watched her walk away, her words ringing in her ears. She hadn't really thought about how people saw them as a couple.

"It's true," Wendy said and picked up her own coffee mug. "You do make a cute couple."

"But you know the truth," Jade told her mother. She didn't need her family to believe in this fake engagement because she might start buying into it herself.

"I'm so glad you're letting us help you get ready for this party," Wendy said, strategically changing the subject.

Or willingly ignoring it. Jade wasn't sure which and wasn't sure what she preferred. But changing the subject was for the best. As much as she didn't want to discuss what to wear to the reunion, she wanted to dissect her complicated nonrelationship with Heath even less.

Wendy patted Jade's hand. "Don't worry. We'll get you all dolled up. Won't we, girls?"

Jade groaned inwardly. That's what she was afraid of. How could she tell her mom and sisters that she didn't feel comfortable wearing the outfits they favored? Yes, they looked glamorous, but she felt like a fake. Like a child playing dress up. She thought briefly of wearing the dress from the Ranchers' Reception, but her mom had already given it a thumbs-down. Not because she didn't look good in it but because she'd already worn it to the summer gala, and she'd attempted to wear it for her date with Heath.

So here she was planning out the strategy for today's shopping trip.

"Maybe we should let Jade pick out her own dress," Sabrina suggested.

Wendy frowned. "And miss out on all the fun?"

And that's why she was going along with this, Jade thought. She hated to disappoint her one remaining parent. She'd been a disappointment to Casper. Been there. Done that. Didn't want to do it with her mom too.

"Do you have any idea what you'd like to wear to this reunion?" Wendy asked.

"Clothes," Jade said but immediately regretted the snide comment. Her mother didn't deserve that, but it was situations like this that made her feel so inadequate. Her mother and her sisters all had an innate fashion sense, and she didn't. She was a jeans-and-T-shirt kind of gal. The only thing she wore that could be describe as fashionable were her colorful and sometimes decorated Chuck Taylors. Like the ones she had on now that she'd ordered off Etsy. They were hunter green and embroidered with fanciful mushrooms. But she figured calling her Chucks a fashion statement was stretching the truth a bit.

"Very funny. Don't worry, we'll help you pick out something fabulous. We plan to make a day of it."

Jade wanted to tell her mother that she was thirty-three years old and could pick out her own clothes. But she knew Wendy and her sisters thought they were being helpful. She hated feeling this way, but shopping with the women in her family only served to show how different Jade was from them.

She remembered Casper telling Wendy to "do something with that girl" and her mom sticking up for her, telling her father that there was nothing wrong with their daughter just because she didn't like to wear frilly dresses or, when she did, she managed to get dirty.

Still doing that, Dad, she silently admitted, remembering the evening of her ill-fated first date with Heath.

She wished she'd been able to connect with her dad before his death, set things right between them, but she hadn't and now it was too late. A regret she'd have to live with. She wasn't about to let anything like that happen with her mother.

Plastering on a smile, she managed, "I'm looking forward to shopping and makeovers."

"Heath won't know what hit him," Wendy said with a triumphant gleam.

Jade suppressed a groan. Her mom was talking like this reunion was an actual party, but Jade saw it as an ordeal to survive. Or was there more to this? Was Wendy hoping to get Jade happily settled in a relationship like her two sisters? She didn't want to think about it. Too afraid of being disappointed.

She needed to keep in mind that her relationship with Heath wasn't real, it was based on a lie fabricated to save face in front of high school bullies. Sure, when he was kissing her, it felt real, as real as his lips on hers. But she knew in her heart that this time with Heath was only temporary.

"Should we go to Houston or Dallas?" Wendy asked after the waitress dropped off their breakfasts.

Jade frowned. "Oh, I doubt if we need to go that far."

"Well, our choices in and around Chatelaine are pretty limited," her mom reminded her. "It's not like we're going to find you a dress and shoes at GreatStore."

Jade started to say, *Why not?* but clamped her mouth shut before the words slipped out. Why make this any harder than it already was by being petty?

"And you'll come to the Castle for a spa treatment before the reunion."

"That's where Alexis and Nina had been." The two who'd started this whole thing. But a voice reminded Jade that this was her own fault. She's the one who opened her mouth.

Wendy nodded. "Yes, we sent invitations out."

"And you picked Nina because she's such an important influencer?" Jade asked.

"I'm sure that was the reason, but I didn't do the picking. I hired a publicist to take care of that. Jade, I apologize for that. If I had known how she'd treated you, I wouldn't have invited her."

Jade shrugged. "She's an influencer and can send a lot of business your way. I understand why she was invited. I only wish I hadn't run into her and Alexis. I wouldn't be in all this trouble now."

"Trouble? I would hardly call it that. You've met a wonderful man and are spending time with him. How could that be a bad thing?"

Because I'm spending time with a wonderful man, that's why.

If she wasn't careful, she'd start believing in the lie herself. And that was asking for trouble.

HEATH SPOTTED JADE sitting with her mother and sisters as soon as he walked into the diner. He still wasn't sure if he should be doing this. Maybe she didn't want to be rescued. What gave him the right to interfere?

He might be out of line, but after listening to Jade last night and hearing the apprehension in her voice over this proposed shopping trip, he couldn't just sit back and do nothing. Besides, if she preferred going with her mother and sisters, she could simply say no to his suggestion.

He glanced across the crowded restaurant at Jade before striding toward them. The look on Jade's face had him going forward. Couldn't her mother and sisters see how miserable she was? She might not thank him for what he was about to do, but he had to chance it.

"Ladies, hello," he said as he approached the table. "I'm so glad I ran into you."

Dahlia gave him a speculative glance. "It's good to see you too, Heath."

Did Jade's sister suspect why he was here? "I hate to intrude on this family moment, but could I borrow Jade for a minute?"

Dahlia smiled at him. "Of course. We don't mind at all. Do we, Mom?"

Heath returned Dahlia's smile, but he was also smiling because he had a feeling she knew what he was doing. She obviously approved. At least he had one ally.

Jade got up and followed him to an empty table, but they didn't sit. "What's going on? Is something wrong? Did—"

Heath cut off her questions with a kiss. He knew Wendy and the others could see him with Jade. Hell, everyone in the place saw that. After he pulled away from Jade's delectable mouth, he glanced over and saw Wendy's grin. Okay, maybe he wouldn't be causing a family rift by doing this.

"Nothing's wrong," he reassured her. "I have to make a quick trip to Houston to personally approve some changes to our drone project."

"Oh, so I won't see you tonight?" Her tone held disappointment.

"That's just it. I'm hoping you'll go with me."

"Oh." Her eyes widened and her gaze locked onto his. Moistening her lips, she said, "My mom and sisters want to take me shopping for an outfit for the reunion today."

"The meeting won't take me long and we could go to Nordstrom to shop and then to supper."

"Nordstrom?" she asked with a twinkle in her eyes.

He grinned. "Yeah, I've heard you can't even trust a town that doesn't have one."

She laughed and glanced back to where her mother and sisters sat.

Now that he'd asked her, he found that he hoped she'd say yes. "I still owe you a dinner. Remember? Not that I didn't enjoy Wendy's lasagna."

She shook her head. "That was my fault."

"Charlie's fault."

"But he's my dog, so ultimately my fault."

He raised his eyebrows. "So you'll come?"

"Hmm. That would mean I'd have to bail out on the shopping trip with my mom and sisters." She chewed on her bottom lip and glanced over at their booth. "But okay.

Why not? I can make it up to them by agreeing to the spa day they want to do."

"You're sure? I don't want to cause any trouble." And he meant it. He reached for her hand.

"It's fine. Really," she said and squeezed his hand as they made their way back to the table.

"Heath needs to take a trip to Houston today and wants me to go with him."

"Why does he need you?" Wendy's brow furrowed.

"Maybe he likes her company," Dahlia whispered and threw her mother a look.

Heath silently thanked Dahlia. "I'm sorry to spoil your fun shopping trip today, but I'd really love Jade's company during the drive, and I wanted to show her the new drone prototypes."

"You do?" Wendy asked.

"Why is that so hard to believe?" Dahlia winked at her sister. "Jade is great company."

"Of course she is," Wendy agreed. "I meant why did he want her to see his prototype?"

Sabrina giggled and Wendy poked her. "I was talking about the drones. That *is* what we're talking about, isn't it?"

"Yes, my company is hoping to use them for help farmers eradicate weeds without spraying fields full of pesticides. I've already started giving a series of talks for the students at Jade's day camps. If she sees what I'm talking about it will be more helpful to plan things."

"That makes sense," Sabrina and Dahlia said at the same time.

Wendy nodded. "Yes, I suppose it does." She glanced at her oldest daughter. "Go ahead, honey. We can reschedule our shopping trip."

After they'd left the restaurant, Heath said, "I hope

I haven't gotten you into hot water with your family over this."

"You might be the one in hot water. They'll start thinking you're serious about all this."

"Who says I'm not?"

Jade blushed. "Well… I…"

Heath decided to let her off the hook by changing the subject. Or was he letting *himself* off the hook? "Last night when we talked, I got the impression you were uncomfortable with their shopping plans."

She blew out her breath noisily through her lips. "I always feel so inadequate when it comes to picking out fancy clothes. They mean well but…"

"That's because you're not being true to who you are. Yes, your mother and sisters are stylish, but so are you."

"Yeah, right." She rolled her eyes.

"It's true." He reached for her hand again and squeezed gently. "If you chose things that were true to who you are, you'd feel more comfortable. Trying to imitate someone else never works."

"You sound like you've had experience." She gave him a look.

They reached his car, and he opened the passenger door for her. "Not with clothes but with my company. I found a niche market with smaller farmers and ranchers rather than the big corporate ones. That's when I was the most successful."

"So, you're more dedicated to helping than getting rich?" She settled in the seat and reached for the seat belt.

"I've been lucky that the money followed, and now I can use some of it for research and development to help smaller family farms and ranches. I'm glad my technology helps large industrial farms and ranches, but I don't want it to stop there. I know right now not all the high tech is affordable for the smaller family farms and ranches, but that's why I'm working on improvements. If I can streamline the process, I can help even the smallest family farm. At the moment, I'm setting up cooperatives so they can share the equipment."

"You mean like renting it out on an as-needed basis?" she asked.

"Exactly. I've created a foundation for the initial layout of funds but after that, I'm hoping the rental fees can support it."

He shut the passenger door and went around the hood of the SUV and slid into the passenger seat.

"Why are you looking at me like that?" he asked when she continued to stare at him. He glanced in the rearview mirror. "Do I have something in my teeth?"

"No. I just thought that when you first came to town that you were like Casper."

"You thought I was like your *father*?" He wasn't sure how to feel about this.

"Yes."

"It's good that I'm not?" At least he hoped that's what she meant.

"Very good. He only cared about the money and chasing what he considered success."

Heath started the engine and eased out of the parking spot and onto the main road. He wanted money and success as much as the next person, but it wasn't his main goal.

Having met his sisters he considered family one of the most important aspects of life. Of course he needed to uncover the truth about the circumstances surrounding his birth before starting one of his own.

As Jade listened to Heath, one thing became clear. She wasn't just falling in love…she had a feeling she'd already taken that tumble.

Now that she'd gotten to know Heath Blackwood, she didn't have to be upset with herself for having a crush on someone who might be like her dad. Someone who chased success to the exclusion of everything else and who wouldn't look twice at her because she didn't fit the profile of the sort of woman a rich man wants on his arm. She could just imagine what her father would have said about her running a petting zoo and camps for underprivileged children.

On the drive to Houston, they talked about food, movies and whatever else came to mind in a meandering and comfortable conversation.

Seeing a traveling carnival set up in an open field on the side of the road made Jade sigh. She'd always loved them but rarely had the opportunity to go because Casper had always said Windhams didn't participate in such low-brow activities. Well, she had and did it every chance she got even if it meant sneaking out to attend.

A thought occurred to her, and she sat up straighter.

"What is it?" he asked.

"I'm not a Windham anymore," she blurted.

"I know. You all changed your last name to Fortune, but it's my understanding that happened a while ago."

"It did."

He glanced at her for a second then turned back to concentrate on the road ahead,

She sighed. What the heck? She may as well explain. So what if he thought she was weird? "I saw that Ferris wheel over there."

He looked over to the field and nodded. "Looks like

one of those traveling carnivals. But what does that have to do with being a Fortune or a Windham?"

She explained how her dad had felt about such activities.

He nodded. "So, since you're not a Windham you can attend all the tacky carnivals you want."

"You think they're tacky?" Disappointment lanced through her.

"Sorry. Poor choice of words. I have never been to one, so I shouldn't pass judgment."

"No, you shouldn't," she said with a little huff.

"I honestly didn't mean to offend you." He reached for her hand.

She seized on something he'd said. "You've never been to one? Ever?"

"Never."

"That's…that's terrible. A giant gaping hole in your life."

He laughed. "I never realized I was so deprived."

"Well, you are. We really should rectify that."

"We should, but I wasn't lying about my meeting."

She heaved a sigh. "And I need to find a dress for the reunion."

"But neither one will take all day," he said. He spared another glance at her. "Or will it?"

"I am not a big shopper. Believe me, I don't plan on dragging you from store to store all day. That was my mother's plan, not mine. Besides, I can always take a rain check with her and my sisters for a day of shopping."

"You make it sound like a fate worse than death."

She stared down at her hands in her lap. "They mean well."

"I'm sure the Ferris wheel will still be there on the way back."

Her eyes lit up. "You mean it? We can stop?"

"I don't see why not," he said.

Today was turning out a lot better than Jade had thought when she got up in morning. But she was finding that any day that included time spent with Heath was a good day.

Their relationship might not last beyond the reunion, but she decided that she was going to jump into every moment as if it were the last—since it very well might be—and enjoy herself.

HEATH WAS GLAD he had given into temptation and invited Jade to accompany him to his meeting with the research and development folks in Houston. She had offered to wait somewhere else while he conducted business, but he wanted to show her his latest prototype. *Show off is more like it*, a voice taunted, but he brushed it aside. So what if it was true?

After showing her the prototype drones, they indeed went to Nordstrom, where she found an understated blue dress that went perfect with the sapphire ring he'd given her. True to her word, she didn't take long to pick out an outfit, including shoes. He bought a new shirt to go with one of his business suits.

"Where would you like to stop for supper?" he asked as he stowed their purchases in the G Wagon. "I didn't make a reservation because I wasn't sure what time we'd be done or where in the city we might end up."

"Well..." She dragged out the word as she chewed on her lower lip. "I'll bet that carnival has corn dogs and funnel cakes."

"You're joking, right? You actually mean you'd prefer deep-fried dogs and pastry to a nice dinner with candle-light at some fancy restaurant?" He honestly didn't mind either way, but he enjoyed teasing her. Lately, when he thought about Jade, he was thinking of more long term than the reunion. He couldn't be sure if she felt the same way, but if he was reading some of the signals right, and lord knew he might be all wrong, this wasn't one-sided.

"What's wrong with corn dogs and funnel cakes? Or cotton candy and candy apples? Ooh, I bet they have those too."

Her enthusiastic comments brought his thoughts out of his head, and he started the engine. "Who knew you were such a junk food junkie?"

"It's not *junk food*, and I'm a connoisseur of carnival food."

He raised an eyebrow and spared her a quick glance as he pulled out of the shopping center's parking lot. "A connoisseur?"

"And don't you forget it." She laughed.

"Duly noted," he assured her.

"So, you really don't mind stopping at the carnival?"

He heard the wistful note in her voice and said, "I don't mind, and since I'll be with a connoisseur, I'm sure she'll steer me to the right booths for amazing food."

"That's the spirit," she said, giggling like a schoolgirl.

As they had done on the way to the city that morning, they chatted easily as he drove through late afternoon traffic and left the city behind.

"It's actually a county fair," he remarked as he pulled into the grassy field doubling as a parking lot.

Without even waiting for him to come around to her side, she hopped out of the Mercedes once he'd parked. "I can't tell you how much I appreciate this," she said as they crossed the field toward the entrance booth.

He took her hand in his and only dropped it to get out his wallet so he could buy entry tickets and tickets for food, rides and games on the midway.

Sticking the tickets in his pocket, he reached for her

hand again. They passed several large canvas tents on their way to the Ferris wheel, which Jade had insisted on riding first.

"It's my favorite," she told him.

"What's the matter?" she asked when he dragged his feet. "You're not afraid of heights, are you?"

"Me? Afraid? No way. It's just that these rides are put up and taken down so many times, there's no telling what sort of wear and tear they're subjected to."

"But that's just it. These people know what they're doing. They're professionals."

He raised an eyebrow and gave her a skeptical look.

She grinned at him. "Look, if you want to stay down here, you can. I won't think any less of you."

"If you go, I go," he said with as much of a glower as he could muster. Despite any misgivings over the integrity of the rides, he was having fun, and he had Jade's enthusiasm to thank for that.

They boarded the Ferris wheel. He wasn't afraid of heights as such; he just liked having his two feet on the ground better. But he meant it; he was going where Jade was.

When their car got to the top, it stopped.

Of course it stopped, he thought ruefully.

"You're supposed to kiss me," Jade told him. "That's the rule if you get stopped at the top."

"It is?"

She gave a firm nod of her head. "Well, if it isn't, it should be."

So he obliged and kissed her. His lips on hers made him forget he was sitting on a rickety Ferris wheel high in the sky. All that mattered to him was her soft, sweet lips pressed against his.

She gasped and pulled away when the Ferris wheel

started to move with a jerk and a rocking motion. Then she laughed with glee and he found himself laughing too.

Apparently, he found a cure for his dislike of heights, and she was sitting right beside him.

After the ride they wandered among the crowd of fair-goers. The smell of grilling meat and deep-fried food permeated the air around them. Not exactly the candlelight and wine he'd envisioned for tonight with Jade, but one look at the excitement and contentment on her face told him this was the right choice. And he had to admit that he was enjoying the evening too. The music from the rides and the buzz of excitement from the fairgoers filled the air and provided a frenetic backdrop to their evening. Jade seemed to thrive on it.

Instead of corn dogs, they stopped at food cart that sold Greek gyro sandwiches. They found a spot at a picnic table and ate their supper. After they'd finished their sandwiches and tossed the trash into a bin, she pointed to a cart advertising funnel cakes, her eyes aglow with enthusiasm. "Look. Dessert."

They enjoyed the funnel cakes while standing to the side of the cart.

"So, what else haven't you had a chance to do at a carnival?" he asked as she munched on her funnel cake.

"You haven't won me a stuffed animal yet."

He groaned. "You do know those games are rigged. And not in the player's favor."

She grinned and hooked her arm through his. "I have every bit of faith in you."

"Wait." Heath reached out and stopped her before she began walking again.

"What?"

He reached over and brushed her cheek with his fingertips. "You had some powdered sugar on you."

"That's the only trouble with funnel cakes."

He wouldn't exactly call it trouble since it gave him an excuse to touch her.

They enjoyed the next several hours at the carnival. Heath managed to win her a small stuffed animal. To his embarrassment, it was one of the tiniest prizes offered. But Jade didn't seem to care. She acted as if it were the most coveted treasure.

"I'll do better next time," he promised.

"I'm perfectly content with this one," she assured him.

And he was perfectly content with the way they'd spent their evening.

CHAPTER TEN

JADE CHECKED HERSELF in the full-length mirror in the master bath. She had to admit that the woman staring back at her looked fabulous, if she did say so herself. Thanks to her mom, she'd spent a greater part of the day at the spa at Fortune's Castle. Evidently she'd received some of the same treatment that Alexis and Nina had enjoyed.

Jade picked up the blue satin clutch purse she'd purchased on the trip to Houston and glanced at herself one last time. Yes, she looked good, but it wasn't her staring back from the mirror. It was a fairy-tale version of Jade Fortune.

But life wasn't like a fairy tale.

"Except for tonight," she told her reflection.

Tonight was *her* fairy tale, and she was going to enjoy it and not worry about tomorrow.

Right on time, a knock sounded at the door, and she went to answer it.

She opened it and stood speechless. Dressed in an impeccably tailored dark blue suit with a pristine white shirt open at the neck, Heath took her breath away.

He frowned and touched the open neck of his shirt. "Should I have worn a tie?"

"What?" She continued to stare for a second longer. Shaking her head, she whispered, "No. You're fine."

"Good." He stepped inside and his gaze swept the room. "No Charlie tonight?"

"He's with my mom. I wasn't sure what time we'd be back," Jade said and shut the door. "Besides, this way there's less chance of any sort of wardrobe malfunctions."

He laughed. "I suppose that's true, but I kinda miss the guy."

"So do I, but believe me, he's getting spoiled by my mom."

Heath stood staring at her, the silence stretching until she finally cleared her throat. "Something wrong?"

She'd been convinced she looked great, but maybe Heath didn't agree. But he'd already seen the dress, so it couldn't be that. She glanced down at herself in case she'd managed to—

"Hey, hey," he said and used his hand to lift her chin and stare into her eyes. "Nothing's wrong."

She swallowed. "Then why are you staring at me?"

"Because you are beautiful." A slow smile spread across his handsome face. "Perfection."

She laughed but was secretly thrilled. "Well, it's obvious that you need those glasses for more than reading. But you do make me feel beautiful. And more than that, you make me feel special."

"That's because you *are* special."

Her chin still captured by his hand, he leaned over and brought his lips in a sweet, reverent kiss.

The tenderness in his touch made her breath catch in her throat.

Lifting his head, he said, "We'd better get going or we'll be late."

HEATH PULLED THE SUV into the parking lot at the country club where the reunion was being held. The large white building was lit up both inside and out. Three steps led to a small landing where double doors were thrown open, inviting people inside.

He stopped at the valet parking stand. "Pretty swanky for a high school reunion."

"Well, it was a swanky high school," she said.

"It didn't change the high school experience though, did it?" he asked. He'd always thought that his circumstances, having a single mother who struggled to provide for her son and being a bit of a social misfit, had been the cause of his experiences. But Jade had helped him to see that wasn't the only reason. Jade had been part of a prominent family, and as beautiful as she was now, he had to believe she'd been attractive in high school. Since meeting Jade, he had to admit she'd changed a lot of his ways of thinking about things.

"Not at all," she was saying.

The valet opened her door, and she stepped out of the SUV. Heath got out and handed the keys to the attendant. Going around the front of the vehicle, Heath met up with Jade and took her arm. "Ready?"

"Again, I want to thank you for this."

He shook his head. "No thanks necessary. This is my pleasure."

And he meant it. Attending a high school reunion might not be at the top of his list of things he wanted to do on a Saturday night, but being with Jade made him happy. It didn't matter where he was, as long as he was with her. The fact he was helping her in front of those snotty former classmates was a plus. The things they'd said to Jade that day still rankled him.

"Did I tell you how gorgeous you look tonight?" he asked as they climbed the steps to the entrance.

"Only about a dozen times."

"Then let's make it a baker's dozen."

Once inside, Jade checked them in at the table set up and manned by a former classmate that she only vaguely remembered.

But it appeared the woman remembered her. "Good to see you, Jade. I was wondering what you'd gotten up to since graduation. Nina and Alexis say you're running some sort of animal thing in Chatelaine?"

"It's a petting zoo," Jade told her as she pulled the backing off her name tag to expose the sticky side.

"She's way too modest," Heath said. He suspected this person wasn't going to treat Jade any better than those other two. He put an arm around Jade's waist. "She also runs day camps and workshops for kids to teach them about how technology is the future for ranching and farming, both important industries for this state."

The woman eyed him closely. "And you must be Mr. Fortune?"

Heath smiled at the woman. "No, it's Blackwood. Heath Blackwood."

He couldn't help grinning, thinking about the Bond movies. Maybe he should have tried out a Sean Connery accent. And totally embarrassed himself.

The woman's mouth dropped open. "You're the Heath Blackwood of Blackwood AgriTech?"

"That's him all right," Jade said proudly.

"Well, we're honored to have you here, Mr. Blackwood."

"And I'm honored to be here…with Jade," he said before they moved on.

They'd barely entered the packed ballroom when Nina and Alexis spotted them.

"Jade Windham… I mean Fortune. You came and you even brought your, uh, fiancé with you," Alexis said when she saw Jade and Heath.

"I hate to let her out of my sight," Heath murmured, putting his arm around Jade.

"I can see why. If she were with me, I'd want everyone to know she was off the market." A short, stocky man wearing wire-rimmed glasses and a bow tie glided up. He grinned. "Is that you Jade Windham? Remember me? Roger Stackhouse. I was president of the Computer Science Club."

Nina and Alexis snorted, but Roger ignored them. He obviously knew them well.

Jade smiled and shook Roger's hand. "Actually, it's Jade Fortune now."

Roger chuckled. "As if being a Windham wasn't enough. Now, you're a Fortune. How did that come about?"

"It's on my mother's side. She found out she was the long-lost granddaughter of Wendell Fortune. My mother changed her name to honor the connection, and we followed suit."

"All of you?" Roger asked.

"All six of us, but with my sisters getting engaged and marrying, they didn't really keep the Fortune names for very long. But my brothers will presumably have it for the rest of their lives."

Roger nodded, then a look of surprised recognition came over his face. "And you're Heath Blackwood of Blackwood AgriTech!"

Heath nodded.

"Well, it's certainly a pleasure to meet you." Roger beamed.

JADE STOOD NEXT to Heath and listened to him and Roger talking about computer technology. She noticed Nina and Alexis roll their eyes and wander off like predators deprived of prey.

"It's been great chatting with you, Roger, but I promised Jade we'd dance," Heath said.

"Oh yeah. Sure, sure. It was good seeing you again, Jade."

The band was playing a slow one and Heath took her in his arms. In his strong embrace, Jade forgot everything else. Even seeing Alexis and Nina again meant nothing.

"I'm sorry for that woman calling you Mr. Fortune. Talk about awkward," she said as Heath glided her around the dance floor.

"It's okay. I actually don't mind not being recognized. It can get old fast."

She gazed up at him and nodded. "I'll bet."

"It's true. You never know if someone wants to talk to you because they think you're interesting or they're just interested in what you can do for them."

Now she regretted her remark. "I guess I hadn't thought about it that way."

"First being a Windham then a Fortune, you must have run into that," he mused.

"Not really. I guess people didn't expect to run into Casper Windham's daughter waiting tables or selling lingerie at Nordstrom. When they'd ask if I was any relation, I usually said no." She didn't want it getting back to Casper, but more importantly, she didn't want to explain why she wasn't successful like her siblings.

"Earning an honest living is nothing to be ashamed of," Heath told her.

"No, but if Casper found out that someone saw his daughter waitressing, he would have gone ballistic. Said I was ruining the family name."

"Well, I never had a family name to ruin," he said.

"I think Blackwood is a very fine name and one you

should take pride in. You're a self-made man and have a lot to be proud of."

A jolt of awareness shot through her when her gaze met his. Judging from the slight darkening of his eyes, he felt it too.

"Thanks."

They danced before and after the lavish meal.

"I have to confess I didn't think I was going to enjoy this, but I am," Jade said as the evening was winding down and people started leaving. Having people envious of her was a whole new experience.

Deep down, she'd been dreading the reunion, but now she was sorry to see it end. Being with Heath and dancing with him was like a dream come true. She felt like a true Cinderella, but like the fairy tale, it was time to leave the ball.

"So I was thinking," Heath began as they waited for the valet to bring the car around, "would you be interested in staying in Cactus Grove tonight?" He held up his hands, palms out. "No pressure. If you don't want to, that's fine."

"You mean instead of returning to Chatelaine?"

"Yeah, we could stay in town or go somewhere else where there's more choice of hotels. You did say your mom is watching Charlie."

"That's true. I wasn't sure how late we'd get back, so I said I'd pick him up in the morning. She wouldn't even have to know we didn't return to Chatelaine after the reunion."

He frowned. "You don't want her to know you spent the night with me?"

"Oh, no, it's not that. I was just saving you her efforts at matchmaking. Since my two sisters are in relationships, she's trying to get me into one too."

"I think I can handle the pressure."

Did this mean he was as interested in her as she was with him? Sounded like maybe he was wanting to take this to the next level. Question was, did *she*? "I didn't bring a change of clothes or any toiletries with me."

He shrugged, his face blank. "The hotel will supply any toiletries you might need. We can shop for clothes for you tomorrow."

Somewhere inside, a voice whispered words of caution. She hadn't known Heath for very long. Should she be doing this?

Any other time or with any other man, she might have heeded the warning voice, but when she was with Heath, nothing mattered except the two of them.

"I'd love to stay here tonight."

They found a hotel within the town limits. As Heath checked them in, he glanced at her, a question in his blue eyes. She smiled and nodded to indicate that she was still on board with spending the night together.

After getting the room keys, he took her hand and led her to the elevator. Once inside, the air seemed to crackle between them.

This was really happening, she thought as they exited the elevator and walked down the corridor. When he inserted the key, they all but tumbled into the room.

He used his foot to shut the door behind them and pulled her into his arms. Their mouths crashed together as he led them over to the king-sized bed.

They toppled onto the bed without losing contact.

All urgency gone, he kissed her slowly, thoroughly, leaving her trembling beneath him. His mouth touched and tasted, overwhelming her until she melted. Jade didn't want the kiss to ever end. She wanted to drown in it. She wanted to lose herself completely.

He kissed, stroked and explored her body making her

feel not just feminine but desired and special. When he had worked her into another frenzy, he ripped open the foil packet. Nudging her entrance, he moved slowly as her body adjusted to him. Another gesture that made her feel treasured. He set a rhythm that had her climbing toward another release. Was that even possible? He put his hand between their bodies and found that sensitive bud. Not just possible...*inevitable*.

"Yes, please." She writhed and twisted on the mattress; the sheets clutched in her fists.

One last powerful thrust, and they simultaneously fell over the edge.

They lay entwined as their breathing slowed, his fingers making lazy trails across her bare skin.

"You're very talented," she whispered.

His gaze riveted on hers, he brought his hand to her face and used his fingertips to trace the sprinkling of freckles across the bridge of her nose and the top of her cheeks. The warmth from his fingers lingered on her skin, raising the hair on the back of her neck.

His mouth captured hers again and she was lost in the tantalizing sensation that was Heath.

JADE AWOKE TO an empty bed the next morning. She glanced around the room, but Heath wasn't there, and the door to the bathroom was open, so he wasn't inside there either.

Maybe he was out getting coffee or breakfast, she thought as she scrambled around on the floor to pick up her discarded clothing.

As much as she loved last night's dress, she wrinkled her nose at having to put it back on this morning.

Before she made it to the bathroom, the hotel door opened, and Heath walked in with several shopping bags.

"You're awake," he said as he came to her and gave her

a kiss. "You were sleeping so soundly, I hated to wake you before I left. I was hoping I'd get back before you woke up."

"I've only been awake for a few minutes."

"Perfect timing." He handed her a bag.

"What's this?" She peeked inside.

"For today. As much as I love that dress, I figured you would prefer being more comfortable for the return home."

She pulled out a pair of jeans, a comfy looking sweatshirt and some underwear. There was even a pair of Converse high-tops in the bag.

"I can't guarantee everything will fit, but I checked your sizes from what you'd been wearing last night."

She threw her arms around him and hugged him. "That's so thoughtful of you."

After showering together, they dressed and went downstairs for a leisurely breakfast before getting back on the road to Chatelaine.

CHAPTER ELEVEN

SEVERAL DAYS AFTER their weekend together in Cactus Grove, Heath asked Jade to accompany him to visit Billy, the boy he'd spoken to during his workshop.

"Is something wrong?" she asked.

"No. I have something for him."

"Okay, he should be home from school by now."

He saw her inquisitive gaze, but he didn't tell her what he'd done. As it was, he was crossing his fingers that the boy would like his gift. He'd never done anything like this before.

Heath parked the G Wagon in front of a small crafts-man-style home in a solid working-class neighborhood of Chatelaine.

They went to the door, and it opened before they could knock. The boy must have seen them through the window. Jade had called ahead and spoke with Billy's mother to be sure they were home.

"You came to see me!" Billy greeted them.

"We sure did." Heath greeted Billy's mother and handed the gift bag to the boy.

Billy pulled a book out of the bag. "What's this?"

"I believe people call it a memory book. Your mom and some people in town gave me pictures and told stories about your dad."

Billy's eyes widened and he clutched the book to his chest. "You mean this book is all about my dad?"

"It sure is. There's even some stuff in there about when he was your age."

"Really?"

"Yes, really."

"And I can keep it? For my very own?" the boy whispered.

"Absolutely," Heath assured him.

"I can't thank you enough for this," his mother told Heath. "Please sit down. Can I get you some coffee? I made a pot."

Billy sat and looked at his book, carefully turning the pages.

They stayed for coffee and some homemade cookies.

Once they were back outside and heading to the Mercedes, Jade turned to him.

"That was so thoughtful of you," Jade told him, her eyes welling with tears.

He shrugged but was grateful for her words. "I only thought of it. Others did the work of gathering the information and putting it all together for the book. They deserve the credit."

"They wouldn't have done it if you hadn't come up with the idea and asked them to do it."

"The kid was worried about preserving memories of his dad. I didn't want him messing up his life because he was worried over something I could easily help fix." He swallowed hard. "Not that I or anybody else could help fix the fact he'd lost his dad. If I could ease his pain some, it's worth it."

"Because you know what it's like not to remember your dad," she murmured.

"I'm familiar with some of what he might be going through not having a father."

Jade stood on her toes and kissed his cheek. "You're a special man, Heath Blackwood."

"What good is all this success if I can't help ease a young boy's concerns?"

"And that's why I love you," she said.

At Jade's words, Heath's hands gripped the steering wheel tighter. He mumbled something, but he couldn't bring himself to say the words back at her.

Back at Jade's log home, he went inside and kissed her as soon as they were inside. After greeting Charlie, Heath carried Jade to the bedroom.

He needed this, needed to be close to her one more time. This was coming to an end. It had to, because he was no closer to finding out the truth surrounding his birth.

But he couldn't let her go. Not yet.

JADE TOLD HERSELF this was his way of saying he loved her. He might have trouble with the words, but he'd shown her with his actions. He loved her as thoroughly as he had the night of the reunion. Once again, she told him she loved him.

Afterward, she snuggled up to him, but something was off. His body might be right next to her in the bed, but she suspected his mind was elsewhere, closed off.

She wanted to take the coward's way out and ignore that Heath had no response to her declaration. She probably shouldn't have said the words so soon, but she couldn't hold it in any longer.

If she didn't ask him about it, he might not tell her, and she could bury her head in the sand, pretend she hadn't said anything. Or claim that it was just one of those things people said and that she didn't mean it in the literal sense. That might buy her some time before he told her they were through and the fairy tale she'd been living would be over.

But she couldn't do that, because she *had* meant it. She was worth more than silence. The ironic part of the whole situation was that being with Heath is what taught her she was worth more than accepting a less than ideal situation.

In hindsight, she knew that if the situation at the Daily Grind with Nina and Alexis had happened today, Jade would probably have handled the whole thing differently. Instead of feeling like she'd been put on the spot, she hoped she would be able to put those two in their place without resorting to lying or pretending she was something she wasn't.

She was proud of the classes and day camps she offered. As Heath pointed out, she was helping shape future ranchers and farmers, and maybe one of her students would end up helping to revolutionize agricultural tech like Heath was doing.

Might as well get this over with, she thought. "So are you going to tell me what's wrong?"

"What's makes you think something's wrong?" He pulled away.

"Because of what just happened."

"What just happened was that we made love. So, why would you think something's off?" he asked, but he had guilt stamped all over his features.

"We didn't make love. We had sex. You went through the motions."

A muscle ticked in his jaw. "Are you complaining?"

"What? No. It's always great with you."

"Then what is it?"

"It's just…it felt as though you were pulling back emotionally."

He opened his mouth, and she held up her hand to stop him. "Let me finish before I lose my nerve. It was as if you were putting walls up, protecting yourself."

"Do you want the truth?" he asked, a muscle ticked in his jaw.

No! I want to stay in this sensual bubble a little longer. "Always…even if it hurts."

His expression darkened. "I'm trying to protect you, Jade."

"Protect me from what?" she asked, fear and anger knotting inside her.

"From me."

Frustration clawed at the back of her throat. "Why would I need protecting from you?"

"Because I know you want a home and family." He ran a hand through his hair.

"And?"

"And… I can't give that to you." He blew out a ragged breath.

"And you know this how, why?" Ice slowly spread through her stomach.

"Because I can't get involved with anyone until I find out the truth about who I am."

"What are you saying?" she asked, searching for a plausible explanation. "You're Heath Blackwood. Entrepreneur, a man who loved his mother, a man who cares about farmers and ranchers. A man who wants to help even the small family farmers with his advances in technology."

He shook his head, and she reached out and touched him, squeezed his arm. "It doesn't matter who or what you came from. All that matters is who you are now."

"That's easy for you to say. You know who your father is and the circumstances of your birth."

"I do, but that doesn't—"

"Yes, it does!" He jerked away from her touch. "You wouldn't understand."

Jade flinched at the anger in his voice, but she refused

to back down. If this was going to end, she would know she at least tried. She'd know she fought for what they had, what they'd meant to one another. She couldn't give up without a fight. Heath meant too much to her.

"Try me," she said, her voice full of challenge.

"I don't know why my father never acknowledged me. My mother would never tell me, and she got upset every time I tried to push for answers so I eventually gave up."

"And that's okay. Maybe you aren't meant to know."

"I have to know, damn it. Why are you so accepting of this unknown?"

"Because I love you, damn it!" As far as declarations of love went, this had to be the worst one so far. What was wrong with her?

His jaw hardened and he glared down at her. "No. You can't. I won't let you."

"You won't *let* me? If that don't beat all, I swear."

"This whole relationship wasn't supposed to be real."

"Yeah, well, I broke the ground rules," she admitted thickly. "It's not like I planned it or anything."

"Thank goodness for small favors."

"That's cruel and beneath you, Heath."

Regret washed over his features and his tone softened. "You're right. I'm sorry. And I'm sorry that you were expecting something more from me. I was quite clear from the beginning that I wasn't looking for long term."

"That's true so there's no need to apologize. That's all on me. My brain heard what you said, but my heart refused to listen."

"You should have listened," he told her wearily.

"Duh. I know that now. Maybe you need to leave." *Because I want to sob and cry.* But she didn't say that out loud, but she did say, "And please take this with you."

She removed the ring and held it out to him.

He shook his head. "I don't—"

"Please."

Reluctantly, he held out his hand and she dropped the ring into it.

She got out of bed and padded barefoot into the adjoining bathroom and shut the door. She threw the lock with a quiet click.

Heath was gone when she finally emerged.

JADE PULLED INTO her driveway and parked. It had been three days since her breakup with Heath. Three days of yawning emptiness, of longing. She squeezed her eyes shut as she struggled to quell the dragging sense of loss threatening to engulf her.

In the beginning she'd tried to protect herself but her feelings for Heath had eventually made that impossible. She was sure he'd developed feelings for her too and that was the sharpest knife of all.

Sighing, she exited her pickup. Life went on, right? She'd stopped at the mailbox station at the end of the road leading to all the properties on the ranch. The envelope looked like a card or invitation.

She opened the envelope and pulled out an invitation. To a wedding. *A mystery wedding.* The whole town had been buzzing about it. It was an invitation, along with a note requesting she bring a photo of herself as a wedding gift. Why would the happy couple wanted a picture of her? That was strange. She didn't even know who was getting married.

The note also requested that the picture be as close a representation of herself as possible. It might be a bizarre request, but it was certainly easy enough to do.

She got out of the truck and went to her front door. Inserting the key into the lock, she heard dog toenails on the hardwood by the door. Charlie was waiting for her. He would probably be angry with her for not bringing him into town with her.

She opened the door, and the dog greeted her. She gave him a hug and an apology for leaving him behind.

After feeding Charlie, Jade brought the box of photos she kept in the bedroom closet into the living room and set it on the coffee table. She slipped her sneakers off and sat on the couch, drawing her feet up under her. Taking a fortifying sip of wine, she pulled the lid off the box.

It was stuffed with photos. Most were old. People these days keep their photo collections on their phones or their computers. But the invitation stipulated one physical copy that Jade felt most represented herself. Huh. Very odd.

She had picked out one of the photos taken of her when she first moved to the ranch and took over the running of the petting zoo. Sitting back on the couch with Charlie napping beside her, she glanced over at the fireplace.

On the mantel was a picture taken of her the night of the reunion along with one of both her and Heath. She rose and went to the mantel. Her smile was a mile wide in the photo. It was easy to see how happy and excited she was. And why not? She'd been with Heath.

Despite how everything had turned out, she knew that was the picture she needed to use as the gift for the mystery wedding. Things may not have worked out in the end, but that night had been magical. Remembering was bittersweet and she knew that someday those memories would be more sweet than bitter.

Her decision made, she called for Charlie and made her way to her bedroom. Maybe tomorrow would be better. Maybe she'd be closer to those memories bringing a smile along with the tears.

CHAPTER TWELVE

HEATH PULLED HIS G Wagon into a spot near the coffee shop. What had gotten into him? Going to see Beau Weatherly wasn't in his nature. As a matter of fact, he'd secretly made fun of the people who did. But after a sleepless night, he was desperate enough to try anything.

Bypassing the takeout window and the seats on the porch that he preferred, Heath went inside and glanced at his watch, Sure enough, Beau was seated at his usual table with his sign that offered Free Life Advice.

He might feel a bit embarrassed by doing this, but he figured the old guy might be the closest he was ever going to get to fatherly advice. He was in luck because no one was waiting to see Beau at the moment.

Heath sat down across from the man.

"Heath," Beau nodded. "Good morning, son."

Heath recalled his earlier thoughts about Beau being a father figure and hoped the warmth in his cheeks hadn't manifested in any sort of blush. Talk about embarrassing.

"So, what can I do for you?" the older man asked.

Heath sighed as if admitting defeat. "I need some advice."

Beau smiled. "That's what I'm here for."

"Yeah, I…" Heath rubbed his jaw. "I'm not sure how much you know about my situation."

"Well, I don't like to pry into your personal affairs, but this *is* Chatelaine, so I probably know as much as you."

Heath chuckled, the act releasing some of the tension that had been building within him. "Small towns. Anyway, I'm debating if I should try visiting Doris Edwards again. I don't know if I should even continue to pursue the truth. I found my sisters and have a…relationship with them."

The word "relationship" wanted to stick in his throat. It reminded him of Jade and what he'd lost. No, not lost. He'd thrown it away. She'd told him she loved him, and he totally disregarded her confession. She'd given him her heart, and he'd handed it back as if it hadn't been the most precious thing in the world.

"Heath? Son, did you have a specific question? I'd like to help, if I can."

Beau's concern touched him. Heath nodded. "I'm wondering if pursuing this thing to find out why my biological father abandoned my mother and myself is the right thing to do. It's been frustrating, to say the least."

It may have cost him the love of his life, but he wasn't about to admit that to Beau. This confessing and seeking advice from the old guy—no matter how wise—had its limits. And Heath had his pride. Thinking back on how happy he'd been when he was with Jade only mocked him now that he'd lost her through his own foolishness.

"Has anything good come of your quest?"

"I found my sisters," Heath replied.

"And that's a good thing?"

"Absolutely. With my mother gone, they're all the family I have left, and I feel blessed to have connected with them."

Steepling his hands, Beau said after a beat, "So, your pursuit of the truth has paid off so far?"

"Yes, sir. I would say it has, but I don't know if continuing to pursue it is the right thing to do."

"Would you be satisfied to know that you stopped trying to uncover the truth?" the man asked. "When you get older and realize the people who are alive today and may have had the answers are gone, will you regret not having pursued it?"

Heath rubbed the back of his neck. The fact he was even asking Beau about this felt like it should be a clue. Trying to deal with Doris Edwards was frustrating, but at least she was here and alive, so he could deal with her. "But what if I learn something I would have preferred not knowing?"

"And what if you learn something you'll be grateful knowing?"

"You've got me there," Heath admitted gruffly.

"Learning the truth won't change who you are or change any of your accomplishments. You'll still be you."

And I'll still have messed things up with Jade.

"You'll be able to go to the woman you love with a clear mind no matter what the outcome is. As I said, son, knowing the truth won't change who you are deep in here," Beau said and tapped his chest.

...go to the woman you love...

Beau's words echoed in Heath's head as he left. Beau was right about that. Was he also right about finding out the truth?

HEATH, ACCOMPANIED BY his sister Lily, rounded the corner of Doris Edwards's daughter's modest ranch house. After speaking with Beau, he called his sisters and told them of his plan to see Doris one more time before giving up. Once again, Lily had insisted on coming with him. At first, he wasn't sure if that was such a good idea, but as she'd pointed out, this concerned the triplets too. Plus, on a practical level, she said that having a woman present might help put Doris at ease.

They'd been told the old woman lived in the rear of her daughter's place.

"Ooh, look, it's a tiny house," Lily said.

"It sure is tiny," Heath agreed as they approached what looked to him like a child's fancy playhouse.

"No, no. It's a real honest-to-goodness tiny home." She shook her head when he gave her a puzzled look. "Like all those shows."

"What shows?"

"Oh, I can't remember them all, but they're on the home improvement networks on cable. Shows like *Tiny House Nation* or *Tiny House, Big Living.*"

"Okaaay," he said, dragging the word out.

Lily gave him a playful poke on the shoulder. "It's a thing."

"If you say so," he said and found himself wondering if Jade watched any of those shows. *No, stop thinking about her, or you won't be able to make it through this interview with Doris.* "I prefer a good football game."

"Of course you do." Lily made a noise with her tongue, then she laughed.

Moments later, he knocked on the door of what he now knew was a tiny house.

"You don't have to do this, you know. Whatever happened is in the past," his sister murmured. "We've all found one another now, and that's what's important."

"I want to try at least one more time." At least seeking the truth surrounding his birth gave him something to concentrate on. He didn't want to tell her how miserable he was now that he and Jade had ended things.

No, that wasn't right. Jade hadn't ended anything; he had done all the ending. She had taken a chance and confessed her feelings. He'd been on the edge of that precipice too, but instead of stepping into the scary unknown, he'd faltered. He'd refused to take a chance on love. On happiness. If he had been braver, he'd be with Jade right now. His lack of courage was costing them both.

Just thinking about what he'd given up was like an ice-cold fist twisting his gut. The thought of not seeing Jade again, touching her, kissing her or simply talking with her sent shards of agony shooting through him.

"It's for the best," he muttered under his breath and knocked again on the door. Louder this time.

"What's for the best?" Lily asked, her gaze on Heath.

"What?" He glanced at his sister, realizing he'd almost forgotten she was with him. Most things flew out of his head when he let himself think about Jade. That's why he needed to stop dwelling on her. Put her, and all thoughts of her, in the past where they belonged.

The look Lily gave him said she knew his mind was elsewhere. "You said it's for the best and I—"

Her next words were cut off when the door swung open to reveal Doris Edwards. The woman wore a purple velour tracksuit and slippers.

"Yes?" Doris peered at them.

"Miss Doris? It's Heath Blackwood. I was hoping to have a few minutes to speak with you?"

At first the elderly woman looked confused, and he feared this was just another wild-goose chase. But he had to at least give it a shot. Beau Weatherly was right. He needed to do all he could to find answers. His personality wouldn't let him just leave it without at least trying everything he could to get to the truth.

"Blackwood?" The woman's brow wrinkled as she squinted at him. She stared for a few more moments and her brow cleared. "Of course. Why, you must be Anne's boy."

"Yes, ma'am. That's me." He gave her what he hoped was a reassuring smile.

"My word but you've grown into a fine young man. Let's have a look at you." Doris pushed her glasses higher up her nose. "Anne must be so proud."

"Well, I—"

"And who's this with you? Your missus?"

"No, this is my sister Lily."

"That's right. There were triplet girls." Doris looked at Lily, then checked the space behind them. "There must be two more just like you."

"There are three of us, but only me here tonight. And we're fraternal triplets, so not exact replicas, but we do resemble one another." Lily gave the older woman an encouraging smile.

"Well, come in, come in." Doris opened the door wider and stepped aside. "Have a seat. You're in luck, my friend from GreatStore came to visit today and brought me some cider and donuts. She remembered how much I love apple cider and cinnamon donuts in the fall. It's so wonderful that I have something to offer you."

Heath sat on the couch with Lily. He started to decline the offer of refreshments, but before he could, Lily elbowed him in the side. He shot his sister a quizzical look and mouthed, "What?"

"That would be lovely, thank you so much," Lily said as Doris scurried over to the other side of the room, where a small kitchenette was located.

"She was very excited to be able to offer us refreshments," Lily told him quietly. "She might be more willing to talk if we accept her hospitality."

"Good point," he said. Maybe having his sister along was a smart move.

As it turned out, it was. Maybe the smartest move of his life. After Doris had served them the cider and donuts, she told Heath that his mother had buried her secret.

"Her *secret*?" he asked.

Doris nodded. "She told me she buried it next to that gnarled oak tree behind the swings. She said she considered the swings her special spot with James."

HEATH DROPPED LILY off and spoke with his other sisters. He explained he was going to see if he could dig up what Anne had buried so long ago. They offered to accompany him, but he told them he was going to ask Jade. He expected some flak for his decision, but they exchanged glances and nodded, wishing him luck with both the Jade and the dig.

He pulled out his phone on the way to his G Wagon after leaving his sisters, opening the screen to Recent Calls. He touched his thumb to the screen and called Jade. She might hang up on him or not answer when his name appeared, but he had to at least try. Doing this didn't feel right without her. *Nothing* felt right without her.

She picked up on the third ring. At least he'd gotten over that hurdle.

"Jade? I know you're angry and you have every right to feel that way, but please hear me out. You can decide what to do after that. I won't pressure you if you want nothing more to do with me."

"What do you want?" she asked after a long moment of silence.

"I'm on my way to the park."

"The park?" She sounded confused.

"I went to see Doris Edwards and—"

"Oh, Heath."

"I know. I know. But please just listen to what I found out."

"All right. I'm listening."

He jumped into the driver's seat and started the SUV.

"She said my mother buried a letter in the park before she left town."

"Say what?"

"She asked Doris to tell James about the letter once his own children were grown. Or if Anne's son ever came looking for information," he explained.

"And you believed her? Heath, you know this could be nothing but a snipe hunt, right?"

"Yeah, I know that, but I at least have to try. If it turns out it's nothing but the nonsensical ramblings of a woman with the beginnings of dementia, I'll drop the whole thing. I promise."

"You could be in for a big disappointment," she warned.

"I know but I have to check it out. And I want you there with me when I do it."

"Why me?"

"Because I can't imagine my life without you." Honesty was the best policy.

She was silent for so long, he was afraid she'd hung up. "Jade?"

"I'm here. I'm just trying to process what you just said."

"Well, I know I didn't act like it the other day, but it's true. I can't imagine being without you. Will you meet me at the park? Please."

Evidently, his please got to her because she heaved a sigh into the phone. "How about if I meet you in the park and we look for whatever this thing is? We don't have to make any decisions or plans right now."

"So you'll meet me?"

"Charlie and I are leaving right now. I'll bring a shovel. I have plenty here at the zoo."

Heath chuckled, realizing he hadn't thought about how he was going to find this note. "Thank you. I can't tell you how much this means to me."

Heath waited next to his vehicle at the park and went immediately to open Jade's door when she pulled in next to his Mercedes.

"Thank you for coming." He reached out.

She put up a hand as if to prevent him from touching. "What if there's nothing here or if there is, the answer isn't the one you want?"

"Then I will deal with it."

She shook her head, her expression sad. "That's easy to say now."

"No, it's not but I'm not going to run away from my feelings."

Her gaze searched his. "I want to believe you. I really do. But…you hurt me."

He couldn't wait any longer. Drawing her into his arms, he urgently whispered, "I'm sorry," over and over again.

He finally pulled away enough to look into her eyes. "I love you, Jade Fortune. I should have said that days ago. I'm damn sorry I didn't."

She gave him a watery smile. "I love you too, Heath."

His heart clutched at seeing that smile. It was like the sun returning after endless days of dreary clouds. He leaned down and kissed her.

Charlie woofed from the back seat of Jade's truck.

Jade used the back of her hand to wipe the tears off her cheeks. "He says he loves you too."

Heath laughed and helped the dog out of the truck. "And I love you too, Charlie. But you're going to have to get used to me kissing your mommy."

Jade went to the back of the truck and pulled out two shovels. "Where are we headed?"

"Doris said it's buried in a box on the south side of the tree."

Jade laughed. "Well, you're going to have to tell me which way is south."

Heath kissed the end of her nose and laughed as well. They went to the tree.

"Charlie, you be the lookout and let us know if you see any cops coming. I'm not sure what the law is regarding digging in the park."

Charlie barked as if he understood his job and went and sat by the tree.

"Are you sure you want to do this?" Jade asked.

Heath used one of the shovels to start digging. "I have to. Beau was right. I won't ever be able to rest until I know the truth."

"What if you don't like the answer?"

Pausing from his task, he turned toward her. "If or when that happens, I'll deal with it. How about you? If I find out that my father never wanted me, how will you feel about me then?"

"How could you think it would matter to me? I know who you are, what sort of man you are. That's all that matters to me." Locking eyes with him, she vowed softly, "I don't care about your birth story. I love the man you are today, Heath Blackwood. You backed me up when I made an outrageous claim, took me to a silly reunion to help me save face, put up with my disobedient dog, helped my friend Billy and helped me put on a wonderfully memorable Halloween for the kids of Chatelaine."

He winked at her. "Wow. I did all that?"

"Yeah. And more."

"And more?"

"You made me feel loved and desirable," she whispered.

"That's because you *are* lovable and desirable."

She gazed at him tenderly. "See? How can I not forgive

you? I know how much not knowing about the circumstances of your birth affected you."

"Breaking it off with you was the worst decision of my life. I hope you can believe that," he rasped.

"I do."

"In that case, how about if we make this engagement official?" Heath asked.

"Are you serious?"

"Yes." He nodded. "I realize we haven't known one another all that long, but I know I love you, and that's not about to change. No matter what happens."

"Maybe we should stop stalling and dig this thing up."

He shook his head. "Not until you give me an answer, because no matter what happens, I want to marry you, Jade Fortune. I love you. Whatever is in here isn't going to change that. That's why I called you before I came here."

"You…" she began and then cleared her throat. "You mean that?"

"Of course I mean it. I'm sorry for the stupid things I said and the way I behaved. I'll spend the rest of my life making it up to you, I swear."

He cupped her face in his palms and sealed his promise with a kiss. After pulling his mouth from hers he rested his forehead on hers and stroked his thumb along her lower lip.

"I forgive you because I love you and want to spend my life with you too." She kissed his thumb and gently pulled away. "Okay, let's find this thing so we can start on the rest of our lives."

They continued digging, and before long, Heath's shovel hit something solid. He dropped to his knees and pulled out a plastic grocery bag. Brushing off the dirt that clung to it, he opened the bag. Moments later, he retrieved a small rectangular-shaped item surrounded by more plastic and secured with duct tape. He pulled out a pocketknife and sliced through the layers of tape. After getting rid of the tape, he unwrapped the rest of the plastic.

Underneath all the protective layers was a black lacquer box with colorful pictures of flowers decoupaged onto the top. The box was attractive, but it was obvious that whoever had decorated the box was an amateur. Had his mother decorated it some thirty years ago?

"What the…?" Heath turned it over several times.

"Wow," Jade said. "It looks like a memory box."

He frowned. "What's a memory box?"

"It's a container people use to store mementos. Keepsakes from someone or something important."

He felt a new reverence for the item he held in his hands. Would this provide more clues to who he was and what had occurred thirty years ago between his mother and father?

With a deep inhalation he opened the lid.

Inside were a jumble of items, including a floppy stuffed brown monkey with exaggerated red lips. Why would his mother have saved something like that? What meaning did it have? He held it up and turned it around. It looked like a cheap carnival toy, the kind that were offered as prizes on those midway games.

"Oh my," Jade breathed out.

"Where did all this come from? I…" his voice trailed off and his gaze met hers over the open box.

"Do you think…?" she asked in a hushed tone.

His eyes widened. "It sure looks like it."

"These are from a traveling carnival. Just like…" her voice broke off too as she stared at him.

He shook his head. "What are the odds?"

"Pretty good I'd say."

Next, he pulled out two admission tickets. That's when he spotted a strip of photos like the kind taken in those photo booths. He lifted it from the box. For a moment he just stared at the two young people smiling and mugging for the camera. His hand shook as he gazed at the pictures.

"I know this is my mother. I have to assume this was my dad." He tried to swallow, but his throat had suddenly closed up. It was as if all the emotion he was experiencing had gathered in that one spot.

Jade placed a gentle hand on his shoulder and peered down to get a closer look. "Has anyone ever seen a picture of James Perry?"

Heath shook his head. "Lily told me the other day that they've never seen a picture of him. Haley tracked down a yearbook photo of their mother through the ancestry site she belongs to. But they haven't been able to find anything for James Perry. Do you think this is him?"

"I would say so, because he looks a lot like you…maybe a bit younger in those pictures," she murmured.

"My sisters are going to want to see these."

"Yeah. This is definitely a treasure trove." Jade sucked in a breath. "Oh, look, Heath, there's writing on the back of the picture strip."

The date was approximately nine months before Heath's birth. The note read, *Memories of our one and only night.*

Lastly, he pulled out a folded piece of paper. Must be the note that Doris was referring to. Would this hold the explanation he'd been searching for?

He leaned over and placed his lips on Jade's in a gentle kiss. Pulling back, he said gruffly, "And it won't affect how I feel about you, but I've—make that *we*—have come this far, I need to read it."

He blinked as moisture gathered in his eyes.

Taking a deep breath, he unfolded the paper and read.

Dearest James,
I'm not planning to send this, but I need to write it
down and bury it forever in our place. I've loved you
from the moment I met you, but I know you've always
considered me just a friend. I'd hoped our one night
together after the carnival would change your feel-
ings. I'll never know if it would have because you
met Leanna just a few days later. That was it for you.

When I saw how in love you were, I knew I'd have
to let you go. And when you eloped after just two
weeks and announced she was pregnant with triplets,
I kept my own secret, that I too was pregnant with
your child. You have given me one of life's great-
est gifts, and I want you to be happy. I don't want
to come between you and your great love or future.

I'm leaving town before anyone knows I'm carry-
ing your son so that there won't be any gossip as you
embark on your new life with Leanna. One day, the
truth may lead our son to you and his siblings. I hope
he can forgive me. I hope you all will forgive me.
With love,
Anne

"Wow," Heath said as he read it over again and handed
it to Jade.

She read it and sniffed. "So sad. Sounds like your
mother loved him very much. A true love that wasn't selfish or hurtful. I'm sorry I never got to meet your mom. She
sounds like a wonderful woman."

"She was. Toward the end of her life, I was frustrated
that she wouldn't discuss my father. But I like to think
that if the cancer hadn't taken her so quickly after the di-
agnosis, she might have. I'll never know, but reading this
makes me believe it to be true. She didn't hate him, she

loved him," he said with a touch of reverence and wonder in his tone.

"Enough to let him go and not to cause trouble for his new family or to put you in the middle," Jade said softly.

"Yeah. I suppose James wouldn't have wanted to acknowledge me if he was newly married and expecting children with his wife." That acknowledgement hurt but he'd known going into this that he might not like everything he found out.

"Maybe, but I think your mother was also looking out for you. Think about it. Even if he and his wife accepted you, you wouldn't be a part of their little family."

"Always on the outside," he mused.

"Exactly." She nodded and placed her hand on his shoulder. "Your mother was doing what she thought best for everyone, and since your father didn't even know about you, he didn't reject you."

"Even if my mother eventually changed her mind, James was deceased, so it didn't matter." He tilted his head, resting his cheek on her hand.

"I'm sure your sisters will also appreciate the story. They'll know how much their father loved their mother, thanks to Anne's letter, and they'll know that their dad was an honorable man and didn't simply abandon you or your mother. This letter shows he'd spent the night with Anne before he even met their mother."

Warmth spread across his chest. He wasn't conceived during an extra marital affair. "You're right. I'm sure they'll be as relieved by all of this as I am."

"Thank you for sharing this with me, Heath." She wound her arms around his neck.

"I wouldn't have wanted anyone else by my side...and I'm talking about forever. I want you by my side for the rest of my life and beyond." He kissed her and held her close. "Thank you."

"For what?" she asked, sounding genuinely surprised.

"For being who you are. For coming here today with me." He blinked rapidly. "And especially for dragging me to that carnival. I wonder if they had as much fun as we did."

"She saved all the souvenirs, didn't she?"

"But she buried them," he said.

"Like I said, she was letting go. Burying the past so she could go forward into the future with you."

They picked up the box and its contents and set it on a bench. Then Heath went back and filled in the hole they'd made and tamped down the dirt.

Afterward, he followed Jade back to her place. They brought the box and its contents into the house.

"About that engagement ring you returned to me," he said once they were inside.

"You mean the fake one?"

He shook his head. "Unlike the engagement, the ring wasn't a fake."

"So, why did you give it to me?"

"I think I knew then that I wanted it to be real. In spite of my misguided belief about needing to know my past," he admitted.

She lifted a brow. "And now?"

"I realize that was a false belief."

"I would never ever hold your birth against you. No matter what we had discovered from that letter."

He reached into his pocket and pulled out the sapphire ring. "I want this engagement to be real. Will you wear this again, Jade Fortune?"

"I would be honored." She threw her arms around him.

He kissed her. Then suddenly pulled away and looked at her.

"What? Is something wrong?"

"I just thought of something."

"Whatever it is, I'm sure we can work it out. Tell me."

"Do you think Charlie will accept me as his dad?"

"What? I…you…" Rational thought was beyond her.

"I'm willing to work at it if he is."

"You can't be serious," she giggled.

"I know how much he means to you."

"But you mean the most. Surely you know that."

"I do, and don't call me Shirley."

She swatted him on the chest. "You're terrible, Heath Blackwood. Teasing me like this."

"I was only half teasing. I know Charlie is important to you."

"He is, but right now he's going to get a chew bone, and we're locking the bedroom door."

THE NEXT DAY, Jade accompanied Heath to his sister Lily's place. After calling her to tell her he had important news that affected all of them, all of the triplets gathered at Lily and Asa's home.

First, Heath announced his and Jade's engagement, and all three sisters flew to her and gave her a hug. They welcomed her to the family and told Heath what a lucky guy he was.

"Maybe I'm the one who's lucky," Jade said.

All three sisters laughed uproariously.

"Despite your being mean to me—" Heath said pulled out the photo strip and carefully passed it to Lily to share with the other two "—I want to share this with you."

The triplets passed the photo back and forth among themselves, tears streaming down their cheeks.

"It's the only picture we have of our dad. We couldn't find him in the yearbook where he supposedly went to high school," Lily said.

"I can't tell you what this means to us," Haley said.

Heath also shared the letter with his sisters. "I wanted you to know the story behind it all. Our father must have been a pretty special guy to have women like both our mothers love him as much as they did."

"Like father, like son," Jade whispered and took his hand in hers.

EPILOGUE

"THAT WAS A wonderful supper, Jade. Thanks so much for inviting us," Lily said.

Jade and Heath, who had moved out of the hotel and into Jade's spacious log home several weeks before, had invited his sisters and their loved ones to supper.

Jade smiled at them. "You're welcome, and I'm so glad you could come. I grew up in a big family, but Heath didn't, and I know he enjoys spending time with each and every one of you."

"When we're not overwhelming him, you mean," Haley added lightly.

Heath looked around the large dining table at his sisters and their families. His gaze came to rest on Jade, and his heart overflowed with gratitude. She had helped him accept the past. He couldn't change what had already happened—no one could—but he could appreciate and love the family he had going forward.

"You're probably wondering why I gathered you all here today," he said and stood up. He couldn't prevent himself from grinning at the puzzled expressions on everyone's faces. Even Jade was giving him a quizzical look. He held up his wine glass. "Man, I've always wanted to say that. Makes a guy feel important."

His sisters all groaned and rolled their eyes at him. Lily threw her napkin at him.

"I have something for each of you," he said and stacked three colorfully wrapped packages on the table.

"But it's not Christmas yet," Haley protested.

"This is just something extra. Not a Christmas gift." He passed them out. "It was something I wanted to do."

Lily opened the gift and immediately burst into tears.

Heath's stomach dropped. Had he miscalculated? "Lily, I'm so sorry. I didn't mean—"

She jumped up and ran to him. Giving him a tight hug, she said, "These are happy tears, you dope. This is perfect."

Haley and Tabitha went to him too. "Group hug," they proclaimed.

"So, you like them?" he asked when they'd released him from the hug.

"That's so thoughtful of you."

"What made you think of it?"

Lily looked to Jade, but she shook her head. "He thought of this all on his own."

"I thought you all might want a picture of our father without my mother in it," he said of the pen-and-ink drawings of James Perry he had commissioned from the photo strip. He'd had the pictures drawn, matted, and framed.

"Heath?" Jade cleared her throat. "Check out that gift for you under the tree."

Heath went to the Christmas tree they'd put up just yesterday. Color rose in his face as he recalled what they'd done in front of the tree once they'd decorated it. There was one lone package under the tree. He brought it back to the table and began to open it.

"Great minds think alike," he said as he held up the drawing of his mother and father. The artist had obviously copied one of the pictures from the strip from the photo booth.

"Now that we know the true story of what happened, I thought you might want that memory," Jade said softly. "We'll be able to tell our children about both sides of their family tree."

He blinked back tears and went to her. He hugged and kissed her, knowing they were forging a bond that wasn't meant to be severed. Ever.

* * * * *

Don't miss the stories in this mini series!

THE FORTUNES OF TEXAS: FORTUNE'S SECRET CHILD

Follow the lives and loves of a complex family with a rich history and deep ties in the Lone Star State.

Fortune's Faux Engagement
CARRIE NICHOLS
September 2024

A Fortune Thanksgiving
MICHELLE LINDO-RICE
October 2024

Fortune's Holiday Surprise
JENNIFER WILCK
November 2024

MILLS & BOON

The Rodeo Cowboy's Return
Cathy McDavid

MILLS & BOON

New York Times bestselling author **Cathy McDavid** has written over forty-five titles for Harlequin. She spends her days penning stories about handsome cowboys riding the range, busting broncs and sweeping gals off their feet—oops, no. Make that winning the hearts of feisty, independent women who give them a run for their money.

Visit the Author Profile page
at millsandboon.com.au for more titles.

Dear Reader,

I love starting new things, and *The Rodeo Cowboy's Return* is book one in my latest Harlequin Heartwarming series, The Rocking Chair Ranch. People often ask where I get the ideas for my stories, and I usually have an interesting answer. But I'm not sure where the original inspiration for this book sprang from. I only know I've wanted to write about a charming and quaint independent senior living community for some time. And because I love writing cowboy romances, of course it had to be a Western setting.

Everett and Macy's romance is a second chance for both of them in more ways than one. Years ago, Everett let Macy down, and she doesn't trust him with her vulnerable heart, or the one belonging to her adorable young son. Only by taking a chance, and Everett proving he's not the same man who once abandoned her, can their newfound love bloom.

The Rodeo Cowboy's Return is also populated with some charming secondary, elderly characters who will make you smile and even sigh. I hope you enjoy reading Everett and Macy's story as much as I did writing it.

Warmest wishes,

Cathy McDavid

PS: I love connecting with readers. You can find me at:

CathyMcDavid.com
Facebook.com/CathyMcDavid
Twitter.com/CathyMcDavid
Instagram.com/CathyMcDavidWriter

CHAPTER ONE

THE RUSTED IRON gate stood open, inviting anyone who approached to enter. Some things, thought Everett Owens, never changed. And, unfortunately, some things did.

Ignoring the stab of guilt squeezing his heart, he drove his late-model cobalt blue pickup truck onto his grandfather's ranch, the tires shooting plumes of dry red dust into the air. A few hundred yards later, the dirt road curved and pasture fences came into view. Three years ago, a herd of Arizona's finest quarter horses would have galloped alongside the fence line, escorting Everett to the outbuildings. Today, the pastures sat empty.

A dozen broodmares and one stallion were all that remained of his grandfather's once thriving horse breeding business. In the wake of the older man's recent heart attack, Everett assumed that the horses would soon have a new owner. The ranch, too.

Help selling off. That must be why his grandfather had summoned him home. Only a few reasons could convince Everett to set foot in Wickenburg, Arizona. His grandfather's health. The ranch and horses. A funeral.

Another funeral, Everett amended.

He shoved the sudden flood of unhappy memories aside and focused on what, according to his mom, might be required of him during this visit. Liquidating Pop's few remaining business assets. Making any necessary repairs and then putting the ranch on the market. Eventually, overseeing the sale. Finding a suitable eldercare facility for his grandfather.

How long would all that take? Everett had no wish to prolong his stay or keep returning. He didn't miss his hometown, and he was sure his hometown didn't miss him.

The outbuildings came into view, shabbier than the last time he'd seen them and crying out for fresh paint. He counted at least a dozen missing roof shingles on the mare barn and stallion quarters. Doors hung crookedly on loose hinges. The hay shed housed at most thirty bales. Barely enough to feed a string of pregnant broodmares and a big, hardy stallion for a week.

Everett's mom had either downplayed the situation or lacked a full understanding of it. She and Everett's aunt Laurel would have been here if not for Pop's objections. Everett was the only one his grandfather had summoned. According to him, a phone call wouldn't suffice. The two of them needed to talk in person.

Aiming the truck in the direction of the house, Everett reduced his speed to a crawl. Pop must have been watching from the back window, for the kitchen door opened, and he shuffled onto the spacious back porch. Shuffled? What had happened to his robust stride? His worn work shirt billowed at the waist where it once strained against the buttons, and his formerly square shoulders now drooped.

Swallowing his shock, Everett parked in front of the freestanding garage behind the house and climbed out of his truck. His mom's worry hadn't been exaggerated.

"Hey, Pop," he hollered and waved.

Most people in town called Winston Connelly by his nickname. If asked, he couldn't remember how or when it started.

"Everett, my boy. Mighty good to see you."

They met on the porch where Everett enveloped Pop in

a fierce embrace. Feeling his grandfather's slighter frame gave Everett another shock.

"Good to see you, too, Pop." He fought the sudden tightness in his chest. "I've missed you."

"Missed you something awful." Pop clapped Everett on the back before releasing him. "You hungry? Thirsty? Can I make you a sandwich?"

It was too early for lunch. "Maybe later," Everett said. "I'll take a cold drink in the meantime."

"You fetch your stuff from the truck and come on in. I'll round us up a couple of root beers."

Pop's favorite beverage. That much was still the same.

Everett did as instructed and carried his duffel and laptop satchel into the house. He passed Pop at the kitchen counter, struggling to pry the lid off a bottle. Everett resisted offering to help—Pop was a proud and independent man—and headed down the hall instead. His cowboy boots echoed on the wooden floor only to be muted when they reached the carpeted guest bedroom.

The quilt that had won his late grandmother first place at the county fair two decades ago covered the bed. Like everything at the ranch, it had seen better days. After setting his duffel and satchel on an old chair in the corner to be unpacked later, he returned to the kitchen.

Midway down the hall, Everett came to a bone-jarring halt. How could he have forgotten about the photo, one of many in a vast collection that stretched from one end of the long wall to the other? Feeling like he'd been kicked in the gut, he stared at the image of his younger and happier self. He and his best friend, Brody, had their arms draped around each other in a congratulatory side hug. Their grinning faces spoke of a good day. A good rodeo. They'd both finished the weekend with first place wins, Everett in bulldogging and Brody in bareback bronc riding.

Eight months later, Brody had died, the result of a head-on collision. Everett's fault. Because of him, the finest man to ever walk the face of the earth lay six feet beneath its surface. Worse, his beautiful wife became a widow, and his yet-to-be-born son was left to grow up fatherless.

Everett attempted to draw air into lungs that refused to function. He shouldn't keep coming back, even as seldom as he did. Too much time had passed for him to make good on his broken promise.

A loud clatter jerked him from the dark hole he'd disappeared into, and he hurried to the kitchen.

"You okay, Pop?"

His grandfather stood over a bottle of root beer lying on its side and emptying its contents into a puddle on the floor. Pop's wizened features twisted into a frustrated grimace.

"Dang blasted bottle slipped out of my hand."

"Don't worry about it."

Everett bent and retrieved the bottle, which he set in the sink. He then ripped a long length of paper towels off the roll and sopped up the mess, disposing the sodden paper towels in a trash bin beneath the counter.

"It's my arthritis," Pop said with a note of dejection.

"I'll lend you this new ointment I've been using. Pretty good stuff." Everett suffered his share of aches and pains. Rodeoing was a physically demanding way to earn a living.

Pop reached for the refrigerator door handle. "Let me grab you another soda. Then we can tour the stallion quarters and mare barn."

Right to business. Okay.

With their drinks in hand, they walked from the house to the barn area at a more sedate pace than in days gone by.

"What did the doctor say at your last checkup?" Everett asked.

"I'm fit as a fiddle."

"Pop, I'm serious."

The older man's chuckle lacked mirth. "I'm doing well enough for a man who almost kicked the bucket. Could've been a lot worse."

"He's satisfied with your progress, then?"

"*She's* satisfied. And young enough to be your sister, iffin' you had one. Says I'm recovering nicely. Then again, I should be. She's got me taking more pills than a grizzly has teeth." He snorted in disgust. "Insisted I give up all my favorite foods. Steak. Bacon. Fried potatoes. Salt, for Pete's sake. Now I have broiled chicken breast and salad for dinner prit near every night."

That accounted for some of the weight loss, though not all. Pop had the appearance of someone who'd been gravely ill for an extended time.

"You sure you're allowed to have root beer?" Everett asked, only half-jokingly.

"Give a poor man a break, will you?"

He supposed they could bend the rules this once. "I won't tell."

As they neared the stallion quarters, a magnificent chestnut trotted out the stable door and into the paddock. Snorting and shaking his head, he came to a standstill at the paddock fence and emitted a shrill whinny that let everyone in earshot know he was king of his domain. With a well-defined head that might have been chiseled from marble, his heavily muscled form displayed a strength and athleticism inherited from the best quarter horse lines.

Pop reached out a gnarled hand to the horse, whose personality instantly changed from that of a lion to a lamb.

"How's my good boy?" He ran his palm along the horse's prominent jaw.

In turn, the horse pressed his nose into Pop's shoulder

and nickered with contentment. There was no doubt of the close bond the two shared. A chip in Everett's carefully constructed armor fell away.

"Champ looks good," he observed.

"He's a beaut."

Doc Bar None Better was the stallion's registered name. After his first win—a halter competition as a yearling—Pop had started calling him Champ, and the nickname stuck.

"I've had help looking after him. And the place," Pop added with a tilt of his chin.

"Your neighbors?"

"Them and some of the folks in town. They keep things clean and tidy for me."

Everett was glad to hear that. Champ was a valuable asset. Selling him and the dozen mares would bring in a lot of money that could be put to good use. Such as nice accommodations in a reputable eldercare facility. A clean and tidy place would also help obtain a good sale price when they sold the ranch.

After Champ had his fill of being doted on, Everett and Pop made their way to the mare barn. Half the stalls were occupied. To Everett's relief, he found the mare barn in the same well-kept condition. Even better, the pregnant residents appeared healthy and content. Pop was fortunate to have such kind neighbors and friends. No way could he care for this number of horses on his own. Cleaning the stalls alone would do him in. Not to mention hauling hay, watering and the countless other labor-intensive chores required with running a ranch. Even with a limited number of horses.

"I need to rest my feet a few minutes."

Without waiting for a response, Pop eased himself down onto one of two worn wicker rocking chairs sitting just inside the barn's wide entryway. Most likely, he needed to catch his breath rather than rest his feet.

Everett joined Pop, taking the other chair. They chatted while finishing their sodas. Everett caught Pop up on his parents' doings and his rodeo career.

"I'm proud of you, sonny."

"Thanks. That means a lot to me."

Where they sat afforded them a clear view of the distant mountains, their gentle slopes a soft green gray typical of late summer. The hot afternoon sun bore down on the parched ground, trying its best to drive all manner of man and beast inside. No wonder Pop felt winded.

After a moment, he said, "There's something I need to talk to you about."

Everett sat up straight. "Yeah?"

Finally, he thought, the reason Pop had summoned him home. Asking for help, admitting he was too aged and infirmed to keep up with the ranch, had to be hard for a proud man like his grandfather. Everett didn't push and let Pop make the request in his own time and own way. It was the least he could do.

"I could use a hand with some things."

"Sure, Pop."

"As you can guess, this place is a lot of work, and my ticker ain't what it used to be."

"Whatever you need. You just have to ask."

The older man relaxed. "All right."

"I've got a job lined up. A youth rodeo coach. But that won't start until January. I have to finish the year out first." And qualify for the National Rodeo Finals in four months. If he did, he'd receive a nice signing bonus. "I told my buddy Rusty I'd rope with him at the Big Timber Rodeo later this month. In the meantime, I can carve out a week or ten days at the most. We'll get this place in order and maybe even ready to put on the market. I can also reach out to a few breeders I know and see if they're interested in Champ or the mares. If you can dig out their registration papers, I'll take pictures with my phone and—"

"What in blue blazes are you talking about, sonny?" Pop drew back and stared at Everett. "I'm not putting the ranch on the market, and Champ isn't going anywhere."

"What are *you* talking about?"

"And as far as the mares go, they aren't mine anymore. I sold them a while ago."

"Sold them!"

"Didn't have much choice. Property taxes and insurance were due. But I still own twenty percent of the foals they're carrying. That was the deal I cut with the collective."

Everett shook his head in confusion. "Collective?"

"I don't want your help selling the ranch. I want you to *manage* it for me. In exchange for half ownership. Only fair your mom and aunt get the other half. Champ would be yours, however. You'd have to keep working with the collective and allow the mares to remain here. That's part of the deal. My hope is you can rebuild the breeding business."

"I don't understand." Everett pushed to his feet. "You're not making any sense."

"What's not to understand? A horse collective bought the mares. I bred Champ to them in exchange for an ownership percentage of the foals. More'n that, they help me with the chores, and I let them keep the mares here. It's a business arrangement."

At that moment, a white pickup truck appeared and drove slowly to the barn, its tires making a crunching sound. Everett went still. He knew that truck. Four years ago, he'd been with Brody when his friend bought it brand-new off the lot in order to surprise his bride.

Not her, please.

"Well, lookie there," Pop said with a happy grin. "We got us some company."

"Why is she here?" Everett choked out the question.

"She drops by most days. She's head of the collective."

By then the truck had come to a stop. The driver's side door opened, and a young woman wearing jeans, boots and a baseball cap emerged. Her long blond ponytail had been threaded through the hole in the back of the cap and swung jauntily when she turned to open the rear driver's side door.

Macy. Brody's wife. No, *widow*.

Everett felt the weight of his guilt, as if he'd been stomped on by a two-thousand-pound bull. That was nothing compared to the blow he suffered when she opened the rear door and lifted out a little boy with dark curly hair and who was the spitting image of his father. With an easy, natural grace, she hoisted the boy onto her hip.

Everett grabbed the rocking chair, feeling disoriented and unsteady from the force of being thrust back in time. When he and Macy had last spoken, they'd been at the cemetery, her pregnancy just starting to show in the somber black dress she'd worn.

She caught sight of him then and reached for the side of the truck, her reaction an exact mirror of his.

No, not exact. Everett's expression was no doubt contorted into a mask of agony and grief. Macy, however, glared at him with undisguised anger.

Her mouth moved. From this distance, he couldn't hear her words, but he could read her lips.

"What are you doing here?"

MACY SOMMERS REMINDED herself to breathe. Five counts in, seven counts out. The coping mechanism was one she'd learned during grief counseling sessions, and it usually worked to restore her calm. Today proved no exception.

Her blurted question to Everett had been purely a knee-jerk reaction. She'd known he would be here. Pop had informed her of Everett's arrival days ago. Still, she'd been unprepared for the shock of seeing him in person after all this time.

Anger bloomed anew inside her. He'd been Brody's best friend and rodeo partner. And then, he'd abandoned her, breaking his deathbed vow to be there for her and the baby. She'd forgiven him, hard as it was. But she didn't trust him. Not for a minute.

"Put me down, Mommy."

Her young son, Joey, kicked and squirmed and wouldn't stop until he got his wish. Still, she held on, wanting to protect him from…from what? Everett? The past? Her own uncertainties?

"Now, Mommy. Please."

Joey was strong for such a tiny human being. He'd wear her out before long, and the last thing she wanted was for him to throw a temper tantrum. Not in front of Everett.

She lowered her son to the ground, and he immediately took off running with the fearless confidence of a two-and-a-half-year-old.

"Pop. Pop."

"Hello, there, youngin'." The old man opened his arms.

Joey plowed into him. Pop hoisted the boy onto his lap and enveloped him in a fond hug.

"I want to ride a horse."

"That depends on your mom." He glanced at Macy and winked. "She's in charge."

"Not today, honey. We don't have time."

Macy sometimes led Joey around the ranch on one of the older broodmares. It was a treat for them both. Joey was a natural and would no doubt grow up to be an avid, talented horseman like his father. If she could just keep him from rodeoing. She couldn't bear it if another person she loved left her behind for a life on the road.

She walked toward Everett, wishing she possessed a fraction of her son's confidence.

"You made it," she said when she neared.

Did he hear the challenge in her voice? Truth be told, she'd half expected him to bail on his grandfather. More than half. He'd bailed on her, after all.

He nodded. "Just got here. Pop was showing me around."

"Don't let me stop you." She retreated a step. "Come on, Joey."

He curled against Pop. "I want to stay."

Her son had a stubborn streak that landed the two of them in frequent power struggles. He also melted her heart with his silly antics, charming personality and sweet bedtime kisses.

Pop chuckled. "I'm happy to watch him while you check on the mares."

"I can't keep imposing on you," Macy insisted.

"He'll only get underfoot." Pop tweaked Joey's nose. "Won't you, youngin'?"

Joey burst into giggles. This was one of the many games he and Pop played, and reason why Macy adored their visits to the ranch. Joey had two sets of grandparents, but Pop filled the role of great-grandfather.

Glancing at Everett, she was struck by his expression, a mixture of tenderness and sorrow and grief. A far cry from his stoic, almost unreadable countenance on the day of Brody's funeral.

Wait. Macy looked closer. Grief, yes, but also guilt shone in his ruggedly handsome features. Did he feel bad about breaking his promise to Brody and staying away?

Did he miss his friend and feel like a chunk of his heart had been ripped out? She hoped so. She hoped, like her, he spent restless nights tormented by regrets.

As much as she wanted to, Macy couldn't go back in time and change what she'd said to Brody that last fateful day. But it was different for Everett. He purposely chose not to honor his commitment to Brody by checking on her and Joey, and his actions hurt. She considered asking him why, only to clamp her mouth shut. This wasn't the time or place.

"I have an idea." Pop grinned in a way that had Macy convinced she wouldn't like what he proposed. "I'll keep an eye on Joey. That way, Everett can help you with the mares while you tell him about the collective. I was gettin' ready to do that when you pulled up."

Macy hesitated, absorbing this latest surprise. Everett didn't know about the collective. She had to wonder what else Pop hadn't mentioned.

Suddenly, she wanted to tell Everett everything. Not only about the collective but also her job and school and how well she'd managed these past three years—all without his assistance.

"Fine." She spun and returned to her truck, refusing to give him a chance to object. From the floor of the back seat, she removed a heavy brown medical bag that resembled a suitcase. Carrying it by the handle, she returned to where Everett stood. "Ready?"

His hazel eyes had always been easy to read. He didn't want to accompany her. Didn't want to be alone with her. But as much, if not more, he wanted to learn about the collective. The latter won out.

He extended his hand. "Let me take that for you."

She tugged the bag closer. "I've got it." As an afterthought, she added, "Thanks."

Assured that Joey was behaving for Pop, she made her way into the mare barn. Everett followed, his slower pace another indication of his reluctance.

"You got your vet tech certification?"

He'd known that was her ambition. "Not yet. I'm close. I'll finish in the spring."

"Good for you."

She stopped at the third stall on the right. A chunky sorrel hung her head over the half door, her ears pricked forward inquisitively.

"Hello, Miss Roxie. How are you today?"

The mare snorted and blew out a gust of warm air that grazed Macy's cheek.

"Better, I take it?"

Roxie swung her head around to nip at her neighbor, letting the well-pedigreed and too-nosy palomino know that her interference wasn't appreciated.

"Quit squabbling, you two," Macy warned as she bent to open the case and remove a stethoscope. When she straightened, Everett stood beside her. Unable to stop herself, she retreated a step. "Oh."

"I didn't mean to startle you."

"I'm not sta… It's…" *Five counts in, seven counts out.* "I've had a stressful morning." That was an understatement. "I'm preoccupied."

"What's wrong with the mare?"

Horse care. A safe topic. Macy slid open the latch and stepped inside the stall, closing the door behind her. "Roxie had a concerning case of colic yesterday."

She ran her hand along the mare's belly, feeling Everett's gaze on her like the glow of a heat lamp. Roxie, along with most of the mares in the barn, was about four months along in her pregnancy. Horses generally carried eleven months. Sometimes less. A year or longer wasn't uncommon. An ultrasound recently had confirmed Roxie's baby was developing normally, but things could, and sometimes did, go wrong. Colic in horses was always concerning and could be quite dangerous for a pregnant mare.

Relieved that Roxie exhibited no signs of distress, Macy pressed the stethoscope's diaphragm against Roxie's belly and listened. Hearing only typical gut rumblings, she moved the diaphragm around, then repeated the process on Roxie's other side. The mare amused herself by nuzzling Macy's ball cap.

"Enough," Macy chided affectionately and stepped away.

She gave Roxie a thorough visual examination, satisfied the mare appeared healthy. Next, she surveyed the stall. Roxie had eaten all of her breakfast, as evidenced by the empty feed trough, and done her business in the corner. Both good signs.

Still, she'd ask Dr. Beck his opinion at the clinic and stop by the ranch after work for another well check. Roxie was much more than a valuable broodmare and a key to her and her son's financial future. Macy treated all the collective's mares like they were her personal pets, spoiling and fretting over each one.

"You still work for Red Hills Veterinary Clinic?" Everett asked when she emerged from the stall.

She relatched the door and turned to face him. "I do. I manage the office. For now. Until I complete my certification."

"How's Dr. Beck?"

"Good. He's very accommodating with my schedule. In fact, I'm on my lunch hour right now. My mom watches Joey when I'm at work. I picked him up on the way here and will drop him off on my way back."

"They still live right down the road?"

"They talk about moving but haven't yet."

He'd been a regular at her parents'. Brody had brought him to the house often for birthday parties and cookouts.

A quick glance assured her Joey and Pop were doing fine. The older man was attempting to teach Joey the names of coins. Penny, nickel, dime and quarter. Which meant she couldn't use her son as an excuse to escape Everett.

"You were going to tell me about the collective," he prompted.

Okay. Business. That was fine with her. "Pop needed money to meet some of the ranch's expenses."

"He told me that much. Before you got here."

"Did he also tell you he'd been selling off horses for years?"

"I was aware of that."

"And you never asked why?" Her accusatory tone sounded harsh even to her.

"He said he was lightening his load. He wanted to retire."

In Everett's defense, Pop probably had said something along those lines. He'd refused to admit he was struggling to make ends meet.

"Your grandfather couldn't keep up with the ranch on his own. At first, he hired part-time help. Then the supply chain crisis drove the price of hay sky-high, and he could no longer afford help. There were repairs and maintenance expenses. The heat pump on the house broke down. The transmission went out on his truck. Eventually, he couldn't pay the back taxes and almost lost the ranch." She noticed a spark of emotion flitter across Everett's face and paused. "Look. It's not my intention to lecture you."

"It's all right, Macy. I deserve a lecture."

She'd heard him say her name a hundred times. Two

hundred. She'd forgotten the way the syllables rumbled pleasantly in that low-timbered voice of his and how she used to love listening to him talk. They'd been so young that summer between their junior and senior years of high school.

Then Everett's dad was transferred for work, and he and his family moved to Santa Fe. Time passed. Macy started dating Brody and fell in love. When she next saw Everett after graduation, they were just friends. Nothing more. Now, they were practically strangers.

Clearing her throat, she continued. "Everyone in town loves your grandfather. He's lived here his entire life. Given to the community. Lent a helping hand to whoever needed one."

"Not many like him," Everett agreed.

"We, his friends, didn't want to see him lose the ranch because of being unable to pay back taxes. But he refused the loan we offered him. So, we came up with another idea. We pooled our resources and formed a collective—I used some of the life insurance money I got—and we bought the remaining broodmares from him."

"That must have cost…"

She could see Everett doing the math in his head.

"Yes. A lot. In addition, Pop retains a twenty percent ownership of the foals, which he'll receive when they're old enough to sell."

"What about any future foals?"

"That will depend. Hopefully, the collective will have enough money after the sale of the foals to pay Pop outright for any stud fees. Or we'll strike a similar agreement with him. Meanwhile, Pop allows the mares to remain here. In exchange, the collective members feed and tend the mares. We cover all their costs, including medical. We also keep up the mare barn and clean Champ's stallion quarters, saving Pop the trouble."

"Wow." Everett pushed back his cowboy hat. "That's something."

"It's a good arrangement for everyone. If all goes well, the collective will make a nice return on their investment and Pop, too, on his share of the foals." At the slight downturn of Everett's mouth, she asked, "What's wrong?"

"Nothing."

"You disapprove?"

"It's not that." He shifted uncomfortably. "Can I ask who else is in the collective?"

"There are five of us altogether. Me, Kinsley Karston, Sheriff Andy, Glynnis Pottinger, and the Hays family. They're the new owners of Hayloft Feed and Tack Store and a valuable addition to the collective. They supply our feed at cost, which is a huge savings."

"The local sheriff is a member?"

"No, no. Nothing like that." Macy shook her head. "His real name is Roy Gleason, and he's a retired real estate broker. But everyone calls him Sheriff Andy. You'll see why when you meet him. He looks just like Andy Griffith from the old TV show."

"Thank you," Everett said, his demeanor changing. "For helping Pop. None of us realized how bad his finances had gotten."

"You know your grandfather. He's very private and not one to talk about his problems. The only reason any of us found out he owed back taxes is someone spotted a notice in the newspaper. If he hadn't paid the back taxes, he'd have lost the ranch."

Everett gave a start, the news clearly unexpected. "I wish he'd told me."

"What would you have done?"

He hesitated. "I'm not sure."

"That's what I thought." Returning the stethoscope to the case, she grabbed the handle and started to walk away.

Everett stopped her before she got two steps. "What does that mean?"

She stared down at where his large, strong fingers rested gently on her upper arm. He immediately let go.

"Sorry."

She nodded, not trusting her voice. Rather than feel threatening, his touch had evoked old memories from their brief period of dating she'd all but forgotten.

"I have to get going." That was only half-true. Dr. Beck had given her extra time off in case Roxie was in distress. "I'll be back around six."

"I can keep watch on Roxie and save you a trip. I'll call if there's any change in her condition."

She wanted to object. But Everett was experienced with horses and would recognize the signs of colic. "Thanks. Guess I'll see you in the morning, then."

"Is your number the same?"

"Yes."

He hadn't deleted her contact info. She'd saved his, too.

They walked to where Pop sat, bouncing Joey on his knee.

"Come on, honey." Macy reached for Joey's hand. "Time for us to leave."

He pouted. "I want to stay."

Pop lifted Joey from his lap and set him on the ground, then, with a low grunt, rose on unsteady legs. "I was hoping the three of us could have a chat."

"About what?" Macy asked, suddenly wary.

Pop grinned. "Our new arrangement."

"I don't understand." She glanced at Everett, who wore a puzzled expression.

"Let's go inside where it's not so hot," the old man suggested.

"Pop." Macy gave him the same warning stare she gave Joey when he was about to reach for something off-limits.

"What arrangement?" Everett asked.

"With you." Pop turned to Macy, his grin widening. "Everett will be taking over management of the ranch and ownership of Champ. The collective will be working with him from now on."

Macy didn't believe her ears. "Is that true?"

She turned toward him, seeing the same shock she felt reflected on his face.

CHAPTER TWO

WHATEVER RESPONSE EVERETT might have given was interrupted by Joey's abrupt loud wailing. He didn't stop to think. He dived forward, grabbed the crying boy and cradled him against his chest.

"Hey, sport. You okay? What happened?" He examined Joey for any obvious signs of injury and found none. Then again, he could fill at most a sticky note with all he knew about kids.

Macy materialized beside him. The medical case lay on the ground where she'd dropped it. "Honey, what happened? Are you hurt?"

With tears in his eyes, the little boy held up his index finger, displaying a small but angry red scratch. "I have an owie."

"Move your finger for Mommy," Macy said.

He did, bending it into a hook. "The chair bit me."

"Bit you? That must have hurt." Her distress visibly drained from her face.

Joey's, too.

"The chair's old," Everett explained. "There's probably a sharp piece of wicker sticking out. Is that what happened, sport?"

Joey tipped his head back and, for the first time, looked squarely at Everett. His dark eyes widened, and he made a little noise that sounded like the beginnings of a whine.

"It's okay. I'm a friend of your dad's."

Beside him, Macy inhaled sharply.

"Well, I was…and a friend of your mom's." Everett tried again. "I'm not going to hurt you. Just ask Pop. He's my grandfather and will vouch for me."

"I'll take him." Macy held out her arms.

"Sure." Everett released the boy. "You be good for your mom, okay?"

To his surprise, Joey smiled at him, stunning Everett again with his resemblance to his late father.

"I'm a good boy."

Macy enveloped him in a fierce hug and kissed his scratched finger. "Yes, you are."

Everett's chest tightened with emotion. The two of them were alone in the world because of him. He was supposed to have been driving the day of the collision outside of Kingman. Instead, he'd been napping in the back seat, the result of celebrating too hard the previous night and getting too little sleep.

He'd never had the courage to tell Macy. Instead, he'd withdrawn from their friendship and rarely returned to Wickenburg, breaking the promise he'd made to Brody minutes before he died in the hospital ER and two hours before his new widow arrived. When she'd sobbed and clung to him, it was all Everett could do not to push her away and run out of the hospital.

"I've got first aid supplies," Pop said and hitched a thumb toward the house. "We can talk while you bandage him up."

"Now's maybe not a good time for a talk," Everett added. "Macy needs to get back to work."

"I have a few minutes." She balanced Joey on her hip. "And I want to know about this new arrangement."

Everett had been afraid of that.

They made their way inside and to the kitchen. He sat

at the table while Macy washed Joey's finger at the sink. Pop returned shortly with some ointment and a bandage. He then retrieved three bottles of water from the fridge, which he set on the table before joining Everett.

When Macy finished with Joey's finger, she put him on the floor to play with an assortment of plastic tumblers and a potato masher she borrowed from a drawer by the stove. He was instantly enthralled.

She'd done this before, thought Everett. Her familiarity with the kitchen told him she was one of those helpful friends Pop had been talking about earlier. It spoke well of her that she didn't hold her anger at him against Pop.

"So, you're taking over the ranch," she said.

"He is," Pop replied before Everett could.

Unscrewing the cap on his water, Everett took a much needed swallow and willed himself to remain calm. Getting upset with Pop would solve nothing. "We haven't had a chance to talk about it yet."

Pop refused to be deterred. "I'm giving him half the ranch and Champ. In exchange, he'll live here and manage the ranch. As part of the deal, he'll honor the agreement I made with the collective."

Macy turned her gaze on Everett, her raised brows asking a silent question.

"Nothing's been decided."

"It sounds like a fair deal." She sipped her water. "And if you don't help your grandfather, who will? From what he tells me, your folks can't return to Arizona because of your dad's job, and your aunt has a brand-new grandbaby she doesn't want to leave."

"Plus none of your cousins have the first clue about running a ranch," Pop added.

"Neither do I," Everett said. "Not really."

Again, Macy raised her brows.

"Bull riding and calf roping aren't the same as breeding and raising horses."

Her stare didn't waver.

Okay, okay. The truth was, Everett did know much more than his cousins. Their riding experience consisted of annual holiday visits to the ranch and trail riding in the nearby hills. And while inexperienced in business, he was the only grandchild the least bit capable of taking over for Pop.

Under different circumstances, he'd jump at Pop's offer. The problem was, circumstances weren't different.

"I can't stay," he said. "I'm entered in the Big Timber Rodeo. It's two weeks away."

"You can skip one rodeo," she said.

"I told a friend I'd be his roping partner."

"He'll find someone else."

"I need to maintain my ranking. If I don't, I won't qualify for Nationals."

"Ah. Nationals." She folded her arms across her middle.

"It's fine, Macy," Pop assured her. "If he can't stay, he can't stay. I'll make it until the end of the year. You and the collective will see to it. Then he can return after the holidays."

The guilt feasting on Everett's insides took another giant bite. "I have a job waiting for me. If I qualify for Nationals, I receive a signing bonus."

"A job doing what?" Macy asked.

On the floor, Joey arranged plastic tumblers into an obstacle course and then drove the potato masher through it. His sound effects made it hard for Everett to concentrate.

"Youth rodeo coach for the Oklahoma Twisters."

She glanced away.

"I need a job," Everett said. "I can't rodeo my entire life."

That got her attention. "Taking over your grandfather's horse breeding business would be a job."

"Yes." But in Oklahoma, he could pretend he wasn't responsible for ruining her and Joey's lives. In Oklahoma, he wouldn't have to see the anger and disappointment in her eyes and be reminded of his failures.

However, in Oklahoma, he wouldn't be caring for his grandfather and returning the favor to someone who had taught him how to ride and rope and set him on a career path.

"Pop and I need to talk—" He started to say in private but was cut off by a buzzing sound.

"Hold that thought." Standing, Macy dug into her jeans pocket for her phone. "It's work." She crossed the kitchen to the other side before answering. "Hello."

Joey paused playing to watch her.

"Look, Pop," Everett said.

"Don't you worry, sonny." The old man grinned, unfazed. "We're gonna figure this out."

Macy returned to the table, but she didn't sit. "I'm needed at work. The vet tech covering for me had a personal emergency and left." She stooped and began collecting the plastic tumblers. "Come on, Joey. Time to go. Give Mommy the potato masher."

Two minutes later, she'd rinsed the items and set them in the sink to dry. Then, she gathered Joey and kissed Pop on the cheek.

"I'll see you in the morning."

"I'll be here." He chuckled and blushed a little.

Everett rose. "I'll walk you out."

"That isn't necessary," she said. "You and Pop have your chat."

"I'll walk you out, Macy."

She lifted a shoulder in a suit-yourself gesture.

Joey dashed ahead of them toward the truck still parked by the mare barn. Macy didn't bother mincing words.

"Your grandfather had a serious heart attack. He can't run this place alone."

"I agree."

"Then, you'll stay?"

Everett wanted to speak first with his grandfather but didn't believe Macy could be put off.

"Pop needs more than help running the ranch. He needs a skilled caregiver. Part-time, at least."

"Hire someone."

"Or I could find a good nursing home."

She stopped in her tracks. "You'd put Pop in a nursing home?"

"I don't want to."

"Really?" she scoffed. "Because it seems like you do. He's giving you the chance of a lifetime. Half ownership of this ranch. Full ownership of a horse breeding business and a championship stallion. How many cowboys on the rodeo circuit do you know who'd give anything to be in your shoes? A lot, I bet. And you're going to turn him down. Why, for heaven's sake? Because your friend needs a roping partner? A possible job? Those are lame reasons." She ground out the last part.

"I gave my word, Macy."

"Your word? When did that become something important to you?"

Her remark cut deep. Deservedly so.

"Or is it only your promises to Brody that you can easily break?" she asked.

"I'm sorry."

Perhaps he shouldn't have told her. But she'd been desperate for a recounting of Brody's last words, and Everett had wanted to comfort her.

"Forget it," she said. "There's nothing you have to say that I want to hear." Without warning, she whirled on him. "But there's something *you* need to hear. If you attempt to sell the ranch, I'm going to do everything in my power to fight you. Not just because Pop deserves more than to be dumped in a nursing home. The collective, and that includes myself, have invested their hard-earned money in the mares. As head, it's my duty to protect our investment. And if we need to hire an attorney to enforce our agreement, we will."

Everett watched her load Joey into the pickup truck and then drive past him on her way out. He had no doubt, if pushed, she would carry out her threat.

"MORNING, SONNY. How'd you sleep?" Pop greeted Everett the next day with a wide grin and a steaming cup of black coffee.

"Not bad."

Everett didn't want to admit he'd slept poorly, spending the night kicking blankets and staring at the ceiling.

His restlessness had nothing to do with the guest room's ancient, saggy mattress and everything to do with his mind's refusal to shut off. Events from yesterday, as well as the past, had replayed over and over like a video on an endless loop.

With, at most, four hours of sleep, Everett found himself easing into the early morning rather than charging full steam ahead. A long shower had marginally revived him. Enough he could fake it and not dim Pop's jovial mood.

Falling into a chair at the kitchen table where Pop had set his coffee, he took a long whiff. It smelled like heaven.

"Better quality sleep than in your truck, I reckon." Pop chuckled.

"A lot better."

Everett had spent plenty of nights zipped into a sleeping bag and wedged between his saddle and equipment trunk. He wouldn't miss that part of professional rodeoing when he retired.

"Thought I might've heard you tossing and turning." Pop stood at the stove where he scrambled eggs in a skillet. "No surprise, considering things didn't go so well with Macy yesterday."

"No, they didn't."

He and Pop hadn't talked after she left. Not about her or the collective or Everett taking over the horse breeding business. He'd needed time to process. Pop seemed to have sensed that and had chosen to avoid the subject. Instead, Everett had spent yesterday afternoon repairing a break in the pasture fence so that Champ and the mares could be let out during the day for some exercise.

Not together, of course. Everett had released Champ when he finished, and the stallion galloped from one end of the three-acre pasture to the other before slowing to a trot, his long mane and tail flying in the breeze. Pop had tried to hide his misty eyes and claimed watching the stallion was better for his ailing heart than any of the pills in his medicine cabinet.

Maybe he was right. There had been a spring in his step for the rest of the day.

As opposed to Everett's feet, which had dragged. If he was to put Pop in a nursing home, there would never again be days when the old man could watch his beloved horse run loose, his hooves kicking up dirt. Everett's actions would put an end to that. One more reason he'd been awake half the night.

Pop placed a heaping plate of eggs and toast in front of Everett. "Eat up. Folks from the collective will be here soon. They like to get an early start." He sat across from

Everett, his own plate holding smaller portions. "That way, they have the rest of Saturday for themselves and their families."

"How long do they usually stay?" Everett took a bite of eggs. "Thanks, by the way. These are good."

"Depends on how much work's to be done and how many of them show up. They don't all come at the same time. The Hays are seldom here. The feed store keeps them busy. They send a delivery truck every couple of weeks with a load of alfalfa and grain. They give me a discount on feed for Champ."

"Macy mentioned that."

"They're good people. Everyone in the collective is. I hate to admit it, but they saved me from going bankrupt."

Pop's honesty surprised Everett.

"I could have lost this place," he continued, his expression sobering. "Then where would I have been? In some county-run old folks' home for people with no money and nothing to leave to my daughters and grandchildren. The ranch I spent my whole life building would belong to a stranger."

"You made the right decision."

Pop had saved his ranch. Except, with only his social security for income and the breeding business at a standstill, he'd be in the same financial straits before long. Property taxes and insurance were due in two months. The collective's resources were limited. Their bailout was a onetime deal.

Everett needed to convince his grandfather to sell the ranch on his terms. If not, the county or the court could force the sale.

Pop stabbed a clump of eggs with his fork. So much for his jovial mood. "We're on the same page, then."

"I'm going to be here a week," Everett said. "Maybe ten days. We've got some time to come up with a plan."

"A plan that includes you staying on?"

He recalled Macy's final words to him yesterday about doing everything in her power to fight him. "What about hiring a nurse?"

"A nurse? I'm not an invalid."

Everett tried a different tactic. "Me staying is an option. But it's not the only one."

"It's the only one that makes sense." Pop pushed his half-eaten breakfast aside. He wouldn't regain any of his lost weight at this rate.

"I told Rusty I'd be his roping partner at the Big Timber Rodeo in Tucson, and that he could count on me."

"You can go and come back."

True. Everett could. But he'd have to leave Wickenburg again right away. If not, he'd risk not qualifying for Nationals and losing out on the nice signing bonus with the Oklahoma Twisters.

He chewed slowly and swallowed, his appetite also waning. "I made a commitment with the rodeo club. I signed an employment contract."

"I bet they'd understand if you told them why you changed your mind. No one would begrudge you taking over a family business. Heck, they'd probably respect you."

"I'm not sure about that, Pop. They're depending on me."

"I'm depending on you."

"I could run the breeding business into the ground. Leave you worse off than you are now."

Pop frowned. "What's the real reason? You can't fool me, sonny. This have something to do with Macy? Nothing's been right between you two since Brody died."

His grandfather had always been astute, and Everett

considered coming clean. Pop might understand and have some good advice to offer. Then again, he could accuse Everett of being selfish and thinking only of himself.

Why was he such a coward? He regularly climbed onto the back of a one-ton bucking bull without the slightest hesitation. Yet he couldn't bring himself to live in the same town as the woman whose life he'd ruined. A woman who, when they were seventeen, he'd adored and was later brokenhearted when his family moved away.

At eighteen, he'd returned to Wickenburg only to learn she was dating his best childhood pal. Everett had stepped aside, choosing to keep two friends rather than lose them, even serving as Brody's best man when he and Macy wed. He'd believed life had turned out as it was meant to be. And then he and Brody were struck by an oncoming vehicle traveling eighty miles an hour. Had Everett been driving, as he should have been, that might not have happened.

"I'm not a smart man," Pop said.

"That isn't true."

"Not book smart, anyway." He rested his forearms on the table and studied Everett. "But I've always been good at reading folks. Your grandma had some fancy word for it. I just like to think I pay attention." His wizened expression softened. "You're hurtin', sonny. Losing Brody was hard on you. And, maybe, you walking away from that crash with no more'n a few broken bones and bruises left you feeling bad and wondering why you were spared and he wasn't."

A jagged pain tore through Everett's chest. When he spoke, his voice sounded like sandpaper on wood. "They call it survivor's guilt."

Pop snorted. "More of them fancy words. But I'd say that sums it up." He sipped his coffee. "The accident wasn't your fault. Or Brody's. That other driver changed lanes when he should've stayed put."

"I…" Everett started to say he was supposed to be the one driving. It had been his turn. "I was napping in the back seat. If I'd been in the front seat with Brody or behind the wheel, then maybe—"

"You'd have died with him? You think that's what he'd want? What Macy would want?"

"No." But given the choice, she might have wished her husband survived and not his friend. "She misses Brody. And seeing me is a constant reminder."

"That girl is a lot stronger than you give her credit for, and a lot more practical. She has a son to raise. She doesn't waste time drowning in regrets or running away from guilt."

Pop was right. He did pay a lot of attention to people. He certainly had Everett pegged.

They both went silent at the sound of a vehicle driving past the kitchen window.

"Looks like the collective is arriving." Pop shoveled the last of his breakfast into his mouth.

Everett did the same, washing it down with his remaining coffee. He then gathered their dishes and carried them to the sink. "You cooked. I'll clean up."

"Fair enough." Pop ambled to the kitchen door where he tucked in his shirt and hitched up his jeans. "See ya outside."

Once he'd left, Everett checked the window, relieved to see the small compact car that had arrived didn't belong to Macy. He needed time to consider and reconsider his conversation with Pop before facing her.

CHAPTER THREE

ONCE THE DISHES were done, Everett retrieved his favorite cowboy hat from the guest room. This one had a handmade leather band with silver-and-turquoise conchos. When he competed, he stuck a turkey feather in the band for luck. He wondered if he'd need that today with Macy.

By the time he reached the mare barn, Pop informed Everett that another of the collective members had arrived—Sheriff Andy. The retired real estate broker was in the back, distributing salt blocks among the mares.

"Hello, Everett!" Kinsley Karston came from the direction of the stallion quarters, pushing a wheelbarrow with a scoop shovel balanced across the top. She must have been cleaning Champ's stall. "Welcome home."

"Hey, Kinsley. Thanks. How's school going?"

"Oh, I graduated last year." They talked a moment before she headed into the mare barn, the wheelbarrow bumping over the uneven ground.

Everett watched her go. He remembered her as a shy and quirky art student with pink hair and an abundance of piercings and who worked part-time in the local craft store. She'd swapped the pink hair for long auburn locks streaked with purple and lost a few of her piercings, along with her shyness.

Wandering over to where Pop occupied the same rocking chair as yesterday, he sat down and in a low voice said, "She grew up."

"Done well for herself, too." Pop wiped his perspiring brow with a red handkerchief, which he then pocketed. "Makes a lot of money selling those metal sculptures of hers in the tourist shops."

"Sculptures?"

"Animals, mostly. Horses. Wolves. Eagles. Roadrunners. Dang things are half as tall as you and cost a small fortune. Doesn't stop people from buying them to put in their front yards or gardens. She won some sort of up-and-coming artist award last fall. Really boosted her sales."

"I was wondering how she had enough money to buy into the collective."

"Talented gal. And a hard worker."

Sheriff Andy emerged from the back of the mare barn after that. Everett got up to introduce himself. The retiree had moved to Wickenburg ten years ago, and he and Everett had never crossed paths.

"Mr. Gleason. Good to meet you." He extended his hand. The salt-and-pepper-haired man did indeed resemble the iconic character from the 1960s sitcom, just like Macy had said, though much older.

"Same here, Everett. I heard you were coming home." He returned the handshake. "And call me Sheriff Andy. Everyone does. Used to have it printed on my business cards back when I was selling real estate."

"Thanks for helping out my grandfather."

"Are you kidding? Glad to do it. The mares were too good of an investment to walk away from. Their foals will bring a pretty penny one day." He tipped his head in Pop's direction. "I've asked your grandfather a dozen times to let me help him sell this ranch. I'm convinced he can get a good price. But he's turned me down every time. Have to respect a man who knows his mind."

Everett nodded, thinking he would file that piece of

information away for later should he convince Pop to sell and move. *When* he convinced Pop.

"Sheriff Andy also handles the collective's finances," Kinsley said. "He's real good at that."

"I try to be useful."

"What can I do to help the two of you?" Everett asked.

Just then, Macy's white pickup drove onto the ranch. She parked behind the mare barn, alongside Kinsley's compact car and Sheriff Andy's luxury sedan.

Everett tensed. He cautioned himself to behave normally and let her take the lead.

Sheriff Andy clapped him on the back, startling him. "You go about your business. There are plenty of us here to handle what needs doing."

"All right. In that case, Pop, I'm going to get busy."

"Kinsley already fed Champ this morning, and I gave him a salt block."

"Good to know."

Everett started toward the stallion quarters. The storeroom was a mess. He intended to start there. Glancing over his shoulder, he noticed Macy watching him. He nodded. She continued walking without acknowledging him, lugging her medical case and with Joey dashing ahead of her as usual.

Okay. It was going to be like that. Everett didn't blame her. He wondered what she'd think of his conversation with Pop over breakfast.

After two visits in two days, Champ was not only accustomed to seeing Everett, he eagerly trotted out from his stall into the paddock, issuing a friendly nickering that turned into a foot-stomping demand for attention.

"Hey, boy. How you doing this morning?"

Everett went through the supply of equine vitamin and mineral supplements in the storeroom and chose two. He added them to a small bucket of grain, the only way Champ would willingly take the supplements. While the stallion munched away, Everett located a screwdriver and tightened the hinges on the paddock gate. Standing back, he surveyed the results, satisfied one less thing on his grandfather's ranch sagged.

Next, he removed pieces of jagged glass from a broken window, swept the aisle with a push broom and nailed down a half dozen loose boards before someone, namely Pop, tripped. When he'd finished all that, he cleaned Champ's hooves and followed that with a thorough brushing.

Periodically, he'd stop in his work and watch Macy, Kinsley and Sheriff Andy. The three collective members seemed to have an established routine and got along well. Joey was in high spirits and amused himself by collecting rocks. Like yesterday, Pop was keeping an eye on the boy. Everett suspected this was a normal occurrence whenever Macy and Joey were there and the reason why Pop had hurried outside right after breakfast. He liked both the company the collective members offered and feeling useful in some small way.

Everett observed Macy returning the medical case to her truck. There, she leaned against the hood and entered information into an electronic tablet. Probably tracking the mares' progress and making notes on their health.

Between caring for the collective's mares, her job at the clinic, vet tech classes and raising Joey, Everett doubted she had much free time. Maybe that was how she coped with her grief.

If so, he understood. He hadn't taken a single break from competing since returning to the rodeo circuit after Brody's death. His schedule provided a convenient reason to avoid returning to Wickenburg and obsessing about the accident.

Finishing writing a list for the hardware store, he decided to quit hiding and ask Macy if she wanted to turn any of the mares out into the pasture. She may be hiding from him, too, but this was business. Giving Champ a goodbye pat on the neck, he started toward the mare barn. At the same moment, another vehicle drove past the house and stopped near where Pop sat.

The collective apparently had a latecomer. Strangely, none of the other members made a move to go over and greet the young woman dressed in scrubs. Not even Macy, who merely offered a distracted hello.

Pop, on the other hand, pushed to his feet with the most vigor and enthusiasm he'd displayed since Everett's return. A broad grin lit his face and took ten years off his haggard features.

"Morning!" he called, a lilt in his voice, and skirted around Joey who played on the ground with his rock pile.

"Hi, Pop." The woman, an apparent health-care worker, opened the SUV's front passenger door in order to assist her unsteady occupant—an elderly woman whose braided white hair reached the middle of her back. At the sight of Pop, her pleasant countenance brightened, much like his did at the sight of her.

Everett ground to a halt, confused by what he was witnessing. He hadn't seen his grandfather this glad to see someone other than family in years.

Suddenly, Macy was beside him. "That's Susan Meyer and her granddaughter Callie. She helps with Susan's care."

"Are they more members of the collective?"

"Oh, no." Macy laughed. "She and Pop are, well, they're sweethearts."

Everett turned to stare at her. "That's impossible."

"Why?"

"Pop doesn't… He wouldn't…" Everett blew out a breath. He honestly didn't know what to say. His grandfather had a girlfriend?

IF MACY WASN'T still mad at Everett, she might have been amused by his surprise and confusion at learning his grandfather was dating. Although, Macy didn't think the elderly pair did much more than hang out together, swap stories about the good old days, discuss their long list of medical complaints and share the latest updates on their extensive families.

Still, they were adorable together. And if all they got out of the relationship was tender companionship, she saw nothing wrong with that. In her opinion, both of them had been widowed for years and were fortunate to have found someone.

Unlike Macy, who had zero intention of dating again. She was satisfied with dedicating her life to raising her son. She owed Joey that. She owed Brody that, too. Especially after the horrible things she'd said to him.

God, if she could only take back their last conversation. All the wishing and tears in the world hadn't changed the fact she'd argued with her husband mere hours before his death, accusing him of being selfish and not caring about her and the baby they'd have in five months' time.

Her throat closed. She couldn't swallow. *Breathe in, breathe out. That's it.*

"How long have they been seeing each other?" Everett asked from beside her.

They continued to stand there, eyes glued to Pop and Susan. Her granddaughter and nurse, Callie Hughes, helped her to the rocking chairs where she and Pop sat down.

Macy found her throat had relaxed, allowing her to

speak. "A while. Before his heart attack. She was so cute, visiting him with us in the hospital."

"He never told me when I visited after his heart attack." Or Mom and Aunt Laurel who had stayed with him for several weeks while he recovered. His mom would have surely told Everett. "They mentioned friends dropping by. No one named Susan."

Macy considered. "Maybe he worried you and your family would be upset and think he was betraying your grandmother."

"We wouldn't think that. We loved Grandma and always will. But she's been gone almost ten years. If Pop has found someone who makes him happy, then we'd support him."

"Good. Because Susan's a really sweet lady. You'll like her. She had a mild stroke a few months ago. I guess she and Pop have recent health crises in common."

"Does she live with Callie?" he asked.

"She has a bungalow in one of those senior independent living communities. Callie drops by every couple of days and takes her to appointments or shopping."

Everett continued to stare, his puzzled expression turning contemplative. For her part, Macy contemplated *him*.

"Are you thinking Susan is the reason he refuses to sell the ranch?" she asked.

"She's gotta be one of the reasons. Pop has always been independent. He hates appearing weak and helpless, which is how living in a nursing facility would make him feel. Especially in front of a woman he cares for. He couldn't stand that."

"Then don't move him."

"But Pop needs help. More every day. What kind of grandson would I be if I left him alone to run the ranch and he had another heart attack, this one fatal? Or he fell, broke his hip and lay on the floor for two days?"

"Then don't leave."

He groaned.

"There are plenty of people coming and going who check on Pop," Macy insisted.

"There are also eldercare facilities in Wickenburg. Some decent ones, from what I researched online."

"You said yourself Pop would be miserable in a nursing home," Macy pleaded. "You can't do that to him."

Everett tensed. "I appreciate your concern and your help. I do. Pop would have lost the ranch without you and the collective." He faced her then. "But his care and what happens to the ranch aren't your concerns. They're my family's. Mine, most of all, because my mom and aunt are depending on me, and Pop asked me here."

Hurt, Macy drew back. Perhaps she had crossed the line a little. But that was no reason for him to put her in her place so firmly.

"Sorry," she muttered.

"No, I am. This is a lot to deal with all at once."

"It's okay." She blamed the residual emotions lingering between them. "And not to nag, but he does have a legal agreement with the collective."

"Which will be honored one way or the other. Either by buying you out or transferring Pop's interest to the new owner of the ranch. I won't let him default on your agreement."

Macy frowned. Everett sounded so businesslike. Which, yes, the collective's agreement with Pop was business. But it was also personal. Didn't Everett realize that?

Maybe he did, for he added, "If it comes to that."

"You're right. It's not my place to tell you what to do. But there must be another solution besides selling the ranch and putting Pop in a nursing home."

"Don't think this isn't hard for me, Macy. It is. I hate

seeing Pop old and sick. It rips my heart in two. He was always so strong and capable and no one smarter when it came to horses. There wasn't a green colt he couldn't break or a piece of machinery he couldn't fix. Not a problem he couldn't solve with hard work and determination. I wanted to be just like him when I was a kid. Heck, I still do. People love him."

"They do. He's the salt of the earth. Kind. Friendly."

Everett chuckled dryly. "And I'm not."

"You used to be, Everett." *You could be again*, she silently added.

"Things changed."

Her throat tightened again. "For all of us."

He reached for her, only to let his hand drop.

She stared at it. "What happened? We used to be close. If I was in trouble and Brody was unavailable, all I had to do was call, and you came. Did I do something to upset you?"

He refused to meet her gaze. "You didn't do anything. It's me."

"You act like you hate me."

"I don't hate you, Macy."

"Am I the reason you've stayed away?"

"No."

He answered much too quickly for her to believe him. The hurt from earlier hit her again, twice as hard. Something had happened. He just wasn't ready or willing to tell her.

She wished he'd let her in. Healing from loss didn't happen overnight. She could attest to that. But pushing away your friends didn't alleviate grief, only deepened it. She could attest to that, too.

"Would you have come home if you'd known about your grandfather's tax situation?" she asked.

"Would me coming home have changed anything? Even if I'd had the money to pay the back taxes and insurance, Pop wouldn't have let me."

"It's not always about money."

"You're right."

"Your grandfather needed his family."

"I'm here now," he answered stiffly.

"Not for long."

Macy reminded herself to resist being judgmental, that family dynamics were frequently complicated. She'd been a teenager the summer she and Everett had dated, and she didn't know his mom well. She'd met his aunt briefly for the first time when she and Everett's mom came out after Pop's heart attack.

Did Everett visit his parents in Santa Fe? Or did he avoid them like he did his grandfather? Why did Macy even care?

For Pop's sake, she told herself. She was fond of the old man. He reminded her a little of her beloved late grandfather, whom she missed.

Everett reminded her a little of Brody. No, that wasn't right. They'd been best friends and rodeo partners, but it was more than that. Being in his company evoked memories. Most, she cherished. Some, she wished she could forget.

"Sonny." Pop beckoned to Everett. "Come on over. There's someone I want you to meet."

"Excuse me." Everett tugged on his hat and retreated.

Macy blinked at the sudden sting of tears. Where had those come from? Mad at herself, she wiped at them with the hem of her T-shirt, ready to claim allergies if someone questioned her.

Thankfully, the collective members were busy finishing their chores: cleaning the stalls, pouring sacks of grain into the feed barrels, cleaning tack and grooming. Macy had given each mare an exam, monitoring their progress and noting it in her charts. To her relief, Roxie had shown no further signs of colic.

"Mommy, Mommy. Look-it." Joey raced over from his nearby pile of rocks, holding out his cupped hands. "I found a snake."

"A snake?" Macy forgot about Everett and their difficult conversation. "Joey, drop it now!"

Snakes were common in the desert, including rattlers. What if her sweet little boy was bitten? Venom would be deadly for someone of his small size.

"No. Look-it." He reached her and opened his cupped hands.

Macy nearly fainted—with relief. Joey had presented her with a yellow-and-black caterpillar. Not a snake.

"Oh, honey." She knelt in front of him. "You scared Mommy. That's a caterpillar. Like in the book Mommy reads you, *The Very Hungry Caterpillar*."

"Can I keep it?"

"I wish we could, but we can't. He needs to eat lots of leaves so he can turn into a butterfly." More likely, given they lived in the desert, this little fellow would transform into a moth. Macy didn't bother to explain the difference to Joey. At his age, he wouldn't understand. "Let's put him over there on that bush. Lots of green, juicy leaves for him to eat."

"I'm gonna call him Stinky."

"Okay." The name Macy used with Joey when she was trying to get him to take a bath. "That's good." They walked together to the leafy bush, which Macy hoped was edible to this species of caterpillar. "Put him on a leaf." She pointed.

Joey did, remarkably careful for a small child. Stinky

clung to the leaf, unmoving except for his wiggling back end. Or was that his front end? Macy let her son watch. After a few minutes, he grew bored.

"I'm thirsty, Mommy."

"Me, too."

She took Joey's hand. At the truck, she removed a water bottle for herself and an organic apple juice for him.

"I wanna open it." He reached up with his hands, fingers extended.

"What do you say?"

"Please."

She handed him the squeeze bottle of juice, and he twisted off the plastic cap. While they both wet their whistles, Macy glanced over at Everett, Pop and Susan. Her granddaughter Callie was readying to leave. She did that sometimes, left her grandmother with Pop while she ran errands or visited one of her home health-care clients.

Why, Macy wondered as the nurse drove away, hadn't she suggested Callie's employer to Everett as a possible solution for Pop's care? Granted, convincing him might take some doing. But Pop knew Callie and had a connection to her through her grandmother.

Unless that made it worse. Pop might resist having someone he knew assisting with his personal needs as tasks like showering and dressing became more difficult. Telling him that Callie was a professional wouldn't make a difference. Not with someone as stubborn as Pop.

How would he fare in a nursing home? Despite receiving training, even the most patient caregivers wearied of grumpy, uncooperative residents, and Pop could be grumpy.

Macy smiled as Pop captured Susan's hand and flashed her a besotted smile. His lady friend beamed in return. Too bad, if Everett did convince Pop to move, they couldn't re-side in the same nursing home. That would make selling the ranch easier. But she had her bungalow and was every bit as independent and resistant as Pop.

Everett had located an old wooden footstool to sit on. The three of them had formed a small circle and were engaged in lively conversation. Well, Pop and Susan were lively contributors. Everett listened more than talked, his features pleasant but lacking animation.

Giving her head a dismal shake, Macy chided herself for what amounted to spying. The thing was, she cared about Pop and Susan and, yes, Everett.

What was she not seeing? He and Brody had been like brothers. They were together the last moments of Brody's life. That had to have been difficult on Everett. Did he suffer from PTSD? Perhaps. And just because she'd made progress dealing with her loss didn't mean Everett had made progress dealing with his.

Returning home, seeing her, must be stirring up all kinds of unwanted feelings he'd avoid given the choice. Which would also explain why he wanted to sell the ranch and leave Wickenburg as quickly as possible.

She sighed. Such a complicated man.

"Come on, honey." She took Joey's empty juice container. "Let's head home. Mommy needs to finish her chores before lunch." Putting their discarded bottles in the truck, she thought about the overflowing dirty laundry hamper, myriad of toys strewn throughout the house and the chapters she needed to read before her next online class. "First, let's say goodbye to everyone."

Joey bounded over to Pop. "We're going home, Pop. Bye."

"You're not leaving already." Pop braced his hands on the rocking chair armrests and struggled to rise, his knees wobbling. "What about lunch?"

Macy wasn't the only one who noticed his unsteadiness.

Everett did, too, and concern knit his brow. The older man had good and bad days. A lot of activity and people put a burden on his heart and tired him. He should probably rest. But he wouldn't. Not until the collective and his lady friend left. At the least, he should get out of the heat. A late monsoon season had sent the humidity soaring, and anyone with a lick of sense stayed indoors enjoying air-conditioned comfort.

"We'll eat at home." Macy thought Pop was referring to her sometimes bringing food for her and Joey.

"Nonsense," he said. "Susan and I are fixin' egg salad sandwiches for everyone. There's plenty."

"Oh, no. That's too much trouble."

Susan gestured to the soft-sided cooler on the barn floor beside her. "I already made the egg salad and brought bread. We just have to throw the sandwiches together."

Pop gave her shoulder an affectionate squeeze. "I have plenty of potato chips and a big jar of sweet pickles. Thought we'd eat early, about eleven, since most everyone needs to get going."

Eleven was an hour away.

Joey tugged on Macy's hand. "I'm hungry. I wanna sandwich."

"I'm not sure…"

"You could take Joey *r-i-d-i-n-g*." Susan spelled out the last word.

She and Pop gazed at Macy with such hope in their eyes. Yet she held out, caving only when Everett spoke.

"Isn't egg salad your favorite?"

He remembered.

Not exactly an invitation, but near enough.

"Fine, but we can't stay late." She really had a mountain of laundry waiting for her. Weekends were never long enough.

"Wonderful." Susan clapped her hands.

Joey, too.

The hard lines bracketing Everett's mouth relaxed, and for reasons Macy couldn't explain, she was glad she'd decided to stay.

CHAPTER FOUR

MACY WASN'T LEAVING. Everett couldn't decide if he was glad or annoyed. Maybe a little of both. As much as she frustrated him, he liked being with her. More than he should.

Some advance warning about making lunch for the collective members might have been nice. Was that a regular Saturday thing or was Susan's visit the reason?

And speaking of Susan, why hadn't Pop mentioned her? No reason to keep their relationship a secret. She was a charming lady who seemed as fond of Pop as he was of her. Like Macy had said, they were a cute couple. And Everett would feel like a heel if putting Pop in a nursing home somehow caused him to end their relationship.

But Pop struggled to take care of himself. Here it was only midmorning, and he appeared ready to collapse. He may reach a point where he had mobility limitations. Or require heart surgery, followed by a lengthy rehab period.

But then again, here they were, planning on making lunch for everyone and grinning from ear to ear. Quality of life mattered, Everett supposed. Still, that didn't stop him from worrying about his grandfather.

Relaxing his features, he focused on the conversation between Pop and Susan. The two were comparing their different arthritis treatments.

In the mare barn, Kinsley and Sheriff Andy continued working up a sweat, though both had taken breaks to talk on their phones. Everett noticed the first few stalls had received a fresh coat of wood sealer, thanks to Kinsley. Sheriff Andy had repaired three saddle racks, showing himself as capable with a hammer and nails as he'd apparently once been with buying and selling real estate.

Engrossed in each other, Pop and Susan all but ignored Everett. Pushing to his feet, he placed the footstool out of the way where no one would trip over it. He considered seeking out Macy only to veto that idea. She'd tied one of the mares to the hitching rail and, given the way Joey skipped up and down the barn aisle, she planned to take him on that ride Susan had suggested.

"You going to be okay, Pop?" he asked.

"Susan and I are heading inside." His grandfather stood and then helped Susan up.

She showered him with a warm smile, which she then turned on Everett. "I'm so glad we finally got the chance to meet. Your grandfather talks about you all the time. He's so proud of you and your rodeo career."

Everett hadn't thought it possible, but he now felt like an even bigger heel. She really was a nice lady. "A pleasure to meet you, too, ma'am."

As the elderly pair ambled toward the house hand in hand, another vehicle drove onto the ranch. Pop saluted as the car passed him and Susan. It then continued to the mare barn where it slowed to a stop. Everett decided the place was beginning to resemble a parking lot. Another regular occurrence?

He didn't recognize either the driver or the passenger and assumed one of them was a collective member. From the rearview mirror, a handicapped parking placard dangled. Before he could wonder about that, the front doors opened, and a gray-haired woman emerged from the driver's side. She immediately hurried around the car to assist her passenger, an unsteady gentleman brandishing a cane.

At the sound of a horse's hooves, Everett spun to see Macy leading a sleek sorrel with an almost perfect white diamond in the center of her face. Joey sat atop the mare, holding on to a strap attached to a bareback pad.

"Look-it, Mommy." Joey wiggled his legs, his face brimming with glee. "I'm galloping."

Macy and the horse walked out of the barn and into the open. "Yes, you are, honey. Hold tight. Don't fall."

Disregarding his mom's warning, Joey leaned forward and hugged the mare's neck with one arm, his cheek pressed against the springy mane. "You're a good horsie."

Everett watched, momentarily speechless. How proud Brody would have been to witness his young son riding, even if he was just being led around by his mom on a docile broodmare.

Macy stopped beside Everett, bringing the past forward to collide with the present. "That's Glynnis Pottinger and her brother Abel."

"I should have recognized him." Everett tore his gaze away from Macy and studied their newest visitor. "He and Pop are old friends."

"Don't feel bad. He has Parkinson's disease. It's taken a toll on him and left him gaunt."

"A lot of that going around. Pop lost so much weight after his heart attack, I hardly recognized him."

She started to speak, only to clamp her mouth shut.

"You're right," Everett said, guessing at what was on the tip of her tongue. "If I had come home more often, the sight of him wouldn't have been such a shock."

Macy nodded. "Well, you're here now."

"Yeah. To take away everything that's important to him."

She touched Everett's arm and stared at him in earnest with those expressive brown eyes of hers. "You won't."

"What if there's no choice?"

"There's always a choice. But don't decide today. Give it a week."

He wouldn't lie. He enjoyed the sensation of her fingers against his skin. It wasn't the first time she'd touched him in a casual way. It was, however, the first time since their breakup years ago he'd felt a small zing course through him.

That was a shocker. From the day he'd returned to Wickenburg after graduation to now, Everett had never considered Macy anything other than Brody's girlfriend and then, later, his wife. This...attraction was new. And unsettling.

"I wanna go faster, Mommy," Joey insisted.

Everett shifted, and Macy's hand fell away. Good. The last thing he wanted was to give her the wrong impression.

"Will you?" Macy asked. "Give it a week?"

"Yeah. I can do that." His temples throbbed. So much had happened in the last twenty-four hours.

Abel Pottinger came just in time, distracting him from his thoughts. "Everett," he called. "My word. Is that you?"

"Excuse me." Everett dipped his head at Macy.

"No worries. I have a little cowboy who's raring to ride." She walked off, leading Joey on the docile mare.

Everett made his way over to greet his grandfather's friend. "Mr. Pottinger. It's good to see you, sir."

They shook hands. Abel's trembled uncontrollably.

"Now, now." He scoffed. "I reckon you're old enough to call me Abel."

"How are you?"

"Been better." He laughed good-naturedly. "Been worse. You remember my sister, Glynnis?"

"I do." He also shook hands with the woman whose resemblance to her brother couldn't be denied—though she was easily ten years younger and a foot shorter. The three exchanged small talk for several minutes.

"Well, I need to get going," she told her brother. "Can I trust you to stay out of trouble?"

Abel made a shooing motion with his free hand, the one not holding the cane. "You run your errands. I'll be fine. Pop texted me and said he and Susan are fixing lunch."

Texted him? When, Everett wondered, had Pop started texting? Or Abel? He grinned to himself, picturing the two old men sitting around texting each other. It was kind of funny.

"All right. I'll be back in an hour and a half. Promise me you won't overdo it." Glynnis gave his shoulder an affectionate pat and then hurried off.

"She's such a mother hen," Abel said as his sister drove away.

"She loves you." Everett wasn't sure how to ask without sounding offensive, so he just asked, "Can I help you sit?"

"I have a better idea."

"What's that?"

"I tag along with you. If you're up to some company."

"All right." Everett nodded. "I'm heading to the stallion quarters."

"Very good. I'll supervise while we catch up." Abel laughed again.

"I need to grab some tools and supplies."

"I'll meet you there."

"You sure?" Everett had his doubts about the older gentleman's ability to travel the uneven ground between the mare barn and the stallion quarters. "If you can wait a couple minutes, I'll just—"

"I'll be fine."

Abel started out walking at a sedate pace, relying heavily on his cane. Everett watched him, wondering if he shouldn't have gone along just to make sure there was no mishap. He didn't leave to fetch the tools and supplies in the mare barn until Abel had safely reached the paddock where he stopped to pet Champ.

Nearby, Kinsley was finishing up with the wood sealer. She had to leave right after lunch to work on a metal sculpture for a client and would return to complete the project another day.

"Take whatever." She made an expansive gesture. "The collective covers all of Champ's stuff, too. That's part of the deal we have with Pop."

"Thanks." Everett gathered what he needed. "Is Abel part of the collective, too? I know Glynnis is."

"Nah. She brings Abel by on Saturdays so he can get out of the house for a while." Kinsley flashed a dimpled smile. "We consider him an honorary member."

Everett hesitated, not wanting his question to be taken wrong. "Is he okay? Getting around the ranch by himself?"

"As long as he's not climbing fences or digging ditches."

"Okay." Everett felt a little reassured. On his way out, he asked, "Is lunch a regular thing around here?"

Kinsley paused in her cleaning and leaned on the push broom. "Pretty much. We all take turns and keep things simple. I'm vegan and always bring chickpea wraps. Everyone eats them, but I'm pretty sure nobody really likes them." She laughed. "I told Pop changing to a vegan diet would be good for his heart. He's not convinced."

"You're fighting a losing battle with him."

She resumed sweeping. "I'm not giving up yet."

Everett sensed the genuine fondness Kinsley and all the collective members he'd met had for Pop. His grandfather was lucky to have the companionship of these people on a daily basis. Another thing he'd lose if he went to live in a nursing home.

At the stallion quarters, Everett found Abel inside. The sun was heating up by the minute, and he'd probably wanted to get some shade.

"You ready to start supervising?" he asked.

"You betcha."

Abel proved to be good company indeed and a decent helper despite his tremors. He was also something of a gossip.

"Your grandpa is a fortunate man. I had my eye on the gorgeous Miss Susan for some time. Pop beat me out."

"Can you hand me a rag?" Everett bent over and applied wide swatches of wood sealer to the stall door with a paint brush. Inside the stall, Champ paced back and forth, snorting and shaking his big head. He disliked the strong smell of the sealer and was letting Everett know exactly how much. After a moment, he trotted through the connecting doorway to the paddock outside.

"Here you go." Abel passed Everett a rag and continued with his story. "They met at the senior center. Susan and I have been attending events there for a while. I dragged Pop along with me one day. This was before his heart attack." The older gentleman sighed. "The pair of them locked eyes, and that was that. The rest of us fellows didn't stand a chance with her."

"Looks like you two are still friends."

"Are you kidding? She wasn't interested in me to begin with. Gotta accept what you can't change. Besides, your grandfather is the only one willing to put up with my shenanigans."

The next hour flew by. Everett caught several glances of Macy and Joey on the horse. Parkinson's disease clearly didn't interfere with Abel's eyesight, for he noticed Everett noticing Macy.

"She's doing well," he said. "All things considered. Raising that boy. Working at the vet clinic. Going to school. Donating her time to the collective. Staying busy is how some people keep the sad memories away."

Everett wanted to ask Abel if he was referring just to Macy or him, too.

"It upset her when you didn't come home after Brody's funeral. She needed you."

"I know." Everett stood, his back aching as well as his heart. "I'm a jerk."

"Maybe things can change now that you're back."

"We'll see."

"She's fond of you. Always has been."

"The feeling's mutual."

"Is it?" Abel grinned. "Because the way you've been watching her, I was thinking your feelings run a mite deeper."

"No," Everett insisted. "Strictly platonic with us."

"You sure about that?"

"Hey, Everett. Abel." Macy appeared at the entrance to the stallion quarters. She had Joey in tow but no horse. At some point she'd removed her ball cap, and her blond hair hung loose around her shoulders. "Lunch is ready."

Everett couldn't move. All he could do was stare. She'd always been pretty. But three years and motherhood had given her a mature beauty.

"Come inside. We're waiting on you," she said and then was gone.

His pulse beat faster. His nerves hummed. Had she heard his and Abel's conversation? What would he say if she confronted him?

Abel took a step, using his cane for support. "We'd better skedaddle. Can't keep your strictly platonic *friend* waiting."

Everett obviously needed to work on hiding his emotions.

MACY STOPPED ALONG the fence midway back to the house. She wasn't ready to face everyone, convinced her face would reveal what she refused to admit to herself. Her heart had pinged when she saw Everett in the stallion quarters, staring at her like she'd walked straight out of his dreams. She'd needed to escape before she embarrassed herself by staring back at him in the same way.

"Hurry, Mommy. I'm hungry."

"Sorry, honey." She bounced Joey on her hip. "I had to catch my breath for a second."

That was an understatement if she'd ever heard one. What was wrong with her? Men had given her enamored glances in the years since she lost Brody. She'd ignored them, which was easy, considering no one had interested her.

And neither did Everett. Which failed to explain the ping. What was different this time? If anything, she was still mad at him for abandoning her and Joey and considering putting Pop in a nursing home. That was not the kind of man who tempted her to share long, lingering glances.

Besides, who was she kidding? After what she'd said to Brody during their fight before he died, Macy didn't deserve happiness with *anybody*. She'd been an awful wife. A terrible person.

She'd accused him of loving rodeo more than he did her. Then, an hour later, the truck he'd been driving was struck head-on by another vehicle attempting to illegally pass. She'd never had the chance to tell him she was sorry. He'd died in the hospital before she got there.

Everett had talked to Brody in his last minutes and promised to watch over Macy and the baby. He'd told her as much, as she cried in his arms, consumed by grief and devastation. Except he'd left for good after the funeral. Far worse, he'd gotten the chance to say goodbye to Brody—a gift denied to Macy and one he'd wasted with a lie. How did he live with himself?

She'd forgiven him eventually. She'd needed to in order to move on with her life. Giving Joey the best life possible was her one and only priority now. That included growing her career by going to school and investing her money wisely, such as in the collective.

The ping from earlier turned into a stab of regret. Macy realized much of her anger at Everett was misdirected. In truth, she was mad at herself. But that didn't change the fact Everett had broken a deathbed promise to his best friend. And now he was about to disappoint his wonderful grandfather.

"Mommy." Joey dragged her name out while leaning his head way backward over her arm. Little children were so trusting. What if she dropped him? "Want down."

"Okay." She put him down, and they started walking.

One minute. That was all the time remaining to pull herself together before facing Pop, Susan and the collective. Hopefully, they'd be too busy with lunch to notice anything amiss with her.

"Where's Everett and Abel?" Kinsley asked.

She'd planted herself at the picnic table on the patio. Across from her sat Sheriff Andy, a paper plate with three sandwich halves and a massive pile of potato chips in front of him. The tall, silver-haired retiree had an appetite that belied his trim physique.

"The food will be gone if they don't get here soon," he said, taking a large bite from one of the sandwich halves.

"They're coming." Macy took Joey inside, where they filled their plates from the spread laid out on the kitchen table.

Pop gestured. "Lemonade's on the counter."

He stood beside Susan like a knight guarding his queen. She'd recovered well after her stroke several months ago, with the exception of balance issues. As a result, Pop rarely let her out of his sight whenever they were together. His devotion was sweet and, in a small way, made Macy believe in second chances.

"Got enough chips there, young man?" Pop asked Joey.

"Mmm-hmm." Joey nodded, unable to speak because of a full mouth.

The back door opened just as Macy finished pouring two lemonades. Abel entered first and then Everett. Both men removed their cowboy hats. Everett ran a hand through his wavy brown hair that he wore shorter than in years past. Macy couldn't recall ever noticing the way the ends curled at the nape of his neck.

She stifled a groan of frustration. This…whatever it was, had to stop. She had two choices. Eat inside on the family room couch—a safe but antisocial option everyone would question—or outside where Everett would likely join them.

Joey gasped. "Mommy. I spilled my potato chips."

She looked down to see half his chips on the floor. Bending, she made a cup with her hands and scooped up the mess. "It's all right. We'll get more."

Everett suddenly appeared beside him. "Here. Let me help you, partner." He took Joey's hand and led him to the table, where he lowered the bowl of chips to Joey's level. "Take what you want."

Joey gazed up at Everett with wide eyes.

"It's okay," Everett said, encouraging him.

Joey reached into the bowl and transferred three large handfuls onto his paper plate, his eyes hardly leaving Everett. Her son tended to be shy at first, though once he warmed up to someone, like Pop, for instance, he showered them with affection to the point of being a nuisance.

How would he act with Everett, should they wind up spending time together? She didn't know how much, if any, experience Everett had with children. He had no siblings, no nieces and nephews. But he could have dated a woman with children. He might even have a current girlfriend that he hadn't mentioned to anyone. Was that the real reason he was so eager to return to competing?

Macy threw away the spilled chips, her emotions awhirl. If Brody had lived, Joey would likely be treating Everett like a favorite uncle. He might also be treating him that way had Everett kept his promise to Brody. She'd wanted that. It was, in a way, another loss. An unnecessary one.

"Let Mommy carry this." She reached for Joey's plate. "You can get the door."

He scampered off.

She nodded at Everett. "Thank you."

"He's a great kid. You've done a wonderful job with him. Brody would be proud."

"I've had a lot of help. My parents. Brody's parents. Friends."

Everett showered her with a tender smile. "I remember Brody saying almost those same words once in a TV interview he gave after a big win in Texas. That he'd had a lot of help from his family and friends. And you, too."

She also remembered that interview. They'd rewatched the recorded show a dozen times. And then, later during their fateful argument, she'd claimed that recording was the only thing she had of him sometimes.

"I… I…"

Macy hurried to the door before she burst into tears. She couldn't remember a more trying lunch. She should have gone home. Was it too late?

Outside on the patio, she sat Joey at the old wooden picnic table with Sheriff Andy and Kinsley.

"You need a phone book to prop up that boy," Sheriff Andy commented. "He's too short."

"What's a phone book?" Kinsley asked.

Sheriff Andy gawked at her. "How old are you? Fifteen?"

She lifted her chin. "I'm twenty-six."

"And you don't know what a phone book is?"

"A book of phones?" she guessed.

"Good grief, girl. It's a book with everyone's phone number in it. People. Businesses. Emergencies."

She held up her cell phone and wiggled it. "I got all that in here. And a GPS. And a search engine. And I can read the newspaper." She pressed a button and aimed the phone at him. "I'm making a video of you right now."

Sheriff Andy snorted a laugh. "You can't sit on a cell phone when you're too short for the table."

Whatever relief their amusing banter had provided Macy instantly vanished when the back door opened and Everett stepped out.

"Where's Abel?" Sheriff Andy asked.

"He stayed inside to talk to Pop and Susan. They're discussing some healthy lifestyle event at the community center. Trying to decide which one of them is worse off."

"Maybe I should get in on that. I need to change my diet. My blood pressure's been off the charts lately."

Macy could relate. Hers, too.

"There's nothing wrong with you, Sheriff Andy." Kinsley rolled her eyes.

"I'm seventy-one. There's plenty wrong with me."

"Wait till you're eighty-seven, like Pop and Susan."

"God willing, I live that long."

That elicited a laugh from everyone except Joey, who didn't understand adult humor, and Macy, whose mouth refused to work because Everett chose the seat directly across from her.

He lifted the top piece of bread on one sandwich half and arranged several potato chips on the egg salad before replacing the bread. Then he took a bite. The sandwich made an audible crunch.

She stared. She'd forgotten about this quirk of his.

He chewed, his brows raised in question.

Beside her, Joey removed the top slice of bread on his sandwich half and layered several potato chips.

"Now you're teaching my son bad habits," Macy said.

"How is putting potato chips on your sandwich a bad habit?"

"Hey, it's good." Kinsley took a crunchy bite of her sandwich made with vegan bread and avocado spread. "I'm going to eat all my sandwiches with potato chips. Try it, Sheriff Andy."

He did. "Not bad."

Macy harrumphed. "You've corrupted everyone."

"Corrupted or inspired?" Everett grinned, the sparks in his eyes the first genuine ones since his return.

She felt a shift inside her. It had been like this once between them. Casual, comfortable joking around. Even after she went from being his girlfriend to being his best friend's wife. He'd treated her like a close friend.

The memory unnerved her. Macy hadn't believed herself capable of ever falling in love again. Brody had been her soulmate. People told her she'd meet someone, someday. But Everett? No. Impossible, despite their brief past.

He was still grinning at her.

"Try it, Mommy," Joey mumbled around another mouthful. Chip particles rained onto his lap. Thank goodness they were outside.

"You know what else is good on egg salad sandwiches, Joey?" Everett asked.

"What?"

"Dill pickle slices."

Joey turned to Macy, his eyes bright. "Mommy, I want dill pickles."

"Maybe next time, honey."

"I'll bring a jar." Everett reached across the table to give Joey a fist bump.

And then Macy's son did something completely unexpected and that caused her to suck in a breath. He returned Everett's fist bump and beamed at him in a way she'd once imagined Joey beaming at his father. It was hard to take, and she fought back tears. Yet, a part of her was touched by this charming interaction.

She contributed little to the conversation after that, hoping no one noticed. Everett chatted easily, making friends with Sheriff Andy and Kinsley, too.

When they were close to finishing their meals, he said, "Tell me more about the collective. I know Macy is in charge of the mares' health. She mentioned the Hays family provides feed at a discount."

"Also supplies," Kinsley chimed in.

"You handle the finances, right?" he asked Sheriff Andy.

"That I do. I keep the monthly books and file the annual tax returns. Though, at this point, we won't have any income until the foals are sold. I also worked with the attorney in drawing up our partnership agreements and creating the LLC."

"Partnership agreements? As in more than one?"

Sheriff Andy nodded. "There's the agreement the members of the collective have with each other and the one the collective has with Pop."

"Right." Everett nodded.

"I handle our social media accounts and website," Kinsley added. "But mostly, we're manual labor. Though, with all of us, the work gets spread out."

"Do you ever disagree?"

"Not often." Kinsley hitched a thumb at Sheriff Andy. "He's a pretty good mediator."

The older man chuckled. "It's easy when everybody's nice and wants the business to succeed."

"Business?" Everett asked.

"Yes, indeed. We all love Pop, but none of us are in this just for fun or to do a friend a favor. We expect to earn a return on our investment. A decent one, at that."

"Makes sense."

"But we won't earn that return on our investment if we have to move the mares and pay a hefty board fee to a different facility. This arrangement works, for all of us, because of our agreement with Pop."

Everett sat back, appearing to contemplate that last remark.

Macy couldn't stop herself and blurted, "Do you understand? If you force Pop to sell the ranch, you'll be causing problems for many good, kind people who helped him out when he was in trouble."

So much for his earlier grinning. Everett sobered. "I understand."

"Okay. Good."

He rose from the table. "And I hope you understand that I won't be strong-armed."

"Strong-armed?" Macy drew back.

"Look, I appreciate everything you've done for Pop. I'm

glad you've told me about the collective, how it operates and its relationship with Pop. But I, *he* and I, need to decide what's best for him and his long-term health. That takes precedence. He had a recent heart attack and nearly died." When Everett next spoke, his tone had softened. "I promise you, I'll look at everything. And we can talk again."

With that, he walked back into the house.

"Hmm. That didn't go as expected." Sheriff Andy exchanged glances with Kinsley, who shrugged.

"Give him time," Macy said, realization dawning and, with it, a sympathy for Everett she hadn't felt before. "He's scared. He's already lost one person he loves. He doesn't want to lose another."

CHAPTER FIVE

EVERETT STOOD IN the kitchen with Pop and Susan, only half listening to them. His mind kept returning to his conversation outside with Macy and the other collective members. Admittedly, he hadn't considered how many others besides Pop would be affected if the ranch was sold.

He tried to concentrate on Susan, who was chatting about an upcoming community-wide garage sale. Her granddaughter and caretaker, Callie, thought Susan needed to downsize, and the garage sale would be a perfect opportunity to sell a few items.

She disliked the idea of parting with any of her treasured possessions as she referred to them, and Pop heartily agreed with her. Everett suspected the conversation was for his benefit—a subtle message that Pop didn't want to sell the ranch.

"It's not as if I use that china tea set," Susan said. "But I've always loved it. And it looks nice on the cherry side table. Not that I need a cherry side table, either." She sighed. "My bungalow isn't big, but I've already donated or gave away roomfuls of things before I moved in. I feel like I'm losing my life, piece by piece."

"I understand completely. Do what makes you happy." Pop patted Susan's hand. He'd finally sat down beside her after everyone had received their fill from the serve-your-self-style lunch. "There's no rush. You're still recovering from your stroke."

"Callie says there'd be less housework if I downsized."

"Don't you have a cleaning service?"

"Yes, but she's worried I'll trip and fall, and she does have a point. My little bungalow is crowded. A person gathers a lot of things over the course of a lifetime."

"You could sell one or two items in the garage sale," Pop suggested. "Not too many and nothing important. Show Callie you're trying."

"A compromise." Susan cupped his wrinkled cheek with her frail fingers. "What a good idea. You're so smart, Winston."

Pop gazed at her like a besotted schoolboy.

Winston? Everett stared in astonishment. Had he ever heard anyone call Pop by his given name? Not that he remembered.

If love were the cure to poor health, these two would be fit as any twenty-year-old. But they weren't fit. The sad truth was, the older one got, the harder it was to look after a house, much less a large ranch. From what Susan said, her granddaughter seemed to recognize this. Susan, too, though she didn't like admitting it. Abel, who'd left to join the others outside, appeared to appreciate his sister's help rather than resent it.

Why was Everett a villain for wanting to lighten his grandfather's load and see him well cared for?

Because five other individuals had invested in a business arrangement with Pop that required him to keep his ranch. That was why. If not, they'd lose their investment.

How would Macy and the rest of the collective feel if Pop had another heart attack while performing some labor-intensive task? One that resulted in his death? Would they blame themselves for pressuring Everett not to sell the ranch? He'd for sure blame *himself.*

He had a sudden urge to get out of the house and clear

his head. Maybe he'd throw a saddle on Champ and go for a short ride. Since the accident, he had a tendency to blow things out of proportion. A change in scenery and a little exercise often helped him calm down and put things in perspective.

On second thought, he'd wait until later. Macy and the others were still sitting on the patio, and he wasn't ready to face them again. Not this soon.

Turned out, staying or leaving made no difference.

The back door abruptly opened, and Macy entered with Joey. She carried a bulging bag with various pockets and zippered compartments slung over her shoulder.

"Hi." She directed her greeting to Pop. "We need to use the restroom."

"You know the way."

Joey ran ahead of her down the hall. Macy followed without so much as an eye flicker in Everett's direction.

That wasn't so bad. He'd expected a fiery glare.

The instant she disappeared around the corner, he said, "Hey, Pop. I'm going to take Champ out for a bit before it gets too hot. You okay with that?"

"He'll love it."

"I'll clean the kitchen when I get back."

"Never you mind about that." Susan shooed him away. "Your grandfather and I have it covered."

Everett needed no further encouragement and hightailed it outside before Macy returned. Yes, that was cowardly. No, he didn't want to face her. They'd already had two difficult conversations today. He wasn't ready for a third.

To his relief, Kinsley and Sheriff Andy had returned to the mare barn, taking Abel with them. They looked to be wrapping up for the day. Everett waved as he walked past toward the stallion quarters. Abel lifted his cane in return. Kinsley and Sheriff Andy gave slight nods. Everett, it seemed, had alienated two more people and given them reason to worry about their investment.

Four hooves on the ground beneath him. That was what he needed to clear his head and look at the situation with Pop and the collective from a different perspective. He understood where Macy and her friends were coming from. And, in their defense, they'd entered into their agreement before Pop's heart attack when circumstances were different. But Pop's health and well-being were a priority. His life might be on the line.

At the stallion quarters, Everett grabbed a halter from where it hung on a post. Champ had trotted inside from the paddock the moment he'd spotted Everett approaching and was waiting at the stall door. The big chestnut must have sensed they were going for a ride because he snorted lustily and stomped the ground with a heavy foot.

Everett slid open the latch and squeezed into the stall, careful not to let the eager stallion escape. "You raring to go, boy? Me, too."

He led Champ to the hitching rail at the end of the aisle where the stallion investigated everything within his tethered reach, his muscles quivering in anticipation of the ride.

For all his nervous energy, the well-trained stallion behaved under the saddle. Once he let off a little steam, that was. Champ didn't have an ornery bone in his body. But he was a big horse and strong-willed, like a lot of stallions, and required the skills of an expert rider. Everett decided to ride the hills behind the ranch where the up-and-down grade would give Champ a good workout in a short amount of time.

After saddling and double-checking the girth, he put on the bridle and fastened the straps. He'd noticed the tack could use a good cleaning and added that task to his mental list. As he worked, he heard the sound of departing vehicles. With luck, everyone in the collective would soon be gone, and he could avoid another encounter.

Untying Champ from the hitching rail, he headed outside. Best to mount in the wide-open should the stallion have a little buck in him. Everett had no desire to be slammed into a stall or tossed onto the concrete floor.

His concerns were for nothing. Champ behaved like a, well, a champ.

"Let's go, boy."

They trotted the length of the long dirt driveway to the road. No holding back on the reins slowed them down, forcing Everett to focus all his attention on Champ. Thoughts of the collective retreated to a dim corner of his mind.

A quarter of a mile later, he turned onto an often-used trail that took him and Champ into the gently sloping hills. Cottontails and jackrabbits both skittered across his path then disappeared into the brush. A red-tailed hawk watched them from its perch in a paloverde tree. Everett kept a lookout for rattlesnakes. Though they were usually more active in the early morning and at dusk, they could be out anytime during the day.

Champ settled into an easy walk, climbing the slopes as if they were no higher than dirt piles. After half an hour, Everett started to head home. The temperature was rising, and he'd forgotten to bring any water.

The moment they reached the road, Champ picked up speed. He was as eager to return to his stall as he'd been to embark on the ride. Everett changed their route on the way back, and they entered the ranch from the pasture gate. Champ pulled hard on the reins, his breathing growing heavy.

"Slow and steady, boy. We're in no rush."

Everett figured he'd check on Pop when he was done

and then drive into town for groceries. An inventory of the refrigerator and pantry this morning had yielded few contents. They'd be out of food in two days.

At the stallion quarters, Everett untacked Champ and cooled him down with a quick spray of the hose. Everett then removed his hat and doused his own head, soaking his hair and neck. The relief from the heat was instantaneous.

After a final rubdown, he returned Champ to his stall. The ride had done them both good. Patting the stallion's neck, he said, "I'll be back at six to feed you dinner."

He no sooner walked outside than he came face-to-face with Macy. Apparently, by returning through the pasture, he'd missed seeing her truck parked alongside the mare barn.

She stood with her hands stuffed in the front pockets of her jeans, an unreadable expression on her face.

"Hey." An awkward silence followed. "I thought you'd left."

"Joey fell asleep on the couch while I was saying good-bye to Pop and Susan. Rather than wake him, I let him sleep and helped Pop with a few chores around the house."

"You didn't have to do that. What about your laundry and studying?"

"I'll finish tonight. And, besides, Joey would have been a grumpy bear if he missed his nap."

"Thank you." Everett shifted his weight and waited. "Was there something else?" he asked when she didn't make a move.

"Yeah, there is."

"Look, Macy." He released a long breath. "Can we give it a day before we—"

"I want to apologize," she said, interrupting him.

That was unexpected.

"I came on too strong earlier."

"I did, too."

"We both care about Pop, and I hate that we're not in agreement." She hesitated. "He told me you're reluctant to turn down the youth coaching job."

"I am," Everett said. "I gave them my word."

"You gave me your word once. That didn't seem to matter."

The bite in her tone hit him squarely in the heart. "You're right. I did."

"This job matters more to you than me and Joey."

He blew out a long breath. "I'm sorry, Macy. I shouldn't have abandoned you."

"Thank you for calling it what it was. Abandonment."

He considered telling her about his part in Brody's death, only to change his mind. This wasn't the time or place. Instead, he said, "If you think the coaching job is affecting my feelings about selling the ranch, you're wrong. My first priority is Pop and his health."

"I agree."

Except it sounded as if she didn't.

"I don't know the first thing about owning and operating a horse breeding business," he said.

"You know more than you think you do. You spent a lot of time here at the ranch with Pop while you were growing up."

He didn't agree but let that go for now. "Whether or not I can run the business doesn't change the fact Pop will eventually need help with his long-term care. And I have no experience with that."

"Few people do when they assume responsibility for a loved one. I didn't automatically know how to care for Joey when he was born."

"Caring for a kid isn't the same as an eighty-seven-year-old man with a stubborn streak."

"You're right." She tossed her ponytail over her shoulder as if to vent her frustration. "There has to be a solution. One that gives Pop the help he needs and doesn't put the collective in jeopardy. Maybe we can brainstorm while you're here."

"Sure. Why not?" When she lifted her gaze to his, hope rather than irritation shone in her eyes. It breached the barriers Everett had constructed around his heart and made him regret his unkind thoughts regarding her motives. "Let's brainstorm."

"Great." She clasped his hand in hers. "I'm sure we can figure something out."

Everett froze. Her fingers wrapped around his sent a shock wave through his system. A very pleasant shock wave.

He quickly snatched his hand away. If she knew that he was the one responsible for making her a widow, she'd hate him forever.

Pain and confusion shadowed her features, and she retreated a step. "What happened, Everett? We used to be friends."

He swallowed, his throat having gone bone-dry. "Nothing."

"Tell me. Please."

Before he could answer, Pop shouted from the house.

"Everett. Macy. Hurry! We need help."

MACY BROKE INTO a run. Everett was faster and beat her to the back patio. There, she discovered him and Pop standing over Susan, who sat awkwardly on the Saltillo tiles, cradling her left ankle.

Everett knelt down beside her. "Are you all right? What happened?"

"She fell," Pop said.

"I didn't fall," Susan insisted. "I took a misstep. The tiles out here are uneven."

"She went down like a ton of bricks, and I couldn't lift her." Pop shook his head in disgust. "Blasted heart of mine. It's useless."

Macy patted his shoulder. "Don't blame yourself. We're here. Everett, can you carry Susan inside?"

All at once, the back door opened, and Joey appeared. Judging from his sleepy expression and the lines indented on his face, he'd just awoken from his nap.

"Mommy?"

"Hey, honey. Miss Susan fell and maybe twisted her ankle. Can you be a big boy and hold the door open for us while Everett carries her inside?"

Joey ducked into the house, swinging the door wide.

"You ready to go for a ride?" Everett asked Susan.

"Really, young man." Her wrinkled cheeks flushed with embarrassment. "That's not necessary. I'm sure I can walk."

Everett didn't argue. He simply hooked one arm under her knees and the other around her waist, lifting her as he stood.

"My goodness," she exclaimed. "You'll hurt yourself."

"I'm fine."

Macy hurried ahead into the house, making sure Joey didn't get in the way.

"I'm hungry, Mommy."

Hungry? They'd just eaten an hour and a half ago. "Give us a minute, honey. Then I'll get you some juice and crackers."

Pop directed them to the couch, hovering as if Everett was carrying priceless cargo, which, in Pop's mind, he was. Pop then gathered two throw pillows. Once Everett had arranged Susan horizontally on the couch, Pop placed one pillow behind her back and the other gingerly beneath her afflicted ankle.

When Susan moaned softly, he fretted. "What do you need, my dear?" He took her delicate hand in his. "Water? An ice pack? Should we take you to the emergency room?"

"A glass of water would be nice." She smiled up at him, and he scurried off to the kitchen.

"I'll help." Joey ran after him.

"I'll go, too, and get an ice pack. Her ankle looks swollen." Macy paused. "I think you should call Callie."

"Nonsense." Susan waved her away. "She'll be here shortly. No need for her to rush. Besides, you'll just worry her."

"Maybe she *should* be worried."

"I'm certain after the ice pack, I'll be good as new."

Macy doubted that. Older people's bones tended to be fragile. Susan might have fractured her ankle.

She crossed paths with Pop on her way to the kitchen while he was returning with the requested glass of water. Because Joey would only continue to pester everyone, she got him juice and some vanilla wafers from a box she found in the cupboard.

"Stay here, honey." She sat him at the kitchen table. "Mommy's going to help Miss Susan." A search of the freezer yielded one of those blue ice packs, which she wrapped in a clean dish towel and took to Susan. "Here, let's put this on your ankle."

With that task accomplished, she returned to the kitchen in order to keep an eye on Joey. Everett joined them, dropping onto an empty chair beside the boy.

"I got booted out."

"Pop is very attached to Susan," Macy said, "and a little possessive."

"Tell me about it."

"You sound mad."

"Are you kidding?" A hint of humor laced his voice. "I'm jealous. My eighty-seven-year-old grandfather has better luck with the ladies than I do."

Did that mean Everett was single? Not that Macy cared. She didn't care one whit.

"Pop has swag. No doubt," she joked in return.

Everett chuckled. Their recent easy, teasing exchanges reminded her of the days when they'd gotten along.

The next moment, they heard the sound of a vehicle outside. Macy checked the window, feeling abundant relief at seeing the SUV.

"Callie's here," she announced.

"Thank goodness," Pop said from the other room.

"Oh, my." Susan sat up and wrung her hands. "I think I might be in for a scolding. Now she'll have the excuse she's been looking for to force me to use a walker." She sniffed. "I don't want to use a walker. They're for old people."

Macy hurt for Susan. No one wanted to think of themselves as getting on in years and losing their mobility.

"I'll go fetch Callie," Macy said. "Let her know we're in here and not the mare barn. Come on, Joey."

"I wanna stay." He hadn't yet finished his juice and wafers.

"We'll only be a minute."

"I'll watch him." Everett gave Joey a friendly jab with his elbow. "That okay with you, sport?"

Joey beamed and nodded.

Macy couldn't quite bring herself to walk toward the door. She was about to leave her son in Everett's care. Only for a few minutes, but in his care nonetheless. Never in a million years would she have anticipated this.

"O…kay." She supposed it was all right. Pop was right there, though he was preoccupied. "Be right back."

On the patio, she waved to Callie, who turned the SUV around and parked next to Everett's truck.

She wore the same scrubs and comfortable shoes from earlier, having come straight from work. Her chin-length hair was scraped back from her pretty oval face with a wide headband.

"Hi." She smiled brightly. "I should have figured with this heat you'd be inside."

"Listen," Macy began when the home care nurse got closer. "Your grandmother had a tumble on the patio."

Concern instantly filled Callie's expression. "Is she hurt?"

"She definitely twisted her ankle. Maybe worse. We wanted to call you, but she refused to worry you."

Callie huffed in frustration as they entered the door. "I swear she's the most obstinate person on the face of the earth."

"Which is why she and Pop get along so well. They're two peas in a pod." Macy opened the door and went in first. A quick glance assured her Joey hadn't come to some horrible harm during his brief time in Everett's charge. "Mommy will be right over there." She pointed. "You behave."

"Mommy, look-it." He held up his hands pressed together. "I made a horse."

Macy didn't understand.

Everett moved Joey's fingers into place. She saw it then, the shape of a horse's head.

"Ah." She smiled. "That's great. Very clever."

"Everett showed me."

"Nice." Where had Everett learned that? she wondered, and then was distracted.

"Grandma," Callie exclaimed while fussing over Susan's swelling ankle. "This is serious."

"It's nothing."

"It's not nothing. You need an X-ray. We're going to the hospital ER."

"No, we're not." Susan's vehemence triggered a flurry of raised eyebrows around the room.

"Grandma, please."

"I think I'd know if I broke my ankle."

"Not necessarily," Callie said, reexamining the ankle. She gently palpated the swollen area. "Does this hurt?"

"A twinge."

"A sharp or dull twinge?"

"It's a twinge," Susan insisted, a note of impatience in her voice.

"Well, you're not yelping in pain." Callie straightened. "Can you put any weight on your foot?"

"I haven't tried."

"Then, let's do it."

Taking hold of her grandmother's arm, Callie sat her up and carefully swung her legs off the couch and onto the floor. The instant Susan's foot met the plush area rug, she let out a soft, involuntary whimper.

"That settles it," Callie said.

"No, it doesn't."

"Be reasonable," Pop interjected. "You're in pain."

All at once, Susan started to sob. "I'm an old, useless woman fraught with health problems. Why would you want to have anything to do with me?"

"My dear." He sat next to her and cradled her hand as if holding a tiny bird. "Nothing could be further from the truth. You are not fraught with health problems. If either of us is, I am. You're beautiful and strong and vibrant, and I'm crazy about you."

Macy didn't know whether to burst into tears or song. Pop and Susan were so cute together.

"Grandma," Callie pleaded. "If we don't treat your ankle, it'll only get worse and might cause permanent damage. You already have balance issues."

Susan sniffed. "I honestly don't think I broke it."

Callie scrunched her mouth, contemplating. "Let me make a phone call. I may have an idea."

While she went outside onto the patio, Macy and Pop convinced Susan to lie back down on the couch and elevate her ankle. Macy readjusted the ice pack, then checked on Joey. He and Everett were seeing which of them could make the bigger juice mustache. Boys, Macy supposed, will be boys.

A moment later, Callie returned. "I have good news."

"I'm not going to the ER," Susan reiterated.

"I called Dr. Alverez from work. You've met her. One of her specialties is geriatric orthopedics."

Susan made a noncommittal sound which Callie ignored.

"She's willing to stop by your place in the morning before her first call. She'll examine your ankle and tell us, in her professional opinion, if you sprained or broke it. Then, depending on what she says, we either go to the ER or not. I'll stay with you tonight. Make sure you're doing okay."

"I guess that would be all right," Susan relented.

"In the meantime, she recommends complete rest, over-the-counter pain relievers, if you need them, icing the ankle and stabilizing it. I have an elastic bandage in my car."

"Wait," Pop interjected. "Doesn't Dr. Alverez live right off of Juniper Lane?"

"How do you know that?" Callie asked in surprise.

"She visited me a few times after my heart attack when I first came home from the hospital. She mentioned it." He glanced down at Susan and patted her arm. "That's not far from here. A mile at most. Much closer than your place."

"What are you saying, Winston?"

"You can't walk on that ankle. Why don't you stay here? In the spare room, of course. There's an old daybed in there."

"An old daybed for an old woman."

The way Pop gazed at her said he thought she was young and beautiful. "You'll be able to rest, and then Dr. Alverez can stop by here in the morning. Which will be much more convenient for her."

"I don't know," Callie wavered.

"Everett will be here." Susan shot her granddaughter a playful glance. "If you're worried that Winston and I will get into mischief."

Macy bit the inside of her cheek to keep herself from laughing.

"It's not that, Grandma."

"I'll be perfectly fine. And didn't Dr. Alverez say I shouldn't walk on the ankle?"

Pop sprang up from the couch with more pep than he'd shown in weeks. "I'll order pizza for dinner. Everett can pick it up. Won't you, sonny?"

"Um, you bet." He probably didn't know how to refuse.

"It's settled, then."

Callie groaned. "I'm feeling outnumbered."

"I won't let a thing happen to her," Pop insisted. "You can count on me."

She smiled, half defeated, half amused. "All right. I'll call Dr. Alverez on the way home. Then I'll come by later with some clothes and your toothbrush and meds."

"Call me," Susan said. "I'll tell you what to pack."

"I have an extra pair of crutches I can bring."

Her features fell. "Crutches?"

"Nonnegotiable, Grandma. You have to keep weight off the ankle."

"All right. You've convinced me."

Everett thought it might have been the other way around. Susan had twisted Callie's arm.

Pop turned to Macy. "Will you and Joey be staying for dinner?"

Her gaze cut to Everett who kept his reaction in check.

"No. Thank you, though," Macy said. "I need to get home. Those piles of laundry waiting aren't going to wash and dry themselves. And I really need to study at some point."

"You sure?"

Again, she glanced at Everett. This time, he nodded. Was that an invitation or him agreeing that she should leave? His vague signals were confusing. She wasn't sure what to do.

Joey made up her mind. He hopped down from his chair at the table. "I gotta go, Everett."

Gosh, the way he talked to Everett, so grown-up like, couldn't be cuter.

"All right, sport." Everett stood.

He accompanied Macy and Joey to the patio after she said her goodbyes to the others. She didn't bother insisting that wasn't necessary. He wouldn't listen.

"About earlier," Macy began while Joey went in search of more caterpillars.

"Can we talk about something different? Give this a rest until tomorrow?"

"I know you're tired of me rehashing the same old thing."

"It isn't that, Macy." His tone changed, reminding her more of the sweet, considerate Everett from before. "After watching Pop and Susan, I feel good. The best I have in some time. I'd like to sit with that for a while if you don't mind."

She could have hugged him in that moment. Thrown herself at him and squeezed with all her might.

Instead, she reached out and captured his hand. "I don't mind, Everett. Not at all."

She expected him to pull away like before. He didn't, and they stood that way for several seconds before parting, their fingers linked. The contented feeling lingered until long after Macy and Joey arrived home. She didn't fool herself, however. She imagined she and Everett were going to butt heads again over Pop and the ranch and the collective. But for this one afternoon, they were of like minds.

CHAPTER SIX

TWO DAYS LATER, Everett awoke to the sound of rain outside his bedroom window. Finally, they'd have a break from the oppressive heat, although, according to the weather app on his phone, a short one. Clear skies were in tomorrow's forecast, which meant the added agony of humidity.

For once, he beat Pop to the kitchen and started preparing breakfast. The old man insisted on playing the role of host, which included preparing all their meals. Everett needed to put a stop to that; Pop was wearing himself out.

Everett had spent the previous morning on chores and repairs around the ranch before running to town. He'd stocked up at both the hardware and grocery stores. Now, in addition to having the necessary material to start work on his long list of projects, the kitchen pantry was fully stocked. Good thing, as Pop had extended Susan's invitation to stay at the ranch with them after Doctor Alverez's visit yesterday morning, and Susan had required very little convincing.

After a thorough examination, the cheerful MD determined Susan had suffered a sprain, not a fracture. She needed icing and rest. If she didn't respond to over-the-counter remedies and her pain continued or worsened, then she absolutely must see an orthopedic specialist and get X-rays. Susan promised, otherwise Callie would never have allowed her grandmother to remain at the ranch.

The home care nurse wasn't crazy about the idea to begin with, but Susan had insisted. She didn't want to put any weight on her ankle. Better she should stay.

They all knew she could have gone home. The ankle was an excuse for Susan and Pop to spend time together. He doted on her, and she let him, enjoying the attention. Everett just chuckled to himself.

"What smells so good?" Pop asked.

"Pancakes."

He ambled over to the stove to inspect Everett's culinary efforts and frowned. "They look funny."

"These are oatmeal pancakes. Very healthy for the heart."

"Sounds terrible."

"You'll like them. Especially when you add the organic maple syrup and fresh strawberries."

"I'd rather add sausage links."

"Sorry, Pop. That's not on the menu."

He grunted. "Last time I send you to the grocery store." The next moment, he broke into a besotted grin. "Good morning, Sleeping Beauty."

Everett didn't have to look behind him to know Susan had entered the kitchen. The soft scuffling sound alerted him that she was using the crutches Callie had brought for her.

"Here. Let me help." Pop hurried to the table, where he pulled out a chair and relieved her of her crutches, leaning them against the counter. "Would you like some coffee?"

"Thank you, dear."

While Pop fussed over his lady friend, Everett finished preparing breakfast. Unlike Pop, Susan complemented Everett when he placed a large platter of pancakes and a bowl of sliced strawberries in front of them.

She clapped with delight. "This looks marvelous."

"Can I at least have margarine on my pancakes?" Pop asked.

"You can have unsalted butter." Everett set a dish on the table. "I tossed that big tub of yellow oil you had in the fridge. Unsalted butter is better for you."

"Says who? I like my margarine," Pop grumbled.

"He's right, dear," Susan concurred. "And, besides, with syrup, you can't tell the difference."

"Well, if you say so." Pop sliced off a generous pat of butter with his knife.

Everett sat across from them and waited until they'd both filled their plates, amused his grandfather had resisted when Everett suggested unsalted butter but changed his mind when Susan endorsed it. Whatever it took to get Pop to improve his eating habits was fine by Everett.

That wasn't all. Pop, Everett noticed, had shaved the last two mornings and wore his best everyday shirts. Susan also took care with her appearance. The evening of her fall, Callie had dropped off a small suitcase containing clothes and toiletries to Susan's exact specifications, along with her medications.

Some people might call Susan fussy. Everett, however, thought of her as a woman who knew her own mind, and there was nothing wrong with that.

Kind of like Macy, who was the definition of independence.

She hadn't really needed him to check on her and Joey these past three years. They'd managed just fine, especially with her parents nearby and Brody's, too. But that wasn't the point. There were things Everett could have done to make her life simpler. More importantly, he'd promised.

"Who from the collective is coming today?" Susan asked, taking a dainty bite of her pancakes.

"Macy, of course," Pop said. "She'll be by on her lunch hour with Joey."

She hadn't come by yesterday. Perhaps she'd taken a day off.

"And Sheriff Andy," Pop continued. "He's hauling a load of manure to the high school. Their landscapers use it for fertilizer."

"What a grand idea," Susan exclaimed. "All natural. And saves the school money."

"Sheriff Andy says it's a tax deduction for the collective. He would know, being the money guy."

Everett had learned that not a single day went by without someone from the collective appearing at the ranch. He'd offered to feed and tend the broodmares while he was here. Macy wouldn't hear of it. The mares were the collective's responsibility. Specifically, *her* responsibility. When he'd countered that the collective helped with Champ, she claimed it wasn't the same thing.

At the end of breakfast, Pop and Susan insisted on cleaning the kitchen. Well, Pop cleaned. Susan sat and kept him company. The arrangement suited them both.

Everett excused himself to tackle more items on his list of projects. The rain had let up, and he wanted to replace the roof tiles on the mare barn and stallion quarters while it was cooler. Plus, this may be his only chance during his stay.

A short time later, he left the mare barn carrying an extension ladder and whistling a tune. Hearing an approaching vehicle, he stopped. Sheriff Andy must be here.

Except it wasn't the retiree's vehicle that pulled up, but rather a small, ancient motor home. The brakes squealed as it came to a stop, and the body rocked. New shocks were in order. A new fender and bumper wouldn't hurt, either. Dents and rust spots peppered the old ones.

Everett set down the ladder and walked over to see about this new arrival. As he neared, he recognized Glynnis Pottinger at the wheel and her older brother Abel in the passenger seat. A moment later, the side door opened and Glynnis stepped out.

"Morning, Everett." She bent and lowered the single metal step.

Abel appeared in the doorway. "How are you this fine morning?" His sister extended her hand, but he waved it away. "Gotta learn to manage on my own."

His descent was a slow process, hampered by his Parkinson's. Everett and Glynnis watched, ready to jump in and help. When Abel had two feet planted firmly on the ground, Glynnis accompanied him to the rocking chairs, which had been moved into the mare barn to keep them out of the recent rain.

"Have a seat, Abel."

He leaned on his cane. "I'd rather stand a bit. Been sitting all morning."

It wasn't even eight thirty.

"Don't tire yourself out," she cautioned.

"You fuss too much."

"You'll get wet if it starts raining again."

Their back-and-forth squabbling held an affectionate note. Glynnis clearly worried about her older brother, and he took her worry as she intended it: evidence of her love.

"Is Pop around?" Glynnis asked.

"He's inside with Susan. They should be out shortly."

She fidgeted, reminding Everett of her brother's involuntary muscle movements.

"I can go inside and get him, if you want."

She sighed. "I should have called first."

At that moment, a car drove onto the ranch, one Everett didn't recognize.

"That's my husband," Glynnis said. "Our daughter went into labor late last night, two weeks early. This is her first baby, and she's nervous. She wants me and her dad there. She lives in Casa Grande."

"Okay." Everett didn't understand anything about having babies, but a daughter wanting her parents there sounded reasonable to him.

"Our son, her brother, was supposed to keep an eye on Abel while we were gone. But he's on a business trip and won't be home until late Friday."

"I don't need a babysitter," Abel grumbled from where he stood.

"Abel, you can't stay alone." Glynnis addressed Everett, "The last time we tried, it was a disaster. He woke up disoriented from a nap and rolled off the couch. He couldn't get up and lay there for almost six hours until we arrived home."

"You're exaggerating," Abel grumbled.

"I'm not." She told Everett, "I know it's last minute, but we were hoping he could stay here until Saturday morning. He'll be okay in the motor home with someone peeking in now and then. It's self-contained. Water and propane tanks. Just need to run a heavy-duty extension cord to an outlet for power. We brought one. He has plenty of food and won't be any trouble. Since he and Pop are friends—"

"It's not a problem." Everett held up a hand. "I'm sure Pop won't mind."

"Really?"

"Really. What's one more houseguest?" Everett winked at Glynnis, then looked over at Abel. "You'll have to help me with my work around here."

Abel, who'd been frowning, brightened. "I can do that.

Used to be pretty handy with a hammer and wrench back before I became such a butterfingers."

"Sounds great, sir. Now, let's figure out where to park this beast. I'm thinking behind the stallion quarters. The ground is level, you'll have shade from the overhang, and there's a motion activated security light on the outside wall."

By then, Glynnis's husband had joined them. "How's it going?"

Her relief was palpable as she filled him in on what Everett had said.

Next, her husband moved the motor home, parking it where Everett indicated. The car was just leaving when Pop and Susan emerged from the house.

"What's going on?" Pop hollered from the patio.

Everett and Abel started walking their way.

"Abel's going to be staying here until Saturday morning," Everett said. "If that's all right with you."

Pop helped Susan to sit at the picnic table. "The more, the merrier."

His grandfather meant it, Everett realized. Pop liked having people around. That was new. He'd led a mostly solitary life since becoming a widower ten years ago. Maybe it had something to do with his heart attack. Nothing like nearly dying to change one's perspective about spending any remaining years in the company of friends and loved ones.

Perhaps Everett could learn something from his grandfather. After the accident with Brody, he'd closed himself off to everyone. In hindsight, that may not have been the best move.

MACY PLASTERED A tired smile on her face. It had been a long day at Red Hills Veterinary Clinic, and she had a long evening ahead studying.

At times, she considered taking a break from school. She was juggling a lot, and she couldn't help but feel guilty about leaving Joey at her parents' so often. Not that he didn't receive the best possible care there. But she spent too many restless nights worrying about neglecting him when she should be sleeping.

Then, she'd recall her vow to give Joey the best life possible. As a vet tech, she could increase her earning potential. And with the money from the sale of the foals next year, she'd be able to start a college fund for him.

"Your total for today will be four hundred and eighty-five dollars."

"What!" The pet parent's mouth fell open in astonishment. "That much?"

"Actually, the final bill came to fifteen dollars less than the estimate of services you signed this morning when you dropped off Taco Bella." Macy slid the document across the counter to remind the young woman.

She huffed. "Are you sure? I don't remember."

"We wouldn't have proceeded with blood work and treatment without your consent," Macy calmly explained.

The woman squinted at the signature on the bottom of the paper as if questioning its authenticity. Macy waited patiently. A lot of people were distressed or panicked when they came into the clinic, especially during an emergency. Then, once the crisis had passed, they were suddenly upset about the money.

Owning pets was a commitment and, often, a costly undertaking. This woman's five-month-old shepherd mix had instigated a tussle with another pup at doggy day care—resulting in a nasty bite on her ear requiring ten stitches and her immediate expulsion from the facility—which might be the real cause of the woman's annoyance.

"Fine." She huffed again and produced the payment app

on her phone, which Macy scanned. "I don't know what I'm going to do with her now while I have appointments."

Macy didn't bother suggesting puppy obedience classes, believing the owner wouldn't listen. Taco Bella was a sweet dog but also big and rambunctious. Not her fault her owner saw no need to enforce socialization skills.

As much as Macy loved dogs, she didn't currently own any. Too much responsibility when her plate was already so full.

One of these days, when Joey was older, she'd get him a dog. And maybe a pony. That was if Everett didn't force Pop to sell the ranch. She'd need an inexpensive place to board a pony. Anywhere else would charge a small fortune.

After processing the woman's payment, a tech led her back to an exam room where she'd be reunited with Taco Bella and receive discharge instructions from Dr. Beck.

Macy sighed and rubbed her temples.

"Hard day?" Jasmine asked. She was another of the clinic's vet techs and always wore a sweater over her animal paw–print smock regardless of the season.

"Yeah. I can't wait until Adam returns."

Their lone male tech was away on vacation for his brother's destination wedding, and he was expected to return on Monday. Macy had been handling both her office manager duties and filling in for the vacationing vet tech whenever a third pair of hands was needed.

"I can't wait for six o'clock," Jasmine said around a yawn. "Quitting time can't come soon enough."

Macy got off an hour earlier. She was the only one at the clinic with regular hours that didn't change from week to week. For that reason, she could stop at the ranch most days for a look at the mares.

She'd skipped going today at lunch. They'd just been too busy at the clinic. According to Kinsley, who'd handled the morning feeding and chores, everyone was doing well. Everett had said he'd watch the mares, as well. She could trust him, right? Just because he'd bailed on her before was no reason to think he would again.

Still, she hadn't been to the ranch for two full days. That was too long for her comfort level. After work, she'd grab Joey from her parents' house and head to the ranch. The half hour she spent there would go a long way toward restoring her peace of mind.

The woman burst from the exam room, Taco Bella dancing alongside her and chewing on the leash.

"Come on," she said in a baby voice. "Let's go to the pet shop and buy you a doggy doughnut. You deserve a treat for being such a good girl and letting the doctor fix your boo-boo."

They tumbled out the door, enamored with each other.

Ah, thought Macy. How quickly pet owners forgive and forget. As do moms and dads, too.

An image of Everett rushing to grab Joey after he'd cut his finger on the old rocking chair surfaced. A dad would do that. Everett may not have much experience with children, but he seemed to have the instincts. Why, then, had he ignored her and Joey after the funeral?

Never getting a straight answer from him only increased her frustration and caused old resentments to resurface. She decided to find a time to raise the subject with him. It's true she and Joey had survived without his help, but that wasn't the point.

She pushed the question away as her cell phone rang. Retrieving it from the front pocket of her smock, she checked the display. Seeing Everett's number, she drew in a sharp breath. He wouldn't be calling unless something was wrong!

"Hello."

"Sorry to bother you at work, Macy."

"What is it?" At his serious tone, her apprehension sky-rocketed.

"It's Roxie. I think she might have colic again."

"What are her signs?" Macy was already charging down the hall toward the office where she kept her purse.

"I found her lying down in her stall about fifteen minutes ago. I got her up, but she went right back down and tried to roll. I got her up again and have been walking her ever since. She keeps biting her side, and I think her gums might be tacky, but she won't let me get a good look."

"I'll be there as soon as I can. I have to pick up Joey first." If not for her parents participating in a pickleball tournament this evening, she'd have asked her mom to keep Joey longer.

"Don't worry. I won't let anything happen to Roxie."

She started to hang up, only to pause. "Thank you, Everett."

"Drive careful. No speeding."

"See you soon."

Before she left, she spoke with Dr. Beck. They discussed colic treatments and Roxie's history. He agreed to come out to the ranch and treat Roxie if necessary.

"Call me anytime, day or night," the perpetually cheery vet told her on her way out the door.

En route to her parents' house, she phoned her mom and explained the emergency. As a result, when she arrived, her mom had packed healthy snacks for her and Joey in case they needed to stay late at the ranch. It was already after five, and he'd get hungry soon. Macy was too upset to eat.

At the ranch, she drove straight to the mare barn. Everett was walking Roxie in the pasture. The mare kept stopping and required encouragement before continuing.

"Come on, honey." Macy unloaded Joey and gave him a box of raisins.

"Where's Pop?"

"I don't know. He must be in the house."

"I'll find him."

"No, Joey. Stay with me."

She briefly wondered if Susan was still here, but then her concerns for Roxie took over. Everett had led the mare to the pasture gate. Macy waved and motioned that she'd meet him in the barn. Next, she removed her medical bag from the truck and carried it over to the barn's front entrance.

"Stay close to Mommy, honey." As much as she hated imposing on Pop, for once, she wished he was here to watch her son. "How's she doing?" Macy asked Everett the second he approached.

"The same."

"Can you hold her for me?"

"Sure."

"Joey, honey, get back here."

He'd started running toward the house. "Wanna find Pop."

"Hey, sport." Everett beckoned Joey with his free hand. "Would you like to go for a ride?"

Joey stopped in his tracks. "I ride a horsie?"

"Well, not a horse. Here. I'll show you. Come on."

The boy tentatively approached. Macy watched, a tad nervous. When Joey was close enough, Everett lifted him in the air and deposited him onto his shoulder.

"Hold tight."

Joey squealed, first with alarm and then with glee as he settled into place.

Macy almost squealed herself. A young boy riding a man's shoulders. Such a natural, normal activity. It was something she'd expected to see Joey do with his father. Not Everett. And, yet, there they were. Both of them wearing smiles, and Macy not at all sure how she felt about it.

Wait, that wasn't right. She was unsure how she felt about *not* being upset at the sight of them together. She was mad at Everett and still didn't trust him entirely. But he was good with her son, and he'd called her about Roxie.

"Okay," she said. "Let's get started."

The first thing Macy did was take the mare's vitals and check for laminitis, as it could mimic colic. She and Everett then discussed Roxie's eating and elimination habits during the day, which Everett reported as being off.

"We shouldn't let her eat or drink, for now," Macy said.

"Right."

Joey had removed Everett's cowboy hat and plopped it down on his own head. "Look-it, Mommy. I'm a cowboy."

"Yes, you are." Macy forced her gaze away from the brown hair curling attractively at the nape of Everett's neck to study the mare, who shifted restlessly from foot to foot. "I'm going to wait before administrating any flunixin meglumine. If she gets worse, I'll consult with Dr. Beck." The anti-inflammatory could sometimes mask colic symptoms. "For now, let's continue walking her and letting her rest every twenty minutes."

"If you want to take over, Joey and I can feed the rest of the horses."

"He can come with me," Macy said.

"I'll go with Everett, Mommy."

"All...right. But, I think you should take him off your shoulders."

"You heard your mom, sport."

Everett passed Macy the horse's lead rope and lifted Joey down. He didn't release Joey's hand.

Macy couldn't quite make herself leave. "Don't let him out of your sight. Joey is a magnet for trouble."

"I'll be good."

Everett winked. "You heard him. He'll be good."

She sighed. Never, ever had she pictured this day. Her relinquishing temporary care of her son to Everett, and her being mostly okay with it.

Twenty minutes later, Macy met up with Everett and Joey in front of the mare barn. They were sitting in a rocking chair, Joey on Everett's lap. Somehow, he'd located the snacks and had given Joey a fruit bar.

"How's she doing?" he asked.

"No change."

"But no worse?"

"Doesn't appear so."

"Ready for a break?"

"I am." Macy tied Roxie to the fence where they could watch her. She then returned to Everett and Joey and plopped into the empty rocking chair.

"Rough day?" Everett asked.

"Very. And it's going to be a rough night. I can't leave Roxie until I know she's out of danger."

"You're not thinking of staying all night."

"I am." Macy pushed with her feet, setting the chair into motion. "Roxie is too valuable and too important to the collective to risk. Colic can be very dangerous for a pregnant mare and her foal."

"What about Joey?"

"I'll take him over to my parents when they get home from their pickleball tournament. He can spend the night there. Then I'll come back."

"What about you?" Everett asked. "You can't stay up all night."

"I have a two-and-a-half-year-old. It won't be the first time. Besides, I have a bunch of reading to do for class."

"No." He shook his head.

"No?" Macy drew back to gaze at him.

"You and Joey stay here. Have dinner with Pop and I and Susan. Then you can bunk on the couch."

"I can't. My reading."

"You can, Macy. Use my laptop to log in to your class account."

"You already have a full house," she insisted. "I heard Abel's staying in his motor home behind the stallion quarters."

"My point exactly. What's two more?"

She hesitated.

"Let us help," Everett said. "Let *me* help."

She almost asked why he hadn't offered before, after Brody died, but she didn't.

And what he did next surprised her more than anything else he had done today. He reached for her hand and held it in his.

The familiar sensation took her momentarily aback, and she almost snatched her hand away. Only she didn't. She liked it too much, and that also took her aback.

They stayed like that for several minutes before she reluctantly withdrew. She shouldn't encourage him when she didn't know how she felt.

CHAPTER SEVEN

EVERETT STOOD AT Roxie's stall, watching the mare stomp her foot and shake her head in an angry demand for water and food.

"Sorry, girl. I get that you're feeling better, but nothing for you until Macy gives the okay."

Roxie wasn't appeased and lashed out with her front foot, kicking the wall. The loud bang startled her neighbor, and the palomino squealed in surprise.

"Enough already of your bad temper, Roxie. Why don't I take you outside where you can't get into trouble?"

Everett and Macy had alternated shifts during the night to watch and walk the mare. Pop, who was delighted at having two more houseguests, had prepared a simple dinner of spaghetti and salad—which Joey loved. Abel had joined them, too, and they all ate on the patio at the picnic table. Joey had loved that, too.

After dinner, Everett took the first shift with Roxie while Susan helped Macy make up the family room couch into a bed for her and Joey. Macy had relieved Everett around eight o'clock after giving Joey a bath and putting him down for the night.

The plan had been for Everett to catch five hours of sleep and then relieve Macy for the rest of the night so that she could then get some sleep. There was only one problem. Eight o'clock was too early for Everett. When he had finally lain down at nine thirty, all he could think about was the moment he spent with Macy, holding hands.

He'd expected Macy to instantly withdraw. Only, she hadn't, eventually letting go to search for Joey. Neither of them had mentioned the hand-holding or what, if anything, it meant.

Everett dozed off after a while. Too soon, his phone alarm played an obnoxious melody that never failed to rouse him. He'd dressed and dragged himself into the kitchen, careful to be quiet. After making himself a large mug of coffee, he'd headed outside to the mare barn. He and Macy had exchanged information on Roxie's no worsening and possibly improving colic before she went inside.

Now, at five thirty, the sun was peeking over the hilltops and turning the reddish-brown ground a glorious bronze.

Everett opened the stall door. "Going to be another beautiful day, Roxie. And hot."

He removed the lead rope from where he'd draped it over the stall door and fastened it to the halter. Because he'd been walking her forty minutes out of every hour, he hadn't removed her halter in between.

Rather than follow him, Roxie banged her nose against the metal waterer, making it clang.

"I know you're thirsty." Everett had turned off the water to her stall the previous evening. Horses with colic sometimes still ate and drank even when they were in pain, which could aggravate their condition. "My guess is it won't be long now." He patted the mare's neck.

The other eleven barn occupants nickered and circled restlessly in their stalls.

"I'll feed the rest of you in a few minutes." He wanted Roxie out of sight when he did. She was already agitated. Seeing her stablemates eat when she had to go hungry would be miserable for her.

Everett finally coaxed the mare out of her stall and into the early morning sunshine. They didn't get far before she jerked on the lead rope, lowering her head and trying to take a bite from a small cluster of dried grass.

"That's not good for you." Everett pulled her head up.

His cell phone promptly rang, and he checked the display before answering, grinning upon seeing his roping partner Rusty's number.

"Hey, buddy, how you doing?"

Rusty's booming voice with its strong Texas drawl filled his ear. "Tell me I didn't wake you."

"Nah, I've been up since one. Got a pregnant mare with colic."

"One of your grandfather's?"

"A friend's." He wasn't about to explain the collective to Rusty. Not now. "She's doing better."

"That's good. Anyway, I just called to find out when you're arriving in Tucson for Big Timber. We need to get some practice time in."

They did. Rusty wasn't wrong.

"I'm not sure. I have to look at my calendar."

His friend must have heard something in Everett's voice, for he asked, "You haven't changed your mind, have you?"

"No."

"Cuz if you have, I need to know now while there's still time to replace you."

"My plan is to leave here by the eighteenth. That'll give us at least three practice days before the rodeo."

"I'm calling you again on Friday," Rusty said, a note of irritation in his tone. "Just to make sure."

Everett must have sounded as unconvinced as he felt, and he grumbled to himself. Rusty had always been a good friend, and he owed him complete honesty.

"I plan to be there, pal. But, there is a chance something might come up. Things are more…complicated here than I anticipated."

"Your grandpa doing all right?"

"The heart attack took a toll on him. And the ranch isn't in great shape. On the chance I get stuck, you may want to ask Chet Lindon or Junior Abrahams to be your backup partner. If I can make Big Timber, I will. But I don't want to leave you in the lurch."

"Okay, okay. I just talked to Junior yesterday. He's interested. So, I'll just give him a jingle."

Everett heard his friend's relief, making him glad he'd been up front. Missing one rodeo wouldn't hurt Everett's ranking much. No worse than if he went to the rodeo and lost in all of his events, which could happen if he had a bad streak.

And he did still have every intention of making the rodeo. What had Macy said? He could go and come back? That did make sense. And it gave him flexibility.

"I hope you're not mad at me, buddy," he said.

"You kidding? Junior's twice the roper you are."

They both laughed at the joke. Everett liked to think of himself as better, but Junior was talented in his own right. And he was available.

"I'll still call you Friday," Rusty said.

"You got it."

By then, Roxie was tugging on the lead rope. She wanted to eat. Everett said goodbye to his friend and started to walk back toward the mare barn. Seeing a flash of movement, he glanced in the direction of the stallion barn. He thought Abel might be up and puttering around. He had a habit of sneaking Champ apple cores and carrot stubs when no one was looking. The thing was, everyone noticed. But they said nothing, letting Abel think he got away with it.

When did Macy normally rise in the morning? Everett checked his phone again and glanced at the house. The kitchen window remained dark, giving him reason to believe everyone inside was asleep. Maybe he'd tie up Roxie, go inside and get another cup of coffee. After the night he'd had, he could use a boost.

"What the—"

He stopped in his tracks as he caught sight of Joey running across the open area between the house and the garage where his and Macy's trucks were parked. A quick visual sweep told him Macy wasn't nearby.

"Come on, girl."

Everett walked briskly toward the garage, Roxie trotting to keep up. He may not know much about kids, but he figured the boy shouldn't be outside by himself, especially this early in the morning. He must have escaped Macy's watch.

"Joey. Hey, sport. Where you off to?"

The little boy stopped and pivoted. "Hi, Everett. Can I ride a horse?"

"You can pet her."

Everett wasn't going to put the boy on a horse, not without his mom there. And he wasn't sure about Roxie. Though normally docile, she had just come through a bout of colic and was understandably testy.

As Joey reached him, Everett bent and opened one arm. The boy held both his out, and Everett scooped him up, holding him close.

"Go slow," he said. "Be careful of her eyes."

Joey did neither. He patted Roxie on the hard ridge just above her left eye and then tugged on her forelock. "Good horsie."

Roxie proved to be extremely tolerant, a trait that would

come in handy when she had a rambunctious foal to contend with.

"Easy, sport." Everett moved to Roxie's neck where
Joey's affection would be less bothersome to the mare.
"What are you doing outside?"

"I don't know."

"Hmm." Everett wasn't sure if Joey misunderstood the
question or really didn't know why he'd come outside,
other than to explore. "I should probably have taken you
back. How about we tie up the horse and go inside."

"Can I tie the horse?"

"You can help me." Everett looked around. "We'll use
that tree over there."

They walked to the paloverde tree. Everett managed
to keep hold of Joey and tether the horse to a low branch
without anyone getting scratched.

"Pull this as hard as you can." He passed the end of the
lead rope to Joey who tugged. The rope didn't need any
tightening, but Joey was thrilled with the task, given his
huge smile.

Yet again, Everett was struck by how much the boy resembled his late father. A renewed tightness formed in his
chest. Yes, he felt guilty that this small boy had lost his
father, and Everett should have been the one driving that
day. But Pop was right. No one could have predicted what
would happen. And the man who'd struck them was driving recklessly, crossing the double yellow line and passing
when no passing was allowed.

He, more than Everett, bore the blame. He, more than
Everett, had to live with the guilt that his actions had cost
someone their life.

This tightness in Everett's chest was also the result of
an unfamiliar feeling: protectiveness toward a child. And
deep regret. He shouldn't have stayed away.

"I'm sorry, Brody," he murmured to himself.

"My name is Joey."

"Yeah, I know, sport."

They started toward the house, Everett still carrying Joey. At the same moment, the back door burst open, and Macy ran outside, shouting as her frantic eyes searched the area.

"Joey, Joey! Where are you? Joey, please answer me." She raced through the patio gate.

"Here we are," Everett called out. "I found him outside and was just bringing him back."

She came to a grinding halt. A sob escaped as her shoulders slumped, and she pressed her hands to her heart. After a moment, she raised her head, visibly more composed.

"You scared Mommy. I woke up, and you were gone."

Everett put Joey down. The boy ran the remaining twenty feet to his mother. "I helped Everett tie the horse."

"You did?" She lifted him into her arms and squeezed the stuffing out of him. Tears glistened in her eyes. "Next time, wait for Mommy." She buried her face in his neck.

Everett stood there. The protectiveness he'd felt for Joey a moment ago expanded to encompass Macy, too. He was suddenly very glad he'd told Rusty to line up a substitute roping partner. Everett didn't want to leave the ranch. Not now. Not yet.

"ENOUGH, MOMMY. No more hugs." Joey squirmed to get down.

Macy wasn't ready to let go. The panic she'd felt when she'd wakened on Pop's family room couch, disorientated and finding her young son missing, had yet to wane. Joey was her world. She'd lost his father. She couldn't bear it if she lost him, too.

"Okay." Releasing a long sigh, she lowered him to the ground. "But you stay right here."

"Can I ride a horse?"

"After breakfast." Macy glanced at Everett, and his tender expression tugged on her heartstrings. "Thank you."

"He was only outside for a few minutes, from what I could tell."

"A lot can happen to a small child in a few minutes. I'm grateful you were here to find him."

Everett nodded. "Me, too."

"I'm hungry, Mommy." Joey pulled on the hem of her shirt, wrinkled from sleeping in her clothes.

"All right." Macy looked around, noticing Roxie tied to the tree. "We need to feed the horses first."

"I'll do that," Everett said. "I was just going to when I spotted this escapee here." He bent and patted Joey's head.

The little boy beamed up at him.

Macy wanted to cry and almost did. Her emotions were all over the place. "How is Roxie?"

"Much better in my opinion. But you're the expert."

"My medical case is still in the mare barn."

"I'm hungry." Joey's voice had taken on a whiny quality.

"I know, but Mommy has some work."

"No." He pouted and crossed his arms over his cute little protruding belly. "No work."

"I have an idea," Everett said. "I can really use some coffee. Why don't I take Joey inside with me. He can have a bowl of cereal while I put on a pot. Meanwhile, you take Roxie to the mare barn and give her a once-over. When Joey and I are done, we'll join you and feed the horses."

"Um…"

It was a decent plan with one exception. She worried that Everett spending time with her son was becoming a habit. Her little boy became quickly attached to people he liked, and Everett may be leaving soon.

Roxie whinnied, reminding Macy of her reason for being here.

"All right," she conceded. "Joey, you be good for Everett. You mind him, you hear?"

"I'll be good." He reached up for Everett's hand, grabbing on to his first two fingers.

"Okey dokey, sport. Let's go."

"Okey dokey," Joey repeated.

They walked off together toward the house, taking a piece of Macy's heart with them.

At the tree, she untied Roxie. By the time they reached the mare barn, Macy felt more like herself. The horse, too, apparently. She instantly buried her nose in the feed trough when Macy returned her to her stall, then came up quickly, a disdainful expression on her face, when she discovered there was no hay or grain.

"I'm going to take that as a good sign." Macy ran her hand along Roxie's flank, observing only a pregnancy curve and no digestive bloating.

The other mares nickered and stomped their feet. No one wanted to wait for Roxie's exam to be over before eating.

"Give us a minute, girls. Let's see if Roxie can have breakfast, too."

Macy found her medical bag where she'd left it by the rocking chairs and conducted a speedy exam. She tried to keep her mind on Roxie, listening to the mare's gut with the stethoscope and checking her gums, but images of Everett and Joey kept distracting her.

What kind of cereal did Pop have? Joey could be a picky eater and would probably consider heart-healthy cereal boring and tasteless. Maybe she should text Everett and tell him to fix Joey a peanut butter and jelly sandwich instead. Did Pop keep fruit on hand? Of course, he did. She should tell Everett to give Joey a banana or apple slices.

Roxie snorted and banged the feed trough with her nose, returning Macy's attention to the exam.

"You're definitely hungry." Macy patted the mare's generous hind end. "Let's try a light breakfast. See how you do with that."

Closing the stall door behind her, she pushed the wheelbarrow outside and across the open area to the hay shed. There, she loaded up with enough feed for all the mares and Champ. She then walked a thick flake over to the stallion quarters. Champ pranced in place with excitement at the prospect of a meal. Finishing with him, she returned to the mare barn where she fed all twelve mares. Roxie got half her usual amount. If she tolerated that well, Macy would give her more in a few hours. Lastly, she turned on the water.

She was just emerging from the mare barn, intending to head to the house and see how Joey was faring, when the back door to the house opened. Her little boy charged outside. Behind him came Pop and then Susan on her crutches. He held what appeared to be two cups of coffee. Giving Macy a good morning wave, they sat at the picnic table where, she assumed, they intended to enjoy the sunrise and each other's company.

Nice, but where, she wondered, was Everett?

"Mommy, I had oatmeal for breakfast." Joey bounded toward her, all smiles and bursting with energy.

"Oatmeal?"

"It was yummy. Everett cooked. I helped."

"Good. Where, um, is Everett?"

"In the house. Can I ride a horse now?"

"Maybe. Let me see. Mommy has to work today."

In truth, there was no need to rush. Macy had called Dr. Beck early last evening to report on Roxie. He'd told her to come in late if necessary. She was grateful, as she really wanted to see how Roxie responded to her light breakfast before leaving. She had to fill the time with something. Might as well be giving Joey a horse ride.

Her heart gave a sudden start at seeing Everett emerge from the house and start toward the barn. He also carried a mug of coffee. No, two. She suspected one was for her.

"Extra cream, right?" He held out a steaming mug.

"Thanks. And yes."

By mutual silent agreement, they strolled into the mare barn. Macy gave Joey an old empty coffee can so he could find more rocks for his collection. That way, he'd stay busy and not find trouble.

"Don't go far," she warned him. "Stay right here where Mommy can see you."

Joey skipped off.

"How's Roxie?" Everett asked.

They stopped in front of the mare's stall. Macy marveled at how their relationship had evolved over the last few days from strained to easy camaraderie. Then again, they hadn't discussed selling the ranch or finding Pop a good nursing home or why Everett had abandoned her after Brody's death. Plus, he'd been a real help with Roxie and intercepted her wandering son this morning. How could Macy not soften toward him?

"She's doing better. Her vitals were good. I gave her breakfast, half her usual amount."

Macy propped her forearms on the stall's half door, studying the mare. Everett stood beside her, right at the edge of her personal space. She didn't mind. If anything, she liked his proximity. That was unexpected.

Or was it? There'd been moments during that long-ago

summer when they hadn't known what to do with the myriad new feelings they were experiencing. She'd purposely
maneuvered herself as close to Everett as possible just to
incite a spark. Then he and his family had moved away,
and her teenage world had crumbled.

Later, when he'd returned to Wickenburg and she was
with Brody, Everett had retreated to the friend zone. He'd
made a point of keeping his distance, she now realized, in
order to ensure things were comfortable for the three of
them. Those were the actions of a decent and caring indi-
vidual. Why hadn't she noticed before instead of taking
him for granted?

"The feed trough's already empty," Everett said. "She
was hungry."

Macy was going to give him the rundown on Roxie,
then changed her mind and instead said what was in her
heart.

"You know, I was heartbroken when you and your family moved away."

His brows rose. "What made you say that?"

"I was just remembering."

He nodded. "The move was hard for me, too. Having
to leave my girlfriend behind, my best friend, my football
teammates, and finish my senior year at a new high school
where I didn't know anyone."

"But you met people."

"Some. I couldn't wait to come back here after I turned
eighteen and graduated."

Except, by then, Macy had fallen head over heels for
Brody.

"It's too bad you couldn't have stayed with Pop," she
said.

"Believe me, I begged my parents. They refused to budge."

"They would have missed you. I can't imagine being okay leaving Joey behind, even for just eight months."

"That wasn't the only reason. They didn't trust Pop to be a reliable guardian."

"Seriously?"

"He was a wreck in those days. Grandma had died less than a year earlier. He was…not himself for a while. Drinking too much. Staying out with his cronies at the bar or playing poker. Leaving every weekend for some horse sale. Mom was sure he'd lead me to ruin."

"He missed your grandmother. Her death was pretty sudden, as I recall."

"Very sudden. She was fine one minute and then the next, she fell and died from a brain hemorrhage."

His voice held a mixture of anger, grief and sorrow. He missed his grandmother, too. She understood what it was like, losing someone you loved with no warning. They both did.

"I'm sorry, Everett."

"Pop pulled himself together not long after that. But by then, I only had another month or two of school. It made no sense for me to transfer at that point. Not when I was planning on returning, anyway."

Had he hoped to pick up where they left off? She doubted it. By Christmas that year, distance and separation had impacted their relationship, and they'd drifted apart, no longer calling or texting or chatting online.

Macy swallowed a painful lump. They couldn't help what had happened; their lives went in different directions. And she'd gone on to have a wonderful marriage to Brody and become mom to an amazing little boy. But she probably could have handled things better with Everett. Warned him before he arrived back in Wickenburg that she and Brody were together.

"Macy?"

"Yeah." She shook her head, rousing herself.

"You looked sad for a second there."

"I was just thinking. Thank you, Everett. Seriously. For earlier. When I woke up to find Joey missing, I nearly had a breakdown." Her voice started to tremble as the emotions from that terrifying moment returned. "I'm probably overprotective, but after losing Brody…"

"Are you okay? You're shaking."

"Am I?" To her shock, she started to cry. A delayed reaction, apparently. "I'm s-sorry. Some days, it's hard." Her glance cut to Joey, who was playing quietly by the rocking chairs. "I didn't sleep much last night." That must be the reason for her high emotional state.

Before she quite knew what was happening, Everett's arm went around her shoulders, and he pulled her close.

"You have a lot going on. And I…" He paused. "I haven't made things any easier for you."

"No, you haven't." She sniffed, on the verge of crying again. "What went wrong, Everett? We used to be friends."

"I want to still be friends."

"Can we find a way?"

"I think so. Maybe."

She turned into him, resting her cheek on his chest. His arm tightened, and Macy sighed. It had been so long since someone held her, and she'd missed it.

Raising her face to his, she said, "I'd like that."

His answer was both unexpected and, Macy realized, may have been what she was secretly longing for: Everett lowered his mouth and pressed his lips to hers. She sighed and melted into the kiss. His arm went around her, drawing her closer. She stood on her tiptoes, giving herself over to the moment.

This wasn't their first kiss, but it might as well have

been. It didn't compare to the awkward, innocent ones they'd shared as teenagers. She reveled in his confidence and his maturity and the changes the years had brought in him.

When she moved her hands to cup his cheeks, he suddenly broke off the kiss and stepped away as if she'd kicked him in the shin.

"I shouldn't have…" He faltered. "I'm sorry."

"Don't, Everett." An apology would turn the lovely moment they'd shared into something tawdry. "There's no need. I wanted you to kiss me."

"That's not it." He swallowed. "I—I've been lying to you, Macy. And I can't keep doing it. I care about you too much. And Joey, too."

Macy felt a chill course through her. "Lying about what?"

"The accident. Brody didn't have to die."

She straightened and stumbled backward, needing to distance herself from Everett more than she'd craved his closeness minutes ago. "I think you'd better tell me everything."

CHAPTER EIGHT

"LET'S SIT DOWN," Everett said, his stomach churning. He'd dreaded this conversation and hoped to never have it.

Macy sent him a worrisome look. "What do you mean, Brody didn't have to die? What are you saying?"

"Please." He gestured to the rocking chairs. No way would he tell her about the accident standing there in the middle of the mare barn. Her knee joints might not be giving out, but his were.

Nearby, Joey played with his rocks, lining them up in a long and crooked row. Everett worried the boy could overhear them, but he appeared focused on his activity, paying no attention to them.

"Does this have something to do with our kiss?" Macy strode to the rocking chairs and claimed one. "Because we did nothing wrong."

"*You* did nothing wrong." Everett lowered himself into the empty chair beside her.

"I understand if you feel like we betrayed Brody, but we didn't. I loved him. I still do. A part of me always will. But it's been three years. I don't believe he'd want me to spend the rest of my life alone. Not that there's anything between you and I," she hastily added. "We had a moment. That's all it needs to be and doesn't have to happen again. Not if we'd, *you'd*, rather it didn't."

"This has nothing to do with our kiss. At least…" Everett drew a breath. "Not *just* the kiss."

"What then?" Exasperation had crept into her voice.

"I like you. I always have. When I first came back after high school and you and Brody were dating, I admit I was jealous."

"I like you, too. When we're not disagreeing." She paused. "Is that what this is about? Are you still trying to convince Pop to sell the ranch and move to a nursing home—"

"No." How could he tell her? Revealing a three-year-old secret was no easy feat.

She began rocking the chair with extra force, his stalling clearly getting to her.

"You said you lied about the accident. I don't understand. I read the police report. The other driver was in the wrong and caused the collision. He was found guilty of vehicular manslaughter and served time, then released early for good behavior. But you know that."

"I was notified by the court."

Everett often wondered how the driver lived with himself. Did he, like Everett, have regrets and play the what-if game? *What if my wife had been killed by someone disobeying a traffic law? What if my three kids had been in the car with her and died, too? What if I hadn't been in such a hurry that day and been five minutes late to my appointment instead?*

"Okay. Tell me about this supposed lie."

Everett closed his eyes. Maybe this would be easier if he didn't have to look at her and Joey over there playing with his rocks.

"Brody wasn't supposed to be driving that day. It was my turn."

The rocking slowed.

"But I was tired and, to be honest, a little hungover. I'd been out late the night before celebrating our roping championship and wasn't in the best shape to drive. Brody volunteered. He told me to nap in the back seat and take over later. He said he had some things on his mind, anyway, and driving would give him a chance to think."

Her face took on a stricken expression, and a small whimper escaped her lips.

"I am so sorry, Macy. It's all my fault." Fresh guilt tore at Everett. "Brody would be alive today if not for me."

"You don't know that." She spoke in a voice barely above a whisper.

"I do. I should have been the one driving. If I hadn't gone to the bar the night before—"

"What, Everett?" she snapped and twisted sideways in her seat to face him. "You'd be dead instead of Brody?"

He waited a beat. "Yes."

"Maybe. Maybe not. You might have left twenty minutes earlier if you weren't hungover and missed the man who hit you altogether. I mean, did you? Leave late because you had a slow start?"

"We, um…" They had left late. Everett remembered Brody shaking him awake multiple times in the hotel room bed and lingering in the hot shower.

"Maybe, if you were the one driving," she continued, "you wouldn't have been distracted by things on your mind, seen the other vehicle coming at you and swerved out of the way in time." Her face distorted into a mask of pain, and a bitter sob broke free. "I can do this all day. I've had plenty of practice over the last three years."

"Macy."

"You're not to blame for Brody's death. I am." The sobs came in force then, making speech difficult for her. Sharp intakes of breath punctuated every third word. "We argued on the phone the night before and again that morning. I was so angry at him. I wanted him to quit rodeoing, stay home and find a regular job. We had a baby on the way. And he was gone all the time. I was sick of having a part-time husband. I accused him of loving rodeo more than me and the baby. Those were the last words I said to him. I hung up on him after that. Hung up on him," she repeated and burst into gut-wrenching tears.

"Macy. Don't cry. Please." Everett scooted closer and rested a hand on top of hers. Rather than pull away, she clutched at his fingers in a desperate need for reassurance.

"He died before I had the chance to apologize or tell him that I loved him."

"He knew you did. Trust me on that."

"I'm a terrible person."

"No, you're not. We were on the road a lot. You were stuck at home dealing with a pregnancy all on your own. That had to be hard."

"I was selfish. He was winning that year and trying to earn enough money for when Joey came along. All I cared about was myself."

"He didn't think you were selfish. He understood."

"Did he tell you that? At the end? In the hospital?" Her voice broke. "You said he made you promise to look after me and Joey, but what else did he say? Did he mention our argument?"

"No. Not a word about that. Before or after the acci-dent. I swear, Macy."

"Was he planning on leaving me?" Pain filled her eyes.

"Absolutely not."

"I don't believe you." She stiffened and tried to draw her hand away. "You two were best friends. You're trying to protect me. Or him."

Everett squeezed her fingers harder. "I would tell you. I swear. Brody never said a single negative word about you or your marriage. Ever. He loved you. More than anything in the world and was fully committed. He couldn't wait to be a father and talked about it all the time."

She sniffed, her composure slowly returning. Everett gave her a moment before continuing.

"He was unconscious right after the crash. I was able to kick open the rear passenger door open and crawl out of the truck. People had stopped to help. Someone called 911. I wanted to get Brody out, but two guys held me back. He was in bad shape, and they were afraid moving him would cause more injury. I tried talking to him through the window. He didn't answer. But we could see he was breathing. Then help arrived."

"You didn't tell me this before," Macy said.

"I probably shouldn't now. It's hard to hear."

"No, go on."

Everett cleared his throat as old memories assaulted him. Three years hadn't softened the blows. "The paramedics took me to the other side of the fire truck to examine me. They wouldn't let me watch. I kept asking about Brody, how he was, and they'd give some generic answer like the firefighters and EMTs were doing everything in their power to save him. We were taken to the hospital in separate ambulances. By the time they let me in to see him…" An intense pressure compressed Everett's chest. Breathing became a struggle. "He was alive but drifting in and out of consciousness. It was during one of his lucid moments when he made me promise to watch over you and Joey."

She nodded but said nothing.

"He asked me to tell you how much he loved you and the baby. I got my phone out and started to call you so he could tell you himself. But he…he lost consciousness again and didn't… It wasn't long after that he…he passed." Everett didn't tell Macy how he'd held Brody's lifeless body and refused to let go, having to be pulled off by a pair of nurses. "The doctor said the trauma he sustained was just too great."

It was the same explanation he'd given Macy when she arrived at the hospital and Brody's parents on the phone.

"God, I would give anything to relive that last day." Macy's tears started anew.

Everett's, too. He'd imagined a dozen different scenarios in his head, but all that had ever gotten him was more guilt and more frustration.

"We can't change the past, Macy. Dwelling on it does no good. Pop recently told me as much, and he's right. Brody's last words were of his love for you and Joey. That's proof enough his feelings for you didn't change because of an argument."

Sniffling, she wiped her tears with her free hand. She had a distant look in her eyes that Everett recognized all too well. He'd seen the same struggle to accept what couldn't be changed reflected back at him in the mirror many times. It had only been since this past week, and since coming home, that this had started to change.

Confessing to Macy and hearing her angst from that final day of Brody's life had lightened some of Everett's emotional burden. He hoped it was the same for her.

THEIR QUIET MOMENT didn't last long.

"Mommy, Mommy." Joey ran over, concern pinching his small features. "Do you have an owie?"

Everett released Macy, instantly missing her touch.

"I do, honey," she said and scooped her son into her lap. "Where?"

She patted the area over her heart. "Here."

Joey leaned forward and touched his forehead to where she'd indicated. "Better?"

"Much better." She smiled and kissed the top of his head. "I love you, honey."

"I love you, too, Mommy. Can I ride a horse now?"

"In a few minutes, okay? I promise."

"Okay." He dragged the word out as he crawled off her lap and returned to his rocks.

"Brody would be proud of Joey." Everett watched the boy playing. "And of you for doing such a good job raising him."

"Is that why you stayed away?" Macy asked. "Because you think you should have been the one driving and died instead of Brody?"

"I figured you'd hate me if you knew the truth and deservedly so."

She started rocking again, albeit much slower. "I have no clue what I would have felt at the time. I might have been angry at you, it's true. But that's because you'd have become an innocent target for my grief and the rage I felt at myself. And that wouldn't have been fair."

"Not sure I agree with you," Everett said. "I made a big mistake."

She studied him then, her expression empathetic and without a trace of the anger she had every right to direct at him. "How hard it must have been for you, surviving an automobile accident when the other person died."

This was the second time since Everett's return that someone mentioned survivor's guilt. Was he that transparent? Or were people more understanding than he'd given them credit for?

He almost brushed off her comment. But Macy didn't need a reason to feel worse than she already did. Instead, he chose to level with her. She'd see right through him otherwise. "I've had some bad days."

"I'm so sorry, Everett." Her eyes misted again. "I should

have realized what you were going through. Looking at me must remind you of Brody and the accident."

It did. That wasn't her fault.

"Stop." He held up his hand. "Do not pile on yourself. You hear me? You couldn't have known what I was going through."

"Well, no one could have known." She sent him a very mild chiding smile. "You avoided us."

"I regret that now for a lot of reasons. Including Pop. I should have been here for him. Kept an eye on him. Maybe he wouldn't have gotten so ill."

"You couldn't have prevented his heart attack," Macy insisted.

"But I might have realized he was in financial trouble before his debt became overwhelming."

"What did you say about being unable to change the past and not dwelling on it?"

"You're right." He might have chuckled if their moods weren't so somber.

"I know there are things about Pop's agreement with the collective you don't like," Macy said. "But it's not a bad deal for him. If the mares produce healthy foals, we all stand to make some money. He'll have enough to pay the ranch taxes and insurance for two years at least."

Pop wouldn't need that if he sold the ranch. The money could go toward his current and long-term health care. On the other hand, if Everett stayed and took over the horse breeding business, he could contribute to those expenses. However, that plan would rely on Everett succeeding at the business, which he'd have to learn almost from scratch. It would also still put Pop in a nursing home, since he'd eventually need more assistance than Everett could provide.

Could there be another solution? His gaze traveled to the two seniors sitting at the picnic table on the patio. They were having a great time. Neither of them was in the best of health, but they were enjoying life to the fullest.

Everett had been that happy, too, before the accident. Macy seemed to be recovering. Mostly. He imagined she had bad days.

"We'd be happy to show you the collective's books and our business plan," she said, bringing him back to the present. "You can see for yourself how solid our plan is."

She wanted to convince him not to sell and let Pop continue to live here. If only things were that simple. But, maybe they weren't as complicated as Everett had been making them.

He didn't want to get into that now. Too risky. Their conversation could go quickly sideways. But now that he and Macy were back on somewhat level ground, he wanted to spend more time with her.

"All right," he relented. "What could it hurt to have a look?" What *could* it hurt?

"Maybe we could get to that brainstorming afterward." She smiled.

He returned it. "I'd like that."

"Good morning!"

At the greeting, they both glanced up to see Abel hobbling toward them from his motor home behind the stallion quarters.

"Hey, Abel." Everett raised his mug. "Can I get you some coffee?"

"Already had a cup with my breakfast, thank you." When Everett started to rise, he shook his head. "You stay put. I see Pop and Susan on the patio. Going to head over and say good morning." He shuffled on, his cane scraping in the dirt. "Morning, young man."

"Hello." Joey swiveled on his bottom and waved.

Everett watched Abel go. Interested in how, in a short

amount of time, Pop had acquired three houseguests, two of them elderly like himself. He marveled again at how happy they seemed as Pop gestured for his old friend to sit with him and Susan.

When you counted the collective members' daily comings and goings, the ranch was like grand central station. And Pop loved it. All Everett had to do was look at the old man to see the joy on his wrinkled face.

Macy rose from the chair. "I'm going to take Joey for a short ride. Then check on Roxie and leave for work."

"All right." Everett also stood.

She paused as if she was uncertain. Finally, she asked, "Do you want to come with us? It's fine if you don't. You're probably busy."

The tightness in Everett's chest had eased. Having a real conversation with Macy, more than their kiss, was responsible. Perhaps the two of them could work through some of their grief and guilt together while he was here.

"I'm not busy. And I'd like nothing better."

Her brown eyes shone. "Okay. Good."

While she fetched Joey, Everett went into the barn and got Butterscotch, the sorrel mare he'd seen Joey riding before. Five minutes later, the little boy was sitting on a bareback pad atop Butterscotch's back, kicking ineffectually with his short legs. The mare cranked her big head around and gave him a withering look, which made no difference.

Everett and Macy walked side by side, their hands occasionally brushing. Neither of them commented on the contact or made an effort to avoid it from happening.

"Look-it, Mommy. I'm galloping."

"Yes, you are, honey."

Macy showered Everett with a warm glance. He was glad his grandfather had summoned him home. Very glad.

A FEW DAYS LATER, Macy sat at the kitchen table with Everett, Pop and Sheriff Andy. Joey played in the family room with a hugely overweight but gentle dachshund that Sheriff Andy was fostering for the local animal shelter. The retired real estate broker had a real knack with animals and had volunteered at the shelter for years. Macy knew this well, as the clinic where she worked often provided pro bono, or very low-cost, vet services to the shelter.

This dachshund, recently homeless when her owner fell and broke a hip, was in Sheriff Andy's care until she lost weight through diet and exercise. After that, a suitable forever home would be found for her. In order to socialize the dog, ironically named Peanut, he took her everywhere with him.

Having met the dog first at the vet clinic and again today, Macy was considering being that home. She still thought a pet of any kind was too much for her busy schedule. But, if Peanut turned out to be as affable and obedient as she seemed, Macy's mom might be willing to watch Peanut, along with Joey, while Macy worked. Might. Time would tell.

Seeing Joey as he rolled around on the family room floor with the dog, the pair of them playing scratch-my-fat-belly-and-I'll-lick-your-face, her resolve was weakening.

"So, as you can see," Sheriff Andy said, pointing to the screen on his laptop, "we're projecting a twenty to twenty-five percent return on our investment."

Everett studied the screen. "That's assuming all the mares carry to term and their foals are born healthy."

"Even if we were to lose one foal, which would be tragic, we'd still see a ten to fifteen percent profit. And as long as the mare remained healthy, we could try again the following year."

"The bottom could fall out of the horse market. That's happened before when the economy soured."

"There are risks in any investment."

"Seems there are a lot of risks in this one." Everett sat back and sipped his root beer. "Pregnancy complications. Birth defects. Disease. Genetic disorders. The economy."

"The mares and Champ have all been tested," Pop interjected. "I have their health certificates."

Macy had to bite her tongue. She knew the meeting would go better if she let Sheriff Andy take the lead.

Everett had accepted her earlier offer to review the collective's books and business plan. To that end, they'd agreed to meet today at four. Macy had arranged to leave work early and brought a bucket of fried chicken along with all the fixings for dinner after the meeting. She didn't want anyone distracted by thoughts of dinner preparations.

Pop was already having trouble concentrating. Susan had returned home yesterday. Her ankle was much improved, and there was no real reason for her to stay. Her granddaughter had come by and collected her.

Macy hadn't been here at the time. She'd heard from Everett that Pop had been down in the dumps ever since. Of course, he'd see Susan again soon. They already had future lunch plans. But he missed her terribly. His gait had slowed in the last two days, and frown lines creased his brow.

Yet another reason why Macy wanted this meeting with Everett to go well. If he felt confident in the collective's agreement with his grandfather, once he learned of the income potential, he would hopefully be more open to remaining in Wickenburg and taking over the horse breeding business.

And then Macy could broach the subject of Pop remaining on the ranch with Everett and receiving home care rather than going to a nursing home. She and Everett had made tremendous strides in their relationship this past week. However, she wasn't ready to test it by tackling a touchy subject too soon.

What if she scared him off? Macy hadn't forgotten his broken promise. She wanted to believe he'd changed or *was* changing. But her trust in him had yet to be fully restored.

"We've tried to cover every contingency," Sheriff Andy continued. "And you can see from our bank account balance, we have plenty of funds to support the mares and their foals for two years."

"Are you taking advance deposits on the foals?" Everett asked.

"We're discussing that. We'd have to get our attorney involved. Have him draw up an agreement."

That remark launched a discussion about the collective's LLC and how it worked. Macy almost objected. That part wasn't any of Everett's business, only their agreement with Pop. But, again, she kept quiet, opting for complete transparency. That was the only way to earn Everett's trust.

"Mommy." Joey appeared at her side. "Peanut wants to see the horses."

"Are you sure?" Macy suspected Joey wanted to take the dog outside to play, and this was an excuse.

"I'm sure."

The meeting wasn't over. "In a little while, okay?"

"Please."

A whine had infiltrated his voice. If Macy continued refusing him, he'd have a meltdown. That wouldn't help the meeting.

"Just for a few minutes." How much could she miss?

"Yay! Come on, Peanut."

Joey returned to the family room and tugged the dachshund along by the bright red collar she wore. For a dog that supposedly wanted to go outside and see the horses, she moved rather reluctantly.

"We won't be gone long," Macy told Everett, Pop and Sheriff Andy.

They hardly glanced up from the laptop screen.

"Take your time," Everett said.

What had them so riveted? She'd been preoccupied with Joey and lost track of the conversation.

Outside, Joey ran ahead toward the mare barn. Macy lagged behind with Peanut. The overweight dog waddled along, her tongue lolling, her tail wagging.

She had a sweet face, Macy decided, and her sable coat glistened in the late afternoon sun. She certainly had the right temperament for a young child, and small dogs were easier to care for, too.

"You think you could develop a bad habit or two so I'd have a reason not to adopt you?" Macy asked.

Peanut raised her head and gave Macy a silly dog smile.

Macy's resolve softened with the beginnings of affection. "I think I'm in trouble."

The dog wasn't the only one growing on her. Everett was slowly worming his way into that soft spot she'd carefully guarded since Brody's death.

She hated the idea of that meeting going on without her. What were they discussing? Everett had impressed Macy with the intelligent questions he asked. Why did he not think he'd be good at taking over Pop's horse breeding business?

In the barn, Joey showed Peanut the mares, which consisted of him running up one side of the aisle and down the other, banging a hand on each stall door with an occupant and saying, "Here's a horse," and, "Here's a horse," over and over. Once the mares realized they weren't going to be fed yet or get a treat, they ignored him.

Everett had let them all out into the pasture for most of the day, giving them a bit of exercise. Macy wished she'd been there. She always liked seeing the entire small herd milling peacefully.

Peanut also ignored Joey. She'd waddled to a corner near the door and was sniffing in earnest. A bug or mouse must have caught her attention. Well, dachshunds were small hound dogs and good hunters. Though, with twice the girth of a normal dachshund, Peanut might not be good at anything beyond sniffing.

Joey joined the dog, dropping to his knees to investigate the corner.

"Be careful, honey. Get back," Macy said. What if Peanut had discovered a snake or a black widow spider? She should see for herself. "What did Peanut find?"

Before she could get there, Joey withdrew his hand and raised it high in the air. "Look-it."

He held an old, decayed chicken bone. Peanut tried to jump up and grab the discovery from his hand but was unable to achieve enough height.

"Joey!" Macy hurried over. "Put that down." The moment the words were out of her mouth, she changed her mind. "No, wait. Give it to me. Don't let Peanut have it." The filthy thing was not only a choking hazard, it was likely riddled with germs and would make the poor pup sick.

She took the bone and walked over to the trash barrel. Peanut danced after her. At this rate, she'd lose half a pound.

"Sorry, girl. When we go back inside, I'll give you a healthy snack, like carrot or apple pieces."

Peanut sent her a pitiful look that Macy was certain had weakened her former owner's resolve and accounted for all the extra pounds.

"I think you're going to be trouble, young lady."

Peanut barked. Joey came over, his hands and jeans from the knees down covered in dirt.

How was the meeting going? Macy really wanted to return to the house.

"Time to go inside, honey."

"Aw, Mommy. Do I have to?"

"What if we take Peanut for a walk?" Five minutes, and she could circle back around to the house.

"Sounds like fun."

Hearing Everett, Macy spun. He looked tall and rugged, his broad shoulders filling the doorway. "Oh. You're here."

"Everett." Joey raced over to him. "Peanut found a bone."

"Really?"

"Mommy threw it away."

"Was it a dinosaur bone?"

Joey burst into giggles. His idea of dinosaurs came from the picture books Macy read to him.

"We're walking Peanut. You want to come?"

"Sure." He smiled at Joey, and then Macy. "If your mom's okay with that."

"What about the meeting?" she asked.

"We're done."

"You are?"

"Sheriff Andy's just leaving. He said to tell you thanks, but he has other plans for dinner."

"Um, okay." Macy hedged. "How'd it go?"

"Good. I'm actually impressed. You and the other members have quite the operation." His handsome smile widened.

Macy experienced the now familiar little ping in her heart. Was it attraction or something deeper? She was afraid of the answer. She didn't feel ready for a relationship, not yet, and Everett didn't seem willing to settle down. If he was willing, taking over for Pop wouldn't be an issue. He'd have agreed in the beginning to stay.

She had to protect herself, and Joey, until he made his intentions clear. Better to squash that ping before it turned into something bigger, like real feelings. The last thing Macy wanted was to get hurt. She was still healing from losing Brody.

"Has your mind been put at ease?" she asked.

"About some things, yes."

"Not others?"

"Let's walk Peanut," he said and gestured. "We have a few minutes before the horses need to be fed and dinner's ready." He chuckled. "And she can't go more than a hundred yards without dropping from exhaustion."

He was right about that.

Like before, Joey led the way. When he wasn't skipping, he extended his arms as far out to the sides as they would go and pretended to be a plane, even providing engine sounds. Peanut lagged behind with the adults.

"I'm thinking of maybe adopting her," Macy said.

Everett did more than chuckle this time. He laughed out loud. "Macy Sommers, you are a pushover."

"She's a good dog."

He just shook his head.

Their interaction was so very reminiscent of days gone by when they were friends. The sensation increased with Everett's next remark.

"Hey, Joey," he called and waited for her son to turn around. "Did anyone ever tell you about the time your dad and I were riding our horses in the desert, and we came across a mountain lion?"

"A lion?" Joey ran back to join them.

Macy expected him to take hold of her hand. Instead, he placed his small one in Everett's.

"Yep. I was scared and wanted to get out of there. Your dad, he was brave and rode his horse right up on that big old cat."

Joey gasped. "What happened?"

"Your dad and that mountain lion stared at each other for a full two minutes. And then, all of a sudden, the mountain lion took off running lickety-split into the brush."

"Lickety-split," Joey repeated.

"It was something else."

Macy had never seen anything like this. Her son completely enraptured with a man other than his grandfathers. And Everett? He couldn't be more charming.

She'd done her best to bring Brody to life for Joey. She'd told many of her own stories, shown him pictures of Brody and videos and magazine articles. Having never had a father, she wasn't sure Joey, at two and a half, understood. Maybe this interaction with Everett would help.

"Tell me another story," Joey pleaded.

"Okay," Everett said. "Might take a while. I have a lot of them. But first. A riding lesson."

"I'm gonna ride a horse?"

"Not quite." He lifted Joey into his arms, and they returned to the mare barn. There, he sat Joey in a saddle on a freestanding rack where it awaited cleaning. "I'm going to teach you how to ride."

Joey gasped with excitement.

"First, hold on to this." He patted the saddle horn.

Joey gripped it tight with both his hands. He was much too small for the saddle, but that didn't seem to matter.

He then moved Joey's legs into position. "Keep these straight, okay? Not all bunched up. That's how cowboys do it."

"I'm a cowboy."

"Just like your dad." He patted Joey's shoulder, keeping his hand there to steady the boy.

Joey gazed up at Everett with undisguised hero worship. The ping Macy had felt earlier sharpened into a stab of pain. She suddenly realized more was at stake here than just her renewed attraction to Everett. Her son was also becoming attached to him. And if Everett left, which he well might, he'd break Joey's small heart. That would hurt worse than Macy's own disappointment.

Tears stung her eyes, unbidden.

Everett turned, and when he saw her, his expression filled with concern. "What's wrong?"

Macy composed herself, deciding to be straight with him. "I just hope you'll be around for a while to tell Joey a lot more stories. You're one of the few connections he has to his dad."

For a second, she thought she might have scared Everett off and that he'd leave them and go into the house. Instead, he continued speaking, a pleasant rumble in his voice.

"When your dad and I were fifteen, we rode our first bulls. And we both got thrown. I lasted two seconds longer than your dad, and I didn't break my arm, either."

They spent the next fifteen minutes with Everett interjecting tips on horseback riding in between feeding the horses and stories of him and Brody during their errant youth. Nearby, Peanut snoozed. When Pop called them for dinner and they sat around the table eating, it felt a little like a family gathering.

Macy didn't want the evening to end.

CHAPTER NINE

EVERETT WENT IN search of the footstool, finding it in the storeroom. He then wandered over to where Pop and Abel sat in the rocking chairs. They'd scooted the chairs inside the mare barn in order to watch the most recent downpour without getting wet. After an overcast, gloomy day, the rain finally made an appearance around four o'clock.

The instant twenty degree drop in temperature was a welcome relief from the sweltering heat and humidity. Everett had gotten Champ in from the pasture only moments before the first fat drops fell and turned the red-brown dirt a deep, muddy rust.

Sitting on the footstool, Everett removed his cowboy hat and shook off the water before replacing it on his head.

"We sure do need this rain," Abel commented.

Pop nodded as he rocked. "That sprinkle the other day wasn't near enough."

Everett's pocket vibrated. He removed his phone and read Macy's text. A small spark of anticipation flashed. He'd been thinking of her nonstop since yesterday and the riding lesson with Joey.

He should have told her he was no longer averse to the idea of staying. The two of them were getting along better. Well, in fact, their brief kiss aside. And after their talk when he'd confessed his part in the accident and she told him about her last gut-wrenching argument with Brody, him being unable to live in the same town with her had ceased being an obstacle.

There were still problems to resolve, and Everett didn't want to get ahead of himself. For one, his uncertainty about his ability to take over the horse breeding business remained. He had no experience—either with running a business or with breeding horses. There had to be more to it than throwing two horses together and hoping for the best.

If they didn't sell the ranch, Pop would be able to advise Everett. Macy could be a help, too, assuming she was agreeable. But what about Pop's medical care? His needs were growing daily. And what if he got worse? As little as Everett knew about the horse breeding business, he knew less about taking care of an ailing octogenarian.

What if he failed to notice that Pop was having another heart attack? Or he grew dizzy and fell while Everett was away from the ranch on business? He supposed he could insist Pop wear one of those medical alert devices, though that would be an uphill battle.

Everett's biggest concern was generating immediate income. If he had to foot all the ranch bills, his savings wouldn't last past the first quarter of the year. Could he accomplish that with the breeding business? To attract new customers, they needed to make repairs to the ranch. He may be a rookie when it came to running a business, but he knew that it took money to make money.

The rodeo coaching job did pay well, and part of him hated the idea of turning it down. Everett believed he'd be good at working with teens and preteens. Too bad he couldn't give lessons here on the ranch. That would require an arena, however.

Though, on second thought, there were other small arenas in town. Maybe he could work with the owners. Give them a percentage of the registration fees in exchange for use of their facility.

Wait a minute. Him giving rodeo lessons in town? He hadn't even figured out his next move when it came to Pop and the ranch.

Rereading the text from Macy, he told Pop and Abel what it said. "Because of the rain, the collective won't be here today."

"I'll miss seeing them," Pop said.

"She's still coming." Everett typed a reply. "She asked if I can help her clean the stalls. I'm telling her she can skip a night. I'll feed the mares and clean the stalls."

"Good idea. She should stay home." Abel squinted at the distant hills. "Roads are dangerous in this kind of weather. Gotta watch out for flash floods."

Everett's phone vibrated again. He read Macy's message out loud. "She insists on coming. Says she needs to put a fresh dressing on Beauty's injury."

The large black had cut her foreleg on a piece of wire in the pasture yesterday. While not serious enough for stitches, the wound did require a daily cleaning and a fresh dose of antibiotic ointment.

"Can't you do that?" Pop asked.

Everett typed into his phone. "I'm telling her now."

"She fusses over those mares as much as she does her own boy."

"What she needs is to find someone new." Abel tapped his cane on the barn floor. "A shame for a pretty young girl like her to spend her life alone."

Everett wasn't sure Macy would appreciate Abel's remark. If she decided to have a relationship with a man, it would be because she wanted to or had fallen in love, not because she was spending her life alone. But Abel meant well. He liked Macy and wanted to see her happy.

Once again, Everett's phone vibrated. "She insists. But she's leaving Joey at her parents'."

"That's smart," Pop agreed.

Everett typed a response.

See you when you get here.

While Pop and Abel chatted, Everett pulled up the rodeo schedule on his phone. He then checked his current ranking, which hadn't changed significantly over the weekend. If he stretched his week-to-ten-day stay to, say, three weeks, he could return to the circuit and, as long as he did well, still qualify for Nationals in December.

The extra time would give him a chance to explore more options, like taking over the business from Pop and arrangements for his care. Perhaps Pop would agree to let Everett speak with his doctors and get the full scoop on his condition, giving Everett a better picture of the situation. Pop could be capable of more than Everett was giving him credit for. Or less. At the end of three weeks, Everett could decide—on that and a lot of things.

He closed the schedule on his phone and texted his buddy Rusty, letting him know he should definitely partner up with Junior for the Big Timber Rodeo. As he hit send, a thought occurred to him. Rusty might make a good coach, too. Would he possibly be interested? Would the Oklahoma Twisters be interested in him?

A short while later, Macy arrived. Standing, Everett motioned for her to park in front of the barn rather than alongside it. Too much runoff water accumulating back there. Her tires might get stuck. And while he wouldn't mind an unplanned stay, she no doubt wanted to return home to her son.

She darted from the truck to the barn, her plastic rain

poncho flapping in the breeze. Inside the barn, she came to a stop and pushed back the hood, revealing a head of damp hair and face glistening with rainwater.

For just a second, she looked like the teenager who, at seventeen, had stolen Everett's heart. He was instantly smitten, like he'd been ten years ago. He also felt some of the same awkwardness he had in those days and struggled for words.

"Do you, ah, need your medical bag?"

"Oh." She glanced at her truck and sighed. "I forgot to grab it in my rush."

"I'll go."

Before she could protest, he dashed out into the rain and retrieved the bag from the back seat of her truck. When he returned, he, too, was soaked.

"You didn't have to do that." She beamed at him.

"No problem." He nodded at the bag in his hand. "Where do you want this? Beauty's stall?"

"Thank you."

Ignoring Pop's and Abel's amused chuckles, he accompanied Macy. They stopped in front of the stall holding a sleek black half-Arabian and half-quarter horse with a long, thick mane and tail. Beauty had been aptly named, and her breeding would produce an interesting foal, especially when crossed with Champ's dark chestnut coloring and heavily muscled body.

From her Arabian ancestors, she'd inherited an often fiery temperament, which explained how she'd gotten into a fix with the pasture fence and injured her leg.

"Hiya, girl." Macy opened the stall door and squeezed inside.

Everett passed her a halter, and a moment later, she led the mare out and into the aisle where there would be more room to maneuver. She tethered Beauty to the hitching rail and then removed the old dressing from her lower front leg. The angry-looking wound didn't appear infected.

It would, however, leave a scar. When the rain stopped, possibly tomorrow, Everett would walk the pasture fence and search for any other sharp pieces of metal or protruding wires.

"If you don't need me," he said, "I'm going to feed the horses."

The rest of the mares were making a ruckus.

"You want to borrow my poncho?" Macy had removed it and hung it from a nearby hook.

"I'll be fine. I won't melt."

She smiled. "I would have disagreed with you five days ago."

"I wouldn't have made that claim five days ago."

She laughed before redirecting her attention to Beauty's injury.

Everett retrieved the wheelbarrow, which had been left outside, and, dumping the accumulated water, pushed it to the hay shed. After feeding Champ first, he maneuvered the full wheelbarrow into the mare barn where the hungry occupants greeted him with eager nickers and restless pacing.

"You're drenched." Macy stood with her hands on her hips. Beauty's leg sported a fresh bandage, and she strained the lead rope, more than ready to eat.

"Proof positive I won't melt."

Macy rolled her eyes, and he went about tossing flakes of hay over stall walls and into feed troughs. Heads dived in, then popped up, jaws working as sprigs of hay stuck out of the sides of mouths.

Macy untied Beauty, and the half-Arabian muscled her way into her stall, unwilling to wait even for her halter to be removed.

"Okay, Miss Piggy," Macy chided, refastening the latch. "Excuse me for getting in the way."

"She's willful, that one." Everett much preferred the generally more docile quarter horses.

"I'm going to give Roxie a quick once-over while I'm here. Can't be too careful with colic."

At some point while they'd been busy, Pop had gone inside the house and Abel had returned to his motor home. Everett had no reason to stick around. Macy, either. He anticipated her heading to leave in order to pick up her son. Only she didn't.

Together, they meandered to the barn opening and watched the rainfall. It had lessened somewhat. Though only about six o'clock, the sun made an appearance, the rays hidden behind a heavy blanket of clouds that gave the impression of it being much later.

Everett decided to tell Macy about his recent decision. "I changed my mind."

She faced him, her expression expectant. "About what?"

"I'm extending my stay in Wickenburg. At least for a few more weeks."

"At least?"

He lifted one shoulder in a shrug. His wet shirt clung to his skin. "We'll see. I'm giving myself some time to explore options."

"What kind of options?" Hope lit her expression.

"I don't know the first thing about the horse breeding business."

"You're smart. You can learn."

"I can," he agreed. "My biggest concern is Pop and his care. Present and future. You know how stubborn he can be and independent."

"I thought your plan was to put him in a nursing home."

"He'd be miserable. And if I were to stay—"

"Oh, Everett." Macy went limp with relief. "I'm so glad to hear you say that. He *would* be miserable. And depressed."

"I'm just not sure what else to do. I searched online earlier. I guess there are caregivers you can hire."

"What about Callie?" Macy said excitedly. "She's great at her job."

Everett shook his head. "I don't know if Pop would agree to that. A young woman… He's a private person. He'd be embarrassed and resist, which would defeat the purpose."

"Total Home Nursing Services has male caregivers."

"Hmm. That might work. I'm hoping Pop will let me talk to his doctors and get an idea of his needs."

"That's a really good idea. Will he?"

"Maybe. If I tell him that me staying is contingent on it."

She grinned. "You'd blackmail him?"

"Not blackmail. Encourage. He wants me to stay. I think he'll be willing."

"I think he will, too. If you want, I can ask Callie for some advice on how to approach Pop with the idea of accepting home care."

"Thanks, but I'll talk to her. After Pop and I have a chat. I'm not going behind his back."

"What if he refuses?"

Everett let out a breath. "I'll cross that bridge when I come to it. But I'd like to think he'll be cooperative if it means me staying."

"You could involve Susan," Macy suggested. "I'm sure she'd have some sway with him."

"We'll see. There's a lot to think about and to research. Guess I need to bone up on horse breeding, too."

"I have a thought." Her eyes sparkled.

Everett tried not to get lost in them—which was easier said than done. She was getting to him. And the feeling was both the same and different than when they were younger.

"I'm listening," he said.

"The collective has enough money to purchase another mare. Me and Kinsley and Sheriff Andy are attending a horse sale in Cave Creek on Saturday. You could come with us. You'd learn a lot."

"Are you taking Joey?"

"Of course." Macy grinned. "He'll have a blast."

Everett wanted to go, but he hedged. "I'm not sure about leaving Pop alone."

"Abel is here. Won't the two of them be all right for the day?"

"I suppose. And Susan's coming by for lunch."

"Which means Callie can check on everyone."

That was true. And Everett was only a phone call away. He could also let the neighbors know he'd be away and ask them to drop by in the afternoon.

"I would like to go," he admitted.

"We can feed the mares and Champ before we leave." Macy spoke quickly, her excitement contagious. "And either Glynnis or one of the Hays can come by and feed at six if we're running late. But the sale should be over by three or four at the latest. We might have to stop for dinner on the way home, though. Joey gets hungry."

How could he say no? Then again, he didn't want to say no. Nothing appealed to him more than spending the day with Macy and Joey, and not just because he'd learn about breeding horses.

"Sure. Why not? Sounds great."

"Oh, Everett. I'm so happy."

He wasn't prepared for what happened next. Macy threw herself at him and wrapped her arms around his neck.

His, naturally, circled her waist. And then he pulled her close as his lips sought hers. She didn't pull away and, instead, leaned into him, giving herself over to the kiss—which lasted and lasted.

"Macy," he said during a pause to take a breath.

"Shh. Don't talk. We can figure this out later. For now, let's just enjoy." She brought his mouth down to meet hers for yet another amazing kiss.

And they remained that way until Pop came looking for them five minutes later.

MACY HADN'T BEEN to the rodeo grounds in Cave Creek for years. She used to frequent it in those days to watch Brody compete. Everett, too. He and Brody had been inseparable as friends and roping partners.

"See all the horses, Mommy," Joey chimed from the back seat and pointed with his chubby finger.

"Yes. There are lots of them."

She shifted in the truck's front passenger seat to check on her son. He'd handled the ninety-minute drive from Wickenburg well. She'd expected him to nap, as they'd risen earlier than usual. But no. Joey had been a chatterbox the entire drive, washing down his bites of dry cereal with a sippy cup of milk.

Everett maneuvered the truck and empty horse trailer through the crowded parking lot. Macy didn't bother telling him where to park. He was more familiar with the grounds than her.

"How are we doing on time?" he asked, studying the side mirrors as he eased into a space, reversed, adjusted and then pulled forward.

"Great. It's only seven forty-five."

Their goal had been to arrive well before the sale started at nine, affording them plenty of opportunity to walk the holding pens and inspect the hundred-plus horses being offered for sale.

Sheriff Andy parked his sedan alongside them, and he and Kinsley emerged. They'd taken two vehicles rather than cram the five of them together in Everett's truck. Sheriff Andy carried a travel cup of coffee, which had been filled at the start of their trip at the gas station on the outskirts of town. Knowing him, thought Macy, he'd be refilling the cup at the concession stand.

"At least we have beautiful weather," the older man commented as he skirted the truck to join Macy.

"The rain the other day helped. It's not quite so hot."

She opened the rear passenger door and removed Joey's portable stroller before lifting him from his car seat. He preferred to walk, but in case he grew tired, she'd have the lightweight stroller available for him to doze in. Her little boy had grown too big for her to carry around for long periods of time.

"Where to first?" Everett asked. He'd locked the truck after making sure Macy had everything she needed.

"The registration booth." She slung her backpack onto her shoulders. It contained Joey's emergency necessities, including snacks and drinks, boredom buster toys, disposable underpants and a clean shirt, along with her wallet and keys. She shoved her phone in her zippered shirt pocket. She needed her hands free and without having to worry about losing anything. "First, we get our bidder number."

They started out. Macy pushed the empty stroller, already having trouble with Joey who refused to listen.

"Don't run ahead, honey. Here, hold on to the stroller. No, don't touch that. Come back, Joey. Right now. I mean it."

She worried she'd lose her voice by the end of the day.

"Hey, sport." Everett motioned to Joey. "Why don't

you walk with me. I need someone to point out all the good horses."

Joey didn't hesitate. He ran to Everett and grabbed his hand.

"I'll go with you, Everett."

"Okay, but we're both sticking with your mom. She gets lost easily."

"I do not," Macy protested, but her smile stretched wide. That was until she noticed Sheriff Andy and Kinsley watching them. Kinsley waggled her eyebrows.

Was her and Everett's mutual attraction obvious to onlookers? She imagined so. They hadn't kissed again since the other day when Pop interrupted them. There had been lingering looks, however, and frequent, not-so-accidental brushing of fingers.

They'd spent the drive here this morning talking about Everett's research on home nursing care and his chats with Pop. The older man had been receptive to Everett accompanying him to his follow-up doctor appointment next week. He'd been less receptive about home nursing care, insisting he didn't need any help. That was no surprise.

At her suggestion, Everett had spoken to Callie and learned from her a better way to approach this sensitive subject with Pop. As a result, Pop had agreed to sessions with a physical therapist and an occupational therapist who would teach him ways to make everyday tasks easier. Both would prolong Pop's independence.

Whether Everett stayed or left Wickenburg, these were good steps for Pop to take. Macy was pleased for him and Everett, who'd expressed a sense of relief. And she was pleased for herself. Forward progress meant a better chance of Everett staying and the collective's agreement with Pop continuing.

They hadn't discussed what the future held for them.

It was too soon. But Macy had already begun picturing what having a relationship with him might look like. As she watched him and Joey walking hand in hand, that picture came more into focus.

Beneath a large canvas canopy marked Registration, they approached a folding table set up in front of the rodeo grounds office. Later in the day, the office staff would process payments for the successful bidders. Macy presented her ID and the collective's credit card. With the paperwork complete, she received her card stock bidder's number.

Assuming they were heading to the horse pens, she was surprised to see Everett registering.

"You thinking of buying a horse?"

"I might." He grinned.

"For yourself?"

"For the business."

"Really?" She suppressed her excitement. He must be considering staying if he was buying a horse.

"I don't know. Just thought I'd be prepared should I see something that strikes my fancy. Maybe I'm just caught up in the excitement."

He glanced around. Macy, too. People were everywhere and from all corners of the horse world. Many wore cowboy hats and ball caps with their jeans. Some sported dress slacks and button-down shirts. Others, overalls or shorts with Hawaiian shirts.

Most of the sellers appeared to be reputable breeders—such as the collective—and horse traders who made their living trading in livestock. Some of them represented stables specializing in cutting, roping or dressage horses. One hailed from the Prescott Valley racetrack. Macy recognized a seller who bought wild mustangs from the Bureau of Land Management and rehabilitated them.

There were also less scrupulous buyers and sellers in

attendance. Those looking to make either a quick buck or unload a sick or injured animal on an unsuspecting bidder. Which was why Macy and the others had come early. A wise bidder inspected the horses up close before they were put in the ring where flaws could be disguised by a clever handler.

Sheriff Andy met them outside the canopy. He carried his freshly filled travel mug of coffee. "Where do we start, boss?"

She blushed slightly at his nickname for her. Macy was the official head of the collective, but she really considered them a team comprised of equal partners.

"That way, I guess." She indicated the pens and set out with the stroller.

"Come on, sport." Everett took Joey's hand. The boy had yet to leave his side. "Where's Kinsley?"

"At the vendor tents." Sheriff Andy walked along beside them, sipping on his mug.

"Buying new tack?"

"Checking out the competition. There's another metal artisan here."

"She should look into renting a tent herself at the next sale," Everett said.

"I bet she's doing that very thing right now."

They reached the first long row of connected pens, each one only large enough to hold a single horse, a mare and her foal, or a pair of yearlings. There were even a few ponies, donkeys and mules.

Attached to each pen, dangling by a cord, was a plastic document protector containing information on the occupant that could include registration papers, health certificates, photos, medical history and information on the seller. Displays sat in front of a few pens with ribbons and awards to show off the occupant's winning potential.

They walked down the first row. Macy only examined the documentation if she was seriously interested in the horse. She was only interested in purchasing a mare, preferably a registered quarter horse. Color and conformation caught her eyes. Temperament mattered. A proven breeder was a plus.

A veterinarian was on-site and could be hired for a consultation if there was a concern. Macy was grateful for her equine knowledge. In addition, Dr. Beck had instructed her to call if she needed advice.

"Look-it," Joey said, his face all smile. "There's Champ."

They all turned to see a horse of similar chestnut color to Pop's beloved stallion that stood in a pen near the end of the row. Only this horse was a mare.

"Let's head over there." Macy took the lead.

The others followed. At the pen, she removed her backpack and placed it in the stroller. She didn't want to be encumbered in any way.

"Hey, pretty girl." She leaned her forearms on the pen's top railing. The horse met her gaze but remained rooted in place. Not a concern. This was a strange place with a lot of strange people. Exhibiting wary behavior was expected.

"You want to go for a ride, sport?" Everett swung Joey up onto his shoulders, probably to keep him busy and out of Macy's way—something she much appreciated.

The mare continued to assess Macy from the center of the pen. Another bidder was also looking at her, a tall, skinny cowboy with a silver belt buckle the size of a saucer.

It was no wonder the mare garnered attention. She was striking. There were other slight differences between her and Champ. The mare's mane and tail were threaded with strands of gold that reflected the sun's light. Smaller and more finely boned, she had a sweet face accented by large dark eyes.

The seller hovered nearby. An old-timer with bowed

legs and a full beard, he appeared to have several horses here today for sale and was going from pen to pen, answering questions for interested bidders.

"What's her bloodlines?" the cowboy asked.

Macy's ears pricked up. Nearby, Everett and Sheriff Andy chatted, though she noticed Everett glancing her way, as if also paying attention. Like before, Joey had removed Everett's cowboy hat and put it on his head, something that greatly amused him and strummed Macy's heartstrings.

"Her sire is out of Double Dun Down," the seller said and removed a sheet of paper from the document protector, which he passed to the man. "Here's a copy of her registration."

Macy knew the name. Most people in the horse business did. She really wanted to see that registration but waited. There was an unspoken rule at horse sales. If the seller was currently engaged in conversation with a bidder, anyone else interested had to wait until the bidder walked away.

While Macy cooled her heels, she gnawed the inside of her lip. After a moment, the mare sidled over and sniffed her arms and gently nipped her skin.

"Hi, girlie."

She reached up and scratched the mare's ears. The seller and the bidder were still engaged in conversation. From what she could gather, the bidder was in the market for a cutting horse. This mare had the right conformation and disposition. Did she have a born instinct for cows? That was less easy to determine in a sale pen.

Some sellers put a saddle on their horses and let potential bidders take them for a short ride. Generally, it was a good sign. This seller offered the option to the bidder.

"Let me have a closer look first," he said.

Macy thought she noticed a shadow of concern cross the seller's face, but it quickly disappeared. He opened the pen door, and the two of them entered. As they neared the mare, she moved away from Macy, presenting her previously hidden right side.

The reason for the seller's concern became immediately apparent. A prominent scar eight inches long ran along her back leg from her stifle to her gaskin.

"What happened?" the bidder asked.

"She was kicked," the seller explained. "Couple years ago. But she's sound. Everything's in her medical records. I had her vet checked just last week."

"How does it affect her performance?"

"Not at all." The seller motioned with his hand.

"What have you been using her for?"

"Mostly, my daughter's been barrel racing on her."

The bidder dipped his head and then retreated toward the pen door. "Sorry, man. She's a dandy, but I can't take a chance. An old injury like that could come back on her out of the blue, and a lame horse doesn't make me any money."

Macy saw her chance. As soon as the bidder walked away, she approached the seller before anyone else. "Can I see her?"

"She's not lame," the old-timer insisted, his expression determined. He hadn't liked the cowboy's insinuation. "I have a good reputation. Just ask the auction company."

"I'm not concerned about the injury, sir. At least, I'm not overly concerned," Macy added. "The mare's breeding and health matter more to me."

"Yeah?" He studied her with a mixture of curiosity and doubt. "And why's that?"

She straightened, wanting, *needing*, to be taken seriously. "Because I'm looking for a broodmare."

CHAPTER TEN

EVERETT HAD KNOWN Macy since they were freshmen in high school and in the same algebra class. They'd been friends much of that time, save for the last three years, and sweet on each other for a short while. But he'd never seen this side of her and, he had to admit, she impressed the heck out of him.

He and Sheriff Andy had stopped talking in order to move closer and observe her in action, conversing with the seller. There was a reason the collective looked to her as their leader, and it was on full display now. She handled herself with confidence and poise. Her expertise was evident in the intelligent questions she asked and thoughtful observations she made. More than once, the seller's brow rose with surprise and admiration.

"I'm thirsty." Joey swayed frontward and backward atop Everett's shoulders. "I want juice."

Everett gripped the boy's legs tightly. "In a bit, sport. Your mom's busy."

"I'm thirsty now," Joey repeated.

Sheriff Andy hitched his thumb at the stroller. "Macy probably has some of those pouch things in her backpack. I'll get one."

"Thanks," Everett said.

Probably a good idea to placate the kid. He didn't need to be out of sorts while his mom was impressing the socks off everyone.

The seller flashed Macy a gap-toothed smile. "Lady Moon Dust here would make a fine broodmare. She's had one foal already. It's right here in her paperwork."

Macy leaned closer. "Is that so?"

She went through the documents with the meticulousness of a police detective reviewing evidence. When she finished, she returned the packet to its place hanging from the railing. Then she entered the pen.

Lady Moon Dust showed no hesitation and came over to greet Macy. The seller extolled, in his opinion, the mare's many fine qualities while Macy conducted a thorough once-over. From what Everett could tell, the horse appeared healthy and well cared for and no more than eight or nine years old.

More interested buyers gathered at the sidelines to watch Macy, awaiting their turn and listening intently. This seller would have no trouble finding an interested buyer today. But would he get the price he wanted? Auction companies that operated the horse sales took a commission, cutting into profits.

"I'd like nothing better than to see her get a good home," Lady Moon Dust's seller said, giving her a pat. "She's a sweetheart."

Macy straightened from inspecting the mare's hooves. "Can I take her out and see how she walks?"

"Absolutely."

That was a good sign. If he'd objected, Everett would have wondered why. Macy spent another twenty minutes with the mare, even riding her bareback around the grounds with no more than a halter. The mare behaved impeccably. Another good sign. When Macy finished, she had one last question.

"How much to you want for her?"

"You offering to buy her outright?" the seller asked.

"Yes, I am. If my partners agree."

Sheriff Andy nodded at her and immediately got on his phone, presumably to contact the other collective members.

Sometimes, at horse sales, transactions were conducted at the pens. It was an accepted practice, as long as the commission was still paid to the auction company. There were benefits and drawbacks to both. A seller might get more in the ring. Or less. No way to tell. And a sale at the pens was guaranteed money.

Five minutes later, Macy and the seller shook hands. Each wore a wide smile. Everett, too. He liked watching her in action and had developed a newfound respect for her. He'd always believed she had potential, even back in high school, and was pleased to see her proving him right.

"Mommy."

Joey would have run to Macy if not for Everett holding him back. The kid had grown tired and bored in the last several minutes, given his pout. This was the point where Everett's lack of experience showed.

"She's almost done, sport."

"Mommy. Hurry, please."

Macy finally rejoined them, beaming from ear to ear.

"Congratulations," Everett said.

"She's a looker." Sheriff Andy hitched a thumb at the pen. "I'm going to take some pictures."

"I missed you, Mommy."

"Sorry, honey." Macy lifted him into her arms and hugged him tight. He laid his head on her shoulder. "Thank you for being so good."

"Can I ride the horse?"

"No. Not here. We don't have your special saddle."

"I wanna go home."

Macy sent Everett an apologetic smile. "He's tired. We were up early."

"I understand. I get cranky when I'm tired, too."

"I appreciate you watching him."

"No problem." Everett reached out and ruffled Joey's hair. He'd reclaimed his cowboy hat earlier after Joey had dropped it twice. "I suppose we could leave. We got what we came for."

"Yes." Macy hedged. "Except it's barely past nine. The sale just started in the ring. It's kind of fun to watch."

"What about Joey?"

"Let's walk around a bit. Find Kinsley. See what she wants to do."

"I vote for breakfast," Sheriff Andy said, returning from the pen.

They'd grabbed stale pastries from the gas station early this morning. Everett wouldn't mind something more substantial.

Macy coaxed Joey into the stroller, bribing him with a toy from the dollar store she'd hidden in the backpack in case of an emergency—an emergency being preventing Joey from having a meltdown.

Her ploy worked. Sort of. They started out walking along the last row of pens. By the time they reached the end, Joey had started to nod off.

And that was when Everett saw him. A tall gray horse with prominent dapple markings that caused him to stop in his tracks.

"Wait a second," he said.

"What is it?" Macy peered past him.

"See that young stallion over there? Next row over."

"He wasn't there before. Must be a latecomer."

Everett's feet were already in motion. Something about the horse drew him. It wasn't just his unusual color and markings or the regal shape of his head. He had an air about him that commanded attention. And he had Everett's.

"Wow, he's something else," Macy said as they reached the pen.

"Pop would call this kind of horse a showpiece."

"He's a little standoffish."

"A lot of stallions are, if they haven't been handled much or handled wrong."

Macy smiled. "And you said you knew little about the horse breeding business."

"I've been around bucking broncs enough to tell this guy isn't mean. He's just had very little human contact. Probably left in a pasture with his dam until someone weaned him and threw him in with a bunch of yearlings."

"And now he's here."

Fortunately, no one else was at the pen. Everett went right to the railing. Unlike Lady Moon Dust who'd immediately approached Macy, the young gray stayed back, staring at Everett with the same intensity as Everett stared at him. He liked that about the horse, despite his wariness of people.

After a few moments, a woman in her mid to late forties approached. With her tailored business attire and expensively styled hair, she looked nothing like the usual horse traders in attendance today. Then again, the rich populated the horse world every bit as much as those hanging by a thread.

"Morning," the woman said.

Everett nodded and touched the brim of his cowboy hat. "What can you tell me about him?" He and the young stallion continued their visual standoff.

"This is Gran Hombre Gris. The hands at my ranch call him Hombre."

Big Gray Man in Spanish. The name fit.

"He was foaled in February of last year," the woman continued, mindless of the dirt on her expensive suede shoes. "Registered quarter horse but, like a lot of them, he has some thoroughbred blood in him going back a couple generations."

Everett could see that in the set of Hombre's eyes, his bone structure and his height, which would only increase during the next year.

The seller removed the paperwork from the packet and handed it to Everett. According to the logo, the woman's ranch was located in northern Texas. Why had she come this far for a horse sale? Everett's curiosity was admittedly piqued.

"Take a look for yourself," she said. "If you're in the market for a stud, he'd be a fine addition to any breeding program."

Everett studied each page before passing them to Macy for her to inspect. By now, Joey was sound asleep. Sheriff Andy had wandered off in search of Kinsley and food, not necessarily in that order.

"Why are you selling him?" Macy asked.

It was a good question.

The woman sighed. "I'll be honest with you. I need the cash. I have two kids in college, and tuition is very expensive."

In Everett's opinion, she didn't look like someone who needed money. Then again, she may have recently encountered financial difficulties. Or her assets could be temporarily tied up—like the collective, which was waiting on the birth of the mares' foals.

"Why *this* sale?" Macy asked. "You're a long way from Texas."

"I had to deliver three horses to a buyer in Phoenix yesterday. Unfortunately for me, the buyer changed his mind about Hombre. Or I should say his wife changed his mind for him. She apparently controls the purse strings.

On a whim, I brought him here rather than taking him all the way home."

"Why wasn't he trained?"

More good questions. Everett could learn a lot from Macy.

"He's young still," the woman said. "Plenty of time for training."

Except training should start as early as possible. If not, bad habits developed. Still, Everett liked the horse and thought he had potential.

"I don't see any genetic testing in the paperwork." Macy riffled through the pages.

A really great question this time. Everett should have paid better attention when Macy was buying Lady Moon Dust.

"My secretary forgot to include those." The seller pulled out her phone. "I had her take a picture and send it to me." She opened the photo and enlarged it for Everett and Macy to read. "He passed. Negatives across the board. I can have my secretary email the result to you. That is, if you buy Hombre."

Here was the moment of truth. Money wasn't an issue. Everett had enough of his own saved up. But did he have the time and willingness to commit to training a young, exceedingly green stallion? That wasn't anything he could accomplish on the road or if he convinced Pop to sell the ranch. Was he ready?

To be brutally honest, his grandfather's business didn't need another stallion. Champ was more than enough. If Everett bought Hombre and then decided not to stay, he'd have two horses to sell.

Macy must have been reading his mind, for she gazed at him expectantly. What if he bought Hombre, decided to stay, and then Pop took a turn for the worst, forcing them to sell the ranch? Everett would then have to add disappointing Macy to his long list of mistakes.

He stepped away from the pen. "I need to think about it."

"You can take Hombre out," the seller said. "He's not broke to ride yet, obviously. But he's good under halter."

"No." Everett shook his head. He was afraid if he got close to the horse, his resolve would weaken. Buying a stallion was a step he wasn't ready to take. Not yet.

"All right." The woman retreated. "We'll be here if you change your mind."

Everett avoided looking at Macy. He didn't have to see her face to know he'd let her down. She'd wanted him to buy Hombre, seeing it as a commitment on his part to stay.

"How about we find Sheriff Andy and Kinsley and get something to eat?" he said.

By general consensus, the four of them agreed to stay for a while before heading home. Kinsley had never been to a horse sale before and was quickly caught up in the excitement. She tried to guess the final sale price for each horse that came into the ring and missed the mark each time.

All around them, bidders called out and raised their numbers in the air. Spotters in the ring kept a lookout, making sure no one was missed. The announcer described each horse as it entered the ring, listing its attributes and giving a bit of history. There were plenty of bargains to be had and a few horses that went for way too much money, in Everett's opinion.

Joey woke up soon after they'd entered the sale area, where they found seats on the bleachers. Like Kinsley, he was swept up in the newness and the excitement. Unlike her, he lost interest quickly. Every distraction Macy presented him with lasted only five minutes at most.

After a while, containing him on the bleacher seat became a challenge.

"What do you say we head home?" Everett said.

"Is that okay with everyone?" Macy looked around.

Sheriff Andy and Kinsley were in agreement. As they were organizing and preparing to leave, Hombre came into the sale ring, led by one of the ring hands. Everett went still, watching. Everyone else did, too.

"I just want to see what he sells for," he said and sat.

"Sure." Macy settled Joey in the stroller.

And then the bidding started. It began slowly. What others saw as misbehaving on Hombre's part, Everett saw as high spirits. A trademark of stallions. The auctioneer tried his best to excite the crowd and get the people to bid. Action picked up a little, but not much.

A seller had the right to refuse if the price didn't reach what they wanted. They'd still have to pay a fee to the auction house. The decision to sell or not was often made in a split second.

"Going once," the auctioneer said. "Going twice."

The price was ridiculously low. Hombre was worth five times that for his breeding alone.

"One thousand dollars."

Macy turned to stare at Everett. Only then did he realize he'd bid and that his hand was raised in the air, the one holding his number.

Bidding resumed with interest renewed. The price went up. Everett didn't think. He just bid.

"Twenty-two hundred," he hollered.

"Over here," a spotter shouted.

A young woman entered the action but fell out quickly when Everett outbid her.

"Going once," the auctioneer said. "Going twice." He

paused for several seconds before banging his gavel. "Sold to number 344."

Everett turned to Macy and felt his mouth break into a wide grin. "I think I just bought a horse."

She grinned back at him. "I think you did, too. What happened?"

"I don't know." He shrugged. "I suddenly realized I wanted him."

He also wanted everything that owning Hombre represented. But he didn't want to think about that now. Not yet.

MACY AND EVERETT headed to the auction office while Sheriff Andy and Kinsley made a final run to the concession stand. Joey wanted to walk, but Macy insisted he stay in the stroller. The crowd had increased in size. Too easy for a small child to get lost.

She bit her tongue as they went along, hoping Everett would mention his future plans for Hombre and, beyond that, his intentions to stay in Wickenburg. He did neither, his only comment wondering if he'd lost his mind for a moment.

"I'm not sure what got into me."

"It can be like that when bidding," she said as they stood in line. "In fact, auction companies count on the electric excitement running through the crowd and your natural competitive spirit to drive prices higher."

"I got a smoking deal on Hombre."

"I think his lack of training scared people off. I'd be surprised if he's ever seen a saddle, much less had one on his back."

What she thought but didn't say aloud was, if Hombre's behavior didn't improve, he'd be of no use, and Everett would have wasted his money. His claims of not being qualified to take over for Pop would have merit. She still believed he could learn the breeding business, but this could be a setback.

Was Everett always this impulsive? She tried to remember and thought yes. It hadn't bothered her before when they were just friends. Now, she had a son and future career at stake. Impulsivity could be a red flag.

After finalizing his transaction at the auction office, they met up with Sheriff Andy and Kinsley at the horse pens. Kinsley took over pushing Joey in the stroller so that Macy was free to lead Lady Moon Dust. The mare came willingly, following Macy as if she couldn't wait to get to her new home.

Hombre was a different story. He charged through the gate and would have escaped if Everett didn't have a strong hold on the lead rope. Once out, he pranced alongside Everett to the parking area, his erect head swiveling in every direction. With the sun reflecting off his sleek coat, Macy had to admit the horse was indeed a looker who would only grow more striking as he matured.

Lady Moon Dust loaded into the trailer with no problem. Everett and Hombre waited a short distance away just in case. When Hombre's turn came, he initially balked. Digging in his heels and snorting angrily, he put his weight on his back end and lowered his head.

After several failed attempts, Everett recruited help from Sheriff Andy and two other cowboys who'd stopped to watch. Between the four of them, they were able to convince Hombre that loading was in his best interest. Hating the cowboy hats they waved at him, the young stallion leaped into the trailer as if clearing a three-foot fence, landing awkwardly with a clatter of hooves.

"Look-it, Mommy." Joey pointed from their safe vantage point well away from the action. "The horse jumped."

"Yes, he did."

"Not the most graceful thing," Kinsley commented. "Everett's going to have his work cut out for him."

Macy almost asked Kinsley if she thought he intended to stay in Wickenburg, then decided against it.

Lady Moon Dust wasn't thrilled at the prospect of a ninety-minute drive home beside Hombre and nipped him several times to let him know. Mares typically disliked the company of stallions except during the time in their cycles when they were ready to breed. Only then did they welcome any attention, and sometimes that was touch and go.

Hombre wasn't deterred and kept reaching over to her side of the trailer, trying to make friends. Weary, she rebuked him with a swift kick that landed on the metal panel separating the two of them. Had Everett anticipated buying a stallion, they would have brought two trailers. With only one, the horses had no choice but to make peace.

"They'll settle down once we're on the road," Everett said, latching the trailer gate and engaging the safety chain. "The motion will distract them."

Soon after that, they left the rodeo grounds behind. Again, Macy silently willed Everett to raise the subject of Hombre or Pop's care or anything having to do with him staying. Instead, he talked about the last time he'd competed at the Cave Creek rodeo arena, the latest family news from his mom and gathering his courage to call Brody's parents.

"They'd love to hear from you, I'm sure," Macy said, reaching into the back seat to retrieve Joey's dropped toy.

"You don't think they'll be mad at me? For not coming around?"

"Absolutely not. They probably think you avoided them because they remind you of Brody and the accident."

"I'm sorry to say, they're not entirely wrong."

Eventually, they reached the outskirts of Wickenburg.

Just as she'd given up all hope, Everett finally raised the subject of Hombre. Sort of.

"Are you planning on breeding Lady Moon Dust now or wait until after the first of the year?" he asked.

"I have to check with the collective first. But I'm going to recommend we give her a month or two to get used to the ranch and her surroundings, make sure no health or behavioral problems arise, then breed her. We can't afford to keep a mare who isn't earning her keep."

"Makes sense." He turned at the next intersection, executing the corner with care so as not to unbalance their passengers in the trailer.

"What about you?" she asked, daring to probe. "Are you going to give Hombre time to get used to the ranch and his surroundings before starting training?"

"Not much time. I need to start working with him right away. He's gone too long without training as it is. With luck, I should be able to tell within a week if I made a good investment. If I can't use him for stud, I'd probably turn him into a gelding, train him and sell him. Hopefully for a profit."

"What about rodeoing and your coaching job?"

"I'm not sure, Macy. I don't have all the answers yet."

What she heard was he had no intentions of staying longer than his original time frame. "You can't procrastinate forever."

"I know that." A pronounced V appeared between his eyebrows.

How could he be impulsive one minute and stall the next?

The answer hit her even before she'd fully formed the question. Because he didn't like confrontations and dealing with unpleasantries. Like coming home after Brody's death. Macy faced her problems head-on and needed someone who did the same.

At the ranch, they drove past the house to the mare barn. Both Sheriff Andy and Kinsley were already gone. Able to drive faster, they'd reached the ranch well ahead of Everett and Macy.

"I can unload and feed the mares," he offered, "if you and Joey want to head home. You must be tired."

"I'll stay." She was tired, but she refused to leave without first making sure Lady Moon Dust was tucked in safe and sound for the night.

By the time he parked the trailer and unlatched the rear gate, Pop and Susan were strolling hand in hand from the house. Apparently, she'd stayed after lunch. Macy noticed the elderly woman still sported a slight limp from her sprained ankle and used a sparkly red cane.

Before long, Abel meandered over to observe the happenings. He'd probably be returning home tomorrow or the next day. His sister Glynnis was due to return from her trip. Too bad, really. Pop would miss the company, and Abel would miss his reprieve from his mother hen sister.

The three seniors stood in the shade of the mare barn to watch Everett unload the horses from the trailer. By now, Joey was refreshed from his long nap and bursting with energy. Macy couldn't take her eyes off him or he'd find trouble.

"Mommy, I'm hungry."

She'd begun to truly wonder if her son had a hole in his stomach. He never seemed to have enough to satisfy him.

"Okay. Okay. You wait over there with Pop while I get something from the truck."

Good thing she'd loaded up on snacks before they left. Glancing over at Everett, she quickly grabbed a package of peanut butter crackers from her backpack.

"Who are you unloading first?" she called out, giving Joey the opened package.

Her answer was a loud banging. Hombre was making his presence known as he shot backward out of the trailer, showing as little grace and agility as when he'd loaded back at the rodeo grounds.

From the paddock, Champ whinnied and raised a ruckus. He'd no doubt smelled the new horses and was ready to challenge Hombre while making Lady Moon Dust's acquaintance. He would get the opportunity to do neither today.

Everett tied Hombre to the side of the trailer, where he alternated between pawing the ground, prancing in place and whinnying.

"I want to give him a few minutes to calm down before I take him over to the stallion quarters. He's young, but I guarantee you he'll act up around Champ."

"Will they be all right together in the stallion quarters?" Macy asked.

"The two stalls are across from each other. That should put enough distance between them. If not, Hombre can stay in the round pen for a few days until they get used to each other."

Macy couldn't help saying, "I always thought stallions couldn't live together. That they fought."

"Some of the bigger horse breeding operations have more than one stallion. Pop did, too, for a while years ago. I remember him telling me they have to be introduced slowly and carefully managed. Hombre's immature enough Champ may not view him as a threat to his position."

"Yet."

"Right. I'm definitely going to have to research stallion management."

"Aren't a lot of racehorses stallions?" Macy asked. "And they race side by side on the track."

"They are. And an agent from the Bureau of Land Management once came to a rodeo. He talked about groups of bachelor stallions banding together in the wild."

"What if Champ and Hombre don't ever get along?"

Everett mulled that over before answering, his brow furrowing. "I suppose I'd have to sell Hombre."

Macy could tell he didn't like that option. Not only had he already developed a fondness for the horse, he wanted to prove himself as a capable successor to Pop's business.

"Your girl is next," he said. "Time to see if she likes her new digs."

Like before at the rodeo grounds, Lady Moon Dust exited the trailer with grace and composure. Macy immediately collected her from Everett and led her inside. She created quite a stir. Her new barn mates reached their heads out over the stall doors in an attempt to catch a whiff or nuzzle noses.

There were plenty of empty stalls to choose from. Macy picked the one next to Butterscotch, confident the older broodmare's sweet temperate would made her a good neighbor.

Dusty, as Macy was already beginning to think of Lady Moon Dust, immediately quenched her thirst with a long pull at the waterer. After that, she explored every corner of the stall, sniffing and digging with her front foot. To the dismay of the other mares, Macy gave Dusty a half bucket of grain. Food went a long way in aiding a horse's acclimation.

She stood at the stall watching the mare. "You're a good girl, aren't you?" She knew she should get back to Joey and start for home. But he was fine with Pop and the others, and Macy wanted a moment to herself.

This day trip with Everett had gone far different that she'd expected. Then again, so had her relationship with him since his return. She really needed to get her head on straight. They'd kissed, more than once, and she'd enjoyed it. There'd been no declarations from Everett afterward, however. Any expectations she had, including those she'd come to after he bought Hombre today, were entirely her own.

"Hi."

She started at the sound of his voice and spun. There he stood alone at the entrance to the mare barn.

"Admiring your new purchase?" he asked.

"Yeah." She collected herself. "I thought you were with Hombre."

"He's fine for the moment."

"Getting along with Champ?"

"I wouldn't say getting along." Everett joined her at Dusty's stall. "The two of them are squaring off from across the aisle. Whether they decide to fight or get along remains to be seen."

Suddenly, Macy was tired of tiptoeing around the subject. "You bought a stallion, one who needs training, without any forethought."

"Yeah?"

"You can't return to the rodeo circuit or head off to Oklahoma and leave Hombre here for Pop to deal with."

"No, I can't." He paused and inhaled deeply, his gaze connecting with hers. "I'm starting to think I can't leave here under any circumstances."

"What are you saying?" Hope flared anew.

"Nationals may have to wait another year. Or, if I show any promise at this horse breeding business, I just might retire."

"Oh, Everett."

"I'm recommending Rusty take my place with the Twisters. He was already on their short list, and I know he's interested."

"That's a great idea!"

"There's still the matter of Pop's care."

"We can figure that out."

"We?" His lopsided smile melted her heart.

"Yes." She went out on a ledge. "We."

"What are *you* saying, Macy?"

"You're not in this alone. I'm here to help in any way I can."

He inched closer. "And if I want more than just your help?"

The moment had come for her to decide. She either took a leap and told Everett how she really felt, or she put a stop to whatever was happening between them in no uncertain terms.

"Like I said." She also inched closer. "You're not in this alone."

And just in case she hadn't made herself clear, she wrapped her arms around his neck and planted her lips on his in a kiss that spoke way more than words could convey.

CHAPTER ELEVEN

EVERETT DROVE HIS truck into town on Monday afternoon, his destination Hayloft Feed and Tack. In addition to vitamin supplements, salt blocks and a training halter for Hombre, he wanted to introduce himself to the Hays, the only members of the collective he'd yet to meet.

He told himself he was simply being neighborly. The fact was, he thought it wise to establish a good relationship with all the collective members in light of him taking over the business from Pop.

Glynnis and her husband had returned from their trip yesterday. However, rather than take Abel home, everyone agreed he'd remain at the ranch a while longer. Pop liked the company, and enjoying a semi-independent lifestyle, it seemed, had a positive effect on Abel. His Parkinson's disease may not have improved, but his mood had flourished.

Plus, leaving Pop with someone else there rather than alone eased Everett's mind. Abel could at least call Everett or dial 911, should anything happen. Same could be said for Pop if Abel had a mishap. The two looked after each other. Everett knew the arrangement wasn't permanent. But in the meantime, everyone benefited.

Was that also true for him and Macy, that their arrangement, for what it was, benefited them both? He'd never forget their spontaneous kiss on Saturday and hoped not to disappoint her. He intended to stay in Wickenburg. And while they hadn't spoken about any kind of future, he wanted a commitment more than a one day at a time kind of relationship. What that would look like, he wasn't sure.

Often, during his and Brody's heyday, they'd visited Scottsdale, Arizona, a place self-dubbed the West's most Western town. Everett considered the name a misnomer. Wickenburg, with its old-time storefronts and boardwalks, cowboy museums, multitude of cantinas and bars, dude ranches and Vulture City Ghost Town just outside the city limits, was far more Western than the highly commercialized Scottsdale.

He'd loved growing up here as a kid and hated having to move. Returning wouldn't be so bad. It might actually be great.

On the corner of West Wickenburg Way and North Mariposa Drive sat a small strip center. Everett pulled in and parked outside the feed store, easily identifiable by the large sign above the shingled awning and life-size fiberglass palomino horse on display in front.

A buzzer announced his arrival when he pushed open the front door, and a chorus of tiny cheeps greeted him. There, immediately to his right, sat a brooder with chicks and ducklings for sale. They bunched together under the light bulb, keeping warm against the store's air-conditioned interior.

Pop used to keep a few laying hens around the ranch years ago. That might be something to consider. Everett would need to build a pen for them. Without a safe place to roost, chickens were vulnerable to hawks, coyotes and other predators.

"Hi. Can I help you?" A jeans-clad middle-aged woman with the upbeat demeanor of a salesperson sauntered over to Everett.

"Are you by chance Brenda Hays?"

"Oh!" Her mouth dropped open and then curved into

a bright smile. "You must be Pop's grandson Everett. I recognize you now. I've seen your picture in the house at the ranch."

"Nice to meet you, ma'am."

"Please, call me Brenda."

When he went to shake her hand, she pulled him into an embrace. "I hope you don't mind. I'm a hugger."

Everett didn't mind.

"Besides," Brenda said, releasing him, "we're practically family. My husband and I belong to the collective, and you're Pop's kin. Which reminds me." She grabbed his arm and escorted him deeper into the store. All around them, customers perused shelves and displays. The store contained everything from equine medications to pet food to Western clothing to gift items. "You have to meet Larry, my husband and partner in crime."

They found Larry in the rear bay, overseeing the loading of a large order of hay and grain into the delivery truck.

"Larry," she hollered to be heard above the din. "Come here. You'll never guess who this is. Everett. Pop's grandson."

Her husband motioned to the young man operating the Bobcat and wearing a Hayloft Feed and Tack T-shirt and then jogged across the bay to join them.

"Everett. Welcome." He didn't insist on hugging Everett when they shook hands. "We've heard a lot about you."

"I want to thank you both for all you've done and continue to do for Pop."

"He's been a good customer since we opened the store," Brenda said.

"And a better friend," Larry added.

They chatted for some time. Everett liked the couple, same as he did all the collective members. He didn't remember such camaraderie when he lived in Wickenburg.

Then again, he'd been young, just seventeen, when he moved away. And from the time he graduated high school, he'd lived mostly on the road.

It reminded him a lot of the community of professional rodeo competitors. There were many similarities. Some people were as close as siblings. Like him and Brody had been.

With the loading finished and the truck dispatched to the customer's address, the three of them returned to the main part of the store, where Brenda gave Everett a tour while Larry waited on customers. Everett's compliments were sincere. He'd been in plenty of feed and tack stores during his life. This one compared favorably.

"You know, we're the ones who brought the collective members together." Brenda beamed.

"No fooling."

They stood near the front door. Everett held a bag containing the supplements and his new training halter. Larry had used a handcart to transport the salt blocks outside, where he placed them in the bed of Everett's truck.

"Well, credit where credit is due. Macy had the original idea. Since we're acquainted with just about everyone in town who owns horses, she asked us if anyone might be interested in purchasing Pop's mares. We were, naturally. Larry's always had a hankering to raise foals, but the commitment was more than we could take on, with the store and two kids active in sports. We put her in touch with Glynnis first. She's one of our best customers. Raises and shows miniature horses."

"Abel mentioned it. He talks about her little critters a lot."

"Kinsley, of course, sells some of her metal art creations here. We take a small commission."

"She's very talented." He'd noticed several of her items on display during the tour. "Does Sheriff Andy also have horses?"

"Him? No." Brenda laughed. "Just those dogs he fosters for the shelter. He joined the collective strictly as an investment. That man is smart as a whip."

"Rumor is he was pretty successful in real estate."

"That was his main livelihood. He also dabbles in stocks and bonds and insurance. All kinds of stuff that goes way over my head." She gestured with her hand. "He advises a lot of us on our retirement and investment portfolios. Made Larry and I a tidy profit on our nest egg."

Everett would have to ask Pop if Sheriff Andy advised him, too. "And he doesn't charge?"

"We've tried to pay him. He refuses. Money, that is. We give the shelter a deal on dog kibble and donate ripped bags that we can't sell. Which we take as a tax deduction. He told us to. Said it's considered a donation to the shelter."

Everett recalled Pop mentioning donating horse manure to the high school and taking a tax deduction was also Sheriff Andy's idea. He was clearly savvy when it came to managing the collective's books. Everett had seen that firsthand.

"He's been a true asset to the townspeople," Brenda continued. "And to the collective. Man has a heart the size of the Grand Canyon."

Everett nodded, storing this new information away. Maybe he could hit Sheriff Andy up with a few of his own questions about the horse breeding business. What could it hurt?

On a whim, he asked Brenda, "You have your finger on the pulse of horse people in this town. Do you think there'd be any interest in youth rodeo classes?"

"Without a doubt. Why? You thinking of giving classes?"

"Tossing the idea around." He'd spoken to the head of the Oklahoma Twisters last evening. She'd taken the news better than he'd expected and felt confident if Randy didn't accept, another candidate from her short list would take the position.

At the door to the feed store, Everett shook hands with Brenda. "Thanks again for showing me around. I'm glad we finally got to meet."

"You're staying on then?" she asked.

"I think so. For now."

"That's great. Pop must be thrilled."

"He is." The memory prompted a grin. Everett and his grandfather had celebrated with root beers on the back patio. Pop had gotten tears in his eyes he'd failed to hide. "There's still a few details to work out."

"How do you feel about giving up rodeoing?"

He'd lie if he said he didn't suffer a small pang of regret when he thought about it. "I may not have to give it up entirely. We'll see."

"You can always enter one of Wickenburg's rodeos."

"I could." The town also hosted various roping events.

Brenda walked him outside to his truck. Everett waved as he reversed and drove away. He made two additional stops before returning to the ranch: the first was filling up at the gas station, and the second was picking up Pop's prescriptions at the drugstore.

When he arrived at the ranch shortly before dinnertime, it was to find Sheriff Andy's sedan parked at the mare barn and not Macy's truck. She didn't come to the ranch every evening. He had no reason to expect her. Only he had.

Maybe he should send a text? Unless that would be misconstrued. Too pushy? Too needy? Too impersonal?

He was seriously overthinking this, the result of being out of practice.

The thing was, he and Macy weren't an official couple. Heck, they hadn't even gone on a date yet. Maybe he should rectify that and ask her out.

Were they ready for that step? What did she want from their relationship? Dating, even causal dating, implied a commitment. He could always suggest a trail ride one morning. There wouldn't be much pressure with that, especially if they took Joey along.

"Howdy, Everett." Sheriff Andy waved as he emerged from the mare barn. He still had Peanut, the fat foster dachshund, and she waddled after him. "I fed Champ and Hombre already."

"Appreciate that. I was running late." Everett met him halfway. "How are they getting along?"

"Seemed like they were more tolerant of each other than the other day." He whistled low. "That Hombre is one fine looker."

"Yes, he is."

The remark reminded Everett to check his phone for any new emails. He'd texted the seller earlier in the day about Hombre's genetic testing results. She'd forwarded the screenshot she'd shown him at the sale on Saturday, but Macy had told him to ask for the actual paperwork. He'd need it for when he began breeding Hombre.

"Pop invited me to dinner," Sheriff Andy continued. "Wish I could accept, but I got a call right before you showed. Something came up."

"Maybe next time, then. We're having turkey meat loaf. It's not bad, but it's not the same as regular ol' meat loaf."

"Better for one's health, though." The older man chuckled. At his feet, Peanut sat and panted, her heavy sides heaving.

Everett put his phone away, disappointed there was no response from Hombre's seller.

"Tell Abel I'll have those CD brochures he was asking about next time." Sheriff Andy paused. "How long is he staying on, if I can ask?"

"Honestly, I'm not sure."

"He seems to like it here. And Pop likes having him."

"True on both accounts."

Sheriff Andy squinted at the house. "It's none of my business, and you can take what I say or leave it." He hesitated. "Would Pop consider letting Abel rent from him?"

"What do you mean?"

"I'm suggesting Abel permanently parks his motor home here and pay Pop a monthly rent. It would be extra income for Pop, and a solution for Glynnis. Abel, too. He doesn't need constant supervision. Not right now. But he can't live entirely alone. I wouldn't have mentioned it if you weren't staying on. Someone physically fit needs to be here to oversee everything."

"I...don't know."

"Might be more than you can take on right now. Your first priority is the business, which has come to a standstill this last year."

He was right. Everett needed to hang out Champ's shingle again. Maybe Kinsley could lend him a hand. Set up social media accounts for him and a website. Pop had always operated by word of mouth. That didn't work as well these days.

"Going to take some time," Sheriff Andy said, echoing Everett's thoughts. "Meanwhile, money's not rolling in. Charging Abel monthly rent could cover some ranch expenses."

"Too bad we can't rent out space to more people. There's a lot of land on this ranch going to waste."

"You probably can. The Conroys down the road rent to his brother-in-law. I'm sure a phone call to the city will better answer that."

"I wouldn't know what to ask."

"I can help you," Sheriff Andy offered. "I used to manage rental properties back in my real estate broker days."

Hadn't Brenda said Sheriff Andy was smart when it came to business and investments? Clearly, he knew something about rental properties, too.

"I'd have to talk to Pop first." Having a renter could solve more than one problem for him. "You sure you're not free for dinner?"

"Not tonight." Sheriff Andy flashed an apologetic smile.

"What about breakfast tomorrow morning? I'd like to discuss this with you. If you're willing, and I'm not imposing. My treat."

"No imposition. I'm working at the shelter tomorrow. Can we meet beforehand?"

"Absolutely. What about the Roadside Café? Seven thirty?"

"One of my favorite places. See you then." Sheriff Andy whistled to Peanut, and the two of them headed to his sedan. Everett checked the time. He had a few spare minutes and wanted to try out Hombre's new training halter.

He also wanted to dwell a little on this potential new venture. If Pop was agreeable, having Abel live on the ranch would mean no backing out for Everett. He couldn't leave two old men alone, much less just one.

Suddenly, he wanted to talk to Macy, too. Get her input.

Digging his phone from his pocket, he gave her a call. She answered on the second ring.

"Hi. Joey and I are just leaving the folks' house."

"You free for dinner tomorrow?"

She gave a nervous laugh. "Dinner?"

"Not what you think. Sheriff Andy has an interesting potential moneymaking venture for Pop, and I'd love your input."

"I'd have to bring Joey. And I can't stay long. I'm observing surgeries early tomorrow morning for my class. Going to be a full day."

"I promise not to keep you late."

"Then sure. I was going to be there, anyway."

"Great. Thanks, Macy."

She paused a moment. "Maybe next time you call about dinner, you'll ask me out."

Any doubts he had about them dating vanished. She was definitely willing to consider taking a step forward with him. And he couldn't be happier.

"Count on it. And you pick the place."

EVERETT MADE A special trip to the grocery store. Macy was coming to dinner, and he wanted to fix something a little more special than the usual broiled chicken breast or turkey meat loaf. Not that he'd veer too far from Pop's healthy diet.

There were also Joey's likes and dislikes to consider. Everett knew the kid liked egg salad sandwiches with potato chips. That was about the extent of his knowledge, however.

Perusing the store aisles and meat cases, he ultimately decided on grilled salmon for the adults—him, Macy and Pop—and hot dogs on buns for Joey. What kid didn't like hot dogs? In the deli section he chose premade heat-and-serve twice-baked potatoes. Lastly, he grabbed a bunch of asparagus in the produce department only because they were easy to grill alongside the salmon.

He was about to hit the checkout line when he remembered dessert. Since there were few things he could get that were on Pop's diet, he settled for a carton of orange sherbet and fresh raspberries. Once, when a bunch of them had gone out to celebrate at a fancy restaurant after a big rodeo win, one of the barrel racers had ordered sherbet and raspberries for dessert. If it was good enough for a fancy restaurant, Everett figured it would be fine for dinner tonight. And Joey would probably like it.

Breakfast that morning with Sheriff Andy had been informative and interesting. Everett had taken Pop along, and the three men had tossed ideas around about how to use the ranch's available acres to make the business even more profitable: from renting some lots to more RVs, to a small arena where Everett could give rodeoing lessons, to turning a far corner of the property into an equipment storage yard. They were just brainstorming at this point, but several of the ideas appealed to Everett, and he couldn't wait to tell Macy.

In the truck, he checked his phone again for an email from Hombre's seller. She'd responded to his phone call earlier, apologized profusely and then promised again to email the test results. So far, she'd failed to keep that promise. Maybe Everett would ask Macy about it tonight.

When he arrived home with the groceries, Pop was waiting for him, a noticeable spring in his step. At first, Everett didn't think too much of it as he put the food away. Pop's mood had been jovial for days, the result of Everett's decision to stay.

Except Pop was acting especially peppy and practically two-stepped around the kitchen. Though, for him, it was more like shuffling. He hummed as he opened two root beers, one for each of them.

"What's gotten into you?" Everett asked.

"I have some news."

He shut the refrigerator door and joined his grandfather

at the kitchen table. Pop had quite liked the idea of Abel staying on and paying a modest rent when Everett suggested it. They'd talked with Abel, who couldn't have been more enthused, and planned on running the idea by Glynnis tomorrow morning when she arrived to take him home.

Everett assumed Pop's news had something to do with that. He couldn't have been further off base.

"I was talking to Susan right before you got home." Pop cleared his throat. "We're going to the movies on Thursday afternoon."

"Nice. You need a ride? I can drop you off. I won't horn in on your date."

"Nope. Got it handled. We're going to take one of those car ride services."

"Seriously, Pop? I can drive you."

"We're going out to eat afterward. We might be late."

Everett tried not to laugh. If Pop and Susan stayed out past eight o'clock, he'd be shocked.

"Besides, it might turn into a special dinner." Pop broke into a wide smile. "I'm thinking of proposing."

Everett almost fell out of his chair. "You're what?"

"I'm going to marry her, if she'll have an old geezer like me. She'd be smart to refuse." Pop's expression turned wistful. "At first, I thought I'd wait until I bought a ring. Give her flowers. The whole nine yards. But then I decided she might want to pick out her own ring. And that way, she can help me pick out mine, too."

"Pop." Everett searched for the right words. "Have you given this serious consideration?"

"I have. She's a wonderful woman."

"I couldn't agree more. But this feels fast."

Pop's grin waned. "We've been seeing each other more'n six months now. You just haven't been around to see."

That part was true.

"I love her, sonny. And she loves me back. She told me." His voice cracked. "The fact is, neither she nor I are getting any younger. Waiting seems like a waste of time that we could be spending together."

Everett wanted to feel about someone special like his grandfather did about Susan. Was that someone Macy? "I'm happy for you, Pop. Really."

"She'd be moving in here. You okay with that?"

"This is your home," he insisted, wondering if he should find another place to live. But then who would care for Pop when the time came? Susan couldn't.

"It's your home, too. Or half yours. As soon as I make an appointment with my attorney. I won't ask you to leave."

"Then I guess the better question is, are you okay living with a third person underfoot?"

Pop chuckled. "We'll try not to disturb you."

Everett didn't want to think about that and tried to wipe the image from his mind.

"I reckon I could move into that bungalow of hers," Pop said, his tone dejected. "If that was our only choice."

"What's wrong with her bungalow?"

"For starters, it's smaller than a matchbox. And there isn't ten feet between her and her neighbor."

"That would be a change for you." His grandfather had lived over fifty years on the ranch.

"Besides, I need to be here to help you run the business."

"You talk like she's already accepted your proposal."

"I'll be lower than an ant's ear if she says no." Pop's grin returned. "But I don't think she will."

"Me, either."

"It won't mean any more work for you. Callie will come by and give Susan a hand, just like when she sprained her ankle."

That was encouraging and a relief to Everett. If Pop accepted Callie's help with Susan, he might be more willing to accept help for himself.

"I do have a favor to ask." Pop looked hopeful. "Any chance you'd be my best man?"

Everett couldn't remember being more touched. "I'd be honored."

"You think your folks and Aunt Laurel would make the trip out?"

"Of course, they will. Uncle Kenny, too," he said, referring to his aunt's husband.

A moment later, they heard the sound of a vehicle. Everett pushed back from the kitchen table. "Macy's here."

"You go say hello. I'll start on this special dinner you planned."

"You sure? I can do it."

Pop shooed him away. "She's waiting on you."

He clapped his grandfather on the shoulder. "Susan's a lucky woman."

"Thank you, sonny, but I'm the lucky one."

Turned out, Macy wasn't waiting on him. Joey had escaped the second she lifted him from his car seat and set him on the ground. It seemed he wasn't alone. A short, fat dachshund waddled after him. The pair made straight for the mare barn.

"Is that Peanut?" Everett asked when he approached Macy.

She blew out a long, weary breath. "It is."

"You adopted her?"

"No. Well, yes." Macy sighed. "We agreed to a week's trial."

"And the dog's not behaving well?"

"The dog is a dream. Housebroken. No bad habits. Sweet as can be. So patient with Joey."

"What's the problem, then?"

"It's Joey. He's incorrigible when it comes to Peanut. Won't listen to a word I say."

"He'll get better once the newness wears off."

"Let's hope you're right." She smiled. "I do like the little scamp. And every kid should have a pet, right?"

"You'll get no argument from me. Remember Pogo?"

Her face brightened. "Your border collie? She was a great dog. So pretty and smart."

"Except she wouldn't leave the horses alone and wore herself out herding them for hours on end."

They strolled into the mare barn where Joey was telling Peanut the occupants' names, making up ones for those he didn't know.

Everett barely paid attention. He had trouble keeping his eyes off Macy. She'd worn her blond hair loose, and he imagined himself running his fingers through it.

In need of a distraction, he said the first thing to pop into his head. "Pop is going to propose to Susan."

CHAPTER TWELVE

MACY SHOULDN'T HAVE been surprised to learn Everett's grandfather intended to propose to his lady love. Especially since Everett had decided to remain and take over the business.

"He told you he's going to propose?" she asked.

"He did."

"When?"

"Right before you got here."

"No, no. When is he *planning* on proposing?"

"They're going to the movies and dinner on Thursday. He's thinking of doing it then. He's in a hurry."

Macy got misty-eyed at the thought of the two octogenarians walking down the aisle. "I'm so happy for them."

"She hasn't accepted yet," Everett cautioned.

"She will. They're in love. It's obvious."

"That's what Pop said."

A thought occurred to Macy. "Where will they live? Or is it too soon to ask?"

"Here, according to Pop. He's not crazy about moving into her bungalow."

"Wow. That's…interesting." She thought a moment. "You know, this could be the answer to your worries about Pop's future care."

"You mean Callie? I've already thought of that. Pop mentioned she'd still come to look after Susan. And, who knows? He might eventually be okay with the idea of having someone looking after him, too."

"That could solve a lot of problems."

"Yeah." Everett hesitated.

"What's wrong?"

"Don't think me selfish because I'm really happy for Pop and Susan. But what if things don't go as planned, their health takes a turn, and I wind up having to look after two elderly people? My skills are limited, and I have the ranch and a business to run. They may need more assistance than I can give them."

"Callie won't let that happen."

"I'd hate to be the reason Pop and Susan don't get married. I can see the positive effect she's had on his health."

Macy liked that Everett's perspective had changed since his return.

"There are some downsides, however," he said. "To be honest, I'm not sure how I feel about living with them. Newlyweds need their privacy, even if they are in their eighties, and I need mine."

She laughed. She couldn't help herself. "I get that."

"I doubt Susan wants to look at my ugly mug every morning and evening."

"I can think of worse things."

"Yeah?" Everett leaned in and traced his knuckles along her jawline.

A small, pleasant shiver skittered up Macy's spine, reminding her of their kiss the other day. Their many kisses, actually. Would there be a repeat today? Once could be blamed on getting lost in the moment. Twice, harder to call it an impulse. Three times? That was something serious and warranted a discussion.

"Mommy, look-it. I'm cleaning."

They turned to see Joey and Peanut. Unable to keep up

with a rambunctious child, the overweight dog had plopped down in a patch of shade near the door and proceeded to pant. Joey had found the push broom and was moving dirt around the barn aisle in an attempt to sweep.

"Thank you, honey," Macy said. "You're a good helper."

With the romantic mood ruined—for the moment, anyway—Macy mentioned something else on her mind. "I heard from Brody's mom yesterday. She said you called."

"I finally worked up my nerve."

"She sounded really glad to have heard from you."

"She invited me to dinner."

"Really?" Macy smiled. "That's nice."

"We have no definite plans." Everett let out a long breath. "It'll be hard facing her and Brody's dad."

"You don't have to tell them about Brody taking your turn to drive on the day of the accident."

"If I'm going to see them again, I think I should. I won't lie to them. They deserve more than that from me."

Macy felt for him. Telling Brody's parents would be every bit as hard for Everett as it had been for him to tell her. And while she believed Brody's parents, like her, wouldn't hold him responsible, she couldn't say for certain.

"If you do have dinner with them, would you like me to go with you?" she asked.

He drew back to study her. "You'd do that?"

"I would."

"Okay. I'll give it some thought."

She could see in his expression that he didn't want to talk about this anymore, and she wouldn't force him. Instead, she changed the subject.

"What's this idea you wanted to run by me?"

Everett instantly relaxed. "I may have a way to bring in extra income."

"Tell me about it while we feed the mares and I give Roxie and Beauty a quick once-over."

Macy listened intently to Everett as they worked side by side. He told her about Abel staying and paying rent rather than leaving, possibly leasing spaces to more RVs and the other ideas under consideration. She concurred they all had potential and were worth exploring.

"I'm impressed, Everett."

"Well, it hasn't happened yet."

"You don't think you'd be taking on too much? You were worried about two elderly people, and now it seems there might be three."

"You're right," he conceded. "That's why I need to do my homework first. And convince Pop to accept home care help from Callie."

To her satisfaction, Beauty's leg was healing well, and Roxie showed no signs of colic. It was just five thirty when they finished. Still a little early for dinner. Rather than go inside, they sat in the rocking chairs. Nearby, Joey entertained himself and Peanut with an old stick and a game of fetch. Only he did more fetching than the dog.

Everett chuckled at the pair. "There's a good chance Joey'll take a few pounds off that dog with all his energy."

"That's actually the goal." Macy rocked slowly.

"I spoke to Kinsley today about a website for the horse breeding business. She's willing to set that up and refused to let me pay her."

"She's a good kid."

"I've also started calling Pop's previous customers and letting them know that we're open for business again. I already have two meetings scheduled for next week."

Macy gave him an admiring look. "I'm impressed."

"I don't want to have to ask the collective for any more funds to cover ranch expenses."

"That won't happen, Everett. You're going to do well taking over for Pop."

"I'd feel better if Hombre lives up to his potential." He sat back, a frown on his face. "The seller still hasn't forwarded the test results. I'm getting annoyed."

"Give it another day."

"Then what? Can I call the auction company? If she fails to supply the results, wouldn't that void our sale contract?"

"I doubt it." Macy shook her head. "Read over the auction contract you signed. I'm pretty sure you'll find a clause in there that basically says all sales are final and buyer beware."

"I was afraid of that." He turned to face her. "Did I make a mistake, Macy?"

"Not necessarily. Don't panic. Give the woman another couple of days. Sellers tend to place sold horses low on their priority lists. Out of sight, out of mind kind of thing. And she mentioned having some financial woes."

"I hope you're right."

She hoped so, too. Not having the testing results would affect Everett's ability to breed Hombre one day. Any customers would want to be assured he was free of genetic disorders.

"How is Abel doing, by the way?" she asked, wishing she could erase the frown from Everett's face. "His legs were bothering him the other day."

"Better. The pain seems to come and go."

"You know, you won't be the only one encroaching on the newlyweds."

"Abel's room isn't right down the hall."

Macy couldn't say what prompted her to suddenly blurt, "Why don't you build a place for yourself?"

"Like an apartment in the barn?"

"Or add a suite onto the house."

"That's a good idea. Except I'd want Pop and Susan to have the suite. Assuming she accepts his proposal."

"You might have to get a permit."

"That's the least of my problems," Everett said. "Changes to the ranch are going to cost money. Money we don't have."

Abel wandered by at that moment on his way to the house. "No worries. I'm not crashing your dinner."

"You'd be welcome," Everett told him.

"I'm just returning the newspaper Pop lent me." He motioned to the paper tucked under his arm. "Got a pot of stew on the stove for me."

With that, he wandered off, but not before stopping to give both Joey and Peanut pats on the head.

"Maybe I should build two bungalows," Everett said with a laugh. "One for me and one for Abel. He can't stay in that motor home forever."

"Or three."

"What would we do with a third bungalow?"

"Rent it out," Macy answered with all seriousness. "Like Sheriff Andy said."

Everett laughed at first, only to sober. "That's either a crazy idea or a really good one."

"You're clever, Everett. You can make this place pay for itself again. You just need to think outside the box."

"You have more faith in me than I do myself."

"I have enough faith for the both of us."

She reached for his hand and squeezed his fingers before going in for a kiss that made her heart sing and give her a whole new outlook on life. Everett didn't hesitate and returned her affection, measure for measure.

When they drew apart a short time later, she couldn't help asking, "What does the future hold for us?"

She thought he might hedge or dodge her question entirely. He didn't.

"I care about you. A lot." He cradled her cheek and skimmed his thumb along her lower lip. "Things with me, with Pop, are a little up in the air right now."

"I get that."

"I don't want to make a promise I can't keep. Not again. You don't deserve that, from me or anyone."

"Which means?"

"I'd say let's take things one day at a time. But that sounds trite, and this, what you and I have, is too important to me to treat it lightly."

"I'm glad to hear you say that."

"This is serious for me, Macy. More serious than any previous relationship I've been in. I don't want to screw up. We need to go slow, however. Pop, the business and the ranch are my priorities."

"And I have mine. I've been building a life for myself and Joey since before he was born. That won't change just because I bring someone new into our lives."

"I wouldn't expect it to. I want nothing more than to see you succeed at your career and will support you however you need. Joey, too."

"You never said, do you want children? Can you see yourself raising someone else's child?"

"I'm new at this. You'd have to be patient with me. But the answer to both is yes. I want a family, whatever shape that family takes."

She leaned her cheek into his palm. "I'm okay with slow, as long as we're moving forward."

He pulled her to him for another kiss. "Count on it."

"MOMMY, MOMMY!" Joey ran across his grandmother's living room and threw himself at Macy. "I missed you."

"I missed you, too, honey." She lifted him into her arms, receiving a big hug and kiss on the cheek. "Did you have fun today?"

"Lots of fun."

As they strolled into the kitchen, Joey told her about his day with Macy's mom. They'd run an errand to the drugstore, where Joey got to pick out a coloring book and crayons, watched Thomas the Tank Engine videos and had Popsicles. Grandpa had called on the picture phone—Joey's word for FaceTiming on Grandma's tablet.

Macy found her mom at the counter, slicing vegetables for a salad. "How goes the grind?" She set Joey down and gave her mom a one-armed hug.

"Hey, sweetheart. Not bad. Joey's tired. He didn't nap long. But otherwise, we've had a nice day."

Most people commented on her resemblance to her mother, and Macy supposed they did look alike. Sometimes she caught herself making the same gestures as her mother and using the same expressions.

"Was work busy?"

She let out a tired sigh. "We had three emergencies today. A tiny Chihuahua needed a C-section and delivered five puppies."

"Five! Isn't that a lot for a Chihuahua?"

"It is for a first litter. Then we had a dog who almost choked to death on a rawhide chew toy and a cat someone shot with a pellet gun."

"Shot? Who would do such a thing?" Macy's mother stopped slicing to stare in astonishment.

"Hard to say."

"Was it a stray?"

"No." Macy shook her head. "The owners found the cat hiding in a bush in their backyard."

"How awful."

From her spot on the back door rug, Peanut waddled over to Macy, tail wagging. Macy picked her up and received another kiss on the cheek. This one wet and sloppy.

"You spoil that dog?" Macy's mom said.

"Me?"

"She is a dear little thing. No trouble at all."

"Maybe you and Dad should keep her."

"No way. But we'll dog sit anytime." Macy's mom cut off a small piece of carrot and gave it to Peanut, who chomped noisily.

"You're not sneaking her any unapproved treats, are you?" Macy put the dog on the floor with Joey.

"Me? No!" Her mom feigned shock at the suggestion. "Only things off the list you gave me. Carrots, apples, green beans and blueberries. We also went on a walk this morning. Joey was excited, but she tuckered out after fifteen minutes."

"Thank you, Mom." Macy gazed fondly at the dog who was nosing around the floor at her mom's feet for a fallen vegetable slice. "I think she may have lost a half a pound since I've had her."

"Well, I could stand to lose some weight, too." Macy's mom patted her round hip.

"You look fantastic."

"Chasing after Joey does burn calories." She returned to her dinner preparations. "You heading to the ranch? I'm making plenty if you want to stay for dinner."

Her mom always referred to Pop's place as "the ranch."

"Yeah. Dr. Beck is meeting me there in…" Macy checked her phone. "Yikes! Twenty minutes. I need to hurry."

"Something wrong with one of the mares?"

"It's their monthly well check. He's seeing another patient right down the road, so it's not out of his way."

"Okay, good. I'll pack dinner for you and Joey."

"I can stop for fast-food chicken nuggets on the way."

"Don't be ridiculous. I have a fridge filled with food."

"You're the best, Mom." Macy felt a surge of love. "What would I do without you?"

"Let's hope you'll never have to find out."

She understood the deeper meaning to her mom's words. She and Macy's dad were there for Macy because she'd lost Brody. But she would have given anything for things to have been different and Macy not to be a widow and a single mother.

While her mom filled some to-go plastic containers, Joey and Macy gave Peanut a bowl of reduced-calorie kibbles, then Macy gathered his things.

"Give Grandma a hug," Macy said at the door. "Tell Dad I'm sorry we missed him and that we'll see him this weekend."

"Before you go…" Macy's mom hesitated. "I talked to Fran today. She called me."

"Oh?"

Fran Sommers was Brody's mom. She and Macy's mom, former mothers-in-law and both grandmothers to Joey, were on friendly terms. A phone call wasn't uncommon.

"They had Everett over for dinner last night."

Macy nodded. "I know. I offered to go with him. He decided he wanted their first meeting to be just the three of them. Less awkward, and no one would feel put on the spot."

"He told her about the accident. That he should have been the one driving. Not Brody."

Macy's heart constricted at the memory of her conversation with Everett on the same subject. "He blames himself."

"He shouldn't."

"I agree."

"Fran was surprised. She had no idea. But she doesn't hold him responsible and told him that."

"I'm glad to hear that. Though Fran has always struck me as the forgiving type. Brody's dad, too. They were always fond of Everett."

Concern filled Macy's mother's eyes. "What about you? How do you feel about Everett's confession?"

"It doesn't change anything for me. I don't blame him anymore."

"Good. That would be a heavy burden to bear. For both of you. Perhaps Everett exercised poor judgment by celebrating too much the night before. But he loved Brody like a brother and must have suffered, thinking he was responsible. No wonder he stayed away. Seeing you and Joey had to have been torture for him."

"I hadn't thought of it that way."

"Well, why *did* you think he stayed away?"

"I don't know. I was just so angry at him for doing it. I never examined his reasons. That was very wrong of me. I see that now, and I should have reached out to him."

"What's the old saying?" her mom asked. "Anger does us more harm than the things we're angry about."

"I'm sad to say that's true. For me, anyway."

"Things are better between you and him, though. Right?"

"Yes." Macy nodded.

"A lot better? You have been spending a lot of time together lately."

Something in her mom's tone put her on the alert. "It's work, Mom. Mostly, anyway."

"Is it?" She touched Macy's arm. "Because if you and he were to start seeing each other, that would be okay."

Her first impulse was to deny whatever her mom seemed to be insinuating. Only she didn't.

"Is this something you and Fran talked about?"

"No. I wouldn't never discuss your dating life with her or anyone without your consent."

"I'd appreciate that."

"So, there is something between you and Everett? I hear the way your voice changes when you say his name."

"A lot has happened since he returned." Macy hesitated, unsure how much to admit. "He's changing. Trying."

"I'm certainly happy for Pop. Everett staying is good for him."

"He's doing much better than before." She hadn't told her mom about Pop's plan to propose to Susan. That was his personal business.

"And I'm happy for you, too, sweetheart. Whatever you and Everett decide." Her mom reached up to cup her cheek, much like she had when Macy was a child. "Brody would want you to be happy and not be alone for the rest of your life."

Macy nodded, a lump forming in her throat and preventing her from speaking. Her mom knew about the argument with Brody mere hours before he died. She'd been Macy's one and only confidante. She'd insisted Macy was too hard on herself and that Brody had loved her body and soul. Something Everett had recently confirmed.

More than that, Everett and Macy had shared the secret guilts they'd been carrying for three years, and it had freed them from their invisible shackles.

Was trauma bonding responsible for their growing attraction? Macy wanted to believe no, that their feelings stemmed from a genuine, positive connection. Nonetheless, she cautioned herself to be careful and not get carried away. She'd worked too hard these past three years building a good life for her and Joey to risk losing it over a miscalculation of the heart.

"Mommy, I wanna go," Joey whined impatiently.

"Okay, honey." Macy hugged her mom. "Thanks for everything."

She loaded Joey in the truck and gave him a cheese sandwich. Peanut rode on the seat beside him, staring at the food with puppy dog eyes in the hopes of receiving a handout.

"I wanna go home, Mommy."

"Sorry, honey. We have to go to the ranch first. Dr. Beck is probably already there. Mommy can't be late." She glanced at the clock on the truck's dashboard. "Later than Mommy already is."

Joey proceeded to sulk, even losing his appetite, which bode well for Peanut who wolfed down the sandwich half he dropped onto the seat. So much for her diet.

Did Macy really need to go to the ranch? Yes, Dr. Beck was checking on the mares, and their health was her responsibility.

But she'd see the vet tomorrow at the clinic and could always get a report from him. If Macy was honest with herself, she wanted to see Everett.

Was her mom right? Would dating him be okay for everyone involved? Macy had never gotten that far in her thinking.

But the fact was, more people than just her would be affected if she and Everett's relationship grew serious. There was Joey to consider, of course. Everett had said all the right things the other night, and she wanted to believe him. But he'd failed her before in a big way. And he did seem to avoid confrontations rather than face them. She needed someone she trusted implicitly. For Joey's sake more than hers.

She had much to think about and had found no answers by the time she reached the ranch.

CHAPTER THIRTEEN

MACY PARKED NEXT to Dr. Beck's truck that had its side compartments open, displaying various veterinarian equipment and supplies. After unloading boy and dog, she remembered her tablet. She'd need that to update the mares' health records.

In the nearby distance, the sun slowly dropped behind the mountaintops, turning the warm golden glow of late afternoon into the soft gray of early evening. The sight never failed to inspire or soothe Macy, depending on her mood. Today, after reflecting on her relationship with Everett, it was the latter.

She cared for Everett. Not the youthful infatuation she'd experience as a teenager. This was…different. Unlike anything she'd felt before. And it gave her reason to believe that finding happiness again with someone was possible for her. Everett knew her terrible shame, yet he still returned her feelings. He gave her confidence that she wasn't a bad person.

Was he here? She glanced around. This time of day, he might be inside with Pop, preparing or eating dinner.

"Stay with Mommy, honey."

Joey dragged his feet, stirring up small clouds of red dust. She didn't blame the boy. He'd had a long day. Her, too. With luck, Dr. Beck would find no concerns with the mares, and they could all leave soon.

"Hi, Doc. Sorry I'm late." She entered the mare barn

and took in the scene. The mares were finishing their evening meal, which meant that Everett had recently been there. He could be as close as the stallion quarters.

"Not a problem," Dr. Beck said from inside Dusty's stall.

"Hope I didn't miss anything important."

The hardworking and caring vet straightened, his round face flushed. "Nothing noteworthy."

"How's Dusty?"

"Perfectly healthy. You can breed her whenever you and she are ready."

"That's good news."

"She's a fine addition to your breeding program."

Exiting the stall, he disinfected his hands with sanitizer, then summarized his exam of the first three mares in the barn. Macy entered the updates into her tablet while Joey attempted to fasten a piece of twine to Peanut's collar, constructing a makeshift leash. The little dog endured this latest torture with her usual patience.

After that, Macy accompanied Dr. Beck as he examined the remaining mares.

"Next month, I'm planning on bringing the portable ultrasound machine," he said with a happy grin. "We can get some more baby pictures."

"That'll be exciting." Knowing for certain the foals were healthy would relieve a great deal of worry for the collective.

They were just finishing with the last mare when Everett's broad-shouldered form filled the barn entrance. Macy saw at once by the shadows darkening his features that something was bothering him.

"Everett." She stepped away from the stall and moved toward him. "Is Pop okay?"

"He's fine. Why?"

"You look… Are you all right?"

"Yeah."

Except he wasn't. She could tell.

"Hello, Dr. Beck." Everett nodded at the vet in greeting.

"Everett." He closed the stall door behind him and once again sanitized his hands. "How's your new young stallion doing?"

"He's fine."

"Do I hear a *but*?"

Everett's gaze found Macy's. "I still haven't heard back from Hombre's seller."

"You're kidding!"

"It's been nearly a week. I think she's ghosting me."

"How can I help?"

"Is there any other way I can get the test results? What if I contact the testing company? Will they send them to me if I show them my bill of sale?"

"I doubt it." She turned to Dr. Beck. "What do you think?"

The vet moved closer. "What happened?"

Everett explained about buying the young stallion at the sale and the seller promising to forward the original genetic test results.

"Can I see what she sent you?" Dr. Beck asked.

Everett scrolled through his phone, then held it out to the other man.

"May I look closer?" Dr. Beck took Everett's phone, enlarged the testing results document and studied it with squinted eyes. "Hmm."

"I don't like the sound of that," Everett said.

Macy concurred.

Dr. Beck tilted his head in question. "Didn't Macy tell me the stallion was around eighteen months old?"

"He is." Everett nodded.

"See this?" Dr. Beck turned the phone and showed Everett. "These results are for a two-year-old."

"What?" Everett grabbed the phone from the vet. "How's that possible?"

"Is the other information correct?"

Everett's jaw worked as he enlarged other areas of the document. "The name's not quite right. Hombre's registered name is Gran Hombre Gris. This says Hombre Gris Gordo."

"I'd say this is a different horse. Compare the document against his registration papers. See if the sire and dam match up."

"I can't believe I missed this."

"The names are similar," Macy said.

"I just zeroed in on the word negative and ignored the rest of the document." Anger hardened his stare. "Have I been swindled?"

"Everett." Macy's stomach knotted. She feared he was right. "I'm so sorry."

"Don't jump to conclusions," Dr. Beck warned. "It could be an honest mistake, and the seller gave you the wrong test results."

"Yeah, then why isn't she answering my calls and texts?" Everett shoved his phone into his shirt pocket. "I'm going to call the auction company. I may have no recourse with them, but they should know one of their sellers is not on the up-and-up."

"Again," Dr. Beck said, "don't get ahead of yourself. Let's assume this was just an oversight, and the seller has kept poor records."

"That doesn't solve my problem. I've invested in a stallion I can't use for stud unless I'm able to guarantee he's genetically sound."

"It's an easy enough problem to solve. Just retest him. It

will cost you some money and take a little time. But I have a kit in the truck and can do it now if you want. The results will take a couple of weeks. I'll try to expedite them."

Everett nodded. "Thank you, Doc."

He retreated to a corner of the barn while the vet went to his truck for a testing kit. Macy joined him, grateful for Peanut and that she kept Joey occupied.

"This is a minor setback," she told Everett.

Doubt shadowed his expression. "The seller lied to me. I know it. Probably because Hombre failed. What will I do if he's a carrier for a condition that makes him unsuitable for breeding?"

"You said before you could turn him into a gelding and sell him. Maybe even make a small profit."

"That'll take six months. He's green as spring grass."

At his dejected expression, she reached out, but he withdrew his arm.

"What was I thinking? I don't have what it takes to run Pop's horse breeding business. I made a stupid, rookie mistake."

"Maybe not. Wait until the tests come back."

"It could be too late by then."

"Too late for what?"

"Me returning to the rodeo circuit. There's still time. I haven't missed my opportunity to qualify for Nationals. And if I make it to finals, I can bring home some decent prize money."

"You'd leave?" Macy tamped down the panic rising in her. This couldn't be happening.

"I don't know. This isn't what I expected." Rubbing his forehead, he closed his eyes and let out a long sigh. "When I screw up, I screw up big."

Macy wanted to argue with him. But Dr. Beck chose

that moment to return with the testing kit, and Joey wandered over to complain again about wanting to go home.

She didn't get a chance to talk to Everett alone before she had to leave, and when she tried calling him later that evening, he didn't pick up. Finally, before bed, he texted her good-night. That was all. Nothing else. Her panic returned, no longer mild.

EVERETT OWED MACY more than a vague text the next morning saying he'd call later. But he wasn't ready to talk to her. Not yet. She'd ask questions he wasn't prepared to answer. He needed time to think and a reprieve from being pulled in a dozen different directions.

What he had done was call his buddy Rusty who was heading to the Big Timber Rodeo in Tucson. Everett needed an ear to bend, one belonging to someone familiar with his situation. But talking things through hadn't given him the clarity he'd hoped for.

When had everything changed? A month ago, he'd had a plan. Qualify for Nationals, win a title and start a new job as a youth rodeo coach. He'd had no responsibilities beyond taking care of himself.

Now, Pop was depending on him to take over the ranch and horse breeding business and, though he refused to admit as much, help with his eventual care. What if Everett left and Pop didn't propose to his lady love? He certainly wouldn't if they were buried in debt and forced to sell the ranch. His pride wouldn't let him.

Then there was Macy. She and Everett only recently confessed their growing feelings and agreed to start dating. That would come to a crashing end if he returned to the rodeo circuit. She wanted a life partner who stayed home. One who kept his promises.

Except, if he couldn't succeed at the horse breeding

business and he was no longer competing, what else did he have to offer her besides a run-down ranch and a pile of bills?

"You're being way too hard on yourself," Pop said. He'd been following Everett around for the past two hours.

"That's a matter of opinion."

"Nonsense," Pop grumbled under his breath. "What about those two appointments you have scheduled this week with my old customers?"

Everett had forgotten about those. "We need more than two customers."

"We'll get them. I've let the business go, and that's on me. But we'll turn things around. I once made a dandy living off this ranch. Isn't Kinsley working on computer advertising?"

Pop was confusing the website and social media accounts. Everett didn't correct him. He was too tired. They'd been going at it long enough that Pop was repeating himself.

Their talk had started during the morning feeding—seeing Hombre stirred a fresh wave of anger at himself and his gullibility—and continued when they'd come inside where Everett ran the vacuum, mopped floors and changed the air-conditioning filter.

These tasks required bending and lifting and standing on a stepladder and were off-limits for Pop. If Everett returned to the rodeo circuit, he'd have to arrange help for Pop. For Abel, too, since he was staying. Maybe Sheriff Andy could lend a hand.

Another solution would be Pop moving in with Susan. He hated the idea of living in her bungalow, but it was better than a nursing home.

Who was he kidding? There was only one solution. He had to earn money, good money, and fast. Rodeoing was the best way to accomplish that, and the only thing he was truly good at. Except that required him to leave after he'd promised to stay.

"There's always a… What do the young folks call it?" Pop asked. "A learning something or other."

"Learning curve."

"That's it."

They were now outside on the patio where Everett had just finished using the leaf blower to clear off debris from the recent rains. He shrugged out of the machine and set it on the ground by the picnic table. Though only 9:00 a.m., the temperature was already in the low eighties.

Today would be another scorcher, which matched his mood. After a restless night troubled by doubts and worries, Everett's temper was easily riled. Most of it was directed at himself.

Was it only the other day that Macy had told him she believed him capable of anything? How wrong she'd been. He couldn't buy a horse without messing up.

Because Pop was breathing heavily, Everett sat down at the picnic table. As he'd hoped, Pop joined him. The heat had been getting to him, too. More so these last couple of days.

"We still have Champ," Pop said when he could speak again. "And Hombre."

So much for Everett thinking their conversation was over. "Like I said before, I may sell Hombre."

"You can't!"

Sometimes his grandfather only heard what he wanted to hear. Everett cut him some slack today, however. Susan wasn't feeling well and had canceled their movie date on Thursday. Pop's plan to propose had been delayed, souring his mood.

"What choice do I have?" Everett asked.

"You're always in such a goll-darn rush. Wait till his tests come back yet."

Hearing the rumble of an engine, they glanced up to see a pickup coming into view. Any hopes Everett had of giving the topic of him returning to the rodeo circuit a rest were dashed at the sight of Macy sitting behind the wheel.

COLLECTIVE MEMBERS ARRIVING on a Saturday were expected. Frankly, Everett was surprised no one besides Macy had shown up. Perhaps they had weekend plans and knew he was here to feed and clean stalls.

Another possibility was she'd told them all to stay away. Less interruptions that way. She did have a determined look on her face. Or was that anger?

Drawing in a deep breath, he steeled himself. He should have called her last night or at least this morning. Too late now.

Pop waved her over the moment her truck door opened and her feet hit the ground. "Morning, Macy."

"Hi, Pop. Everett."

"Hey." He stood.

She opened the rear passenger door. The next moment, Joey bounded over. Unlike his mother, he beamed at Everett. Peanut waddled after him, the opposite of bounding.

Macy brought up the rear. She wore her usual ponytail and ball cap, and her gaze was directed at him. He could feel the invisible daggers she fired at him from where he stood.

"Everett!" Joey reached him and grabbed his legs, his version of a bear hug. "I wanna ride horsie."

Everett bent down and ruffled the boy's hair. "It's a little too hot today to go riding. You can help me put Hombre in the pasture. If your mom's okay with that."

"I'll help."

Everett suspected Joey didn't understand everything he'd said but wanted to go along regardless. As Macy neared, he gave the boy a nudge. "Go to say hi to Pop."

Joey did, taking Peanut with him.

"You're the first to arrive," he told Macy. "No one else is here yet."

She cut right to the chase. "Can we talk?"

For a man in his eighties, Pop had no trouble reading the room. Or, in this case, the patio. Pushing to his feet, he said, "Joey, you want some lemonade? Come into the house with me. And bring that dog of yours before she has heatstroke."

"Can I have cookie?"

"I'm not allowed to have cookies. How 'bout a bran muffin?"

"No muffin for Peanut," Macy called after them without taking her eyes off Everett.

"It is hot out here," he said when they were alone. "You sure you don't want to have this conversation inside?"

Her reply was to sit at the picnic table.

"I take it that's a no." He joined her, dropping into the seat beside her. "I'm sorry I didn't return your call."

"Calls. Plural."

"Okay."

"Are you avoiding me?" she asked.

"More like procrastinating."

She drew back to study him. "Wow. I didn't realize talking to me was so difficult."

Everett adjusted his cowboy hat, a stalling tactic. Uncertainty and anxiety had plagued him from the moment Dr. Beck had discovered the genetic test results from the seller were for a different horse. No calming exercises or silent talks with himself stopped the building tension.

He'd thought Macy, more than anyone, would understand how he felt. She'd suffered her own bouts with uncertainty and anxiety. Only she wasn't acting like she understood, and that only increased his anxiety.

"Pop's been hammering at me all morning."

"Really?" She gaped at him. "Your response is to deflect?"

"I haven't had a free minute to call you," he said, recognizing how lame his answer sounded.

"Seriously? You couldn't find five minutes?"

"I wasn't ready to answer your questions."

She paused, then nodded. "Okay. That, at least, is an honest response."

"I still don't have any answers."

"About staying?" Her voice rose.

"That. And about what's best for Pop. The ranch, the horse breeding business. Any of it."

"Does that include us?" Her gaze on him didn't waver, although uncertainty flickered in her eyes.

Everett refused to lie again. He'd done that once before and caused her a world of hurt.

"Yes."

"I see."

"Any decision I make," he said, "any direction I turn, I'm going to hurt someone or make them mad or disappoint them. Probably more than one person."

"Don't you think you're being a little dramatic? *Any* decision?" Her brows rose. "Really?"

"Pop's breeding business is a shadow of what it used to be. It needs an experienced person in charge, and that's not me. I proved that when I bought Hombre."

"You'll learn. You're smart."

Everett shook his head, frustrated. She wasn't seeing the whole picture. Or she refused. "Time and money are in short supply. With me living on the ranch, we need to bring in enough income to support two people. And that's in addition to all the upcoming expenses and necessary repairs. And then there's the cost of home health care for Pop, if it comes to that."

"What if you got a job?" Macy asked.

"There aren't many openings in Wickenburg for a retired rodeo competitor."

"What about a wrangler for one of the ranches? Or the Hays might hire you."

He would not ask the Hays for a job. Like Pop, he had his pride. "Neither of those jobs would pay enough."

"So, you'd leave?"

Until that moment, he hadn't decided. As he talked to Macy, the answer became clear. "Yes. Temporarily."

She shook her head. "I'm clearly missing something, because I don't see how abandoning Pop to fend for himself and turning your back on the business and the ranch is a solution."

"I can earn quick money rodeoing. Enough between now and the end of the year to pay the insurance and taxes. Abel's rent will cover Champ and Hombre's expenses. And Pop won't be alone. I'll arrange for Callie to check on him and as of next month, Sheriff Andy will be living here."

"Sheriff Andy?"

"He told me at breakfast the other day that he's selling his house. Until he finds a new place, he's putting his stuff in storage and parking his RV here. It was only going to be until November, but I think I can convince him to stay until the end of the year."

Macy crossed her arms over her middle. "What if you don't win your events?"

"I'll come home." But that wasn't an option he wanted to consider. They needed the money. He had to win.

"The collective can help. We have some funds set aside—"

"No." Everett cut her off before she could finish. This wasn't a subject up for debate. "But thanks for the offer."

"Everett—"

"This isn't your problem to solve."

"It is, in a way," she said. "We have to protect our investment."

"Which is what I'm trying to do. Protect your investment. Pop almost lost the ranch once before because of unpaid taxes. If that happens again and the county forces a sale, you won't have a place for the mares and foals. Then what will the collective do?"

She drew in a long breath before continuing. "I just think there are options other than you returning to rodeoing. Champ has a stellar reputation. It won't take long to bring in customers. You already have two appointments. What about them? Are you going to cancel?"

"Pop will cover for me."

"Talk to the Hays. Not about a job," she hastily added. "Advertising in their feed store. I'm sure they'll let you."

"That's a good idea. I'll stop by before I leave town."

She heaved a sigh. "You are more stubborn than anyone I know. Even your grandfather."

"I'm not stubborn. I'm a realist. I ran the numbers last night." He'd created a spreadsheet on his laptop after Pop went to bed. He was by no means an expert, but he didn't think his calculations were that far off. Sheriff Andy agreed when Everett called him. Much to his dismay, the retired real estate broker had reported his less than encouraging findings from the city about renting out space. It was doable, but the permits would require a lengthy application process, cost substantial fees and take two to three months. "We're going to need twenty thousand dollars over the next few months. And that's a conservative estimate."

When she started to speak, he interrupted her.

"Until the foals are sold and Pop gets his share, which is, at minimum, eighteen months away, this place will be running on a shoestring. And that's only if I can bring in enough income and nothing unexpected happens."

"What if you sold Hombre?"

"You know what I paid for him. At most, I'd get enough to support the ranch for a month."

She lifted her chin. "You're just going to give up, then?"

"I'm not giving up. I'm trying to salvage a bad situation the best way I can."

"Which also happens to allow you to qualify for Nationals."

"This has nothing to do with Nationals."

"But if you do qualify, you'd go."

He tried to slow his rapid breathing. Though they were outside, it felt like the walls were closing in on him. He'd experienced the same sensation before in the months following the accident.

"I would go. If I place in the top three of any event, the prize money would be enough to carry the ranch for six months. That would give us the funds we need to make repairs and me time to learn the business. Also to train Hombre and sell him for a profit."

"You're chasing a pipe dream, Everett, and betting your grandfather's health, his business and this ranch on it."

He heard the bitterness in her retort, and it cut deep, reminding him of a phone call not long after Brody's death when he'd told Macy he wasn't returning.

"If, after a month or six weeks, it looks like I'm not going to qualify for Nationals, I'll come home."

Macy averted her gaze; her posture stiffened. "You got it all figured out."

Everett didn't blame her for being mad at him. "I don't

want to sell the ranch and put Pop in a nursing facility. I thought that's what you wanted, too."

"It is."

"Me temporarily returning to the circuit is the best way to accomplish that."

"When would you leave?" she asked.

"Today. I called Rusty earlier. I can still make the Big Timber Rodeo in Tucson."

Team roping was out of the question. Rusty had partnered with Junior. But Everett could enter bulldogging and tie-down roping, both events he excelled at.

Macy's features tightened. She was fighting to control her emotions. "You didn't waste a single second. You must really want to get away."

"I don't." He leaned toward her. She backed away, and he didn't push. "I'll be back. I promise."

"Will you?" She turned to face him then, tears brimming in her eyes. "Because I've heard that line before at Brody's funeral, and then you abandoned me."

"It's different this time."

"Is it? What about us, Everett? What happens while you're competing and saving the ranch? Do we see each other whenever you decide to come home? Are we still dating? On break?"

Here was the hardest part of his plan. "I'm not in a good place right now to make any kind of commitment, and you deserve that."

"I do. I absolutely do." The hurt in her eyes belied the strength of her words.

"I'm sorry, Macy. Try to look at this from my perspective. I don't have much going for me except a ranch that, unless I manage a minor miracle, will soon be in worse debt than it currently is and a business that I may drive into the ground. That's not what you deserve, either."

"My feelings for you don't hinge on how successful you are."

"I won't saddle anyone with my debt. You especially."

She hooked her leg over the picnic table seat and stood. "It sounds to me like your mind is made up. I don't see reason to continue this conversation."

Everett also stood. This hadn't gone well, which was why he'd wanted more time to think things through before talking to her. "I disappointed you before. I don't want to do it again, and I'm afraid I will."

"Right. I get it. A small hurt now rather than a big hurt later."

"Can we talk again in a few weeks? I'll be home after the Amarillo Rodeo."

"No. No." Her composure began to visibly fray, and she waved a hand in the air. "I don't know why I thought this time would be different. You leave when the going gets tough. Just look at your track record."

"This isn't like before." He rubbed his forehead where a headache threatened to morph into a migraine.

"It's exactly like before. You just refuse to see."

"Macy. Please."

"Whatever you got to do to live with your guilt." She walked away only to turn back.

Any hopes Everett had that she'd had a change of heart were dashed with her next words.

"Please tell Pop I'm going to do the chores and ask him if he'd mind watching Joey and Peanut?"

"I will." His chest ached. Not as much as the pain he'd obviously caused her. How was it possible to mess up so badly when all he'd wanted to do was solve problems?

"You know what hurts the most, Everett? You didn't talk to me first. You made your plans without a single thought of me."

It wasn't like that. He'd felt cornered, and their conversation went sideways. But he didn't say that. "I should have. You're right."

"That's not a quality I'm looking for in a life partner." She walked away then.

He debated going after her only to reconsider. He'd let her down. Nothing he said would redeem him.

Thirty minutes later as he was packing, he mentally replayed the scene between them over and over.

Maybe it wasn't survivor's guilt that had kept him away all those years or not having the courage to face her. Rather, he had a fear of failing. At business and, more importantly, failing those he loved.

And in the end, it became a self-fulfilling prophecy.

CHAPTER FOURTEEN

MACY HAD ABSOLUTELY zero intention of going to the ranch today. In fact, she might not go tomorrow, either. Yes, she was that mad at Everett. Not that he was there. He'd left yesterday for the Big Timber Rodeo. She'd watched him from her hiding place in the mare barn. His truck had hardly disappeared in a cloud of red dust when she headed into the house, grabbed Joey and Peanut, managed to avoid Pop's probing questions and drove straight home.

Fortunately, Larry Hays had volunteered to handle last evening's feeding. He'd been stuck covering for their driver who'd left work early to deal with a family emergency. As the ranch was already on the schedule for their regular hay and grain delivery, he hadn't minded feeding the mares and stallions.

Macy hadn't felt guilty asking Glynnis to handle the morning feeding, as she'd already had plans to take her brother Abel to an early breakfast and then church service. Neither had Kinsley minded when Macy phoned and asked her to feed the horses this evening.

Everett would be home in a few weeks. Maybe by then Macy's anger at him would have cooled, and she'd see his point of view. Not today, however.

She should have been able to sleep in and spend the morning catching up on things around the house. Except that hadn't happened. Nothing had gone her way since her argument with Everett.

Joey, apparently picking up on her sour mood, had been determined to test her patience from the moment she'd loaded him into the truck yesterday. Her often sweet and biddable little boy was either misbehaving, refusing to co-operate, pitching a fit or tuning her out.

He'd woken her twice during the night with his crying, complaining of a tummy ache. Macy could relate. She'd had her own tummy ache to contend with—namely, Everett.

The thought of him made her groan aloud. It was three years ago all over again. The same emotions she'd experienced back then rose anew to torture and torment her.

In the end, she'd told Joey he could sleep with her, hoping that snuggling with her darling son would ease both their troubles. It hadn't. Not hers. In the morning, splotches stained her pillow, remnants from where her tears had dried.

Why did Everett have to leave? Macy pondered the question while she stowed Joey's toys in the multicolored cubicles lining a wall in his room. In a way, she kind of, sort of, understood his reasoning to put the brakes on their relationship. He did have more pressing priorities, and she had no wish to add to his struggles. But they could have remained friends until the timing was better. She'd have gladly waited.

It was the fact that he was running away that annoyed her. He was putting his rodeoing career ahead of Pop's breeding business and the ranch.

If he'd stayed in Wickenburg, he could have immediately focused his energies on building the breeding business and likely brought in clients quickly. Instead, he'd jumped in his truck and driven to Tucson.

He had better come back, Macy thought and ground her teeth, feelings from three years ago returning. It was one thing to abandon her and Joey. If Everett abandoned Pop, she'd never forgive him.

Finishing in Joey's room, she went to the kitchen in search of Joey, only to stop dead in her tracks. Leaving him alone in his current mood for even a few minutes had been a big mistake.

"Look-it, Mommy." He beamed up at her, so proud of himself. "I fed Peanut."

"Joey. Oh, no!"

Somehow, he'd breached the cabinet's childproof lock, or she, in her preoccupied state of mind, had left it open, and dumped the entire open bag of dog kibble onto the kitchen floor. Peanut, having suffered reduced portions for the last several weeks, now gorged herself. She inhaled each little round nugget with the speed and efficiency of a hand vacuum set on high.

"Peanut. Leave it."

The dachshund ignored her and continued to feast. So much for Sheriff Andy's assurance that she was trained in voice commands.

Macy bent and scooped the dachshund into her arms. Peanut whined and wiggled in an effort to free herself.

"What am I going to do with you?"

The extra food likely wouldn't undo the results of Peanut's healthy diet. But Macy had promised Sheriff Andy she'd take good care of the dog and not overfeed her.

"She hungry," Joey said.

Macy bit her tongue and drew in a calming breath. She would not snap at her son. He was a child. Exactly two years and seven months old this past Friday. He didn't know any better. And she had left him alone in a kitchen with an unlocked cabinet.

"Come on. Be a good boy and help Mommy clean up. But first we need to shut Peanut in the bathroom."

Macy was just returning the broom and dustpan to the pantry when her cell phone rang from where it lay on the counter. She reached it a split second before the call went to voicemail and saw Glynnis's name on the display.

"Hi. How's it going?"

"Fine," the older woman said. "Hey, listen, I was just leaving after dropping off Abel when I heard a distressing sound from the barn."

"What do you mean by distressing?"

"Hard to say. Grunting, I guess? It's Roxie."

Macy's heart rate quickened. "Is she acting colicky?"

"Maybe. I'm no expert. You want me to call Dr. Beck?"

"No." Macy put her earlier determination to avoid the ranch aside. The health of the mares was too important. "I'll be there in thirty minutes. If need be, I'll call him."

"Should I stay? I have to head home soon. My son and his family are coming over for a birthday cookout. But I can hang around here for a little while."

"I'll call Pop. Ask him to keep an eye on Roxie until I get there. You go on."

They disconnected, and Macy rushed to get out of the house. She called her mom on the way and asked if she could drop off Joey. Should Roxie have colic, Macy might be there well into the evening and, more importantly, need to focus all her attention on the horse. Besides, a change might do her cranky son some good.

Once behind the wheel, she phoned Pop and explained things to him. "Do you mind waiting with Roxie until I arrive? I'll hurry."

"Sure." He coughed and coughed again. "No problem."

"Are you all right, Pop?" She didn't like the way he sounded.

"I'm fine. Just tired." His voice trailed off. "Feeling my age today."

"Yeah. I hear you."

He'd probably had a bad night, too, worrying about Everett and sad he'd left for the rodeo. Plus, it was another warm day.

"Thanks, Pop. I'll see you soon."

Having been forewarned about her grandson's mood, Macy's mom greeted Joey with a frozen yogurt bar. He grabbed the treat with both hands and shoved it into his mouth. Macy kissed the top of his head, avoiding sticky smears on her face.

"And nothing for Peanut that isn't on her diet," she said as she climbed back into the truck cab.

The dog sat at her mom's feet, wearing a forlorn expression.

Macy forced herself to remain unmoved and reversed out of the driveway. She really couldn't tell what had her more on edge at the moment: her son's fussiness, Roxie's possible bout with colic, her concern for Pop or her anger at Everett. This was not a good day.

At the ranch, she drove straight to the mare barn, parked and grabbed her medical bag from the rear seat. Pop sat in one of the rocking chairs, his shoulders slumped. Nearing, she noticed his alarming pallor.

"Hi, Pop. Are you okay?"

"Don't bother with me. Go check on that mare."

"You sure?"

She couldn't help herself and put a hand on his forehead. It didn't feel especially warm to the touch. Nor did he sound congested. His breathing was short, however.

"My stomach's been giving me fits all morning," he said. "I must have eaten something that didn't agree with me."

Macy hesitated, torn over what to do. Finally, she said, "Give me a minute. I won't be long."

Inside the barn, she hurriedly checked over Miss Roxie. If the mare had been showing signs of distress earlier with Glynnis, she appeared perfectly fine now. The stethoscope revealed only normal gut noises, and the mare presented alert and interested and calm. She exhibited no signs of pain when Macy palpated her sides, and an inspection of the stall showed normal elimination habits.

"What's up, girl? You just playing games with Glynnis? Getting her upset over nothing?"

Roxie nuzzled Macy's hair, not seeming the least bit distressed.

"All right." Macy sighed. "False alarm, I guess." She shrugged. "Better I came here for no reason than didn't come and you lost your foal. Or worse."

She scratched Roxie between the ears before exiting the stall. There, she returned her stethoscope to the medical bag.

"Maybe I'll come by this evening just to be on the safe side." So much for her vow to stay away.

Lifting the bag by the handle, she started out of the barn. There, she saw Pop still sitting in the rocking chair, his head bent forward. She started toward him.

"Roxie appears fine. I think I'll—" She stopped short. "Pop?" When he didn't respond, she dropped the bag and covered the remaining distance at a run. "Pop! Pop!" She bent over him and shook his shoulder. "Pop, answer me."

"Yeah. Yeah." His voice came out in a strained whisper.

"What's wrong?"

"My chest. It hurts."

She saw then he cradled his left arm. Terror seized her, freezing her insides. "Hang on, Pop. I'm going to call for help."

He didn't object, which Macy took as an indication of how bad he felt.

Straightening, she dug her phone from her pocket and dialed 911.

When the dispatcher answered, she shouted into the phone, "I have an eighty-seven-year-old man with me. I think he is having a heart attack."

EVERETT LIFTED THE saddle off his borrowed paint horse and carried it to the storage compartment in the front of Rusty's trailer. He then grabbed a stiff currycomb and began rubbing the dried sweat from the horse's hide. Tired from a full day's work in the rodeo arena, the paint lowered his head and snorted with contentment. Though tied to the side of the trailer, it was unlikely he'd go anywhere.

"You did good today, boy." Everett patted the horse on the neck.

"You, too," came a voice from behind him. "For someone out of practice. Second place in tie-down roping was respectable."

He turned to find Rusty's wide, affable grin aimed at him. The lanky cowboy, his plaid shirt and denim jeans dusty from a full morning competing in the arena, carried two foil-wrapped burritos and two cans of soda.

"I've done better," Everett said. He'd been disappointed in his bulldogging performance, coming in tenth. And he didn't want to think about his poor showing in bronc and bull riding. He had no one to blame but himself, thoughts of Macy distracting him.

"Well, that's true." Rusty handed one of the burritos to Everett, along with a soda. "But you kept yourself in the running for Nationals in two events. That's not nothing."

And the tie-down roping prize money would cover his expenses for this weekend and next weekend, too.

They sat down to eat, Everett on the wheel well of the

trailer and Rusty in a rickety lawn chair that had seen more than a hundred rodeos.

"Thanks for lunch, by the way." Everett took a bite of his burrito. He wasn't hungry, but he didn't want to offend his friend, who'd been nothing but good to him. That included listening to Everett spill his guts the previous evening in their hotel room when they should have been getting a good night's sleep in preparation for today's competition.

"Mind if I make an observation?" Rusty asked.

"Not at all. I can use some insight."

"Money is replaceable. You can always get more. Family isn't. Once you lose someone, they're gone for good."

"You think I should quit rodeoing."

Rusty's goofy, yet friendly, features fell. "You know my dad died of cancer when I was twenty."

"Yeah." Everett ached for his friend. "Sorry, man. That had to be rough."

"His last wish was for me to win a title. He didn't get it because I spent the last five months of his life home, with him, helping my mom with his hospice care. I set my rodeo career back two years."

"I remember."

"And I've never regretted a single moment. Those five months with my dad meant everything to me. To him, too."

Everett sat back, ruminating that.

"I'm not telling you what to do, pal." Rusty finished off his burrito and crumpled the foil wrapping. "I'm merely telling you what I did. A heart can't be in two places at once."

"Are you talking about my grandfather or Macy?"

"Take your pick."

Everett nodded. The advice had merit. "You sticking around for the bull riding finals tonight?"

"Wouldn't miss it." Rusty hadn't qualified, either. But he'd remain to support his friends and join in the celebrations afterward. "Aren't you?"

"I'm tired. Gonna hit the sack early."

"Suit yourself. It promises to be a good time."

Everett pushed off the wheel well and extended his hand, shaking Rusty's. "Thanks." He didn't elaborate what for, and Rusty didn't ask.

When he reached for the paint's lead rope, Rusty said, "Don't worry about him. I'll take him to the pens with my horse."

Everett smiled. "Sure? You don't want to keep that pretty redhead waiting."

Rusty laughed. "How'd you know?"

"You never change."

Everett got into his truck, turning on his phone as he did. He always shut it off when he was competing, avoiding any interruptions. Beeps and buzzes signaled a slew of incoming voicemails, texts and emails.

Before he had a chance to read even the first one, his phone rang. Macy's number appeared on the display, and his nerves ignited. Why was she calling? Was this his chance to apologize and give a better explanation?

He put the phone to his ear. "Hi, Macy."

"Everett! Thank God. I've been calling for hours."

His heart pounded at the strain in her voice. "What's wrong?"

"I'm with Pop. We're at the hospital."

"Hospital!"

"They think he may have had another heart attack."

"How bad?"

She started to cry. "I don't know. They won't tell me anything. I'm not family. He was conscious when the ambulance took him away."

"You were there?" He started the engine. "At the ranch?"

"Yes. He didn't look good, and when he complained of his chest hurting, I called 911."

Turning sharply to the right, Everett exited the parking area, the rear wheels of his truck fishtailing on the loose dirt. "I'm leaving right now. I should be there in…" He mentally calculated the drive time. "Two and a half hours."

"I'll stay with him. Call you if there are any updates."

Relief flooded him. "Are you sure, Macy? What about Joey?"

"He's at my mom's."

"Okay. Thank you." He didn't deserve her kindness after the way he'd treated her. In the past and recently. But, he reminded himself, she was doing this for Pop. Not him. "Do you know, does Pop have his phone with him?"

"Yeah. Why?"

Everett merged into traffic on the main road. "Maybe you can ask the nurses to have him call me. If he's able to, that is."

"I will."

"He may not realize he can give permission for you to sit with him."

"Hold on," Macy said. "I'll ask the person at the front desk." There was a lengthy pause followed by muffled voices. After a moment, she said, "They'll give a message to his care team."

Everett let out a long breath. "Good. Good." He'd feel infinitely better knowing Macy was with Pop.

"The woman did tell me it'll be a while. Pop's having some tests."

Everett gripped the steering wheel tight with both fists. Having tests sounded both scary and optimistic. His grandfather was alive, but was he at death's door?

"I hate to ask another favor—"

"Anything, Everett. What do you need?"

"Can you call my mom and update her? I'm about to get on the freeway and don't want to be distracted." Since the accident, he had a strict rule about not using the phone, even on Bluetooth, during demanding traffic situations.

"Of course."

He recited the number for her. "Tell Mom I'll call as soon as I have a chance."

"Drive safe. Don't take any risks."

"Thanks again, Macy." There was so much more he wanted to say, but the access ramp to the freeway was directly ahead, and this wasn't the time. "See you soon."

They disconnected after that. Everett berated himself as he drove along. He should never have left the ranch. His actions had been selfish and thoughtless. The stress he'd caused Pop had likely triggered the heart attack. He'd never forgive himself.

The irony of the situation wasn't lost on him. Three years ago, he'd been by Brody's side, waiting for Macy to arrive. Now, he was the one driving like crazy trying to get to the hospital before something bad happened, and she was with his loved one.

He clung to hope. Pop had to survive. *Please, God, don't let history repeat itself.*

When his phone rang a half hour later and Macy's number appeared on the truck's dash display, he nearly swerved off the road. Fear sliced through him as he hit the answer button.

"How's Pop doing?"

"I'm with him now," she said. "He's a little groggy from whatever they gave him. We're waiting on the cardiologist to go over the test results."

Relief made him weak. "I'm glad you're with him."

"He wants to talk to you. Hold on a second."

After a pause filled with rustling, Pop's gravelly, slurry voice came on the line. "Hiya, sonny."

"Pop." Everett's throat filled with a burning sensation, and his eyes blurred with unshed tears. "How you feeling?"

"Been better. My ticker's giving me trouble again."

"You're going to be fine."

"Damn straight I am." The feebleness in his voice didn't match the conviction of his words.

"I'm on my way. I'll be there soon."

"How'd you do? Win any buckles?"

Leave it to his grandfather to ask about the rodeo in his condition.

"Second in tie-down roping."

"That's my boy." Pop's chuckled ended on a cough.

"We'll talk more when I get there. You rest."

Pop wasn't finished. "Your mom called. She's thinking about flying out here. I told her not to rush. I have no intention of dying anytime soon."

"I'm holding you to that, Pop."

"Susan is, too. I hated telling her I was in the hospital, but when I didn't answer my phone, she got worried and called Macy."

"Susan cares about you, Pop."

"All these folks making a fuss over me." He sighed. "I'm a fortunate man."

He was. Had Everett handled things differently with Macy, he might even now be considering himself a fortunate man, too.

A deep voice abruptly sounded in the background.

"Seems I gotta go. The doctor ordered some more goll-darn tests just to torture me."

"I'll be there real soon, Pop. Wait for me."

"Where would I be going?" The hoarseness in his voice

let Everett know his grandfather understood what he really meant.

"I love you."

"Love you, too, sonny. And I'm mighty proud of you. If I'm off getting a test or something when you get here, Macy's gonna give you a hug for me."

"I'll collect that in person when I see you."

Before he could say more, Macy came on the line. "The orderly took Pop."

"Okay." Everett cleared his throat, emotions getting the best of him. "Do you know what kind of tests he's having done?"

"He's had an EKG already and another electro-something. Blood work, and they gave him some medications. I think the doctor said this last one is a cardiac catheterization? He talked fast, and I had trouble understanding him."

Everett didn't know what a cardiac catheterization was and didn't like the sound of it.

"I'll keep you posted if there's any change," Macy said.

"How's he doing? Really?"

"Hard to say. I mean, his spirits are good. But whatever happened definitely took a toll on him. He doesn't seem to be in any pain or much pain. They have him hooked up to oxygen and a heart monitor and a bunch of other machines."

"How are *you* doing? Being in a hospital… It can't be easy for you." Which made her willingness to stay with Pop even more meaningful.

"I'm hanging in there."

"I shouldn't have left yesterday. Maybe this wouldn't have happened."

"You won't get an argument from me," she quipped, and then softened her initial stern tone. "You couldn't have prevented his heart attack, Everett."

"I've put him through a lot the last few days."

"He's been under stress for a long time."

Did she believe that or was she just being nice and secretly holding him responsible for this latest medical emergency? She was still mad underneath her helpful exterior. He could tell. The important questions were, did she hate him and could she ever forgive him?

"Look," he began hesitantly. "Can we talk when I get there?"

"I don't want to rehash yesterday."

"Neither do I."

She sighed, which did nothing to reassure him. Neither did her next comment. "We'll see."

He lost their connection then, having traveled into a mountainous area notorious for faulty cell phone reception. Their call, especially the way it ended, had left Everett with a pit the size of a grapefruit sitting in the bottom of his stomach.

Only seeing Pop, being told by the doctor that he would be all right and talking to Macy would ease his awful discomfort.

CHAPTER FIFTEEN

SHORTLY AFTER POP returned from his latest test, the attending doctor breezed into the ER room to review the results. Macy stood to excuse herself and give them some privacy, but Pop insisted she stay. She supposed he wanted someone with him should the results be grim.

Thankfully, they weren't. Mostly, anyway.

"I initially suspected you had a mini heart attack," the young, haggard-appearing doctor said. "And a mild one at that."

"A *mini* heart attack?" Pop blinked in confusion. "What in tarnation is that?"

"Much like a regular heart attack. Just on a smaller scale and with less damage."

Scratching the two-day stubble shadowing his jaw, he studied the monitors tracking Pop's cardiac vitals. Macy had been watching them, as well, listening to the steady *beep, beep, beep*. Not that she understood what the numbers meant and gave a start whenever an alarm sounded.

"But your tests have all come back normal," the doctor continued. "In fact, pretty good for a man your age. You'll need to follow up with your regular cardiologist as soon as possible. And we'll keep you overnight for observation, just as a precaution."

"What happened to me, Doc? I'm telling you," Pop insisted, "I had a heart attack before. I know what it feels like. I swear to you my chest was about to burst open."

"My guess is a panic attack."

"A what?"

"Panic attacks can mimic heart attacks. Have you had them before?"

"I... I...don't think so. Maybe. When I was first widowed, I had some pretty rough nights. I figured it was grief getting the best of me."

"Did you ever seek professional help?" the doctor asked.

"Nah. I fought my way through."

"Well, panic attacks are common after the death of a loved one. They do occur less frequently in the elderly, and there's usually a cause." He scratched his stubble again. "Have you been under any stress lately or more stress than usual?"

"A little. Yeah." He gave a half shrug. "Something has been weighing heavy on me."

Everett leaving, thought Macy. Pop had been counting on him to stay. Everett returning to the rodeo circuit must have worried Pop to the point that he'd suffered a panic attack.

She'd be angrier at Everett if not for their phone call earlier and imagined he was spending the entire drive to Wickenburg berating himself. Besides, what mattered the most was that Pop would be okay.

"You're going to need to find a way to reduce your stress," the doctor said. "Your health depends on it. Next time could be the real thing."

Pop smiled. "The only way I can think of to do that is to quit procrastinating and get down on one knee."

"What!" Macy's mouth fell open. She had jumped to the wrong conclusion. Everett leaving wasn't to blame. Pop was stressed over proposing to Susan!

"I've gotten myself more tangled than an old fishing line this past week," Pop said. "Ever since I decided to ask my sweetheart to marry me."

Macy, clenched her jaw to stop herself from laughing.

The young attending also fought to hide a smile. "Well, I recommend you ask her before you put yourself in the hospital again. And you can consider that doctor's orders."

They chatted for several more minutes with Pop asking questions and the attending patiently answering them. He suggested Pop investigate coping methods to help with stress, such as walks, meditation, chair yoga and breathing exercises.

"I like to nap," Pop said.

The attending couldn't hold back and chuckled. "That works, too."

After he left, Pop drifted off, no doubt a response to his enormous relief. Macy took the opportunity to step outside and phone Everett. When the call went straight to voicemail, she sent a text telling him that the doctor had good news and to please drive carefully. She'd fill him in on the details when he arrived. She figured either he was out of range or his phone battery had died.

She next called Everett's mom and brought her up-to-date. Then she did the same thing with her mom.

"I'm glad to hear that," her mom said. "Panic attacks are no fun, but at least it's nothing life-threatening. What a relief that will be for Everett."

"How's my little man doing?"

The question elicited a long, mournful moan. "Honestly, not great. I'm not sure whose fuse is shorter, his or mine."

"I'm sorry. He doesn't always do well with changes in routine."

"No worries. Your dad and I endured much worse when you were his age."

"You always told me I was an angel," Macy protested, pretending to be offended.

"You had your days."

"Well, Pop should be moved to a room soon. They're keeping him overnight for observation. I won't be much longer, and I'll head home the moment Everett gets here. I'm guessing another hour or so."

"No rush. If you want," her mom suggested, "Joey can spend the night. You'll be tired when you get home."

"But I can't pick him up until tomorrow after work."

"That's all right. I have some errands to run tomorrow. He can come with me. We'll stop by the library for story hour." She paused as if thinking. "You know what? I'll call Fran. She might like to meet us there."

Macy's heart filled with love. Her mom was always thinking of Joey's other grandmother and strove to include her in activities. "You're the best. Have I told you that lately?"

"Not in a week or two."

The orderly appeared then, a short, wide man with a big smile. "Someone here called for a ride?"

Pop instantly roused.

"I have to run, Mom," Macy said. "They're moving Pop."

"Tell him hi from us and to get well soon."

Macy waited outside the new room while the orderly helped Pop change from his clothes into a hospital gown. Once he was settled beneath the bedcovers, she joined him, encouraged by his complaints about not having his own pajamas to wear.

"Darn thing doesn't close in the back."

"I'm going to the gift shop to get you a toothbrush and toothpaste," she said. "Anything else you need?"

He ran his fingers through his thinning white hair. "I could do with a comb, if it's no trouble."

"None at all."

She was about to leave when there was soft rapping on the door. Both she and Pop glanced up.

Pop broke into an enormous smile. "Well, hello, hello."

"Are you feeling up to a visitor?" a gentle voice asked.

Macy immediately jumped out of the chair and moved aside.

Pop levered himself to a sitting position, looking five years younger. "I am now. Come in, come in, my dear."

Susan entered, beaming. She tottered to the side of the bed. "You gave me quite the scare, Winston."

"Gave myself quite the scare, too."

"I'm glad you're all right. What would I do without you?" She bent and kissed him sweetly on the lips. His gnarled hand went up to tenderly stroke her hair.

A lump formed in Macy's throat, and her heart melted.

"You two have a nice visit," she said, feeling like a third wheel. At the door, she paused. "Susan, where's Callie?" She assumed Susan's granddaughter had brought her.

"She went to find some of her nurse friends."

"Okay. Maybe I'll run into her." And be able to extend the lovebirds' private time. "Can I bring either of you a cup of coffee or soda?"

Her question fell on deaf ears. Susan had taken a seat in the chair beside the bed. She and Pop were talking, their heads bent together, their eyes fixed on each other.

Macy started down the hall, her mind on Everett. She'd hoped, for a brief while there, that the two of them might have a relationship like Pop and Susan's. But then her hopes had been dashed.

Was it too late? Seeing Pop and Susan, her optimism had risen. Maybe it was never too late. But if she and Everett were to reconcile, they had to reach a compromise, and therein lay the problem.

THE HOSPITAL'S DOUBLE entrance doors whooshed open as Everett approached. He charged inside as if being chased by a swarm of angry hornets. Cool air-conditioning struck him in the face, but he didn't stop until he reached the information desk straight ahead.

"Which way is room three forty-one?" he asked the woman behind the computer terminal. Macy had texted him Pop's room number a short while ago.

"Down the hall and to that first bank of elevators." The woman pointed. "Avoid the one on the right. That's a service elevator."

"Thank you."

A line was already forming when Everett reached the elevators, including two people in wheelchairs. Five minutes later, he stepped onto the third floor. Glancing at the room number signs on the walls, he turned left. Doctors in lab coats, nurses in scrubs and patients in bathrobes blurred together as he hurried past them.

At last, he reached Pop's room. But rather than enter, he ground to a sudden halt at the door. Susan sat with his grandfather, their hands clasped and speaking quietly. Neither of them noticed they had company.

Everett didn't mean to eavesdrop, but he couldn't help hearing.

"Oh, Winston," Susan said, her voice tremulous. "I'm glad you're all right. Promise me you'll take better care of yourself from now on."

"I promise. We'll take care of each other."

"I know we haven't been seeing each other that long…"

"Long enough to know how I feel about you." He raised her hand to his lips for a kiss. "I love you, Susan. I didn't think I'd ever say those words again to a woman. Can you believe it? An old man like me being in love? But I am. Head over heels."

"I feel the same way, Winston. I love you, too." She rose up from the chair and kissed him full on the lips.

When they parted, Everett saw a handsome young man in the wrinkled face of his grandfather. Susan's smile radiated joy. She must have seen the young man, too.

Everett should step away and give them some privacy. He couldn't, however; the sight of them transfixed him. This was what he wanted for himself. What he might have had with Macy if he hadn't allowed his fears to get the better of him.

"Susan, my sweet." Pop stroked her papery cheek as if it was fine silk. "None of us can predict how much time we have left on this earth. Whether I have a single day or ten thousand remaining, I want to spend every one of them with you."

"Me, too, Winston."

"I had something else in mind, much more romantic than a hospital room. After today, I figure I shouldn't waste another moment."

"Wh...what are you saying?"

"I'd get down on one knee if I could."

"Winston!" Her eyes widened.

"You are precious to me, my love. I realize I have little to offer you other than my heart and a roof over our heads. But I think, between the two of us, we can cobble a wonderful life together."

"I agree." She dabbed at the tears falling down her cheek.

"Will you marry me and make me the happiest man alive?"

"Yes. Of course, I will. I was ready to ask you to marry me if you didn't get around to it."

They laughed and kissed and clung to each other.

"I don't want to wait," Pop said. "You think we can get the minister from your church to come here tonight and marry us?"

"I'm not marrying you in a hospital room, even if it was possible." She gave his arm a playful punch. "I want a real wedding."

"All right. Anything for you. Just don't make me wait too long."

"How about a month?" Susan suggested. "September twenty-second. That's the autumn equinox. The first day of fall, which is my favorite season."

"Sounds like a good day to tie the knot."

Pop and Susan kissed again. Everett couldn't stop grinning. He wanted to bust into the room and shout his enthusiastic congratulations, only he hesitated. This was their special time. The last thing they needed was an interruption.

Retreating a step, Everett turned and nearly knocked into Macy. She held a paper cup of coffee. If not for the lid, she would have spilled the contents all over herself.

"Whoops," she said and pulled back.

"Come on." Everett took her by the arm and led her down the hall. They dodged the same blur of hospital personnel and patients as when Everett had arrived.

"Wait," Macy exclaimed. "What's going on?"

"Pop and Susan need some alone time." He spotted an alcove with visitor chairs. "Let's sit over there."

"That's why I left the room and went to the gift shop and the cafeteria." She raised her other hand, which held a plastic bag. "So they could have some privacy."

"They're not done talking yet." He dropped down into a seat. When she just stood there, he gave her a look.

She sighed and sat. "Fine. Okay."

"Pop proposed."

Macy gasped, only to brighten. "He did? What was her answer? Tell me she accepted."

"She did. They didn't notice me standing there. I saw the whole thing."

"Aw…" Macy looked ready to cry. "That must have been so sweet."

"It was." He relayed the details. "But act surprised when they tell you. They may not like that I overheard."

"Oh, I doubt they'll mind. They're too happy to care."

"Tell me what the doctor said about Pop." With all the excitement of the proposal, Everett had almost forgotten.

"Pop had a panic attack."

"A panic attack? You're kidding."

"According to the doctor, they can present like a heart attack." Macy spent the next several minutes filling Everett in on what the doctor had said and Pop's need to reduce stress.

She smiled. "Pop says his nerves about proposing were responsible."

"Is that really the reason?"

"It's true."

"Me leaving for Tucson didn't help matters."

"Probably not." Her tone was a mixture of teasing and seriousness.

"I regret it. For more reasons than leaving Pop alone," he admitted.

Some of the light in her eyes dimmed. "Well, now that Pop and Susan are getting married in, what, a month you said? You won't have to worry about being gone so much. They can watch out for each other. Plus, Abel and Sheriff Andy will be there," she added. "Along with Callie stopping by."

She didn't understand, Everett realized. *She* was the "more reasons" he was talking about.

"Macy. That wasn't—"

He stopped himself midsentence. What did he intend to say? That, like Pop and Susan, the obstacles he and Macy faced didn't matter? That they cared about each other and they could make it work no matter the difficulties?

No. The fact was, he still had nothing to offer her beyond the hope that one day things might improve if he could pull a rabbit out of a hat. Even if she was okay with a business and ranch barely hanging on, Everett wasn't. He had to bring more to a relationship before committing. A steady, decent income. A promising future. Security. Stability. Dependability. He and Macy could only survive so long on just love.

Before he could take her hand and explain, a loud male voice called out, "Everett. Macy. There you are."

They turned in unison. Sheriff Andy and Kinsley approached, wearing worried expressions. Sheriff Andy carried a thick portfolio.

"How's Pop?" Kinsley asked when she and Sheriff Andy approached.

Everett stood. "Better. He didn't have a heart attack." He gave them the condensed version of what Macy had told him.

"Good to hear," Sheriff Andy said. "It could have been much worse."

"Thanks for coming." Everett once again marveled at the fondness the collective members had for his grandfather. Pop was a lucky man to have so many good friends. Friends, Everett was ashamed to say, that had been there for him when Everett wasn't. That, however, was going to change.

"Can he have visitors?" Kinsley asked.

"Susan's with him now."

The young woman raised a hand. "We don't want to cut in."

"I'm sure it's okay. She's been in there for a while."

"I can check if you want," Macy offered.

"Why don't you go with Kinsley?" Sheriff Andy said. "Pop may not be up to a crowd. We can take turns. Besides—" he clapped Everett on the back "—I've got something to show Everett."

He wasn't the only one who sent Sheriff Andy a curious look. Macy's eyebrows rose high, but she said nothing and just linked arms with Kinsley before they ventured down the hall.

"Let's sit." Sheriff Andy motioned.

"This sounds serious." Everett returned to his previous chair.

"Not at all. I have good news. Made a few calls to some of my old contacts at the city regarding a multiuse permit for rentals on the ranch."

"We can get one?"

"Absolutely. Bear in mind, the fees are the fees. No change to those. But I think we can speed up the application process, thanks to my contacts." Sheriff Andy opened the portfolio he'd brought with him and extracted a stack of papers. "I printed these out for you. Here's the permit application. I can help you fill it out. And a map of the ranch, along with all the acreage." He pointed with his finger. "There are restrictions. A certain percentage of the land must remain natural and untouched. But you can, for instance, turn this parcel here into, let's call it, a mini RV rental park. Running power and water wouldn't be difficult. You'd have to install a second septic tank."

"That sounds expensive."

"It's not cheap." Sheriff Andy named an estimate.

Everett gave a low whistle.

"I have contacts in the construction business," the retiree said, "who will give you the friend discount."

"There's no way Pop or I can afford that. Discount or not."

"I've also included an application for a low interest

government-assisted loan for small businesses." He riffled through the stack and removed several sheets from
the bottom. "You can't beat these rates. I also threw together a very rough income and expense projection. You
should be able to pay off the loan in five years and still
bring in a small monthly profit to supplement the horse
breeding business."

"You did all that?" Everett was torn between being
shocked and impressed.

"Rental properties are one way I used to earn my living."

Everett hedged. "I get this was my idea. But that was
before I knew everything that was involved. It's a lot and
a big commitment."

"That's true. But it will also bring a big reward."

"But I know nothing about running a rental business,
even a mini RV park."

"I do," Sheriff Andy said. "And I'm your second customer after Abel. You just need four or five more of us."

Everett thought of Pop and Susan, Abel and now Sheriff Andy. "If they were all retired, we could have our own
senior living community."

"That's a great idea!"

"I was kidding."

"You know what the biggest problem senior citizens
have?" Sheriff Andy asked. "We're not ready to be put out
to pasture yet. We can still be useful. We want to be active
and engaged and learning. It's why I joined the collective
and volunteer for the shelter and like helping folks with
their investments. It's why Abel would rather stay in his
motor home at the ranch where he can interact with people every day than at his sister Glynnis's. Because we're
living, not just existing."

Everett studied the older man. "You've given this a lot of thought."

"I looked at where Susan lives, and I realized that's not what I want. Stuck for the rest of my life in a shoebox."

"I hear the place has tennis and pickleball courts and a swimming pool."

"I'm not a man of leisure. At the ranch, I'll be working every day."

"Cleaning stalls and delivering manure to the high school." Everett chuckled.

Sheriff Andy was far more serious. "It's more than that. I'll be part of something bigger. Contributing to the running of the ranch and feeling valued in return. I'm not the only one, either. If you put six RVs on this parcel—" Sheriff Andy again pointed to the map "—you'll change six people's lives for the better."

Everett closed his eyes for a moment and, like Sheriff Andy had suggested, tried to picture it. It wasn't hard. He could see the RVs and their owners living contentedly in a small community. Then, he saw dollar signs.

"The money part scares me," he admitted. "What if this were to fail? Me and Pop would be worse in debt with a loan to pay off."

"There's always risk in every business venture. I won't lie to you and say differently. But ask yourself this. What's the worst that could happen?"

"I just said it. Be in worse debt."

"Then what?"

"Me and Pop go broke?"

"Okay, now you're broke. What next?"

Everett didn't like where this conversation was going? "We'd have to sell the ranch."

"Right." Sheriff Andy smiled. "You'd be no worse off

than you are right now. No worse off than before the collective entered into an agreement with Pop."

"That's not true," Everett said. "We'd have put out a lot of money installing a second septic system and utilities to a mini RV park that tanked."

"Okay. There is that," Sheriff Andy conceded. "But what if you succeed?"

Everett knew his limitations. "I can't do this all on my own. There's no way."

"I'll be there to help."

"I can't ask you to do all that for nothing."

"I wouldn't." Sheriff Andy laughed. "I don't work for free."

"We couldn't afford to pay you."

"I'd take my salary in the form of free rent."

Everett picked up the spreadsheet. "Which would reduce the income."

That earned him a huge grin from the other man. "See. Look how fast you're learning. Yes, it would. The loan would take an extra year to pay off. But isn't it worth it to have a manager living on-site?"

A mini RV park that supplemented the horse breeding business. Was it possible without putting the ranch further into debt? Everett worried he'd be taking on too much. But with Sheriff Andy's guidance, he wouldn't be operating blind.

He thought of Macy. Knowing her, she'd love the idea and not only because it meant that Everett would be staying. And with a second business bringing in a monthly income, Everett would feel like he had more value to bring to a relationship.

"I need to discuss this with Pop," he said. "He and Susan...the two of them are serious about each other. Very serious."

The light of understanding shone in Sheriff Andy's expressions. But before they could continue the discussion further, Callie appeared.

"Hey, guys. I'm here to fetch Grandma."

After that, things happened fast. Callie took Susan home. Everett and Sheriff Andy visited briefly with Pop, who was growing tired by then, while Macy and Kinsley went down to the sitting area to wait. At least, that was what Everett assumed.

"You get some rest, Pop," Everett said and bent down to hug his grandfather.

"I love you, sonny,"

"I love you, too, Pop."

When Everett and Sheriff Andy emerged from the room, only Kinsley was there.

"Macy had to go home," the young woman reported.

The stab of disappointment hit Everett hard. He'd hoped to talk with her about the mini RV park. Then again, maybe he shouldn't say anything until he'd discussed things with Pop. For all Everett knew, his grandfather would veto the idea. The ranch was his, after all.

And then what would they do?

CHAPTER SIXTEEN

MACY ENTERED HER parents' kitchen after another long day of work that had started with her observing surgeries. For once, her dad was there. He and Joey sat at the kitchen table and from all appearances were making a mess. A stack of copy paper sat at her dad's elbow, and a pile of crumpled balls littered the tabletop.

"Hey, Dad. Hi, honey."

"Look-it, Mommy. I made an airplane." Joey launched a poorly constructed paper airplane into the air. It nose-dived onto the kitchen floor.

"I see." Though tired from a long day at the vet clinic, Macy plastered a smile on her face. This had to be her dad's idea. "That's…something." She bent and picked up the plane, returning it to Joey and kissing him hello.

"Join us?" her dad asked. He launched his plane, which ascended and sailed across the kitchen to land on top of the refrigerator.

Joey broke into laughter.

She kissed her dad on the cheek. "Thanks, but we should hit the road."

Her mom entered the kitchen in time to hear Macy. "Going to the ranch?"

Peanut waddled after her. Though still overweight, the dog had lost a pound since being in Macy's care—due in large part to them sticking to her prescribed diet and Peanut following Joey wherever he went.

"I ride a horse!" Joey threw his hands up in the air and rocked forward and backward in an imitation of riding a horse. He had nothing if not a one-track mind.

"Sorry, honey. We're not going to the ranch tonight. Mommy has to stop at the ATM and pick up a prescription on the way home." Not that Joey knew what either of those things were.

He let his arms drop and made a sad face.

"I can't believe it." Her mom opened the refrigerator and removed a glass pan of marinating chicken, the unnoticed paper airplane inches from her head. "You've never gone four days without checking on the mares."

"Sheriff Andy and Kinsley are keeping me updated."

"How long are you planning on avoiding Everett?" Her dad launched another plane, this one at Macy.

It hit her in the arm, bounced off and crash-landed at her feet. Peanut pounced on the plane, snatched it in her teeth and ran under the table where she promptly shredded the plane into tiny pieces. No one stopped her.

"I'm not avoiding Everett." Macy removed the plane from atop the refrigerator and, crumpling it into a ball, tossed it into the pile of rejects.

Her dad winced. "Ouch. That was my best design yet."

"I thought you and Everett had a nice conversation at the hospital the other day," her mom said.

"We talked. And we were nice to each other."

But, Macy thought grumpily, the conversation hadn't gone anywhere. At least, it hadn't gone where she'd hoped it would—namely a discussion of where they stood. She'd thought he'd been about to say something when they'd been interrupted by Sheriff Andy and Kinsley.

"And he hasn't spoken to you since?" Her dad helped Joey fold a piece of paper into another plane.

Her mother emitted a soft sound of distress. "That doesn't sound like Everett."

"He's texted me a few times," Macy said, disgruntled. "Stuff about the mares or repairs he's making to the mare barn."

He hadn't suggested they continue their conversation. Nor had there been a declaration of love. Not that she'd expected one. An invitation to coffee, perhaps.

Whenever she wasn't preoccupied, she'd replay their last conversation in the hospital, searching for clues and finding none.

Why had Everett abruptly clammed up? What changed? Was he expecting her to make the first move?

"He must be mad at me," she mused aloud. "I did leave the hospital while he was in with Pop."

"Without saying goodbye?" Her mom moved the chicken to a baking sheet.

"I couldn't stay. He knew that." Did he? In hindsight, she should have stuck her head in Pop's room and at least motioned to him that she was heading home.

"Texts." Her dad harrumphed. "Why do people these days have such a problem with calling?"

"You should go to the ranch," her mom said. "I don't understand why you refuse. This is a simple misunderstanding."

Macy should probably call, like her dad suggested. Give Everett an opening for that talk.

She blew out a long breath. "I wish I knew for sure if he was staying or not."

"Ah. So now we're getting to the heart of the matter." Her dad demonstrated to Joey how to launch this newest plane. "You want assurances."

"Is that so wrong?"

"Of course not, sweetheart," her mom said. "What's the last thing he told you at the hospital?"

"He was saying how him returning to rodeoing might have contributed to Pop's stress."

"I imagine he felt guilty."

"But he wasn't responsible for Pop's panic attack," Macy insisted. "I told him that."

"Guilt can't always be rationally explained away."

"He's waiting for you to show up in order to talk to you in person," her dad said. "And you're avoiding him."

"You're not acting like someone who likes him," her mom added. "The exact opposite, in fact."

"Do you want him to chase you?"

"No!" Macy glared at her dad. "I'm not insecure. I don't need a man's attention to feel good about myself."

"What then?"

"I'm confused. He hasn't exactly given me a reason to feel confident in us."

Her mom nodded. "That's reasonable, and, frankly, you should tell him as much."

"You should ask him what he was doing at Town Hall the other day." Her dad passed Joey a fresh piece of paper.

Macy was certain she'd misheard. "What are you talking about?"

"I ran into Everett on Tuesday. I was submitting my company's bid for the new park project's zero maintenance landscaping."

"Why was Everett at Town Hall?"

"He said he'd dropped off a permit application for the ranch."

"What kind of permit?"

"He didn't tell me, and I didn't ask." Her dad pushed back in his chair. "Why don't you call and find out?" He exchanged glances with Macy's mom. "Do we sound like a broken record?"

"Joey can stay with us," her mom offered.

Macy was wild with curiosity about what kind of permit Everett had applied for. "If I ask him, he'll know you told me."

Her dad shrugged. "He told me why he was at Town Hall. He didn't act like it was a secret."

True.

"I just wish he'd reached out to me." The insecurity Macy had denied having coursed through her. She must really care for Everett for him to be able to put her through such an emotional wringer.

"I'm not defending Everett or his actions," her mom said. "He's made mistakes. He should have come around after Brody died. But he hurt almost as much as you after the accident and carried a terrible burden with him."

"I've forgiven him for that."

"Okay. But let's look at all he's dealing with. His grandfather's health. Running the ranch and the business. Stepping up and doing the right thing after being absent for three years."

"I get that."

"Then cut him some slack and stop playing games." Her dad wagged a finger at her, which Joey mimicked.

Games? Macy ground her teeth together. Was she?

Her mom came over and put an arm around her shoulders. "It's normal that the idea of a new relationship can cause some hesitation. Especially for you. Anyone in your shoes would be afraid of losing someone again."

Macy wasn't sure she liked how her mom saw inside her to her greatest fears.

"I'm fine with spending the rest of my life alone."

"Were fine," her mom said. "Then Everett returned, and you started thinking maybe you didn't want to do that."

"It's not just me anymore. I have Joey to consider. He's fond of Everett and could wind up hurt if things go badly."

"But think how much his life could be enriched if things go well." Her mom smiled encouragingly. "I'm willing to bet Everett is going through all kinds of uncertainties of his own. And if he's anything like your dad, he's putting unnecessary demands on himself."

Everett *was* like that, Macy conceded.

"Go to the ranch," her mom urged.

"We men are proud creatures," her dad interjected. "Everett's always had only one thing, and that was rodeo. He measured his success by how well he does in the arena. By leaving rodeo behind, he's venturing into unfamiliar territory. That can be pretty nerve-racking for guys like him who have always been confident in their abilities."

How was it that her parents seemed to know Everett better than her?

"Okay." Macy drew in a deep breath. "You win. I'm off to see Everett. But I'm taking Joey with me."

"Are you sure?" her mom asked. "We're more than happy to keep him."

Macy paused. If she was doing this, if she was putting herself out there, then she had to go *all out*. None of this "let's see how Everett reacts first" or hinting at her feelings. She'd tell him what was in her heart, her expectations in a relationship with him, and if he wasn't interested or couldn't reciprocate, then that was the end for them.

Though her stomach clenched in anticipation, she squared her shoulders.

"Joey's my son. Can't have one without the other. If Everett and I are going to discuss a potential future, he needs to understand that."

"I'll send some peanut butter and jelly sandwiches with you," her mom said.

"Thanks, Mom." No amount of protests would stop her mother from feeding her and Joey.

Ten minutes later, they were on their way to the ranch, Peanut riding alongside Joey in the back seat.

Macy mentally rehearsed what she'd say during the entire drive. Every word flew out of her head when she pulled into the ranch and saw the layout of stakes and yellow tape to the west of the pasture. Parked beside it sat a bright orange machine used for digging trenches.

Hombre stood in the pasture, staring at the machine as if it might come to life and devour him.

Macy hit the brakes on her truck. What in the world...?

CHAMP STOOD IN his stall, his large brown eyes glued to Everett and his ears pricked forward.

"Don't worry, boy." Everett paused in his work and rolled his shoulders, trying to ease the kinks. He then removed a red handkerchief from his back pocket and wiped off the sweat dampening his brow. He'd been hard at one task or another for the last four days. "Nothing bad is happening."

Champ snorted and shook his head. He clearly didn't agree.

"If this plan has any chance of succeeding, Sheriff Andy and I need a place to work. There's no room in the house for an office. Not with Pop and Susan getting married soon and her moving in."

The newly engaged couple had set a date and were busy arranging their small church wedding. Their days were also filled with packing Susan's belongings and moving the items she was bringing with her to the ranch. The rest would either be given away to family members, donated to charities or sold.

Pop was clearing out space in the house for her and getting rid of the junk, as he called it. He wanted his new bride to decorate to her liking and make the place her home. Everett went along, his one job to help with their combined garage sale this coming Saturday.

Sheriff Andy was coming out of retirement to not only manage the mini RV park but to help Susan sell her bungalow.

"Glad I kept my broker's license current," he'd told Everett the other day.

Champ suddenly pivoted and trotted through the connecting door to the paddock. Like Hombre, the big chestnut had been keeping watch on the construction staking and delivery of the trencher.

Hombre had recently discovered the mares not far away and was fascinated with them, though he was too young to understand the root of his fascination. Dr. Beck had called Everett to let him know the genetic testing results should be available either late today or tomorrow morning. Everett's nerves jumped every time his phone pinged with an email notification.

Whether as a second stallion in residence or a gelded saddle mount, Everett had decided to keep Hombre. His training was coming along, and Hombre showed a keen aptitude for learning. Thanks to their early morning lunge line lessons in the round pen, he was already responding to voice commands and had accepted a bareback pad.

"Hello? You around, Everett?"

"Hey." Hearing Macy's voice, he straightened. At the sight of her entering the stallion's quarters, his pulse rate spiked. "I didn't hear your truck."

"I parked at the house. Pop and Susan said I'd find you here."

"Um…yeah."

An awkward silence fell on them. That hadn't happened since they were teenagers when he'd returned to Wickenburg and learned she was dating his best friend.

He should have done more than send a few short texts. More than that, he should have prepared himself for this moment.

"Where's Joey?" he asked, breaking the silence.

"Inside with Pop and Susan."

Everett nodded, still tongue-tied.

Macy hitched her chin toward the outside. "What's going on with all the yellow tape, and is that a trencher? My dad said he saw you at Town Hall. Something about a permit application."

This he could talk about without any awkwardness. "Come on. I'll show you."

He started toward the cordoned-off area. Hombre trotted to the pasture fence, his long tail swishing side to side. Whatever was happening, he wanted in on the action. Champ whinnied a greeting to them from the paddock.

At the edge of the yellow tape barrier, Everett gestured. "Welcome to Rocking Chair Ranch."

Macy turned to stare at him. "Rocking Chair Ranch?"

"That's what Susan is calling it, and Pop likes the name. I like it, too. It fits our vision."

"Your vision?"

"This is going to sound crazy." He gave an anxious laugh. "Considering I was the one insisting I have no business experience."

"I'm confused."

"It started with Abel staying in the motor home and then Sheriff Andy in his RV. He's parking his RV along-

side the garage until construction is done and Rocking
Chair Ranch is officially open."

"You're building an RV park?"

"A small one. Six spaces for very specific residents."

"Now I'm really confused," she said.

"We're going to be a retirement community for senior
citizens. That's what the permit is for. Abel and Sheriff
Andy are our first two renters."

"I'm...speechless."

"Sheriff Andy is going to handle the books and all the
office work in exchange for free rent. I'm in charge of construction, maintenance, sales and everything else." Everett
summarized the plan for running power and water lines to
the parcel, the digging for a septic tank, and the pouring
of concrete pads. Also, what he imagined Rocking Chair
Ranch would look like when it was up and running. "This
won't be your standard retirement RV park. We'll have
one big difference."

"What's that?"

"All the residents will have part-time jobs," Everett
added with a grin. "Rather than get paid, they'll receive
reduced monthly rent. They'll work as many or as few
hours a week as they want or can, in whatever capacity
they're able. Feeding and cleaning stalls, maintenance and
repairs, groundskeeping, tending the community garden."

"A garden?"

"That was my idea. Gardening is good for mental
health. That's something older people struggle with. Even
Pop admits to having bad days."

"You've been researching again." Macy's eyes sparkled.

"Some."

"You mentioned the horses. The collective takes care
of them."

"There'll be more soon," Everett said. "Clients boarding their mares here for breeding. I can't ask the collective to care for them. That's not part of the agreement."

"We don't mind."

"Sheriff Andy insists the residents will like caring for the boarding horses," Everett said. "And we're all here to help each other. I also have a long list of improvements I'm going to start on when money becomes available. I plan on building a gazebo with an outdoor barbecue area and picnic table. Maybe even a hot tub."

"I can see that."

"The idea is for Rocking Chair Ranch to be a real community with the residents more like one big extended family. Rather than sitting around in a nursing home, the residents will be active and, in a small way, contributing to their support by helping around the ranch. If all goes well, Callie and one of the male caregivers from Total Home Nursing Services will visit weekly to handle any of the residents' medical needs. We won't abandon anyone just because they're old or ill."

Macy glanced around, taking everything in. After a moment of silence, she exclaimed, "I love it! Oh, Everett. I have goose bumps. I'm serious."

"I thought you might."

"You are a kind and wonderful man." Her voice broke.

"Well, it's still business, and I hope a profitable one. The monthly income should enable me to fund the repairs to the ranch and expand the horse breeding business. That's my goal, anyway. With eleven available stalls in the mare barn, I can start right away. My first client is bringing his mare by this weekend."

"All this in just a few days." Macy shook her head in astonishment.

"There's a lot of work ahead."

"Rocking Chair Ranch is going to be a huge success. I always knew you had it in you."

Her praise warmed him. "This isn't a one-man show. Pop has to stay healthy because I need his expertise. And Sheriff Andy's, too."

"Can I ask a financial question? And you're not obligated to answer," she hurriedly added.

"Sure."

She waved her arm to encompass the entire staked-off area. "Doesn't all this require money?"

"Which is why I almost didn't agree. Sheriff Andy had to convince me a low interest loan was the way to go and agree to walk us through the process." Everett winced. "I worry about making the monthly payments."

"I would, too," Macy agreed, more somber now.

"Though, because the ranch is in Pop's name, he's the one who ultimately decided. And the low interest rate was too hard to pass up."

"How long until you open?"

"Optimistically, two months. Realistically, more like three. Which is about how long it will take to obtain the permit, assuming there are no hiccups. In the meantime, Larry Hays's brother-in-law has agreed to start digging the trenches for the power and water lines. Sheriff Andy is obtaining bids for the concrete pads and the septic tank."

"How can I help?" Macy asked.

"You and the collective are already doing enough."

"Come on, Everett," she insisted. "What else?"

"Spread the word. If you know of anyone looking for a quality, proven quarter horse stud, send them our way. The horse breeding business is the quickest source of income and we need some."

"I saw that Kinsley has your web page and social media

accounts up and running. That should help. Did you ever talk to the Hays about advertising in their store?"

"Brenda said to bring over a stack of flyers and she'll put them on the counter by the register."

"You have flyers?"

"And business cards. They're on order. Kinsley designed them. Said I needed them. And she created our new logo."

Macy brightened. "I can't wait to see it."

Until now, Everett hadn't realized how much her support meant to him. A kind of contentment settled around his heart.

"And what about rodeoing?" she asked.

"I'm hanging up my spurs and lariat for now. Maybe for good. I think I'm ready to settle down in one place."

"Settle down," she repeated as if not quite believing him.

"It's true, Macy. I've given you reason to doubt me, but I'm serious this time. Too many people are depending on me."

She considered that before asking, "How do your parents feel about Rocking Chair Ranch?"

He tried not to read too much into her unenthusiastic response. Clearing his throat, he said, "Mom's thrilled. She's eager to see the changes when she and Dad fly out for the wedding. My aunt, on the other hand, is concerned. And I understand. She's worried Rocking Chair Ranch will be too much for Pop and hard on his health."

"I think it'll be just the opposite. Pop will thrive. He's a people person."

"I agree."

"Does him marrying Susan have anything to do with your aunt's concerns?"

"It might." Her astuteness impressed Everett. "My aunt isn't entirely on board with the engagement."

"Why? Susan is a lovely person."

"She worries they're marrying for financial reasons."

"Financial reasons?" Macy frowned. "What? She thinks Susan's a gold digger?"

"Well…"

"Nothing could be further from the truth."

"I told my aunt as much," Everett said. "And that Susan's willing to sign a prenup. But Pop won't hear of it. He says they don't need a prenup, as he's still planning on transferring ownership of the ranch, half to me and half to my mom and aunt."

"I'm sure your aunt is just looking out for Pop," Macy conceded. "Older people can be susceptible to scammers and swindlers. That isn't Susan, however, and your aunt will change her mind once she meets her. She's coming out for the wedding, isn't she?"

"Insisted she wouldn't miss it. And I think she'll feel better when gets a look at the place."

"She will. This will all work out." Macy took a step back and gave Everett a long once-over. "I have to say, you've impressed me."

"Pop and Sheriff Andy are the brains behind this operation. I'm just manual labor. In fact, I was clearing out the storeroom in the stallion quarters for an office when you arrived."

"You're a lot more than manual labor. You're the driving force behind this new venture."

Her words lifted him in a way nothing had in a very long time. Taking a chance, and uncertain of her response, he closed the distance between them.

"About that talk I wanted to have."

She surprised him again with her answer, and not in a good way.

"First, I have a question."

"What's that?"

"Let's get out of the sun."

Without answering, she walked in the direction of the mare barn. Everett's heart began to hammer. The short walk gave him just enough time to wonder if this was what Pop had experienced when he'd had a panic attack.

CHAPTER SEVENTEEN

INSIDE THE MARE BARN, Macy pivoted to face Everett. She hadn't planned on confronting him when she first arrived at the ranch. But then he'd made what stuck her as an overture, and she'd seen the eagerness in his expression. It had reminded her of the look he'd worn at the hospital the other day right before they were interrupted.

No way could she go on another moment without clearing the air between them and, more importantly, getting reassurance on where the two of them stood. If they stood anywhere at all.

"Why didn't you tell me about Rocking Chair Ranch before now?" she asked. "Honestly, Everett, if I hadn't come here today, I'm not sure when I would have found out."

"That's a fair question." He cleared his throat. "I wanted to tell you."

"What stopped you?"

Around them, the mares shuffled in their stalls as if vying for the best position to watch the entertainment. The sun drifted slowly toward the mountaintops, taking the remaining daylight with it and casting the interior of the mare barn in shadows. Sparrows pecked the ground in a last search for food before darkness fell while owls stirred from their hidden roosts, readying for the night's hunt.

"Is it because I left the hospital while you were in with Pop?" she asked, giving him an opening.

He lifted in a shoulder, more in surrender, it seemed,

than uncertainty. "I figured you took off because you didn't want to talk."

"That's not true, Everett. But I can see where you'd jump to that conclusion. My mistake."

"Then why did you leave without saying goodbye?"

Now it was her turn to say, "Fair question." She released a long breath. At her parents earlier, she'd claimed her reason was to get home to Joey. She realized now that wasn't true. "When you left for Tucson, that hurt."

"I know. I'm sorry."

"It makes no sense, I know, but when Brody died, it felt like he abandoned me. Same when you didn't come home after promising you would. Though, that was a genuine abandonment. Then you left for Tucson. I couldn't take it a third time. I'm not that strong. I need someone in my life I can depend on."

"I wish you'd told me."

"Would you have stayed?" she asked.

"I'd like to say yes. The truth is, I'm not sure. I was in my head at the time and doubting myself."

Macy swallowed, stalling for time. His honest answer had thrust her right back into that day they'd argued, and the awful pain coursing through her.

After a moment, she spoke. "I wasn't ready to hear you ask for another chance. I needed more time, and I was afraid that was the reason you wanted to talk."

"It was. You're right."

"I didn't want to agree to something I wasn't ready for, because, and I mean this sincerely, I can't live in fear that you'll leave one day just because we hit a rough patch."

"I'm not going anywhere. Pop has given me an incredible opportunity. And with Sheriff Andy's help, I can build a life and a career. I'm learning to forgive myself for the accident and accept I wasn't to blame. I'm repairing burned bridges with Brody's parents. And I'm committed to caring for Pop as he ages."

He hadn't said what she most wanted to hear. "What about us, Everett?" She needed to know. She wasn't jumping off this ledge alone.

"I care about you, Macy. More than that. I can see us together forever."

"Really?" A thrill rose in her.

"I'm staying. Not just for me and Pop, but for us." He was cut short by his phone dinging. "Sorry. I need to check this email."

"Really, Everett? Now?"

"Hold on." He tapped on his phone screen. "This will just take a second."

"I don't believe this is happening." She started to walk away.

"It's from the equine genetic testing facility. Doc Beck told me to expect it."

She came to a grinding halt, her annoyance instantly fleeing. "What does it say?"

"The print is small." Everett's features knit in concentration as he enlarged the document and continued reading.

"Everett?"

"The seller wasn't lying!" He broke into a spectacular grin. "She did just send the wrong results. Hombre tested negative across the board."

Macy let out a delighted gasp. "That's wonderful news."

Everett whooped and, grabbing hold of Macy by the waist, swung her in circles. "We have two healthy stallions. I didn't make a mistake buying Hombre."

"I'm so happy for you." Her head spun and not just from Everett twirling her. When he finally set her down, she blurted, "Maybe Dusty can be his first mare."

"He won't be ready for another six months, and the collective may have other ideas."

"I can ask."

He smiled tenderly at her. "Let's wait until next year. I'm planning on entering Hombre in some halter and saddle classes if his training continues to go well. He needs a few wins under his belt to raise his value."

"I guess we'll use Champ, then, and modify our agreement with Pop."

"With me," Everett said, grinning. "Pop transferred ownership of him to me."

"Ooh. I like the idea of us joining our businesses."

She didn't need to worry about Everett misreading her signals. Looping an arm around her waist, he pulled her flush against him and lowered his mouth to hers. "I like the idea of that, too."

She stopped him with a finger to his lips. "I need to hear it. What exactly are you saying? Because I won't settle for anything less than a committed relationship."

"We pick up where we left off and start with dating. See if you can stand my company for more than thirty minutes at a time."

"If I can't?" she asked jokingly.

"That's the end for us, I guess."

"And if I can?" She tilted her head and wrapped her arms around him.

His voice lowered, his meaning clear. "We're going to spend so much time together, you'll be sick of me."

"I doubt that."

"Let's test your theory." Again, he lowered his mouth to hers.

And again, she stopped him before he could kiss her. "There's something else you need to know. A condition, actually."

He paused. "Should I be worried?"

"It's Joey. He and I are a package deal."

"I wouldn't have it any other way," he said before claiming a kiss that let Macy know in no uncertain terms he was in this with her for the long haul.

When, minutes later, they broke apart, Macy swore her feet weren't touching the ground. A pleasant sensation bloomed inside her. No, that wasn't quite right. It emanated from her heart and spread to the tips of her fingers and toes. She realized this was the beginning of love. Or, more likely, the young teenage love she'd once felt for Everett evolving into a mature love.

He nuzzled her cheek, seeming unwilling to release her. She wasn't all that eager herself to end their moment. This was once in a lifetime, and she wanted it to last as long as possible.

"I'm falling for you, Macy. If you haven't figured that out yet."

She nuzzled his cheek in return, enjoying the outdoorsy scent of him, the strength of his muscled arms and, most of all, the look in his eyes that reflected his words. "I'm getting that impression. Which is a good thing," she added, "because I'm falling for you, too."

"The first of many things we can agree on."

Several of the mares abruptly snorted and tossed their heads in alarm. The next second, Joey came racing into the mare barn, bursting with energy.

"Mommy, Mommy. Where are you?"

Macy slid from Everett's embrace. "I'm right here, honey."

"Hey, sport. What are you up to?"

"Everett!" Joey ran straight for him.

Everett grabbed him under the arms and swung him in a circle, not unlike he had Macy. When he set Joey down, the boy cried out, "Again."

He obliged, then asked, "Where's Pop?"

"He is coming." Joey pointed.

The three of them stepped outside the mare barn just as Pop was helping Susan into one of the rocking chairs, which were sitting in a white circle cast by the exterior floodlight.

He glanced at them and called out, "Sorry, Joey got away from us."

"No worries." Macy reached for Everett's hand and clasped it in hers.

He sent her a look that asked if she was sure about this. Pop and Susan might be in their eighties, but they were both sharp as tacks and would notice.

Her answer was to squeeze his fingers.

"Well, lookie there," Pop said, easing himself into the other rocking chair. "Appears there's gonna be another change around here. Though I can't say I'm surprised."

"Took the two of you long enough." Susan delivered her comment with a mischievous wink.

Joey looked at Macy's and Everett's joined hands and took hold of Everett's other hand.

A sentimental lump formed in her throat as she leaned her shoulder into Everett. Her gaze took in the ranch and the many new beginnings. Pop and Susan. Rocking Chair Ranch. Hombre. The revived horse breeding business, which would soon rival what it once was in the past.

Best of all, there was her and Everett and their freedom from past secrets and guilt. No longer afraid to face the future, her emotions soared. Thank goodness her rodeo cowboy had returned.

EPILOGUE

Three Months Later

AT A LOUD banging on the door, Everett hollered, "Hold your horses. I'm coming."

He examined his freshly shaved face in the tiny mirror over the compact bathroom sink. Satisfied, he placed his new Stetson on his head and adjusted the fit. For a final touch, he stuck his lucky turkey feather in the hatband. Pop had insisted Everett look the part of a business owner when meeting with customers for the horse breeding business or Rocking Chair Ranch.

The Stetson and feather must be working, for there wasn't an empty stall in the mare barn, and that included the horses owned by the collective. Champ's services were booked for the next several months, and before long, Hombre would be ready for those who wanted to cross their mare with a striking gray with distant thoroughbred bloodlines.

The young stallion's training was starting to pay off. Last weekend, he'd won his first ribbon at a local horse show. Third place, which wasn't bad for a start. Soon, Everett would advance Hombre from the lunge line to light saddle work, depending on when the vet cleared him for riding. The bones of a two-year-old horse needed to be well developed before bearing extra weight.

The banging sounded again, and a deep voice hollered

through the door, "What in tarnation is the holdup? You're keeping everyone waiting."

Everett recognized his caller as Abel. "All right, already."

He opened the door, allowing a blast of brisk November air inside the horse trailer's compact living quarters. He'd been looking for a way to move out of the house after Pop and Susan married two months ago, wanting to give the newlyweds their personal space. When his buddy Rusty asked if Everett could store his horse trailer at the ranch until he found a buyer—he didn't have a place for it in Oklahoma with the Twisters —Everett had made his friend an offer on the spot.

The living quarters were cramped, but they were also temporary. Susan had insisted on using a portion of the money from the sale of her bungalow to build an attached suite onto the ranch house for her and Pop with its own separate entrance. Pop had balked at first, refusing to let her spend any of her own money. Eventually, he'd agreed when Everett suggested they reimburse Susan with regular payments out of the business proceeds.

Construction was scheduled to start after the first of the year. That way, after Pop and Susan moved into the suite, Everett wouldn't feel like he was living on top of them or that his irregular hours interfered with their quiet routine.

Eventually, sometime next year, once they were on steadier financial ground, Everett planned on building a small rodeo arena on a back acre of land. Besides giving lessons, he'd rent out the arena for those needing a practice facility or a venue for their event.

"Let me get my jacket." Everett retrieved it from the hook beside the door.

Abel shuffled back a step, giving Everett room to climb

out of the trailer. "It is a might nippy out today. Hope that doesn't keep the guests from showing up."

"Not a chance." Everett had checked the weather forecast a dozen times during the past few days. "Going to be a clear and sunny day."

He donned his jacket as the two of them walked from the spot where Abel had once parked his motor home behind the stallion quarters. The ancient vehicle had been replaced with a newer, larger RV with all the bells and whistles.

Abel's was the first RV in Rocking Chair Ranch, moved in weeks before the grand opening—which was today. Sheriff Andy's was next after he moved out of his house and put it on the market. All six spots were now rented, the residents having signed year-long leases. The proceeds were enough to cover taxes and insurance and meet the small business loan's payments.

Everett drew a small salary from the horse breeding business while Pop and Susan had their social security and modest investment incomes. They weren't rich, but they had more than enough to get by. And once Hombre was old enough to start breeding, and the foals were sold in a year or so, they might actually be doing well for themselves.

"You look spiffy," Everett told the older gentleman as they approached the patio, where rented tables and chairs had been set up to accommodate the over one hundred expected guests.

"Not every day I get to attend a big shindig. Had to pull out my best Western shirt and jeans. Glynnis bought me this jacket special for the occasion."

"I don't suppose our new retired schoolteacher resident, who just happens to be single, has anything to do with it."

"Not just a schoolteacher. Did you know she taught equine science classes at the community college?"

"I did. She'd going fit in just fine here."

"She promised to save me a seat at the party."

Everett chuckled. "So, it's serious between you two?"

"We'll see." Abel's steps were a little less wobbly, and his shoulders a bit squarer.

Amazing what effect the prospect of romance had on a person's health.

A couple dozen people were already milling about. Just as many were inside, judging by the noise level. The collective members had spent the past three days helping Everett, Pop and Susan prepare. The house had been cleaned top to bottom, furniture rearranged to accommodate folding chairs, and the family room decorated for a belated wedding reception. Banners and streamers hung on the walls. Gold and silver confetti covered every flat surface. Helium-filled balloons had been tied to the backs of the kitchen chairs. A four-tier wedding cake with a pair of ornamental white doves for a topper sat on the counter. Bottles of champagne chilled in the refrigerator.

Pop and Susan had stuck to their original plan and gotten hitched two months earlier at her church in a small, intimate ceremony. Afterward, they spent four days honeymooning at a charming inn in Wickenburg. Today, their many family members and friends were here to wish them well on their journey as a married couple.

Upon seeing how happy Susan made Pop and his improved health, Everett's mom and aunt had fallen instantly in love with her and given their full support of the union. Susan, in turn, couldn't be happier in her new role as stepmother and stepgrandmother.

The newlyweds had one strict rule for their guests: no gifts. They had everything they possibly needed. Instead, they asked for donations to the animal shelter where Sheriff Andy volunteered. Already, a stack of multicolored envelopes filled a crystal bowl on the side table, some of them quite thick and likely containing a cash donation or gift card that could be used to buy food and supplies for the shelter.

Everett motioned for Abel to go ahead of him onto the porch. The older man made a beeline for Rocking Chair Ranch's newest resident. The former teacher sat in a chair, holding a cup of punch in one hand and a plate of nachos in the other.

Sheriff Andy and Glynnis's husband supervised the grill. Before long, they would be serving fajitas to hungry guests. The outside banner, strung along the wall, featured Rocking Chair Ranch's new logo, which Kinsley had designed and that resembled a livestock brand.

Fielding greetings and congratulations, Everett wound his way to the back door. It opened just as he was reaching for the knob, and the woman who emerged threw her arms around him.

"Everett. Don't you look handsome."

"Hey, Mom." Giving her a quick kiss, he released her. They stepped out of the way of other people coming and going inside. "Thanks again for flying out so soon after the wedding. It means a lot to me and Pop."

"Are you kidding? I wouldn't have missed the grand opening for the world. I'm just sorry your dad couldn't be here. Work wouldn't let him take more time off."

"It's all right." Everett glanced around. "The party's livening up."

"Pop says to expect another fifty or sixty people. I'm not sure where you're going to put them all." She stood on her tiptoes and leaned close. "I really like Macy. I always did, but I like her more now."

"Me, too."

"And Joey is so cute. Such a charmer." She nodded at

the door. "He's in there, wrapping everyone around his little pinkie."

"Takes after Macy. She has me wrapped around hers pretty tight."

His mom touched his arm. "I know you haven't been dating long, but I'm hoping it's serious."

"It is."

"Really serious?"

"Really serious, Mom," he answered.

"Because if you two were to…" She let the sentence drop.

"I promise, if we were to, you'll be the first to know."

"No pressure," she said on a wistful sigh. "I'm just excited for you. And proud enough, I could burst."

"Thanks, Mom. That means a lot to me."

"I have to run. I told Susan I'd check on the ice in the coolers. See if we need to make a run to the store for more bags." She dashed off, and Everett went inside.

"Everett!" Joey scurried over to him. "You're here."

"Hey, sport." He scooped the boy up into his arms as naturally as if he'd been a part of Joey's life since the day he was born.

"I'm gonna ride Dusty later." The gentle mare had become his favorite.

"We'll see. That's up to your mom."

"What's up to me?"

Macy appeared from around the corner, a vision in a turquoise sweater that brought out the flush in her cheeks. Everett fell for her again, as he did every time he saw her.

He opened his arm and she went to him, fitting perfectly against his side as if they were made for each other.

"Joey wants to ride Dusty," he said.

"Not today, honey." She tweaked his nose. "We're having a big party."

"Tomorrow?" Joey asked, his expression hopeful. He'd recently learned the word and used it to counter almost every no Macy delivered.

"Okay. But not too early." She snuggled closer to Everett. "We're going to need our rest after today."

Suddenly, he couldn't wait another moment to be alone with her. "Hold on a second." Carrying Joey into the family room, he deposited him on the couch with Susan and Pop, who were holding court among the guests. "Can you watch him for a second?"

"Of course." Susan patted the boy's head.

"Be right back, sport." Everett grabbed Macy by the hand and drew her down the hall to a secluded nook.

"What are you doing?" she asked, a laugh in her voice.

"This." Cupping her cheeks in his palms, he lifted her face to his for a searing kiss that left no doubt about how much he wanted to be with her today and for the rest of their lives.

"What was that for?" she asked, slow to pull away and a little breathless.

"We've been taking things slow. And that's fine. I've had a lot going on. You've also been busy and are going to get even busier when your classes start up again in January. But you need to know something, sweetheart. I'm in love with you. Not falling. I'm there. Totally. All the way up to my ears."

"Love." She said the word as if savoring it. "Is that so?"

He touched his forehead to hers. "This is the part where you say it back."

"It is?"

"Yes. Unless you don't—"

"I love you, Everett. More than I ever imagined."

He kissed her again, long and hard. "Don't ever tease me like that again. My system can't take the shock."

"I won't. I swear."

"Good. Because when I propose someday in the future, I'm going to need a straight answer from you."

She drew back, her eyes wide. "Propose?"

"Someday," he repeated. "Just giving you fair warning." He dropped his hands only to wrap his arm around her. "Nothing would make me happier than being your husband and Joey's stepdad. It's not my intention to replace Brody in Joey's life. He has a father, and I will do all I can to keep Brody's memory alive. But it would mean the world to me to help raise Joey in the way Brody would have if he was still with us."

Her features softened. "Oh, Everett. I do love you."

As if hearing his name, escape artist Joey came running down the hall toward them, his sneakers pounding on the hardwood floor. Seeing them, he pulled up short.

"Mommy. Everett. There you are."

"Here we are," Macy said, sending Everett a look that said they'd continue this conversation later when they were alone.

They returned to the party then, Joey walking between them, Everett and Macy each holding one of Joey's hands. Judging by the tender and sentimental expressions on every face, there wasn't a single person in the room who didn't recognize what Everett knew with complete certainty.

He, Macy and Joey were a family, now and forever, and nothing would ever change that.

* * * * *

A NOTE TO ALL READERS

From October releases Mills & Boon will be making some changes to the series formats and pricing.

What will be different about the series books?

In response to recent reader feedback, we are increasing the size of our paperbacks to bigger books with better quality paper, making for a better reading experience.

What will be the new price of Mills & Boon?

Over the past four years we have seen significant increases in the cost of producing our books. As a result, in order to continue to provide customers with a quality reading experience, the price of our books will increase to RRP $10.99 for Modern singles and RRP $19.99 for 2-in-1s from Medical, Intrigue, Romantic Suspense, Historical and Western.

For futher information regarding format changes and pricing, please visit our website millsandboon.com.au.

WESTERN

Rugged men looking for love...

Available Next Month

The Maverick's Christmas Kiss Joanna Sims
A Proposal For Her Cowboy Cari Lynn Webb

A Fortune Thanksgiving Michelle Lindo-Rice
The Rodeo Star's Reunion Melinda Curtis

 LOVE INSPIRED

The Cowboy's Forgotten Love Tina Radcliffe
The Cowboy's Inheritance Julia Ruth

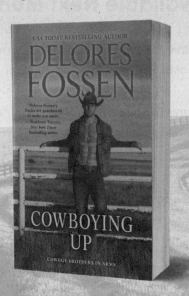

Keep reading for an excerpt of
THE BILLIONAIRE'S CINDERELLA
HOUSEKEEPERE
by Miranda Lee — find this story
in the *After Hours Temptation* anthology.

CHAPTER ONE

'So, you're looking for a live-in housekeeping position, are you, Ruby?' the lady asked.

Ruby heard the scepticism behind the woman's
words. She'd heard it before from the other employment agencies she'd been to. They'd all taken one look
at her, along with her less than impressive résumé, and
told her they didn't have anything suitable on their
books right now.

'Yes, that's right,' she replied, already knowing
she'd drawn a blank again.

Ruby suppressed a sigh. If she couldn't get a live-in
position, then she'd have to take Oliver up on his offer
for her to stay on at his place. Liam had offered to have
her too, but really, she didn't want to live with either
of her brothers. Neither of their apartments were what
you would call spacious. Besides, Oliver's long-time
girlfriend, Rachel, lived with him, and Liam's new
girlfriend, Lara, had just moved in with him. They
needed their own space, as did she.

'You do realise,' the woman said kindly, 'that
Housewives For Hire doesn't often have such a position available. We specialise more in part-time casual

housekeeping. Rarely live-in. Most of my girls are married women who want to earn money whilst their children are at school.'

'I see,' Ruby said in a flat voice. Obviously, it had been a mistake to come back to Sydney and try to embrace real life again.

But before Ruby could say goodbye and go, a phone buzzed on the desk and Barbara, the owner of Housewives for Hire, swept it up, mouthing an apology to Ruby as she did so.

Ruby didn't really listen as the conversation was rather one-sided. Barbara just said *yes* and *hmm* a lot whilst tapping on her computer, so Ruby tuned out, putting her mind to the problem of what she would do now, because blind Freddie could see she wasn't going to get a housekeeping job in Sydney. She'd been a fool to think it would be straightforward to get such a position.

Going back to her nomadic lifestyle, however, no longer appealed. It had served its purpose for the past five years, giving her the time out she'd desperately needed. But when she'd turned thirty on her last birthday, a yearning had started growing inside her, a yearning to settle down and do something worthwhile with her life.

Not marriage. Lord no. Ruby shuddered at the thought. After the fiasco with Jason a few years back, she'd decided that marriage would never be her lot in life. Because marriage meant loving and trusting a man with her happiness, and Ruby simply couldn't see that happening.

And let's face it, Ruby thought, *Jason wasn't the*

only member of the opposite sex to have a strike against him. Your father sowed the seeds for your distrust when you were only nineteen, with your first serious boyfriend, Bailey, compounding your negative feelings shortly after.

It was inevitable that she would eventually come to the decision to rely on herself, and herself alone. Jason had just been the catalyst that had propelled her into adopting a totally celibate lifestyle, which Ruby found she actually quite liked. She enjoyed the freedom from the emotional complications associated with boyfriends and sex.

To her surprise, she found she didn't miss either. Not one little bit.

The idea had finally taken hold that she could become a social worker. Over the past few years of travelling and working all over Queensland and northern NSW, she'd come across a lot of unfortunates who could have had different lives if someone had given them a helping hand.

The only problem with this was that social workers these days had degrees.

Gradually, Ruby had come up with a plan. It had seemed so simple on paper. She would return to Sydney and get herself a live-in housekeeping position, not because she really wanted to be a housekeeper but because that way she wouldn't have to pay rent. Rents in Sydney, she knew, were exorbitant, and she didn't have enough savings to pay a bond, plus the first month's rent in advance. On top of that, she could spend her spare time doing an online course to get herself into a university so that she could study for a social science degree.

In her head, by thirty-five she would be a qualified social worker. Ruby knew she was intelligent and if she put her mind to it, she could do just about anything.

Unfortunately, her plan seemed to have one fatal flaw. No one would hire her as a housekeeper, not even here in Sydney where there were loads of such positions advertised. Ruby suspected her lack of experience in such a position was the main reason for her always being turned down, although one of the agencies had hinted that she looked too…sexy.

Now that had really floored her, though, now she thought about it, she had come across this opinion once or twice before over recent years. Lord knew why. Okay, so she had what was considered a good figure nowadays but she wasn't even pretty.

Ruby shook her head ruefully when she thought back to her teenage years. No one would have called her sexy back then. Lord no! The opposite sex hadn't given her a second glance when she was at school. And why would they? She'd been all puppy fat and braces, along with the lack of confidence that went with puberty. It had taken every bit of courage she possessed to apply for a job at a local fast-food place. But from then on her confidence had grown, confidence that had nothing to do with looks. It annoyed her that people couldn't see past the obvious to who she was inside.

Oh, well. Ruby accepted she would *have* to live with one of her brothers for a while till she could get a job as a waitress or bar staff—jobs she was well qualified for and where looking sexy would be an asset. Once

she had enough money she would look for shared ac-
commodation, hopefully with a room of her own so
she could study in peace.

It wouldn't be as good as her original plan of being
a live-in housekeeper but it would have to do, Ruby
decided as she waited for Barbara to finish her call.
A potential client, it sounded like.

'I see,' Barbara said slowly. 'So this won't be a permanent position, Mr Marshall. Your usual housekeeper
will be coming back to work for you eventually.'

Ruby couldn't hear what Mr Marshall said to this.

'Actually,' Barbara went on with a glance Ruby's
way, 'I do have a girl who might suit you very well.
Yes, she has excellent references.'

Ruby nodded enthusiastically at this. She did have
excellent references. Ruby was a good worker, and as
honest as the day was long. Employers were always
sorry to see her go.

'She's actually here now. Would you like to talk to
her? Good. Her name's Ruby. Here she is.'

The ball's in your court, Barbara's eyes seemed to
say as she handed Ruby the phone.

'Hello?' Ruby said after a swift swallow. She was
not a nervous person, but she did so want this job. Even
if it was only temporary. Because then she would have
experience as a housekeeper on her résumé, which
would lead more easily to getting another housekeeping position.

'Hi, Ruby,' Mr Marshall said in a deep and very
masculine voice, the kind of voice you mostly associated with radio announcers and soul singers. 'First
things first. Have you done housekeeping jobs before?'

Ruby was about to say no when she had a light-bulb moment. Really, why hadn't she thought to mention this before?

'Not professionally,' she said briskly. 'But I ran the family household for seven years from the age of eighteen till I was twenty-five. My mother was ill at the time,' she raced on before he could ask why. She didn't add that her mother had actually died of ovarian cancer a year after she'd finished school, her precious father leaving it up to Ruby to help her shattered younger brothers through school and then university. The rotten mongrel deserted them two months after the funeral to live with his rich mistress in her fancy city penthouse. Yes, he'd given them the family house to live in and, yes, he'd paid the bills, but that had been the extent of his support.

'I did all the cooking and cleaning,' she added, in case Mr Marshall thought they'd been rich enough to pay someone to do that.

'Your mother must have been very proud of you,' he remarked. 'And is she well now?'

Ruby blanked from her mind the grief that still consumed her whenever she thought of her lovely, brave mother. 'No,' she bit out, gritting her teeth at the same time. 'She passed away. Cancer.'

'Bloody cancer,' Mr Marshall muttered, then was silent for a few seconds. 'Sorry,' he said at last. 'My wife died of cancer. Still, no use going on about it, is there?' he continued gruffly before she could make any sympathetic noises. 'Only makes things worse. What's done is done. So, how old are you now, Ruby?'

'Thirty.'

'I see. And what have you been doing with yourself since your mother's death?'

Clearly, he thought her mother had died fairly recently and not a decade earlier. Ruby decided not to enlighten him as it would only mean answering awkward questions that weren't really relevant to this interview. She hated talking about that time in her life. *Hated* it!

'Well, I've always worked part-time in the hospitality industry,' she explained, 'even when I was at school. So once I had the opportunity I took off by myself, travelling all over northern NSW and Queensland, working in various resorts and clubs. I've done lots of things, from serving behind the bar to waitressing to the occasional bit of work as a receptionist. But I'm a little tired of that life, so I've come back to Sydney to find suitable work whilst I study for a degree in social science.'

'That sounds very commendable. And you sound like a very nice girl. Not that Housewives For Hire ever recommends any other kind. I have it on good authority that they're very reputable, so I'm sure you'll be fine for the job. Unfortunately, I'm in London on business at the moment and I won't be back in Sydney for over a week. I hate leaving my house empty so this is what I'll do. My sister lives in Sydney in a nearby suburb—I live in Mosman—and she has keys to my house. I'll contact her and have her meet with you there tomorrow morning. She can show you the house and answer any questions you might have about me. But if you want it, then the job's yours, Ruby.'

If she wanted it? Of course she wanted it. Wanted it like crazy! He sounded like such a nice man. 'Oh,

Mr Marshall, that's wonderful. I'll do a good job. I promise.'

'I'm sure you will. Now hand the phone back to Barbara for me so I can give her my sister's details. Yes, yes,' he said impatiently to someone in the background. 'I won't be long. You go down to breakfast and I'll join you there.'

Ruby handed the phone back and just sat there, dazed and elated, whilst Barbara spoke to Mr Marshall and tapped some more on her computer. Finally, the woman hung up and turned her swivel chair to face her.

'You're a lucky girl, Ruby,' she said with a smile on her face. 'Mr Marshall is none other than Sebastian Marshall, head of Harvest Productions, which you may or may not have heard of.'

She hadn't, and shook her head in the negative.

'They produce several highly successful television shows,' Barbara went on. 'I'm sure you'd have heard of them. *Australia at Noon… What Word Am I?* The soapie *Elizabeth Street*. But the jewel in their crown is *Battle at the Bar*.'

'That's a very popular show,' Ruby agreed, despite only having watched it the once. But she'd heard a lot about it and was always meaning to watch the series some more. The hero, or anti-hero really, was a lawyer named Caesar Battle who defended the sometimes indefensible and often won. A loner, he was an enigmatic character who worked hard and played hard but still had an integrity about him that was very likeable. Women lusted after him. Men wanted to be him. The show had won countless awards, especially for its handsome main actor whose name eluded her.

'I'm sorry it's only a temporary position,' Barbara continued, 'but it's better than nothing.'

'*Much* better,' Ruby agreed with a smile.

'The job won't be too hard, either. Mr Marshall is a widower, with no children.'

'So how old is Mr Marshall?' It had been impossible to tell from his voice. A widower, however, suggested someone elderly.

'Forty, according to the internet,' came the crisp reply.

'Goodness. That young.' Ruby suddenly thought of her father, who'd been forty when he began having an affair. A dangerous age, forty. Or so she'd been told.

Thinking of her father always made Ruby angry. Angry and cynical and just a little wary, when it came to her dealings with men. The last thing she wanted was to stuff up this job by presenting herself with the wrong look.

'Does your company have a dress code?' she asked. 'A uniform perhaps?'

'No. My girls wear whatever they like. Though under your circumstances,' Barbara added with a knowing glint in her eye, 'I would suggest dressing conservatively. Professional.'

Ruby glanced down at her outfit, which she considered reasonably conservative. Yes, the skirt ended above her knee and the top did show a hint of cleavage but by modern standards it was hardly provocative. Still…

'That's very good advice,' she said. 'Thank you.'

'Sensible girl,' Barbara praised. 'Now, I'll just contact Mr Marshall's sister and we'll make arrangements for tomorrow.'

Subscribe and fall in love with a Mills & Boon series today!

You'll be among the first to read stories delivered to your door monthly and enjoy great savings.

WE SIMPLY LOVE ROMANCE